RIPPLES

WILLIAM ELLIOT HAZELGROVE

D0306211

Pantonne Press, Inc.
329 West 18th Street
Chicago, Illinois 60616

RIPPLES

A Pantonne Press Book
Pantonne Press, Inc.
329 West 18th Street.
Chicago, Illinois 60616.

Copyright © 1992 by William Elliot Hazelgrove

For information: Pantonne Press, Inc., 329 West 18th Street,
Chicago, Illinois 60616.

Library of Congress Catalog Card Number: 91-62677

ISBN 0-9630052-9-4

All of the events and characters depicted in this book are fictional.

Printed in the United States of America.

The author is grateful for permission to reprint an excerpt from
"RIPPLES" by Tony Banks/Mike Rutherford (Both PRS) © 1976.
Used With The Permission of ANTHONY BANKS LTD./MIKE
RUTHERFORD LTD./HIT & RUN MUSIC (PUBLISHING) LTD.
(ALL PRS). Administered in USA & CANADA by HIDDEN PUN
MUSIC, INC. (BMI). All Rights Reserved. International
Copyright Secured.

First Edition Published March 1992.

Many thanks to Jeffrey Hellyer for his invaluable assistance.

RIPPLES

To

*My mother and father for
telling me that I could,*

and to

*Kitty Lynn for showing
me what it all was for.*

Sail away, away,
Ripples never come back.
They've gone to the other side.
Look into the pool
Ripples never come back.
Dive to the bottom and go to the top
To see where they have gone.
Oh, they've gone to the other side.

— Ripples

RIPPLES

1

As I have gotten older, I have become increasingly aware of the painful inadequacies of the people around me, to whom I alone have assigned great expectations. It is no fault of theirs if they should fall short of this imaginary level which I set for them and they knew nothing about. My mother told me once it will come as quite a surprise to realize the world is not composed of people such as myself, and that if I survive the ensuing crisis I just might learn something. She was right. I was surprised, and can only hope that I have learned something.

The first real step on my road to discovery was during the summer of my eighteenth year—the summer I spent out east with Christian. It is at his feet that I lay the blame for my exaggerated expectations of people—and yet, simultaneously, my salvation. When the critical fork in the road appeared it was Christian who forced my hand to the high road.

Christian and I were partners of a sort, fellow journeyers through the tangled woods of youth and illusion. Moreover, Christian and I were friends. He was the type of friend you have only once in life. It seems there is a closeness in youth that becomes diluted when later mixed with adulthood. I suppose commonality of purpose is a factor in friendship; there are so many more options as one becomes older.

We spent that summer along the Maryland shore. There was a lighthouse with faded red stripes against a colorless white. The lighthouse turned out to be Christian's barometer on how far he could stretch that elasticity of life that goes under such names as daring or courage.

Many years later I went back to that lone sentry on the beach. The lighthouse was still there, cutting a dark figure against the gray sky. The entrance was an old wooden door we used to push open. I walked up to see if it would spring open for me the way it had in my youth, but the door had been modernized — wood being discarded for the efficient finality of steel — and the basic truth I found years before inside was now locked away forever.

I'm getting away from my story now, so we should go back to that summer — really it was the last summer. But I should go back even further, back to when it all started — six years before, when I first met Christian. We were twelve. It was during a football game that I began to learn what expectations were all about.

The sun-hardened football came sailing through the air — a perfect pass into my hands. I pulled the ball to my chest and could see victory near the giant oak tree that marked the goal line. I wasn't twenty feet away when the sturdy ground rose up to meet me.

"Damn!"

I hoisted myself up off the ground just in time to see the person who had snatched my glory. He was a foot shorter than myself and jogging jauntily back to his teammates. I stared at him as I limped back to the huddle.

"Good catch, Brenton! Too bad you couldn't score," our quarterback called as I came to the huddle.

"All right guys, let's go with a run. . . . Brenton, you want to carry it again?"

"Sure. . . who was the guy that tackled me?"

Our quarterback looked over.

"Christian Streizer. Speedy little guy, huh?"

"Yeah."

I bent down among my three teammates and a drop of sweat fell from my nose to the steamy ground. The wet heat was on everyone's face as the high Maryland sun heated the coastal air.

"Brenton around the right end on two. Let's see if we can score this time."

We lined up.

"Hut one! . . . hut two! hike!"

Our quarterback took the ball and pitched it to me. I started my sweep around the end, pulling the football in against my chest. The air rushed over my wet skin. I saw open field to the goal line and ran faster, pumping my arms, trying to get more breath from the thick air. Quick footsteps raced up next to me — someone cracked into my side. I skidded along the grass as the ball squished out of my arm.

The football landed a foot in front of my face. I watched helplessly as two hands scooped the ball up and my tackler from before ran toward the other goal line and then across it. I struggled to my feet as the game ended. Everybody was already heading home to eat lunch or get something to drink.

I watched my nemesis as he walked toward me. He sauntered past, nodded, then started alone across the field. I ran after him.

"*Hey*—that was some run," I called.

"Thanks," he said, shrugging.

3

"What's your name?"

"Christian."

"Brenton," I said, walking with him.

We started across the golf course we played football on. I glanced at him. He was smaller than I was, but very compact. A rippling of tight muscles ran between his stomach and chest before branching out to his arms and neck. His brown hair was long on top and razor close on the sides, which made his head look enlarged. But his eyes were what really struck me—black-lashed and pale green, they penetrated with a depth I had not seen before.

I was bigger, I'd say by a good five inches, and definitely heavier, with some softness about the stomach and arms. My own shock of curly red hair was quite out of sync with the poker-straight quality of his mop. Freckles dominated my face, and the sunburned, fair complexion of my particular color contrasted to his tanned skin. But I thought my head to be a regular shape, and I preferred my own brand of light-blue iris to his odd green.

I glanced at him.

"Do you play much football?"

"Nah," he answered, barely opening his mouth.

"Pretty good run for not playing much."

He shrugged.

"Nope, don't play much."

We walked in silence for a couple of minutes. I looked at him.

"Haven't seen you in school...are you in the seventh grade?"

"Uh-huh."

"Do you have Miss Sloam?"

He nodded as he walked with these tight little steps.

"I have Miss Stort...she's all right. I transferred in."

He looked at me.

"You transferred in?"

"From Virginia, just last month."

He nodded and was silent again.

I tried several more times to start a conversation, but he just answered in these short sentences. The sun was relentless—a hot breath of baked grass and soil came up from the golf course. I was beginning to regret that I'd even bothered to talk to him. He looked into the white heat, then turned to me.

"—got a question for you."

"What's that?"

He paused, looking around casually.

"You ever kill anyone before?"

I stopped and stared at him.

"What?"

He stopped.

"Did you ever kill anyone before?"

I shook my head and let out a short laugh.

"No. . ."

"Oh," he said, nodding.

We started walking again. The cicadas called out in the hazy green distance of coastal heat with a loud buzzing. I looked at him to see if there was some nuance of a smile, a hidden smirk that would give away his hoax. He just looked straight ahead and kept on with the same sense of purpose in his walk that he had begun with. He was carrying his shirt, swinging it around off both of his shoulders. I wiped my brow and noticed the heat didn't seem to bother him at all. I cleared my throat.

"Did *you* ever kill anyone?"

He squinted into the distance and didn't break his stride.

"Once."

I eyed him suspiciously.

"Where?"

"In a pool," he replied, with no flicker of emotion in his voice. I paused.

"How'd you do it?"

"Easy."

And then he didn't say anything more.

By this time we were walking along the secluded part of the golf course. The grass had turned brown from the heat and it was too hot for any golfers to be out. I noticed with some discomfort that my former teammates were nowhere to be seen. There were only some houses looming in the distance beyond a high fence that ringed the golf course. He started to talk again.

"I was at the pool one day with my mother. It was real crowded, a Saturday I think," he said, squinting his eyes in thought. "I was in the shallow end with a kid named Dickie Thomas. We were having a splash battle. . .then we started to wrestle." He took a long, deep breath. "We began wrestling underwater, holding each other under real long. So I held him under once *real long*." He paused and took another deep breath, the kind people take when they're about to say something that bothers them.

He had wrapped his shirt up into a rope and held it slung around his neck. He was talking in this low monotone—I wasn't exactly believing him, but I was getting nervous. We had slowed our pace way down and there wasn't a soul around.

"Dickie started to fight to come up for some air—I started to wonder what it would be like to kill someone. . .so I kept him under," he said, holding his hands down in front of him. "The pool was crowded and I knew nobody would see me. After a while he quit struggling and went to the bottom. I just got out of the pool, and the lifeguard took Dickie out. . .they thought he had drowned on his own," he said, shrugging.

He was quiet for a moment. I felt I should say something, but couldn't speak.

"It was all right, though. . .I mean killing someone," he added, looking at me again.

I cleared my throat.

"Well...your secret is safe with me—I'm not going to say anything...so don't worry," I said quickly, feeling my heart thud.

He didn't say a word, but came to a complete stop. He turned and stared at me strangely. I halted. My legs felt wobbly as I stood facing him. A suffocating wave of heat came across the wide expanse.

"I can't let you go—you know too much."

A trickle of sweat moved slowly down my side. "Oh no!...Don't worry! *Lots* of people kill people—it's nothing...really!"

He shook his head slowly.

"I can't risk it."

He quickly looked around the deserted golf course. The small pea of terror in the back of my brain became larger and developed into outright panic.

"Well...well—what are you going to do?"

He looked down, then dropped to his knees and tackled me. I fell back. He slid up my body and started choking me.

"I KILLED HIM AND NOW I AM GOING TO KILL YOU!"

I struggled against the grip he had on my throat, pulling at his arms frantically and trying to get my hands under his. His hands tightened on my throat and I felt the stiff grass prick the back of my neck. I tried to hit him but he held his face down and my fists fell harmlessly on his head. I was becoming too weak to struggle. His green eyes stared down at me as my vision clouded.

He jumped off.

I sat up coughing and gasping for air. Christian pointed at me, laughing.

"Were you *scared!* Oh boy—did I have you going! I can't believe you thought I killed someone!"

He rolled on the ground and pointed at me, his face becoming red from laughing.

"You're an asshole!" I said, wanting to spit on him. "You oughta

7

be locked up, you know that?"

I rubbed my neck and continued to curse him. I had been set up in the worst way.

"I can't believe how gullible you are," he laughed, the veins in his neck sticking out. "You really believed I killed someone! Wait till I tell everybody!"

I had no idea who "everybody" was, but I imagined football stands of people gathering and laughing at me. I jumped up.

"You better not tell *anybody!*"

He shook his head.

"Why? — what are you going to do about it? You *believed* me the whole way."

"I didn't believe you . . . nobody would believe a dumb act like that! If you tell anybody. . . you can find someone else to play football with!"

I had no idea what kind of threat that was, but it seemed to make him pause.

"I'm going home, and you better not say anything," I warned, trying to regain my lost dignity.

I started to walk back across the field.

"Hey Brenton!"

I ignored him.

"Hey Brenton!"

I stopped and turned around.

"What?"

He had his shirt slung around his neck and was pulling on the ends.

"D'you want to come over for lunch?"

I seized the moment.

"With *you?* You gotta be kidding!"

I took some pleasure from the look on his face and started walking again.

"Hey Brenton!"

I kept walking.

"BRENTON!"

I turned around. He was still pulling on the ends of his shirt and pushing back with his head.

"C'mon—it was just a joke. . .we're having tuna fish."

"So what?"

He shrugged.

"Tuna fish. . .and cake for dessert."

I squinted at him.

"What kind of cake?" I asked grudgingly.

"Chocolate."

I considered this as some momentum came to my side.

"You promise you aren't going to tell *anybody* about what happened?—even though I didn't believe your stupid story about killing someone."

He nodded.

"I promise."

I stared at him and considered walking off with victory in hand, but I walked over.

"All right—but you better not say anything!"

A smile broke across his face. We started walking again.

"Just moved here, huh?" he asked after we had walked for a while.

"Uh-huh. . .over the summer."

He nodded.

"That's something. . . we've always lived in Baltimore. I'd like to have lived somewhere else."

I nodded. Christian glanced at me.

"You aren't still mad, are ya?"

"Nah," I lied.

"Yes you are, I can tell."

"No I'm not!"

He looked ahead, hesitated, then flung himself to the ground in

9

front of me. He grabbed his throat and started choking himself.

"What are you doing?"

"I'm letting you get even with me," he answered hoarsely.

He continued choking himself. I watched him as his face turned red.

"All right . . . maybe I'm not mad anymore."

He looked up.

"You sure?"

He started choking himself again.

"I'm sure!"

He jumped up. There were red marks on his throat from his own hands. I stared at him.

"I told you I didn't believe you anyway . . ."

He looked at me and grinned.

"C'mon Brenton, you believed me . . . admit it."

I shook my head.

"You're crazy — it was the stupidest story I've ever heard!"

He shrugged.

"It doesn't matter now, we're even."

I nodded.

This was true, we were even, but only by his graces. Right from the start there was a fairness that he enforced. He didn't want any type of advantage to tip the scales in his favor. Christian wanted a fair match — even in terms of personality.

I ate lunch with him on that first day in awe of their sprawling, four-story home. Christian was an only child. His mother was a short woman who talked a lot while adjusting various diamonds and gems, lamenting how the world had become so small now that she had traveled around it three times. I met Christian's father at some point. He spoke little, but moved quickly with the sense of purpose that is the possession of self-made men. Christian called him "sir" and so did I.

Christian's room occupied almost the whole top floor of the house. Annie, their live-in maid, lived on the floor below in a room next to Christian's parents. Even while I envied his large room, I felt it was too much space for one person.

My own home wasn't shabby, but we didn't possess the money Christian's family had. My father's side of the family at one time had been well-to-do. The money had come from my grandfather who was a lawyer, civic leader, and politician of some significance in Virginia. He died when my father was a boy and the money was squandered to the point where all my father inherited was an unsecured loan. My own impression was that our family was always one step behind my father's next check, so there was the understanding that times were good during the month and tight at the end.

My father was something of a history buff—mostly the history of the South. His thick books lined one wall of our den in Civil War splendor. At the end of long days of being on the road for his Industrial sales job he came back and smoked his pipe, refighting the War between the States. He had wanted to be a lawyer, but slept through the admissions test. Marriage and a child served the final blows to his judicial aspirations. He became a salesman with the initial assumption that it was temporary and law was waiting in the wings until the family "got ahead." But the job became the vocation, his pipe smoke mixed regularly into the dusk, and I was left to forge into the present on my own.

When I turned ten, my mother decided that television impinged on our family's sense of culture and the set was sold. That space in our living room was replaced by a bookshelf, and at an early age I had to depend on the dusty imaginings of men long-passed for any entertainment. I developed a certain independence and quietly looked for a new role model. I needed someone able to compete in the tough game that life was becoming. Someone grounded in the present. Christian seemed to be the answer.

Soon after we met, Christian asked if I wanted to go with him and his family to Ocean City for the weekend. Ocean City used to be connected to the state, but a hurricane punched a hole through the connecting strip and it became a five-minute drive across the bridge from the mainland. This was my first visit to the island I would come to know very well.

The fascination of Ocean City was the boardwalk, a wooden conveyer belt that ran along the beach on one side and in front of the stores, hotels, and restaurants on the other. The warm salty air of the ocean floated along the boardwalk carrying the smell of hot dogs, popcorn, seafood, and the hot-pretzel carts that rolled up and down.

Christian took me on a tour down this long wooden trail that shimmered into the distance. Our bare feet plunked on the hot boards while the ocean crashed along the beach, pulling people onto the yellow sand that ran between wood and water. We moved quickly down the sun-hot boardwalk that smelled like telephone poles in summer.

That night we walked toward the rides at the end of the boardwalk. The beaches cooled under the warm blanket of ocean air and the heat of the day glowed in the faces moving through the night. The roar of the ocean occasionally broke through the din, then quickly receded back into the night. A yellow Ferris wheel turned in the distance and excited children screamed the delight of the people on the boardwalk.

Christian said there was something he wanted to show me before we got to the rides. He wouldn't tell me what it was until we were almost there. A group of people looked out at the beach from the edge of the boardwalk. We made our way to the front and saw a sculpture made entirely out of sand; it was the Virgin Mary. A single blue light lit the sand figure against the ocean darkness.

"What do you think of that, Brenton?" Christian whispered next to me.

I stared at the blue sculpture.

"How can anybody do that with sand?"

"I don't know," Christian shrugged. "But somebody does."

"Have you ever seen him?"

He shook his head.

"Some old man who lives by the bay does the sculptures—nobody ever sees the guy from what I've heard. I guess he comes real late at night to make a new sculpture and pick up the money."

"The money" was a bucket full of coins on the edge of the boardwalk. The pail was full and new coins clinked as they were thrown in.

"You mean that bucket of money stays here all night and nobody watches it?" I asked.

Christian nodded slowly.

"Yup. No one has ever stolen it."

We stood looking at the peaceful figure and then started walking again on the boardwalk. There was something about the scene that made me want to stay.

"I can't believe nobody takes the money."

"Ahh— you don't have any faith, Brenton. You have to believe in people."

"I do," I protested.

Christian shrugged.

"Then believe it."

I paused.

"Maybe he comes real early sometimes," I suggested.

"Maybe. . . "

I looked behind us—the blue light was small in the distance.

The rides on the pier occupied most of the night. We made our way slowly back down the boardwalk and stopped to look at the sand sculpture again. I looked closely at the Madonna of sand. Her veil was perfectly sculpted, melting back into the hill she lay upon. A small nose and mouth were formed out of curves of wet sand. Her eyes were serene and her head lay against clasped hands. A crowd had gathered as usual and the bucket was full of money. I looked at the bucket that would sit out all night until the old man came and got it.

"Wonder what he looks like?"

Christian turned to me.

"Who looks like?"

"The old man who does the sculptures."

Christian shook his head slowly and turned back to the figure of sand.

"Nobody knows."

We started walking again. Christian was quiet and I watched the lights far out on the ocean. A green light moved with us in the darkness.

"I've been thinking," Christian began slowly.

"About what?"

"About what you said about the old man — about never being able to see him," he continued, looking straight ahead.

"Yeah, so?"

He hesitated.

"I know a way we can see him!"

"How are we going to do that?"

He turned to me excitedly.

"After my parents go to sleep tonight we'll sneak out and go down to the sand sculpture and hide under the boardwalk. He's gonna come sooner or later and we'll be there."

I nodded and looked at him.

"You sure we can get out?"

"Sure we can — we just have to be real quiet is all."

I turned around and looked down the boardwalk at the small blue light, then at him.

"All right, but if your parents wake up—"

"Don't worry, they won't."

Christian smiled. We walked on as the surf hit the beach loudly and then faded away again. I looked for the green light out on the ocean, but it was gone.

We went to bed early, then slipped quietly out of the bedroom after his parents had gone to bed. There was only the steady tick of the clock in the kitchen and the soft roar of the surf outside. Christian quietly swung the front door open. We stepped outside onto the cool cement of the walkway that was open to the air on one side. Christian left the door slightly ajar. We ran toward the elevator in the salty night air.

We moved through the ocean mist and far down the empty board-walk I could see the small blue beacon. Christian stopped suddenly.

"Uh-oh, we've got trouble."

"What?" I gasped, skidding to a stop.

He motioned ahead. A policeman walked out of the shadows and was coming toward us on the boardwalk.

"My father will kill me," Christian whispered.

I had visions of Christian's parents coming down and bailing us out of jail. The policeman came abreast of us, nodded, and kept walking. I let out my breath.

"That was close!"

Christian wiped a line of sweat off his brow with a trembling hand.

"Yeah—let's go."

We started running again and reached the sculpture. The Virgin Mary was dark with moisture, and the metal pot of money was wet.

"C'mon . . . let's get under the boardwalk," Christian motioned, jumping off into the sand.

We positioned ourselves partly under the boardwalk, but even with the sand sculpture and the money. From our hidden spot we could see anyone who came to get the money. A half-hour passed and nothing happened. We settled in for a long wait.

Christian laid back in the sand and I molded a small mound to lean my head on. A foghorn brooded from a distant lighthouse and the ocean nudged the still night with its soft rhythm. Halos of mist hovered over the lights on the boardwalk.

"I wonder what it would be like to live at the beach," I murmured, feeling sleepy.

"Don't know — pretty great probably." Christian sat up and looked out to the ocean. "My father would never let me do it though."

I looked at him.

"Why not?"

He shrugged.

"— just know he wouldn't. Not till I was real old . . . like college maybe."

I nodded.

"Your dad's pretty strict?"

"He isn't too bad. . . . I just always have to do well." He turned to me. "Your dad ever hit you?"

I thought for a moment.

"No — not that I can remember."

Christian nodded.

"You're lucky."

I looked at him.

"Your dad ever hit you?"

"Yeah . . . when I do something, he does."

"With his hand?"

"Hand, or his belt."

He turned over and put his finger in the sand.

"What's he hit you for?"

"Different things." Christian shrugged. "I remember one time I had been out wrestling around with Jimmy from down the street and fell down on some glass and cut my knee real deep. I had to sneak in the house and try to close it—it's this scar here." He pulled up his leg and pointed to a thick white line that ran across his knee.

"I thought I had it closed and all, but I woke up in the middle of the night and the whole sheet was red with blood." He paused. "I tried to stop the bleeding, but in the morning Annie came in and found the sheet. I knew I was in for it then. They took me to the hospital and I got twelve stitches. . . . Dad beat me pretty good that time."

"Why'd he hit you—you didn't do anything."

Christian shrugged.

" 'Cause I didn't tell him. . .and if I told him he would have hit me for cutting myself."

"That doesn't make any sense."

Christian smiled ruefully and laid down in the sand.

"Mom says he does it 'cause he was poor as a boy and his dad used to beat him. I guess my dad's family was real poor. . .they only had beans and molasses to eat for dinner and he had to quit high school and go to work—his dad was a drunk."

"Your dad drink?"

Christian shook his head.

"No—but mom says he thinks I have so much more than he did when he was growing up, and that's why wants me to do well in everything."

He was silent for a moment. I looked around at the darkness under the boardwalk, then at him.

"Well listen, if you ever need to stay at my house, 'cause he's hitting you or something. . .you can."

Christian nodded and stared up at the dark sky. He turned to me.

"You know, I'm not really afraid of anything but him."

"Really? I'm afraid of a lot of things."

Christian sat up and squinted.

"Yeah, like what?"

"Like fighting maybe. . . "

"Ah, everybody is afraid of fighting."

"No," I shook my head. "It's different than that."

"What do you mean?"

I shrugged.

"I don't know. . .just different."

Christian was silent. He laid back down, then we talked of living at the beach till we fell asleep. I woke up and heard taps on the wooden planks. The wet, rubbery smell of rain was in the air and I moved further under the boardwalk.

"Gonna be a big storm," Christian whispered from the darkness under the boardwalk.

"How long have you been awake?"

"A while — just wanted to see how long you would sleep in the rain."

"Thanks."

Lightning flashed. A spidery blue light touched the ocean and rain swept across the beach, drumming on the boardwalk. Water dripped down on us from the openings between the planks. I looked out at the rain.

"You think he would come in this?"

Christian shrugged.

"He's got to. I'm going to take a look."

He went out into the rain and stopped.

"Hey Brenton!"

"What?"

"Look, it's him!"

I came out and he pointed to the boardwalk. Near the blue light was an old man hugging a greasy wet coat around him. His pants sagged and his shoes didn't have laces. His beard was a stubble of gray and a wet hat hung down on the sides of his head. He glanced up and down the boardwalk, then picked up the bucket of money and started pouring the coins into his coat pockets.

Christian jumped up on the boardwalk. The old man stopped and stared. I came up next to Christian and the man moved back a step, putting his hands in his pockets with the change. The rain was soaking all of us.

"What do you boys want?"

"We just wanted to see you," Christian explained.

The old man squinted and pointed a craggy finger at us.

"Ain't it past your bedtimes?"

Christian put his hands up.

"We just wanted to see who made these figures out of sand — are these sculptures hard to make?"

The old man looked at him, then at the eroding sculpture. An understanding spread across his face.

"Well, uh, why no, they ain't . . . you jest have to spend time is all," he said, taking his other hand out of his pocket. Christian shook his head.

"Well, it's something. I'll bet it's really hard—"

A whistle split the air, then light swept through the rain. The old man turned and ran off the boardwalk into the darkness of a street. The whistle blew again and a policeman ran up. He shined his flashlight down the street, water bouncing off his black slicker.

"Were you boys talking to an old man?"

"—yes," Christian nodded.

"That damn Wiley! . . . He got away again."

The policeman clicked off his light and turned to us.

"What are you two doing out at this time of night?"

We looked at each other, then Christian shrugged, pointing to the sand sculpture.

"We just wanted to see who the sandman was."

"You what?"

"—see who made the sand sculptures . . ."

"Who's Wiley?" I asked.

The policeman's face hardened.

"He's a bum! Always taking people's money," he said, glancing down the dark avenue again.

"Is he a crook?" Christian asked slowly.

The policeman turned.

"Yeah, he is. . . . Are you two going to tell me what you're doing out?"

The rain was running off the brim of his hat in a steady stream. Christian cleared his throat.

"Does that Wiley make sand sculptures?"

"Sand sculptures!. . . Christ! I don't know — maybe if he can get money for it he does. Now you kids get the hell out of here or I'll take you to the station and call your parents."

"Yes sir," I said, grabbing Christian's arm.

"But what about the sand sculpture?" Christian whispered.

I motioned to where the Virgin Mary had been.

"What sand sculpture?"

Christian stared at the smooth hill of sand the figure had become in the rain.

"Come on, Christian — let's go!"

"But. . .the sandman."

The sky rumbled and the beach lit up around us.

"I'm giving you kids to the count of three to get out of here."

"Let's go, Christian!"

I started dragging him down the boardwalk.

"One. . .two. . . "

Christian threw off my arm and started walking. I glanced back once at the blue light and was relieved to see the policeman had left. We walked in silence.

"Well, I guess we found out who the sandman is," I said tiredly.

Christian turned and looked at me.

"What do you mean?"

"Well," I shrugged. "It's that Wiley guy—he takes people's money. . ."

Christian pushed me down on the wood of the boardwalk. He was on top of my chest and his face was inches from mine.

"What do you mean! That wasn't him! Don't ever say that!"

He pushed me and then walked quickly down the boardwalk. I got up slowly and rubbed my leg where I had fallen. I started angrily down the boardwalk and decided to be done with him after this trip.

We walked separately till Christian stopped at a bench just before his parents' place. I approached him warily.

"Hey Brenton—I just had an idea!"

"Are you talking to me?"

He smiled and nodded. I kept walking.

"Well, I'm not talking to *you!*"

"Listen . . .," he began.

"Forget it. You're a *jerk!* Go find someone else to beat up."

Christian scratched his head and looked down the wet boardwalk. It had stopped raining. A mist had come in from the ocean and was flowing past the boardwalk lights.

"You don't have to be that mad," he said quietly.

I turned to him.

"Oh yeah? Let me push *you* down!"

He shrugged and smiled.

"Go ahead."

"Yeah . . . right."

Christian fell down on the boardwalk.

"C'mon—jump on me."

I looked at him.

"I ought to jump on your head."

"Go ahead—I won't stop you."

I stood over him.

"You're nuts."

He jumped up.

"You want to hear my idea?"

"No. . ."

"Look!"

He pointed down the beach and all I could see was the red beam of a distant lighthouse.

"What—I don't see anything."

"The lighthouse!" he said, jabbing his finger in the air.

"So. . .what about it?"

"There's another lighthouse next to it—it's real old and you can climb up in it and—"

"You've *done* this?"

"No. . .but I know a bunch of guys who have, and they say you can get outside when you get to the top and the view is great!"

I looked at the distant lighthouse.

"It looks pretty far, Christian."

"We could hitch a ride down the highway, and—"

"You want to go climb it, *now?*"

"Sure—we'll be back by dawn," he said, putting his hands up as if it was all very logical.

I shook my head.

"I don't know, Christian, I—"

"Come on—how many times are we out at this time of night?"

I protested some more, but from the look on his face I knew it was no use. Christian had made up his mind. I knew this was enough to set any plan in motion.

We reached the Ocean Highway and started walking. Christian's plan had one minor flaw: there were no cars to hitch a ride with. Finally, a car came down the highway and we put out our thumbs. The car stopped and an old man motioned for us to get in. I climbed in front.

"What are you boys doing out at this time of night?"

"Exploring," Christian answered.

"Exploring, eh? Well, it's a heck of a time to be exploring," he said, starting to drive again.

The old man drove slowly with both hands gripping the wheel.

"The missus is in the hospital in Salisbury, so I stay till she goes to sleep and then come back in the morning," he said, looking over his thick glasses.

I nodded.

"Have you lived in Ocean City long?"

"All my life," he said, tapping the wheel lightly. "I leave a lot now that the wife is sick."

I looked at him.

"I hope she isn't too sick."

The old man stared straight ahead and paused.

"I hope so, too."

The measured lines of the highway slipped beneath the headlights as we drove to the far side of the island. White sand ran alongside the car and occasional drifts reached halfway across the road. Weathered cottages hunched between long stretches of vacant beach and the slats and wires of a red erosion fence blurred into one. Rusted, red-and-white NO TRESPASSING signs flared out of the darkness along the beach road as we passed wooden structures that loomed up against the early grayness. Christian pointed these out as old World War II observation stations. The old man came to a point that we thought was roughly even with the lighthouse and pulled to the side of the road. A faint line of light touched the ocean along the horizon.

Christian and I got out of the car.

"Good luck exploring, young fellas," he called out the open door.

"I hope your wife gets better," I said.

He nodded.

"Thank you — she will, God willing."

I shut the door and he drove away.

"Nice old guy," I said, watching the car disappear down the highway.

"Sure was," Christian nodded, looking toward the beach. "— I think we go this way."

He started toward the flashing red beam in the distance. We climbed the ridge of sand just before the beach, the tall weeds brushing dew on our legs. I looked and saw we had gone past the lighthouse.

"We went too far," I yelled at Christian, who was ahead of me. He shook his head.

"The old lighthouse is further down."

Christian ran up the crest with a burst of energy and I followed him. We reached the top; a wide, virgin beach spread out before us. The ocean collapsed on the shore and sizzled back. The old lighthouse was black against the gray sky.

We stumbled down toward the tower. The newer lighthouse flicked on and off silently in the distant morning light. Christian sprinted ahead and reached the bottom.

"I'll bet this thing used to signal to ships a long time ago," he said, leaning back and looking up. I leaned back and followed his gaze up to the dark glass top of the tower.

"God — it's old."

The faded red stripes on the sides of the lighthouse were chipped off in patches. Large, metal NO TRESPASSING BY ORDER OF THE COAST GUARD signs were posted on both sides of the entrance. Christian walked up to the door.

"Christian — maybe we shouldn't go in."

He waved.

"Don't worry about it. If the door is locked, we won't go in."

The wooden door had a lock that was corroded and rusted.

Christian pushed his weight against the door and the hasp pulled out of the wood.

"I guess we were meant to go in," he smiled, as the door creaked open.

We walked into cool, briny air that smelled faintly like damp, rotting wood. Tiny threads tickled my nose; I brushed a spider web from my face. A wooden table and chair rested by a stairway that spiraled up into the darkness.

"Come on," Christian whispered.

He started climbing the stairs in the dark.

"You aren't going *up* there?"

"Of course! Come on."

I considered not going up the steps, but this was the main thing that intrigued me about Christian: he had nerve, or maybe even courage, and this went directly to my own deficiency. I had no choice but to follow.

Our shoes tapped on the iron stairs. Christian spiraled around the musty stairwell above me in the blackness. Our footsteps echoed up and down as we climbed higher. I looked over the railing at the faint light from the open doorway far below and held on tightly.

"Brenton—there's a platform you're coming to," Christian called from the darkness above me.

I stopped.

"Where?"

"Just keep going!"

I kept climbing until his hand pulled me against the wall.

"Now—there's a small ladder and then a trap door," he said, his voice echoing crazily.

"How can you see?"

"I felt it with my hands. . . . I'll go first."

He started up the ladder. I watched him warily.

"Are you sure you want to do this?"

25

"Of course."

Morning light was coming through some sort of opening above us. Christian's outline was on the ladder. He pushed at the trap door above him. It opened and light poured down onto the platform. Christian went up through the opening, then peered down at me.

"Come on," he said, motioning.

I went up the ladder cautiously and pulled myself through the trap door. We were inside the light room.

The machinery of the beacon filled the space. The dawn light was in the thick glass lens. Behind the lens was a silver reflector the size of a kitchen table with large, spiraled filaments that were black with dust and age. Greased cogs were below the reflector and connected to a bulky, dust-covered gearbox. Corroded cables ran from a black switch box on the wall to the motor that had powered the light.

I stood in the well of the trap door. The floor was rotted in several places and had completely given out in front of the door leading to the platform outside. This was the opening of light I had seen from the stairs below. The only way to get outside was to jump over the dark hole.

"I'll bet the view outside is great!" Christian said, looking at the door. He stood flat against the wall. I stared at him.

"You're not going to jump over that?"

"Sure — why not? It's only about four feet across."

"It looks bigger."

"Nah." Christian crouched down. "Wish me luck."

"You're crazy!"

Christian took a deep breath, crouched down further, and then exploded toward the hole. It was a perfectly executed leap. He cleared the hole, practically hitting the door, and turned around.

"See? Nothing to it — go ahead!" he said from the other side.

I looked at the hole and shook my head.

"I can't do it."

"Why not?"

" 'Cause I'll fall. . . . I know it," I said, not looking up.

Christian stared at me.

"Aren't you going to at least try?"

I looked at the hole again and thought about trying to jump it. I looked up at him. "I can't do it."

"You mean you won't try."

"I mean I'll fall through!"

Christian shook his head.

"You don't know that—I'll grab you."

"No, I'll fall."

"How do you know till you try?"

I stood for a moment.

"I just know."

"Just *try*, Brenton. I promise I won't let you fall."

I took a deep breath and knew I had to at least attempt to get across the hole. Christian demanded that. I wanted to tell myself that deep down I did possess the courage to do it. I moved slowly from the trap door and stood flat against the wall with the hole in front of me. Christian coached me from the other side.

"Just crouch down and *jump!*"

My heart pounded. Sweat was running down the sides of my chest and I couldn't get any saliva in my mouth.

"C'mon, Brenton—there's nothing to it."

I nodded. Pricks of sweat stung my face. I wiped a trembling hand across my forehead. I had no energy at all. Just to move my legs would require some miracle. I peered into the blackness and nausea moved through me. There was no courage, no reserve of unqualified nerve to help me through this—I was paralyzed.

"I can't move," I said weakly.

"You aren't going to jump?"

"I mean I can't move," I said, trying to get some air to keep from

27

passing out.

I saw the hole and myself falling through the darkness to the ground beneath. I was dizzy and felt myself sway.

"Christ, Brenton!"

Christian jumped back across the hole. He landed next to me and grabbed my arm.

"Are you all right?" he asked, his voice far away.

He led me to the trap door while spots and circles moved across my vision. It wasn't till I was standing on the ladder that the world became right again.

"I'm all right—just felt lightheaded," I said, trying to act as if some physical defect had intervened and prevented my jump.

"Can you go down?"

"Sure," I nodded.

I considered turning around and declaring I would try again, but I knew I wouldn't. It was there now. Christian had proved one of my own doubts. I did lack the nerve that in crucial moments would come to the rescue and allow a person to do what was required. My own suspicions had just been confirmed.

We made our way back down the steps silently and went back to the highway to hitchhike home. Neither of us spoke of the lighthouse again and the summer proceeded along. But I had a defect now, something that I had only suspected before. Christian possessed what I wanted, and if I studied him long enough I might get it too. All I had to do was stay around him. And as far as I could tell, there was nothing to keep me from doing that.

2

The train climbed the endless mountains of Pennsylvania and far ahead the whistle broke the still mountain air. I sat by the window, watching the mist turn gold from the twilight that slipped quietly behind the mountains. I turned and leaned back in my seat, listening to the rolling tracks that pushed the midwest farther behind. The east lay ahead.

I was excited and apprehensive about my trip. I was headed east to visit Christian for the summer. I should probably back up a little and tell what had happened before all this. I went to Ocean City with Christian for two more summers. During the third summer, my father decided better opportunities lay elsewhere and we moved to Chicago. Christian came to visit the first year and I went back to Baltimore once. We wrote back and forth, but eventually it was reduced to a phone call every few months. By the time my senior year in high school came, it had been three years since we had seen each other.

Christian called in April and asked if I would be interested in working for a summer in Ocean City. I had ideas of going somewhere before college, so I took his offer and was due to leave for the east in June.

In retrospect, the four years in Chicago had gone by quickly. I felt I had grown more in those years than in all my previous years put together. Still, I found the speed of events disconcerting: Just as suddenly as I graduated, I found myself on the train headed east with no time to think about anything.

I tapped my little finger against the train window and thought about Christian. A school flew by the window and I saw an empty football field. I remembered a conversation from long ago with Christian. It was during our last year together.

We had both just started attending the Hawthorne Boys' School and we were in the middle of trying to make the football team. On the second day of school we were marched out to the football stands in the hot sun.

"Men!" Coach Reginald yelled, calling us to attention.

He was the eighth-grade coach for football; a man that controlled our destinies. His hair was slicked back and his large face was tan in the sunlight. Coach Reginald was a big man with an impressive stomach that he clasped his hands across when talking. He had his hands on his stomach now.

"Men — Hawthorne Eighth Grade Football has a proud tradition of winning," he said, shifting his girth back and forth on his feet. "And men," he said, looking down. "I don't want any losers on my team — the losers can go to intramurals. . .I won't hold it against you."

Mr. Reginald unclasped his hands and looked up.

"I'm glad to see, men, there are no losers in the Hawthorne eighth grade. But some of you will be sent over to intramurals, and I want you to work your butts off when you get there so next year you can play on the class team."

He put his hands back on his stomach.

"So, are we going to have a winning season, men?"

"Yes sir!" the Hawthorne eighth grade roared.

Hawthorne was primarily a school of athletics and the biggest sport was football. The school boasted outstanding credentials academically, but the real test was on the playing field—a Hawthorne Man was primarily an athlete. We had to make the team.

The next day we received our equipment and went through the usual hitting drills. I was bigger than most of the other eighth graders and thought it would be no real problem to make the team. Christian was smaller than a lot of the guys and I knew he would have to work extra hard.

Several weeks passed. We were hitting the practice dummies and sweating heavily in the September heat. Coach Reginald surveyed our progress. Most of the cuts had already been made and I was confident I would be on the team. Coach Reginald walked by and I hit the tackling dummy extra hard. He turned to me.

"Brenton—go join the intramurals," he said with a flick of his hand, pointing across the wide field.

I turned and stared at him, but he was already walking on. I thought maybe he was talking to someone else and looked around.

"Heathersfield, *move!*" someone yelled.

I was standing in the way of the drill. I started to walk very slowly across the field. That was the longest walk of my life. My career at Hawthorne was over. I thought I had done an adequate job at keeping my weakness covered, but it had done me in just the same. Coach Reginald had detected the faulty strut that would break in some crucial game. He had done what was best for the team. I was to join the too fat, the too skinny, and the too weak of heart that made up intramurals. I had been cut from the team and was now on the outside of things.

The last day of cuts was on Friday of the second week after I joined intramurals. All of the guys who had made the squad now knew it and went home for the weekend feeling very good. Christian had made the team and was in an amiable mood as we walked home. Autumn had come with brown leaves falling into the streets and the crisp air smelling of burning logs. I struggled with my cloth bag that was full of books.

Christian looked at me.

"You're quiet, Brenton."

"Hmph," I grunted.

I loosened my tie and wished I had never heard of Hawthorne. We walked along in silence. Even the sound of our hard shoes on the cement bothered me. Christian started whistling.

"Will you cut out the whistling!"

Christian was silent for a moment.

"Is it the team?. . .Is that what's bothering you?"

"No!"

"Yes it is. That's what's bothering you," Christian said with this irritating smugness.

"No, it's not! Will you just leave me alone!"

He shrugged.

"You just didn't try hard enough. . ."

"Shut up," I muttered.

"What did you say?"

"Nothing."

"Yes you did, you—"

"I said, *shut the hell up!*"

Christian grinned and shook his head.

"It's not my fault you didn't make the team—you just didn't try hard enough—"

"SHUT UP!"

I threw my books down on the ground and stepped in front of him. Christian stopped. He put his books down on the ground slowly and stared at me. The wind picked at his tie and a car went past. Perspiration cooled on my upper lip as the sun went behind a cloud and the dry leaves hissed above me. Christian waited. I reached down and grabbed my sack of books. I pushed past him and didn't stop till I was home.

I didn't talk to Christian for the next two weeks and we both looked the other way when we passed at school. I struggled through intramurals, where going to practice every day was a reminder of my failure. It was a strained muscle that came to my rescue when a short, fat tackler fell into me, and—for the first time—a decent tackle occurred in intramurals. I struggled to my feet as the pain cut through my back.

I was injured and couldn't practice. I sat on the hill around the field for a few practices, making it look as if I was counting the days till I could return. After a while the coach didn't seem to care if I showed up for practice or not. I took to walking around the campus during that hour.

It was on a rainy Friday afternoon during practice that I went down to the old building known as the Slave Quarters. It was the English building, but it had supposedly been the residence of slaves when the school was a plantation. I knew the English classes weren't in session and I could pass the hour alone. The rain was coming down hard by the time I reached the building. I walked onto the small front porch and pulled a chair to the banister. I sat down and put my feet up on the railing.

I watched the intramuralers slogging around in the misty rain on the practice field. I was glad it was raining; I would have felt out of place on a sunny day. For the first time I considered leaving school to start over somewhere else, hoping that I wouldn't be benched as unceremoniously as I had been at Hawthorne.

I didn't hear the two instructors walk up till they were behind me.

"Looking at the rain, Brenton?" Mr. Reefe asked, motioning for me to stay seated.

It was Mr. Reefe and Mr. Lant, my math and science teachers.

"Yes sir."

"Aren't you supposed to be practicing?"

Mr. Lant motioned to the small squad of boys huddling on the wet field.

"Yes sir, only I hurt my back and have to take some time off."

They were quiet for a moment.

"You know — I have seen a lot of athletes never recover from injuries," Mr. Reefe remarked.

Mr. Lant nodded.

"Yes, it's too bad when that happens."

"The worst is when the injury is in the head."

"Oh right — it spreads; soon they can't get out of bed," Mr. Lant continued.

My skin became warm. I shifted uncomfortably in the chair.

"Well, there are always a few bad apples in every bunch . . . sometimes they just slip through with the rest," Mr. Reefe finished slowly.

"They eventually get washed out though," Mr. Lant added.

I opened my mouth but felt like someone had just knocked the air out of me.

"I guess they do," Mr. Reefe nodded. "Such a waste of time."

A deep hurt was spreading up from my stomach and making my throat tight.

"We ought to go, Mr. Reefe, and let poor Brenton nurse his back."

"Get a lot of rest, Brenton."

"Yes sir," I replied weakly.

They walked off into the drizzle. I brushed hot tears off my cheeks and was glad they had stood behind me. I sat for a long time just staring out at the field. I wiped my eyes again as someone ran under the overhang.

Christian brushed the rain from his coat. He was headed for the locker room for team practice and held his tie in his hand. I looked quickly at the field. He stood for a moment, then cleared his throat.

"What are you doing?"

I shrugged.

"Just watching the rain."

"Oh," he nodded.

He slapped his tie against his hand.

"Aren't you going to practice?"

"No! My back hurts."

"Oh, that's too bad. . . .You told the coach, huh?"

"Yes. . .but everybody thinks I'm faking it anyway."

I held a hand up to my face.

"Who thinks you're faking it?"

"Mr. Reefe and Mr. Lant do," I muttered, trying to keep my voice steady.

"How do you know?"

" 'Cause they were just out here and they said so!"

Christian was silent and the rain sizzled around us. I could hear him slapping his tie against his palm. He shifted his weight several times.

"Brenton . . . forget about those guys —they're just giving you a hard time."

"I know."

Christian paused.

"Look, Brenton, it doesn't matter what they think. You know if you're faking it or not, so forget those guys. It's not worth it."

I looked at him.

"Not—worth it?. . . Not worth making the team, huh? Easy for you to say."

Christian took a deep breath.

"I'm not saying making the team's not important, but . . . maybe for you it's not."

I looked up at him. Christian was pulling the tie between his hands.

"— besides . . . if it was a matter of talent you would have made it."

"What are you talking about?"

"I mean that you have more natural ability. . . I just try harder."

He stared at me with clear eyes and I knew Christian was just saying what he thought was obvious. I nodded slowly and looked down.

"You'd better get to practice, Christian, before you get in trouble."

I pulled my hands down across my face.

"That's all right," he said, shrugging. "It'll wait."

We sat in silence. I turned to him.

"You ever hurt your back?"

"No — but I broke my finger one day in practice," he said, holding up a bent pinkie.

"Really — you broke it?"

"Sure. Try and straighten it."

He held it out to me and I gingerly tried to straighten his little finger.

"See — it won't straighten. It healed that way," he said, nodding.

"Did you stop playing?"

"Nah."

"Didn't it hurt?"

"Sure, but you just ignore the pain — you get used to it."

I nodded slowly and turned to watch the intramuralers falling down in the mud. I took my feet down off the railing and stood up.

"— maybe I'll go back to practice."

"What about your back?"

"It's all right . . . I might be able to catch the end of practice," I said, shrugging and putting my hands in my pockets.

Christian stood up and put his tie around his neck.

"All right—let's go."

We ran through the hard rain to the locker room.

The year progressed and somehow I got through intramurals. Football ended and we had Christmas break. I went over to Christian's on Christmas Eve. We made our way across the whiteness of the snow-covered golf course and reached the woods that bordered the country club. An old railroad trail went into the woods. All that was left of the tracks was one of the rails and some rotted wood.

"Where do you think these tracks lead to?" I asked, looking down the white path.

Christian pushed his hat back on his head, exhaling a long steamy breath into the frozen air.

"Don't know. My dad says a lot of these tracks are from when they used to bring coal in. Wanna follow it and see where it goes?"

"Sure!"

We started following the slight rise in the snow that marked the tracks. The snow had melted in the sun then refroze when the temperature dipped. Our boots cracked the hard surface, scrunching through the snow. We left a trail across the smooth surface, following the train tracks up a hill where they abruptly stopped. I looked down the hill.

"Where'd the tracks go?"

Christian walked ahead.

"There was a trestle here at one time. Look, see those concrete pillars at the bottom of the hill—that was the foundation for the trestle. It crossed over and continued on the hill over there."

I followed his line of vision.

"Oh yeah."

"C'mon, let's go look at the trestle."

I followed him down the hill to the first concrete pillar. Christian grabbed hold of an iron rung sticking out the side of the trestle.

"Hey, it's a ladder going up the side." He looked up the concrete structure and then turned to me. "Let's climb to the top."

"I don't know—looks kind of shaky to me."

"Ah, come on—nothing to it. You go first and I'll follow so if you fall I can catch you."

I looked up at the iron rungs that led to the top, and then at Christian.

"Go on! You can do it, Brenton."

I shook my head and grabbed the first rung. I started up slowly.

"Just don't look down!" Christian called.

I concentrated on the cement in front of me and climbed very slowly. I stopped in the middle. We were even with some distant church steeples. I wondered how he had gotten me into this.

"Just concentrate on the next rung, Brenton!"

I started moving again and finally reached the flat area on the top of the trestle. Christian came up and we brushed off the snow and sat down. There wasn't much room at the top and we sat close to the middle, looking out over the snowy vista of church steeples poking above frosted trees and small white houses that ran as far as we could see. Bells chimed in the distance.

"Jesus—what a view!"

"We are up here," I said, scooting closer to the center.

Christian nodded.

"Just think, at this time tomorrow it will be *Christmas.*"

"Yup, tomorrow we'll know what our presents are," I said, hugging my knees.

Christian nodded and kicked some snow off the top.

"I would hate to fall off this thing," I said, looking over the side.

"You aren't kidding; on the day before Christmas, too."

"Maybe you wouldn't get killed, but you'd definitely break some bones."

A gust of wind blew some snow off the trestle.

"I wonder what it's like to die?" Christian murmured.

I looked at him and shrugged.

"Nobody's ever come back to talk about it."

"I wonder if you can come back and talk to people who are alive?" he said slowly.

"I guess so — maybe that's what hauntings are."

He sat for a moment, then turned to me.

"I'll make you a deal: If you die first, you come back and tell me what it's like. And if I die first, I'll come back and tell you!"

I paused.

"I'm not sure it works like that . . . but all right."

We shook on our pact.

The sun was starting to slant down in the west and it was getting cold. We climbed down and headed home. Christian and I walked back to our neighborhood and felt the safety of familiarity. The large homes were already lit up and Christmas trees twinkled out from the windows. Chimney smoke was in the air and colored lights lined the houses and trees.

There was only an orange glow in the sky and I started humming "God Rest Ye Merry, Gentlemen" very softly. Christian joined in and we didn't really know the verses, but we knew the refrain. We walked with our arms around each other, singing, "Ohhh tidings of comfort and joy! Comfort and joy! Ohhh tidings of comfort and joy!"

The rest of the school year passed quickly, but maybe that was because I found out we were to move in June. The months slipped by, and then it was the day before the move. Christian and I headed off together after I let my sister know where we were going in case I had to help pack some more. I gave her directions to this small creek. We rode our bikes to the woods and laid them down next to the trail that led back through tall weeds.

Summer had come again. Hot stagnant air rose from the weeds and dragonflies scattered angrily as we tramped back into the woods. Christian led the way. I watched the calves on his legs flex as we walked and noticed the dark hair starting to appear on his legs.

We came to the edge of the creek. The gurgling water flowed slowly under a large oak tree that reached out over the water. A rope traveled down from a thick branch to a tire hovering above the greenish brown water that was brackish around the edge of the creek. Water spiders skittered across the surface and June bugs buzzed low over the creek. Frogs croaked in the high grass around us. The uncertainty over moving fell away.

Christian waded into the water and sank down to his waist. He grabbed the tire. I sat down and felt safe with the sun-splashed plants and trees around me. The move was far away and there was only the slowed time of deep summer.

"Hey Brenton, are you going to swing or not?" Christian asked, standing in the water.

I shook my head.

"You go first, then I'll go."

Christian waded to the shore and climbed the muddy bank with the swing. He stretched the rope as far as it would go, then turned and jumped onto the tire. The tree branch dipped with his weight as the rope swung down and then out over the water.

"Ahhhh," Christian screamed as he dropped off the tire into the muddy creek.

He splashed down and jumped up. I grabbed the swing as it came by the shore.

"That was a lousy swing! I'll show you how it's done."

I pulled the swing back as far as possible, took a running start, and jumped on top of the tire. The swing roared down the bank, swooping low over the water. I slipped off into the bath-warm creek.

"Oh, *great* swing!" Christian scoffed.

He took the tire swing and lined up again. He paused.

"You know—I still can't believe you're moving."

"Neither can I," I admitted, sitting in the shallow water making mudcakes. "Go, so I can have another turn."

Christian took a running start and I caught him square in the chest with some mud. He looked at me as he went down in the water. He popped up with a handful of muck and threw it. I ducked.

"BRENTON—C'MON BRENTON! YOU HAVE TO PACK!"

Christian stopped and we stared at each other in the water. The summer left.

"That's your sister?"

I nodded.

"ALL RIGHT, I'M COMING!"

We started washing off the mud silently. Christian looked at me.

"Hey Brenton, let's go one more time."

"I gotta go pack," I muttered, washing my hands in the water.

He waved the whole move away with one hand.

"Come on! One more, and listen, this time we'll get the thing to go really high by both of us going on it at the same time!"

I looked at the swing, then at Christian. He ran his hand through his dripping hair. The cicadas buzzed out across the slow June day.

"Do you think it'll hold both of us?"

"Of course! Come on—one last time."

He grabbed the swing and brought the dirty tire over to me.

"All right—one more time."

He nodded and grinned.

"One more."

We decided the best way was to face each other and hang on to both sides of the tire. Christian would jump onto the top of the tire and I would put my feet in the hole. We walked the tire up to the highest point on the muddy bank and grabbed the rope. Christian nodded to me.

"All set?"

"Yeah."

"Let's go!"

We jumped up and Christian hopped on top of the tire as I slipped my feet in the ring. The swing started down. The tree creaked and protested under the weight. I held on tightly, suspending the weight of my body with my hands. I heard my sister call again, but it was too late — we were gone.

The swing hit its low point and started to climb. The rope strained as gravity and the elements played havoc with the umbilical cord holding us. We approached the apex of our swing and the view was terrific. At the highest point Christian screamed, "Jump!"

We crashed down into the water, and the swing came back empty. . . .

I heard something fall into the aisle of the train and turned from the window. A woman sitting across from me had dropped a package. I picked it up.

"Oh, thank you!"

She smiled. Her face was red and her brown eyes were warm. She had on a green polyester outfit, the kind that larger women sometimes wear.

"Where are you going?"

"Baltimore," I answered, handing the package back to her.

"Thank you very much. We're going to Baltimore, too. Would you like some bread?" she asked, unwrapping a large loaf of homemade bread from tin foil.

"No thank you."

"Nonsense!"

She handed me some bread.

"My name is Dorothy and this is Chester," she said, motioning to the man next to her.

Chester leaned forward and nodded. He rested his large hands on a dark wooden cane.

"Chester just had surgery. Throat cancer—they had to remove his vocal cords, so you can understand why he's not talkative."

"Oh."

"Well, at first it was a blessing—I didn't have to listen to his nagging anymore. But ever since I gave him a pencil and paper, I've been bombarded by notes."

She laughed violently and Chester smiled.

"We have had our bouts with trouble. I've had fifteen different operations for cancer," she said, taking out a Kleenex and wiping her brow.

"Fifteen?"

"Oh I know, in and out of the hospital, it gets tiresome," she sighed. "I guess they just can't seem to get it all. My saving grace has always been my children. I can thank the Good Lord for giving me them. We had thirteen you know."

"Thirteen—"

"Oh yes—Chester and I had our hands full, I can tell you that. Now I have ten grandchildren." She dabbed her eyes with the tissue and sighed again. "Times were hard, especially when Chester was hurt in the mine and couldn't work anymore. There were days when I didn't know where the next meal was coming from..." She paused. "But we always managed to scrape through some way."

She looked at me and her eyes brightened.

"Now just look at us! Ten grandchildren and more on the way. Yes—we were blessed with a lot in our lives," she continued, nodding. "And when our time comes, I'm sure the Good Lord will take care of us, I do believe," she murmured, a small cloud moving through her eyes.

I excused myself to go to the washroom.

"Come back and talk to us. I want to hear all about you!" she called as I bounced down the aisle.

I found the door to the bathroom and went to the mirror. I tried to gauge how much I had changed in the last three years. My curly hair was longer now and more unruly, and I was taller, but not quite as lanky. The door opened and I started washing my hands.

A well-dressed black man came in with his son and guided him to the toilet.

"All right, over here, son."

I looked up in the mirror and he nodded to me.

"Where're you headed?"

I looked up again.

"Baltimore."

"Summer vacation?"

I nodded.

"I'm going to spend the summer at the beach—Ocean City, Maryland."

The man leaned against the wall and jingled some change in his pocket. He had on a suit vest with his shirt sleeves rolled up.

"Man, that's great!" He shook his head, his lips pressed together. "I hope I can give my son the chance to do that."

The boy came out of the stall and his father took him to the sink.

"Are you going to school?" he asked, turning on the water.

"I start college in the fall."

"All right boy, dry your hands." He turned back to me. "Do you know what you want to do?"

I shrugged.

"Not really. . . .I'm going to take a lot of different classes."

He sat down on the edge of the sink and looked at me. He was light-skinned and his eyes had laugh lines at the corners.

"I'm in insurance. . .this vacation is a bonus for selling the highest dollar amount of policies annually." He stared at me intently. "My goal is to make a hundred thousand dollars a year by the time I am thirty-five." He raised his eyebrows. "My next goal is to retire when I am fifty, and spend my days in a cottage beside a lake with a sailboat moored nearby."

His son leaned against him.

"Then I can send my boy to any school he wants." He placed his hands on his son's shoulders. "It's a long way off, and sometimes it seems like a long, hard road, but then . . . ," he nodded, building back up. "I know if I work hard enough — it will happen." He looked at me closely "We can do whatever we want . . . if we're not afraid."

He smiled and shook my hand.

"Good luck to you in your endeavors."

"Thanks — you too."

He left the bathroom and I stood for a moment thinking. His determination was so complete . . . I wondered suddenly what would happen if he didn't meet his goals. The train blasted its horn far ahead as a warning to all those concerned.

I went back to my seat and Dorothy had fallen asleep. I nodded to Chester, then looked out the window. I thought of the two different views — one person looking back and the other forward. The train went over a switch with a loud clack. A blue and green signal light flew by the window, then disappeared into the receding darkness.

3

I stood in the wet, warm air of the train station and looked for Christian. I told him half past four, but the train had been late. I glanced at my watch a few times and checked the station clock on the wall — it was five o'clock. I hadn't eaten any lunch and really was too nervous to eat.

The people that had come in on the train with me had already scattered to their destinations. I looked at my watch one more time and turned around to look across the station. I saw someone standing by the ticket windows. He had on a blue blazer and a tie. His hair was brown and combed to the side and he looked to be just under six feet. I started walking toward him and a defined jaw and cleft chin became prominent. He stared at me with pale green eyes, smiling as I walked up.

"Hey Christian!"

"Brenton," he said, nodding.

We shook hands, then neither of us spoke for a long, awkward moment.

"How was the train?"

His voice had dropped a couple of octaves and was doing strange things to vowels.

"Fine, fine."

He looked at his watch.

"—we'd better get your bags."

"—all right."

We both felt the relief of something to do and walked along in silence to the luggage area with our hard shoes tapping against the marble floor. I pointed out my suitcases and he snatched one of them

"Come on, we're going to have to hurry to make it."

"Make what?"

He glanced at me and started walking.

"My sports banquet. I told you about it, didn't I?"

"I don't remember anything."'

Christian snorted and shook his head.

"Same old Brenton—head in the clouds. And where did you get that stupid accent?"

"Mine!" I cried out. "Where did you get *your* stupid accent?"

"I don't have one. It's the way you used to talk till you moved up to 'Chi-CAH-go.' "

"Well, you ought to hear the way you say it—'Chicagooo.' "

Christian laughed.

We reached the parking lot and took off in his sports car, arriving at the banquet in record time. I recognized the country club as our football field from years ago. Christian went to sit with the other athletes and I talked with his parents at their table. The conversation lulled and I sauntered over to a buffet table and started eating meatballs from a silver tray. I nodded to some people I faintly recognized from Hawthorne. I speared a group of meatballs on one toothpick and placed them in my mouth.

"Are those very good?"

I turned — two wet blue eyes blinked innocently at me.

I pointed at the meatballs and nodded.

"Oh don't stop eating on *my* account."

I swallowed.

"I'm done!"

I stared at her. She tossed her smooth blond hair off her shoulder with a slight twist. A single highlighted wave of hair flared at the part and then melted back into the stream. She looked like she was about my age.

"Do you go to Hawthorne?" she inquired, examining the table.

"No — I used to though."

"Oh," she said, turning up a small, freckled nose.

She flicked her hair again with a twist of body and shoulder. There was a tightness about her figure, as if someone had sculpted her with an eye toward balance. She bent forward and picked up a piece of celery. A tanline and a gold pendant rested just below her neck.

"What school do you attend?" I asked.

"I don't."

"No?"

"I'm a rich countess who doesn't have to go to school."

I was treated again to the twist of her body as she moved some infinitesimal hair back into place. A wave of rich scents moved across the air with each flick.

"Really?"

"Oh yes. . . but occasionally I will make an appearance at Bryn Mawr," she said, taking another bite of her celery.

A tiny gold watch hung on her wrist next to a bracelet of stones. It was the kind of bracelet I had seen my mother wear before.

"Merely for show, of course," I suggested, forgetting by now the banquet, Christian, and the east.

"Of course."

I tried to keep my eyes off her lips as she reexamined the food table.

"So what brings you here?"

"I—" I cleared my throat. "I'm out for the summer—from Chicago," I said, sort of swallowing the word Chicago.

"Chicago?"

"Right—Chicago."

I could see that any reason for leaving the Eastern Seaboard was a mistake to her.

"I'm visiting Christian Streizer," I added quickly.

"Christian Streizer," she said slowly.

"We're leaving for Ocean City tomorrow."

She was quiet, then looked up with saddled mirth in her eyes.

"Well so am I, Mr. Chicago man."

A man approached the podium and started to speak. She flicked him away with her hair.

"Well, I hope I see you in Ocean City," she whispered, and then went back to wherever she had come from.

I went back to the table and then realized I didn't even know her name. I looked hurriedly around the dark room, but didn't see her anywhere. I held on to her last whispered sentence, "I hope I see you in Ocean City."

The next day we left for the beach. Christian's loaded-down Spitfire whined down the evening-drenched country road. We cut through the heated fields of Maryland and the Eastern Shore lay in the distance. The young, warm air roared over the convertible.

After the sports banquet there had been a quick succession of parties. Christian had been given all sorts of awards at the banquet, and carried his badges and trophies home in a bag. We had talked some, but this was the first time we'd really had a chance to catch up.

I listened as he talked about the girls he had gone out with. He had done it; "it" being what I hadn't. And he had done it in a lot of places and in a lot of different ways.

"What about that one girl you wrote about last summer. . . you said you wanted to marry her?"

He shrugged.

"Ah — it didn't work out," he muttered, putting his sunglasses on top of his head. "She was a bitch."

His face darkened and then he started talking about a girl he had done it with while driving his car. I listened and tried to reconcile Christian's experiences with my own. I didn't tell him about the public schools of the midwest, where not only was a coat and tie not required, but T-shirts and jeans were a sort of uniform. I had been teased when I called teachers "sir" and "ma'am" — my accent standing out among the flat nasal twang of the region. I had attended a school with girls, but it wasn't till a certain football game, and what I later admitted was a lucky break, that I started to date regularly. But I graduated, still not having managed what Christian had done with several girls.

Christian seemed about the same, and we began where we left off. His father had grayed, but this had not diminished his determination of what Christian's future would be. Christian reeled off his future plans with such enthusiasm that I became envious I didn't have such a clear path. He would attend the University of Richmond's business school and then take over his father's business.

"So, you'll take over the business?"

"Oh sure. . .there was never any question of that." He nodded. "At least to my father there wasn't."

"What about to you?"

Christian shrugged.

"I don't know — seems as good as anything else to do." He pressed down on the accelerator and the car shot past two other cars on the road. "Anyway, that's what I'm going to do," he said, slowing down.

"You did well in sports?" he asked above the wind while handing me a beer.

"Yeah."

I took a long drink from the cool beer and leaned back. We rode in silence for a while just drinking. Christian looked over.

"How'd you do in football?"

I sat up.

"Had the most total rushing of any fullback in the conference."

"How much was that?"

"— what?"

Christian turned down the music.

"How much total rushing did you get?"

I told him and he shrugged.

"Must not be much of a conference, Brenton — our back, Tim Weller, had that much."

I stared at him, but he kept his eyes straight ahead.

"How about wrestling?"

"I went to state."

He nodded.

"How many schools were in your state tournament?"

"What's it matter?"

A surge of irritation moved into the lull of the beer. Christian glanced at me innocently.

"It doesn't . . . I guess."

I sat back in silence, listening to the wind and looking out to the passing fields. After a few minutes I had calmed down and told myself Christian didn't mean anything by his questions.

He looked over.

"Saw you talking to Jane Paisley at the banquet."

I turned.

"Who?"

"Jane Paisley — at the sports banquet," he said, glancing at me and then back at the road. "I saw you talking to her."

"Oh—that's her! I didn't know her name." I nodded. "I was going to ask you about her."

"Why's that, Brenton?"

"—why's what?"

"Why do you want to know her name?"

I looked at him.

"Why do you think—she was great looking! She said she's going to Ocean City this summer, and so are we—"

Christian laughed and shook his head.

"*That's* funny."

I squinted at him.

"What?"

"*You* asking Jane Paisley out."

I sat up.

"What do you mean?"

Christian shook his head and turned down the radio again.

"Brenton, Jane Paisley is probably the richest girl in Rudland Park."

"*So—*"

"A lot of guys more qualified than you have tried to take her out."

Christian swerved into the left lane, passed a car smoothly, and then cut back into the right lane. A flush of warmth came up over my face.

"What do you mean—'more qualified'?"

"I mean guys from Hawthorne with a lot of bucks," Christian said, staring down the cooling highway. "She's a deb, Brenton."

"What—"

"A deb, as in debutante," he said, looking at me and raising an eyebrow.

"Big deal."

Christian let out a loud breath.

"I know lots of guys who have dated her. . .she gets them to fall in love with her, and then she gets rid of them."

The sound of the car came up.

"She seemed nice to me. . .if she doesn't want to go out with me, she doesn't have to."

Christian was silent and kept his eyes straight ahead. We passed a field bathed in red twilight.

"I'm just telling you for your own good," he finished.

I shrugged.

"I don't see a date hurting anyone."

Christian shook his head slowly.

"You'll never be able to handle her, Brenton."

I stared straight ahead, my face hot. I thought coming out to see Christian was a big mistake.

"We'll see," I murmured.

There was a long silence filled by the droning car. Christian shrugged.

"It's no big deal. . . just thought I'd tell you."

"Sure. . .no big deal, Christian."

I stared out at the passing fields. Christian glanced over and cleared his throat.

"I thought we'd go canoeing at the end of the summer. . . ." He looked over again. "Down the Susquehanna — to the ocean, like we talked about that time. . .remember the first time we went canoeing?"

I looked out, ignoring him, but remembering the Susquehanna and a warm day years ago.

"Paddle on the right, Brenton!"

"I am!"

"It doesn't feel like it. . ."

"Look Christian, just steer the stupid thing and leave the paddling to me."

"Quick! Paddle on the left; we're headed for that *rock!*"

I started paddling to get away from a small boulder in the river.

"How about a little rudder — I can't do everything," I shouted.

I watched the canoe drift helplessly toward the rock.

"I've been ruddering — paddle on the *left,* Brenton!"

"Christian, we're going sideways..."

"I know, I know —"

"We're going to hit the rock."

"No we're not. *Paddle!*"

"You can stay and fight it out. I say every man for himself."

I jumped into the knee-deep water and left Christian to his fate.

"Brenton!..."

The canoe hit the boulder and promptly turned over. Christian tried to jump out at the last moment, but only succeeded in going for a swim in the warm Susquehanna. I grabbed the stern of the canoe and the paddles as they came floating by.

It was my first time canoeing and Christian's third or fourth. His neighbor had asked us if we wanted to go canoeing with him and his wife on the Susquehanna River. The Susquehanna was a river thirty minutes outside of Baltimore. We had started out together, but somehow Christian and I couldn't seem to keep the canoe straight and we were quickly far behind.

We dragged the canoe to shore and I pulled my shirt off in the warm sun. The river moved silently along the rocky shores. Thick forest loomed up on both sides and a steamy haze hovered over the trees in the midday sun. I sat down on the rocks to watch the slowly moving river and see if I could skip a rock more times than anyone else in the world.

"Brenton, what the hell are you doing?" Christian griped, examining the water-filled canoe.

"Skipping rocks. What are you doing?"

"*Canoeing* — come on, we just started."

"One more rock—not a bad skip, huh?"

I watched my rock skate across the water.

"That was rotten."

"O.K., let's see better."

Christian left the canoe and we both began skipping rocks. His rock skipped the furthest. I sat down and looked at the river.

"I wonder where the river goes?"

Christian shrugged.

"Guess it eventually gets to the ocean. That's where most rivers end up," he said as he got a rock to skip a smooth five times.

"You mean we could canoe all the way to the *ocean* by staying on this river?"

"Not us; somebody that knows how to canoe could."

"Yeah, but if we knew how to canoe, we could make it to the ocean?" I asked, pointing down the river.

"Uh huh; but this thing probably goes into another river first, and that one maybe leads to the ocean."

"But eventually they'd lead to the ocean "

"Eventually — but who knows where you'd end up if you tried something like that."

Christian held a rock up and examined it.

"I'd like to do it! Just to prove it could be done."

"Oh, it could be done," Christian nodded, whipping his arm and letting his rock fly. "Damn!"

His rock skipped twice and sank.

"You really think so?"

"Oh yeah. You'd need all the provisions and stuff, but it could be done."

"Yeah—let's try it!"

"Take a lot of planning," Christian said, squinting out at the water.

"Well, we could plan it out—"

We sat in silence thinking of what a voyage like this would entail.

"I say let's do it!" I said, standing up.

Christian nodded.

"Sounds good to me."

"Let's start planning when we get home."

"O.K."

I sat back down and looked at the rocks.

"I wonder how much food it would take?"

"Probably a lot."

"Yeah — probably."

"Probably take a good week to do it."

I looked at him.

"A week, huh?"

"At least!"

I felt the glow start to fade and brooded on the obstacles in the way of our greatest voyage.

"I don't think we can do it," I admitted.

Christian nodded and looked at me.

"We'll do it someday, Brenton — I guarantee you."

"Yeah?" I asked, looking up.

"Sure. . .I promise."

The conversation faded and the noise of the car came back. I turned in from the passing fields and looked at Christian. He nodded.

"So what do you think, Brenton?"

"About what?"

"About canoeing down the Susquehanna. I got a map, and the river really *does* go into the ocean. Maybe we could canoe all the way down."

I nodded slowly.

"Let's do it . . . you promised me anyway that we would someday."

He looked over, then nodded.

"I did, didn't I?"

"That's right . . . you *owe* me."

He grinned, pressing down on the accelerator. The whine of the engine rose in the warm evening as we raced toward summer.

4

My apartment turned out to be behind a glittering disco palace. The rent was low and it was only two blocks from the beach where Christian and I would work. Christian had arranged for us to have two beach stands for the summer. "It's one of the best jobs in Ocean City, Brenton! All you do is sit on the beach all day long," was the way he had described it.

A stand consisted of a blue box on the edge of the boardwalk. In the box were rafts, umbrellas, and chairs. People came off the boardwalk and rented whatever they needed on their way to the beach. Christian's stand was on Tenth Street and was a good stand because of the amount of people that used the Tenth Street beach. I ended up on First Street, next to a long pier of carnival rides. My beach was never more than half full.

We could also work a few nights a week at the disco in front of my apartment. Pella, a Greek woman, owned it and she was a friend of the Streizers. I knew the beach stand would probably not give me enough money. Christian was living in his parents' condominium for the summer, but I had to pay rent — so I took a job at the disco as well.

My apartment faced away from the ocean and onto a parking lot and a dumpster. There were no windows, just an old, oversized air conditioner that rattled all night and dimmed the lights when it started. A wave of musty air came out when I opened the door and found a surfboard in the middle of the room. This was the first sign I had of my roommate. He was a Hawthorne Man to be sure. He came in from the beach just as I was unpacking.

"Sheldon Greely," he announced, holding out his hand.

His sun-bleached hair and dark tan made him look like he had spent a summer at the beach already. There was a permanent white line from his sunglasses over his eyes.

"Brenton Heathersfield — I guess we're roomies for the summer," I said, shaking his hand.

He picked up his surfboard and leaned it against one wall.

"Christian told me you were coming down . . . he said you went to Hawthorne for a while —"

"I did for a year and then we moved," I said, sitting down on the bed and watching him quickly change.

He nodded.

"Well, it only takes a year to get it in your blood."

I was tempted to ask what, but then thought better of it.

"Christian tells me you have a beach stand on First Street," he called from the bathroom while running a hand through his hair to form a part.

"Yeah — it's not a very good stand, at least that's what Christian told me. I took a job working the door of the disco for a few nights."

"Well at least you have a stand. I'm just down a little way from you. I guard on Fifteenth Street," he said, rubbing some Old Spice on his face hurriedly.

"A guard. . .oh, a lifeguard."

He grinned.

"That's right."

He had on a red shirt with "Crab House" printed above the pocket.

"Have you been doing that long?"

"This is my second summer."

I motioned to his shirt.

"You have another job too?"

"I waiter a few nights." He slipped his feet into some thoroughly worn shoes. "Well, have to go — nice meeting you."

"Nice meeting you," I called as the door shut.

I turned to the room. The air conditioner shuddered to life and assumed a steady rattle. The apartment was small but would do for the summer. Sheldon's belongings consisted of nothing more than his clothes, lifeguard gear, and surfboard. I finished unpacking.

That night I walked up to the boardwalk and looked at the ocean. It had been four years since I had been to the coast. The boardwalk was covered with people moving through the balmy night. I sat for a while on a bench just watching the excited rush of vacationers, then walked down onto the beach and toward the roaring ocean.

The sand still held the heat of the day and was warm against my bare feet. The lights of the boardwalk faded till there was just the blackness of the ocean. I walked across the hard wet sand that endured the surf. A wave collapsed and sizzled up the beach. I walked into the water, feeling the sand running under my feet. The green and blue lights of wandering ships moved across the night sea. A white apparition flew through the darkness and the gull let out a cry. Somewhere a foghorn warned ships of the coast. I felt the pull of the vastness that lay before me. I was on my own for the first time, and I wondered what life would bring.

The summer had its own momentum with long, hot, lazy days at the beach stand and nights spent drinking in bars or working at the disco. My first day at the beach stand was a learning experience. I went out early in the morning and walked down the boardwalk. I finally came to the end where my blue box sat forlornly in the middle of the beach. The combination lock was old and rusted, sand grinding inside as I turned the dial. To my amazement the lock released, a drop of water squeezing out when it opened. I swung the painted wood cover up and a spider scurried into a dark corner of the box.

A warm breath of heated rubber escaped as I started pulling out rafts. Many of the rafts were flat or only partially inflated. Some had big tears in the rubbery cloth material. I pulled out the umbrellas and stacked them next to the box, seeing the rips and holes in them. The first thing I had to do was carry all the umbrellas down to the beach and set them up. This was so a customer would go sit under one.

I carefully piled the umbrellas on my shoulder and made the long, sweaty trek down the beach to the ocean. I started to drill the umbrellas into the sand just beyond the surf. The sun blazed off the colorless sand till my eyes stung with salt and my skin was slippery wet. Finally, the last umbrella was leaning into the breeze. I ran for the ocean and plunged into the cool morning water, then made my way back up the beach to wait for customers. I placed an umbrella next to my stand and put a chair under it. This was where I would ride out the summer.

I settled back into the beach chair, pulled out a ragged copy of *Gone with the Wind,* and dug my feet into the sand. I looked up and there was someone with long light-brown hair and baggy blue-and-white shorts ducking under the umbrella. He paused in the shade. A customer—I stood up.

"May I help you?"

"Um, no, I don't think so. . . .are you Brenton?" he asked, flicking his hair out of his eyes and blinking twice.

"Yes."

"I'm Calamitous Receiver—actually my first name is Dwayne, but everyone calls me Calamitous. I'm a friend of Christian's. Um, he said you were coming back east for the summer. . . I thought I'd introduce myself." He paused. "I stayed down here last summer with Christian."

He flicked his hair again and blinked. I remembered Christian mentioning on the ride down a friend of his that he had hung around with last summer.

"I've—I've got a beach stand down a few blocks from yours," he stammered, looking at me with vague eyes.

"Nice to meet you." We shook hands. "Have a seat."

Calamitous plopped into a beach chair. His hair was continually falling into his eyes and he kept flicking his head to keep his vision clear. He looked down the beach, then turned to me.

"Christian says you used to go to Hawthorne."

"I went for a year and then moved—you went to Hawthorne?"

"Yeah. I'm headed for Duke next year," he said, digging a hole in the sand with his foot.

I noticed how white he was for being at the beach and how his shorts hung loosely around his skinny legs.

"You going to join the lacrosse league this summer?"

"I don't know—haven't played in years, and they don't have lacrosse in Chicago."

He looked up.

"You're kidding!"

Calamitous flicked his hair twice and blinked three more times.

"Everybody runs track."

"Track, huh?" he repeated, sounding disappointed.

"It's not too bad. Do you play lacrosse?"

"Um, no—I have a bad knee, can't really play any sports because

62

of it, but I follow lacrosse closely."

"Oh."

"Christian was one of the best center midfielders Hawthorne ever had!"

"Really?"

"The University of Richmond is lucky to get him," he continued.

"I'm sure they are," I murmured.

"But a lot of schools wanted him," he continued. "I just don't think he wanted to go to a big university. University of Richmond has a good academic reputation."

"Huh!" I said, looking past him.

"Although . . . I don't think Christian cares about school. Sports is more his thing and sometimes—"

"*Well*—I think I see customers," I said, standing up and looking down the beach.

I saw some kids sitting under an umbrella. I couldn't have cared less, but I didn't want to hear any more about what Christian was going to do from this skinny, white, hair-flicking person.

"I have to get going anyway," Calamitous said, standing up. "I have some kid watching my stand—nice meeting you."

He shook hands weakly, more of a light grasp.

"Nice meeting you."

He moved off into the bright sand and I started walking down the beach, glad to be away from him. I turned to look back and he had barely gotten on the boardwalk. I had never seen anyone move so slowly.

Christian and I headed down to the beach that night with a six-pack and some cigarettes. We jumped from the boardwalk, kicked our shoes off, and walked toward the summer moon that laid a path to the center of the ocean. The cooling sand rushed over our feet and we sat down just beyond the surf.

I opened a beer for myself and handed one to Christian. He shot the bottle cap off into the ocean as I lit our cigarettes. A white sand crab skittered across the blue surf looking for food in the cover of darkness. I watched the surf come up and take him to the sea. We just sat listening to the ocean and drinking our beer.

"Your friend Calamitous stopped by my beach stand today," I said after a while.

Christian nodded.

"He said he was going to."

"Seems like an O.K. guy—different."

"Yeah, I guess he is different...but he's real smart."

"Yeah—seems like he would be."

I watched some phosphorus sparkle in the surf. Christian smoked quietly.

"Calamitous will end up being a brain surgeon or something."

I nodded, watching the ember burn away some uneven paper on my cigarette.

"I wonder what we'll end up doing—you ever think about that?"

Christian was making white smoke rings in the dark.

"Sure."

I looked out at the ocean and watched a green light crossing the dark horizon.

"I sometimes wonder exactly where we will end up—you know, where we're headed."

Christian shrugged.

"I know I would just like to stop—and not go on."

I looked at him.

"What do you mean?"

"I mean, sometimes I just don't want to go any further—I like where I am now. Who cares about college and getting older and work..."

"I wish I had cared a little more about college—maybe I would have gotten into a decent one."

Christian looked at me.

"That's not a good school you're going to?"

I shrugged.

"It's all right—it's a state school. If I had gotten better grades things would have been different."

"I had to fight for my grades," Christian said, shaking his head. "If my mother hadn't written all my papers I don't know what I would have done."

"She wrote your papers for you?"

"Of course—I can't write. My grades would have been shit without her. . .she got me through math, too." Christian laughed. "The old man sure would be surprised to know she was behind that honor roll."

"But you got the grades. . . . I just wish somebody had been there to kick me in the ass when I needed it—like your father does for you."

"You don't want my father—*believe me.*"

I shrugged.

"I don't know. . ."

"He controls everything, Brenton. . . . I had a job at a radio station, just cleaning up and stuff. One day the station manager walked up to me and asked me how I like my dad's station. I just looked at him and he told me that my dad owns the major part of the station." He shook his head. "It's like I can never get away from him. . .at least you can do what you want."

"You can too."

He shook his head, pulling on his cigarette.

"No. . .I can't."

I looked out at the ocean. I thought Christian still had choices. He could go to any school he wanted, his family had money, he had girls after him—these were the kinds of choices to have. Yet here

65

he was talking about how hard things were going to be.

Christian laid on his back and held his cigarette above him.

"I don't see why we should have to go beyond this summer. I don't think I should have to work harder in college and then go out and work harder still at a job." He rolled over and looked at me. "I like the beach—why can't we just stay here?"

"I suppose there's no real reason...but you can't stand still either."

He shrugged and turned to his back. I drank my beer and looked out to the ocean. A big wave broke and the water came up and touched my feet. We sat in silence looking out at the speckled night sky that arced across the wide curve of the ocean. A foghorn sounded and the red beacon of a distant lighthouse swirled toward us with a quick blink. A blue light hovered further down the beach.

"The sand sculptor is still here?"

"Oh yeah—I still have never seen him." He hesitated. "I wonder if there even is one."

"There has to be—*someone* makes them," I said, looking at the blue light.

"Maybe," Christian conceded. "But it's probably just some guy who does it for the money."

"What else would he do it for?"

Christian let out a short laugh.

"I don't know. . . 'cause he likes doing it."

I looked down and burrowed my foot into the sand.

"Maybe he does."

"Maybe," Christian said, smoking quietly.

We sat a while longer until Christian got up and said he felt like walking. We started along the shoreline. The lighthouse swept across the beach in front of us. I looked at the blue light on the edge of the boardwalk.

"I wonder if we'll see the sandman this summer?"

Christian looked toward the light.

"You never know. . . ."

We walked on, our voices drowned by the sonorous surf.

5

The night I met Duke a furious storm rolled in off the ocean so swiftly people barely had time to pull down the storm shutters on their cottages. The rain swept in with the wind and came across the beach in sheets of water. Signs rocked back and forth along the boardwalk while store owners scurried to check anchor wires. Just as quickly as the storm came, it went on to the interior and the sun broke through in the west. Excited children ran outside and rode their bikes down the wet planks of the boardwalk.

I watched the twilight gleam off the water that leaked from a sagging gutter outside the front door of the disco. It was my second week of working there. I was to meet Christian at his apartment later and was waiting for the other doorman to arrive.

A shimmering white Corvette rumbled up to the front door. A man with a tan face under a Stetson emerged from the car and came toward me. He took long steps and his cowboy boots clicked loudly against the wet pavement. A white shirt with swirls of green stitching caught the last light of the day as he tipped his hat back and two laughing blue eyes centered on me.

"Hey, partner! We're in the same business!"

I stared at him.

"What business is that?"

"Why hell! I'm the doorman at the Tanqueray Club down the street!"

I hadn't heard of it.

"We doormen have to stick together!" he continued, with a wide smile and a hard clap on my back. "Where you from, buddy?" he asked, pushing his hat back further on his head and running a hand over his dark face. He placed one boot up on the step and looked around as if he was expecting something. I looked around also. He turned back to me.

"Oh . . . Chicago."

"Chicago, that *cow town!* " He slapped his leg and shook his head. "Well, I'll be goddamned!"

I expected him to say he had been on big cattle drives into that "cow town." I wasn't sure if he was a real cowboy or one of Ocean City's strange characters. He pulled a wooden match out of his shirt pocket and popped it into his mouth.

"Been a while since I've been to that town," he said, leaning back against one of the posts holding up the awning.

"Where are you from?"

"Where am I from," he repeated, looking at me with these eyes that held the high plains and drifting, sleeping prairie towns. He looked back out into the parking lot. "I'm from everywhere, buddy. Everywhere and anywhere is my home," he said with another laugh and a "Goddamn."

I motioned to his glowing machine.

"Nice car."

"Yep, she is," he said, slipping his hands in his back pockets. "She's been good to me—never dies and moves when she has to. I thought about gettin' rid of her, but I'd never get something that trusty."

I nodded at the loyalty of his car, which could just as easily have been his mount. He shifted the match in his mouth.

"How long you been workin', pard?"

"Just last week."

"Just get into town?" he asked out of the side of his mouth, tipping his hat to a woman walking into the disco.

"Yeah."

He nodded slowly and hooked his thumbs in his pockets.

"This town's all right," he growled. "Little small for this cowboy, but hell, I ain't gonna be here *forever*," he said, winking.

I looked at him.

"How long have you been here?"

"Too long," he muttered, and then he laughed. "I mean—not long enough to get all the *fillies* in this town, buddy," he yelped, jumping down off the step and grabbing on to his oversized belt buckle. He adjusted his hat and pulled it down low. "Well listen—I gotta go." He reached into his top pocket and produced a card. "Here is a VIP card," he said pronouncing the VIP distinctly. "It's for the club— just show it and you're in free, buddy."

I took it reluctantly because I knew I should reciprocate with a card of my own.

"I don't have a card to give to you."

"Aw *hell*, pard! Don't worry, you'll do something for me some-day," he said with a wave as he put his big frame into his white stagecoach. He leaned out the window, revving the engine. "Didn't catch the name, pard."

"Brenton," I hollered over the roar.

"Mine's Duke, and you come and visit me at the club any time,

Brenton, all right?" he called, lighting a cigarette.

"All right—I will!"

He motioned to another group of women walking by.

"Make sure you don't get jumped by any of these fillies."

"I won't."

"All right, boy," he said, holding a hand up as he screeched away.

I watched his car disappear and felt I had met the last cowboy.

I headed over to Christian's. The air had cooled and I liked the rough, clean feel of my jeans and button-down shirt. I reached the boardwalk, took off my shoes, and walked down the weathered, smooth planks. The beach glowed a dusky gold and the waves were tipped with the last slanting rays of twilight.

Christian's condominium faced toward the ocean. It wasn't very large and there was always some crisis going on that made it seem even smaller. I walked down the beach and saw Christian and Calamitous on the balcony. They motioned they would come down to the boardwalk. I had already accepted that Calamitous was along for the summer.

They came downstairs and we piled into Christian's Spitfire. We sped through the warm ocean air, cramped into the two seats with Calamitous hovering above the stickshift. The car protested at the extra weight as Christian wound out each gear.

"Where're we headed?" I yelled above the engine, the wind, and the radio.

"We're going to see a girl I know—we'll drink there first," Christian yelled back.

"It's one of his concubines," Calamitous smirked.

Christian grinned and turned the music up louder. We shot down Ocean Highway.

We reached her apartment after a stop to pick up some beer. She scampered around the dark apartment picking up various things.

She had pulled-back hair and small brown eyes. We cracked open the beers. Calamitous had a grin on his face each time he looked at her.

"So, how you doing?" she asked me in her squeaky New Jersey accent. "Christian told me loads about you — this place is a mess. I just don't have the time what with work and going to the beach. Oh well . . . have a seat anywhere — if you can find one," she offered, although we already had.

Christian finished his first beer and crushed the can. He tossed it into the garbage then sauntered into the bedroom. Debbie — that was her name — watched him nervously, then turned to us.

"You two make yourselves at home — the beer is in the refrigerator, and turn on the television if you like," she said, standing up.

Debbie looked around quickly, grabbed her cigarettes off the table, and disappeared into the bedroom. The door shut with a loud bang and I was sitting with Calamitous. We stared at each other for a moment — I jumped up.

"How about another beer, Calamitous?"

" — no thanks," he said, raising his full beer.

I went into the small kitchen and opened the refrigerator. There were just a few half-empty condiments and our open twelve-pack of beer. I looked about the kitchen. A fan whirred on the counter with a humming squeak. I went back into the room with a beer and turned on the television. I flipped through the channels, clicked it off, and picked up a magazine.

Calamitous sipped his beer. I was annoyed with Christian for disappearing and leaving me with Calamitous. If he wanted to be with this girl, he didn't need me along. I considered leaving, but fifteen minutes later Christian and Debbie reappeared.

We ran through the beer we had brought. Christian had drunk six by himself, Calamitous had barely touched his one beer, and Debbie and I drank the rest.

"I guess we need more beer," I said to no one in particular.

Christian was leaning against a wall.

"Yeah, let's get some more," he agreed, walking to the couch.

Christian picked up a long pillow that was shaped oddly like a bat. He started tapping Debbie with it.

"Christian, are those love taps?" She smiled.

Christian grinned and then whopped her on the back, knocking her cigarette out of her hand.

"Christian, stop that!" she said, standing up. "I'm not a punching bag."

"Christian stop that!" he mimicked, resting the pillow by his side.

Debbie bent over to pick up her cigarette and Christian hit her again. She jumped away.

"Christian!—please!"

"Oh, it's not hurting you—don't be such a baby," he laughed.

She started to sit down and Christian hit her across the side of the face.

"Damn it, Christian! Give me that thing!"

There was a red mark on her cheek. She stood up awkwardly, holding a hand in front of her.

"Come and get it."

She lunged at him and dropped her cigarette again. He laughed, side-stepped her, then hit her in the back of the head. Her head popped forward like a puppet's.

"Almost got me," Christian laughed, ducking from her grasp.

Christian started hitting her all over. He laughed hysterically till his face was red and the veins were standing out on his neck. Debbie desperately tried to grab the pillow from him, but he just hit her more. I stood up.

"Hey Christian—ease up!"

He turned and swung the pillow straight at my head. I moved, but it caught me on the right ear. The pillow was solid.

"Ease up, Christian! Ease up, Christian!" he mimicked, laughing wildly, his eyes green and red slits.

I tried to defend myself as he swung again and hit me on the side. "Cut it out!"

I made a grab for the pillow and missed. He was still laughing and swung from the left. I caught the pillow, yanked it out of his hand, and threw it across the room. A lamp shattered into a blue flash pop and tinkling glass. There was quiet. I stared at Christian and heard my own heavy breathing. A benign look came over his face.

"Jesus, Brenton! You don't have to get mad. I was just kidding." He said this so innocently I almost believed him.

"Yeah right, Christian," I nodded. "Just kidding."

Christian and I stood facing each other. I sat down and Debbie started talking again like nothing had happened. Calamitous sat on the couch staring straight ahead and I wished I hadn't come at all.

We left at some point and I was silent in the car. Christian looked over a few times. I stared out the windshield and watched the night rush by. I thought that maybe I shouldn't have interfered — after all, he knew this girl and she even kissed him when he left. Maybe she liked it when he abused her. Still . . .

"You know, Brenton, I was only kidding around back there," Christian said, glancing over. "I mean, she knew I was kidding. . . it was nothing to get mad about."

He glanced at me again. I shrugged.

"How was I to know. . .she looked scared to me."

"Ahh, she might have been a little scared . . . I don't think we should let it ruin the night."

I nodded slowly.

"So who said anything about ruining the night?"

"She likes it when Christian beats her," Calamitous added. "She thinks it's *kinky.*"

We laughed and Christian pressed down on the accelerator.

The bar on the boardwalk opened to the ocean and was called The Outlet. All the locals were already there. A "local" was not really a local at all, but someone who was working for the summer in Ocean City. All the locals were tan and wore long, baggy shorts and surfer shirts. Christian and Calamitous seemed to know everyone and I stood by the bar wishing for a deep tan and baggy shorts to blend in.

I squinted into the blue-lit haze and noticed a girl sitting on the other side of the bar. She was talking to someone next to her. A slender hand reached up and flicked her hair back. It was the girl I had met at Christian's awards banquet . . . I couldn't remember her name. I lowered my head and watched her, searching for any differences a debutante might exhibit. The same highlighted blond wave shimmered in her hair and a white bracelet stood out against her already brown skin.

I finished my drink and looked over at Christian and Calamitous who were still talking with a group of people. I turned and watched her for a few more minutes, then took a deep breath and plotted my course of action. I walked through the smoky din of blaring music and quick conversations, half hoping she would be gone when I reached her side of the bar.

I came up behind the girl she was talking to. My confidence left when her friend abruptly got up and walked away. She faced the bar. I had a glimpse of slender tan legs that led up to khaki shorts and a white polo shirt. I thought of leaving, even as I pulled out the empty stool and sat down. She turned to me. Her eyes were hazel in the light.

"Ah — didn't we meet at the Hawthorne sports banquet?" I asked loudly.

She looked at me for a moment.

"Did we?. . . Oh yes, you had your mouth full — no wonder I didn't recognize you."

She turned back in and picked up a silver cigarette case off the wet bar and tapped a cigarette out. She handed me the lighter and I lit her cigarette with a trembling hand. She inhaled deeply, letting the smoke out of her mouth in a smooth, even manner.

"Do you plan what you're going to say?" she asked, holding the cigarette aloft and crossing her legs. "If you do, I'd come up with a better opening line than 'Don't I know you?' "

She put the cigarette to her lips again. Her velvety skin looked as if it had never been exposed to anything harsh.

"But. . . I had seen you before."

"So why state the obvious," she said, relieving the cigarette in an ashtray and holding her pink wine.

"Well, I am more of a—"

"Straight-approach type of guy?"

I lapsed into silence. She reached over, squeezed my arm lightly, and smiled. I started again.

"I saw you and wanted to talk to you. . .so here I am."

She put her wine down.

"There—that was better."

She tapped me lightly on the arm again. I leaned against the bar. She drank some more of her wine.

"What's your name?"

"Jane—yours?"

"Brenton."

She paused and fingered her smoking cigarette.

"That's a pretty name, Brenton—like a field wet with dew." She looked at me from the sides of her eyes. "Well, how do you do?" she said, putting out her hand.

"Fine," I said, holding on to the soft little hand. "You sound poetical."

She looked at me.

"I read a lot—don't you?"

She looked alarmed that I might not read and released my hand.

"Oh God! Morning, noon, and night. It's like a religion with me!"

"Oh, and he reads—I'm in luck," she murmured, taking a final pull on her cigarette from pursed lips that wrinkled for an instant.

Her girlfriends came back and said they were leaving.

"I have to leave . . . it was nice talking to you, Brenton," Jane said, standing up and becoming more accessible when she did.

Now was the time, but her girlfriends were an audience, and did the bar just get quieter?

" . . . is there a number where I can call you?" I asked, my voice bringing the bar to a halt.

"I don't know about that," she said, putting her purse over her shoulder.

"I mean I—"

"But there is a phone number in the book under Paisley."

"Oh—well fine, that's . . . just fine," I repeated stupidly.

"Good-bye, Brenton," she called, waving.

I watched her slender hand disappear out the door. There was a vibration inside me as I sat down. The girls I had taken out in Chicago were nice, but they were always telling me I was "just a friend." Now here was this beautiful debutante of the East telling me I could find her number in the phone book. The summer was shaping up very well.

I smiled and looked up and there was Christian. He was leaning against the wall staring at me. I stared back, then he turned slowly away.

6

I met King at the end of my first month in Ocean City. It was a slow Wednesday night and had been raining since the afternoon. I watched the rain come down in the parking lot in front of the disco. King walked up out of the thundering darkness and ducked under the awning. He nodded to me then leaned against a post. A comb flashed through his wet, greased-back hair. He pulled off his leather jacket and slung it over his shoulder. An unlit cigarette appeared in his lips as he looked into the parking lot.

His smooth skin and sculpted features might have looked effeminate if the rest of him could have been ignored. A white T-shirt stopped where a blue tattoo began on one arm, and black pants reached down to black boots. His eyes were dark and brooding. He wiped some water off his leather jacket and lit the cigarette in his mouth, clapping the lighter shut and putting his coat back on. He smoked, watching the rain.

"It's coming down tonight," he said slowly.

I looked at him and then out to the rain.

"It sure is."

"People don't like to come out in the rain, that's for sure," he said, flashing the ember of his cigarette.

I nodded again and looked out to the rainy darkness; somebody was making his way across the parking lot to the front door. The man staggered under a street light, then became a silhouette again. He lurched toward me and I stood up off my stool as he came into the light.

A breeze pushed some stray hair from his forehead back to the bald spot it had fallen from. His glasses were fogged with condensation; yellowish red eyes surfaced out of the haze, looked at me, then receded behind the misty lenses. His mouth was moving continually, and what had been a pressed suit was now just wet, drooping cloth.

He paused, breathed heavily, then came forward. I put up my hands, knowing I couldn't let him in.

"I'm sorry, sir—you can't come in here."

He let out his alcohol-laden breath in my face and stepped back. His mouth kept moving and his eyes surfaced again.

"Why not?"

His jaw shook as he stepped back. He adjusted his glasses with a measure of dignity. I could feel my heart beating and I ran my fingers against my slippery palms.

"Because. . .you're over-served, sir."

His eyes bulged indignantly behind his glasses.

"WHAT DA YA MEAN I CAN'T COME IN!"

"Sir. . .I—I think you have had enough to drink."

My voice sounded weak. He lunged forward.

"I'LL TELL YOU WHEN I'VE HAD ENOUGH TO DRINK!"

He pushed past me with flailing arms—a mindless hand slapped across the side of my face. I fell back as someone stepped into his path. The drunk stopped.

"Hey! — what's the big idea?"

I felt stupid standing to the side but I didn't know what to do. The man stared at the drunk coolly.

"He said you couldn't come in."

The drunk squinted, then adjusted his glasses. He fell back down the steps into the rain and turned around.

"Come on punk! I'll take ya on . . . *I ain't afraid!*"

He took off his coat and it fell onto the slick parking lot.

"Who the hell are you? — I'll take you on . . . C'MON, I'LL DO IT!"

The man flicked his cigarette out by the drunk and stared at him without moving.

"Mister — if I come out into that parking lot, you won't leave it."

His hand rested easily near a bulge in his back pocket. It was long and shaped like a knife. The rain danced on the parking lot around the drunk. An occasional car went by on Ocean Highway with a wet, splattering sound. The drunk man stood with his arms out, alone in the dark parking lot. His arms slowly came down to his sides. He mumbled something about "punks," and then nearly fell down picking up his coat. He staggered off into the rain. I breathed in relief.

"Hey, thanks a lot," I said, still shaking. "I wasn't sure about that guy."

I sat down and tried to calm myself.

"No problem," he said, lighting another cigarette.

He stared out as before. I looked over.

"Uh, do you come here much?"

"I bartend here," he said, flicking his head back.

"Oh — *you work here* . . . I didn't know," I said, feeling more stupid. "I just started . . . my name's Brenton."

He nodded.

"King," he said, pushing back some hair that had fallen onto his forehead.

I knew he was not the kind of person you shook hands with. He returned to looking out in the darkness. I glanced over again.

"Worked here long?"

"Too long."

He turned and looked at me, as if he had seen me for the first time.

"You're not from around here."

"I live in Chicago."

He nodded and frowned a little.

"Chicago's a good town."

"— where you from?"

"Tennessee," he answered, looking at me as if he expected some sort of challenge.

"That's a good place."

He suddenly laughed

"It sure is."

He finished his cigarette and turned to go in.

"Hey — thanks again," I called.

He just held up his hand as he went inside.

I came to know King better after we worked a couple of nights together. He usually took his breaks out front.

"Daddy was one poor-ass farmer!" he said one languid night when I asked him what Tennessee was like, and he gave me the first clues to his past. "Times were hard, but it was the best part of my life," he said, watching the cars go by.

We sat smoking. I had borrowed a cigarette from him once, and now whenever he lit up he would hold the pack out for me.

"I can still see my daddy coming home from the fields. He loved that place and put his soul into the land. When they took it . . . it broke him."

I nodded.

"Did you know him well?"

He shook his head.

"I was young — he drove a truck . . . then he just took off in that rig and never came back," he said with a bitter smile. "Don't blame him — they took away his life. Momma moved us up to Salisbury, just over the bridge. Shoot, nothing ever happened there, so I started coming to Ocean City when I could hitch a ride."

I nodded again, breathing in the warm salty air that always smelled like fried food in the evenings from the restaurants across the street.

"I don't know — one time I came and just didn't leave. I bought her and started bartending to pay the bills," he said, motioning to his car glowing in the dusk.

It was the pride of King's existence — a 1955 Chevy Bel Air. The car was a deep, mirror blue and had been restored to showroom grandeur. I stared at the dark ghost. It looked like a whisper of the past.

"She's beautiful!"

"Yeah — took a long time to get her back in shape, but she's there. I wanted something perfect . . . something I could call my own and nobody could mess up."

"I think you have it there."

King nodded slowly.

"I have part of it, and when I get the other part straight, I'll get out of this miserable town," he muttered, staring into the twilight.

King looked at me, then smiled as if he had been caught doing something. He walked back in. I looked out to the dark car that waited in the dying light.

I managed to call Jane Paisley. I found her number after several botched attempts with an exasperated directory assistance operator. I placed the call and someone answered.

"Hello?"

"Hello—is Jane there?"

There was a hesitation on the line.

"—yes. . .this is Jane."

"Jane—um. . .this is Brenton."

A pause.

"I'm sorry—"

"Ah—the bar. . .I met you at a bar—Brenton? Hawthorne sports banquet. . .then a bar. . .a week ago."

"No—I'm sorry . . you must have the wrong number."

I heard everything Christian had ever told me. It had been a mistake to call. A prickly heat broke out across my face.

"No. . .," I began again. "—this *is* Jane Paisley—*right?*"

"Yes it is."

"This is BRENTON! You know. . . I was eating meatballs at the sports banquet. . ."

Jane giggled.

"Oh, *Brenton!*. . .I thought you said Benton." She laughed more. "I was just kidding—how are you?"

"Fine!"

There was a pause on the line.

"Well. . .the reason I called was—"

"*Yes!* "

"What?"

"You were going to ask me out, and I accept—when do you want to go out?"

I opened my mouth.

"How about tonight?"

"Oh. . .fine—is eight o'clock all right?"

"—sure! I can be there."

"I live at Seacrest Apartments, on Twenty-eighth Street—oh, apartment 2E."

"Great . . . I'll be there," I said, licking my dry lips and wanting to hang up the phone quickly before my victory vanished.

"You are so *smooth!* How did you ever get me to go out? Ciao!"

I hung up and stared at the phone. I had the sensation of coming up out of a dream and wanting to go back. I couldn't believe it had gone so well . . . I wondered if Jane had orchestrated the whole thing. . . .

I picked her up at eight, or rather I walked over to her apartment. Jane answered the door looking calm and in control. My hands were wet by the time I reached her door, and I had a headache from running over possible conversations.

"I'm going out with a man! Inform the police if I'm not back by morning," she called to her roommates as she came out the door.

She smiled brightly at me. I managed a weak smile back with a garbled "You look nice."

"Thank you!"

Christian's words whispered through my mind again, "You'll never be able to handle her, Brenton."

We started walking down her street toward the boardwalk. I tried to think of even one of the conversations I had planned but I couldn't think of a thing. I watched Jane walking next to me, her dress a blue pastel in the evening light and her hair more golden against her brown shoulders. Two diamonds glinted beneath her ears.

I tried various starts at conversation, but each one died from its own effort. I was nervous. Just as we came to the boardwalk, she allowed me a respite.

"So, are you enjoying the summer?" she asked, the wind holding back her hair for her.

"Oh yeah . . . hard to believe Christian and I have been here a month already."

"You both have beach stands?"

"Christian has the better stand — mine is down on First Street and his is on Tenth. He has a lot more people on his beach than I do—which means more money," I explained stupidly.

She nodded slowly.

"You don't have many people on your beach?"

"Well . . . some, but if I want business I have to hustle a lot more and get people to come off the boardwalk at my beach."

I was talking too loudly.

"Are you a hustler?"

"No . . . not really," I said, feeling my conversation had no timing at all.

She then slipped a soft, tanned arm through mine as we came to the bar.

"Just as long as you don't hustle me," she whispered.

I was hopelessly lost . . . the warm wind blew the evening toward night.

We drank and talked, and the nervousness of before slowly left.

"So why did you move?" she asked after her second Chablis and my fourth beer.

I cleared my throat.

"So my father could get a better job—more money."

"Oh—" She paused. "Daddy would do the same thing, I suppose . . . I mean for money."

I nodded and looked at her.

"Where are you going to college?"

"Princeton. Where are you going?"

"Just a small state school."

She paused again.

"College is college," she said, taking a sip of her wine.

I nodded. With the word "Princeton" all my nervousness of before had come back.

"That's great you're going to Princeton."

She looked down at the bar and nodded quickly.

"It's just a school, Brenton," she said softly.

"Yes, but a damn good school...I can think of worse places to go."

"I do want to be with the best of my generation," she said, her blue eyes icing over.

The room came up in a sweaty, smoky haze of people struggling through their daily lives. Jane looked as if she had forgotten about me.

"But it's just a college," she said quickly. "Oh, let's not talk about school...it's the *summer!*"

She reached over, squeezing my hand on the bar, and I glided back into her world.

"Here's to tonight and the rest of the summer!" Jane proposed, holding up her glass for a toast.

"Here's to it!"

I clinked my beer against her glass and took a long pull as she finished the rest of her wine. She put the glass down, then turned to me with her lips glistening.

"Let's talk about you," she whispered, squeezing my arm.

"All right...let's see — what can I tell you about me..."

"You read."

"That's right! — I read."

Then I couldn't think of a single book I had ever read. The drinks came and went many times till the night slipped away and finally it was just her and me.

"Well, I think all the great American writers are dead," Jane said, filling in for me again.

"Really?"

"Oh yes...there aren't any true creative geniuses left...except for myself."

"Are you a creative genius?" I asked, my face close to hers.

"Yes — would you like to read some of my poetry?"

"I would."

"You can't . . . you'll have to wait for the book — but then you can," she added with a smile that made me want to kiss her.

Her eyes melted into a misty sky color.

"I await the day," I said, moving closer to her.

"It will take a while, so I hope you are patient," she murmured, her breath the sweet-bitter smell of wine.

Nothing moved. I was sure she would hear my blood pumping. An acceptance came into her eyes and I glided across the space between us. Her head tilted slowly and the bar was at the end of a long tunnel. I leaned over and felt the softness of her lips parting; there was a slow-moving train that pulled into a cloudy station, then sighed as it stopped. We kissed and I thought it would never stop. We came apart once. Her eyes opened slightly, then we kissed once more — the bar came back down the tunnel and it was very loud.

I was out of my chair and nearly on top of hers. I sat back down unsteadily. Jane took another sip from her glass, slipping her hand into mine. She flicked her hair and glanced around, then gazed at me and squeezed my hand.

"Well . . ."

"So . . . ," I followed and we laughed.

"What were we talking about?" I asked, feeling a humming inside me.

"I don't know."

She slipped her other hand in mine.

"Must not have been very important."

"Must not have," she whispered and we kissed again.

Somehow we left the bar and ended up on the boardwalk. Fog was coming in from the ocean and the mist flew by the globe lights. It was well past one o'clock. Occasionally someone would come out of the mist and then vanish back into it again.

We had drunk steadily. The alcohol pushed back everything and there was just this girl. Jane and I moved unsteadily, stopping many times and then restarting.

"Brenton," Jane murmured breathlessly as we came apart. "Let's go down to the beach," she whispered, moisture glistening on her cheeks.

There was a roaring in my head and I could only nod.

We walked down into the mist. The lights of the boardwalk faded as the ocean moved around us. For a moment we saw nothing, then the surf rushed up beneath us and the ocean erupted as if a veil had been lifted. Jane stepped out of her moccasins and held them in her hand, walking into the warm, giving water. Phosphorus collected around her feet like anklets of starlight. She stood in the glowing mist, looking out to the ocean.

Jane bent down and came up with a small white shell.

"Look, Brenton — isn't this a pretty shell?" She handed it to me. "For you . . . to remember me always."

"Wait a minute."

I dipped my hand down into the rushing surf and found a shell. I handed it to her.

"For you, to remember me."

She looked at it and held it to her cheek.

"Oh! It's a baby conch! I love these!"

I dipped my hand back into the water, looking for more shells.

"Let's go for a swim, Brenton."

I felt my stomach tighten into a knot. I heard Christian's words again, but they weren't clear this time.

" — sure."

Jane threw her moccasins behind her and smiled at me. She reached up and slowly pulled her dress over her head. Jane stood in the glowing surf with her breasts white against the tanline from her suit. Her underwear was a light band against her thighs. She tossed the dress back to the beach and her gold pendant caught the moonlight that slipped through the mist. I pulled off my shirt and when I looked again she was running into the surf and her underwear was in the sand.

I tore off my pants and looked around the mist-shrouded beach. I waded into the water, then dove into a wave. My head cleared from the cool water. Jane was swimming toward me with her hair smoothed back and her features soft and aquiline, as if sculpted out of cream. Her face came up and I kissed its salty wetness. I put my hands on her waist, pulling her to me. Her thighs and breasts pushed against my body. The water rushed out, going down to our waists, then came back as we moved out further into the ocean. I looked at her and couldn't stop the strange roaring in my ears.

"It's all right," she whispered, opening her legs as she floated on her back in the surf.

I pulled her to me, her eyes glistening with moonlight. I hesitated; she sat up. A puzzled look came across her face, then an understanding.

"You're a virgin—aren't you?"

"No. . .not really. . ."

"Here," she whispered, reaching a dripping hand out of the water.

I took hold of her hand and she pulled me into her. The ocean surrounded us and everything was warm and there was only the sound of the white surf rushing up into the night.

7

A line of pink and gold crept up over the ocean and chased the night into the west. The darkness left a lifeguard chair silhouetted against the painted horizon. I watched the morning come and still was not sure the night had ever happened.

We had fallen asleep in two chairs at my beach stand under an umbrella. I turned from the dawn and looked at Jane who was still sleeping with a beach towel wrapped around her. I had been awake for hours and pulled out the pen and clipboard I used for rentals.

"What are you doing?"

I looked at her and shrugged.

She smiled and moved her hand in a small wave. "Have you been awake long?" She yawned.

"Just a little while."

"Mmmm . . . ," she nodded, observing the morning. "What a gorgeous sunrise."

"It sure is."

She turned back to me.

"What do you have there?"

I looked down at my clipboard and shrugged.

"—just a few verses..."

She smiled again and raised her eyebrows.

"May I see?"

I shifted in the chair.

"Well, actually it's for you anyway, but it's not really finished."

She held out her hand.

"Let me see."

She took the clipboard and put it in her lap, pulling the towel around her against the morning dew. She looked up.

"May I read it out loud?"

"If you want..."

She began, her voice husky and soft from the night.

> "Vacant, dark beaches, sitting
> on the edge of a continent.
> Two figures against the blowy night
> with a wine's content.
>
> "Unspoken words looking for shells,
> one looks for and another tells.
>
> "Ocean and ecstasy,
> trails of memory's debris.
> The morning rises—
> lost, but upon the
> blowy beaches of we...."

Jane leaned back and smiled, her eyes wet.

"Thank you, Brenton...it's beautiful."

She hugged the clipboard to her. I leaned over and kissed her while the sun brought in the day.

I once counted how many days we spent together and came up with thirty-five. I don't remember much about the first two weeks with Jane except it was continuous, with the day falling into night and then into the next day. Sleep wasn't something I got much of or cared to. I drifted around thinking of when I would see Jane next.

Jane came up to my beach stand during the days and read under an umbrella. There was talk of a job, but I don't think she ever did work, besides filling in occasionally for one of her girlfriends at a surf shop. Mostly she did what she wanted, and what Jane liked to do was buy things. She bought lots of things, and on these shopping sprees I was amazed at the way she picked out a half-dozen shoes, five new bathing suits, jewelry, or whatever she wanted. The plastic cards that bore her name never resulted in any bills that I saw her pay.

Jane was generous with me. Many times when she bought shorts, I received shorts, and colored surfer shirts started to pile up in my drawer. We ate dinner up and down the boardwalk and Jane paid for the meals, waving away my protests with a card dropped onto the waiters' trays.

But it was the evening swims that I remember most. After I closed the stand — when the sun was touching the tops of the waves and the beach was empty except for a few surfers — Jane and I would go swimming.

"Brenton — someone will see!"

"There's just that lady on the beach and she can't see — the water is up to our waists."

"You don't think anyone can tell?"

"How could they? We're just holding on to each other."

"Well . . . all right — it's off . . ."

"Mine too — "

"Let's swim out further."

"All right."

We moved out together into the ocean.

But Jane was different from me and there were times when our differences were hard to ignore.

"Look at that bed!"

"Where?" Jane asked, frowning as she peered in the store window.

I pointed against the glass.

"The large bed, the water bed right there."

"That?"

"Water beds are great!"

A long pause.

"A water bed . . . you must be kidding!"

"No . . . you don't like water beds?"

She took a step back.

"Oh—they're fine I suppose . . . for some people." Jane looked at me. "*You* must like them."

"Well . . . yes."

Jane turned her head up.

"I personally couldn't think of anything worse," she said, glancing with distaste at the large bed in the window.

"Well, I mean—I would never *get* one."

"Well, I should hope not."

I knew Jane had grown up with money and there were parts of her world that I didn't understand, but then it didn't seem to matter. Jane liked to have fun, and we spent many nights at The Outlet; then came the moonlit swims where we woke up to a shivering dew in my beach chairs.

I was in love; I knew that. The summer had changed.

A heat wave came into Ocean City in July and a warm, humid glove hovered over the resort town. The ocean breeze just rearranged banks of warm stagnant air, while the gray planks of the boardwalk gave off a hot breath of pine tar from the broiling sun.

I watched some children run through waves of heat rising from the sand, then stop and jump on their towels, looking reproachfully at the white desert around them. They stood for a few moments, then took off again running down the beach. I wiped a line of sweat from my lip and looked up at the umbrella that protected us from the heat. There was a small hole in the top of the canvas; a white-hot beam of light came down into the shade.

Jane was reading a book. Her foot rested in the sunlight; a bright-red enamel gleamed on her toes. She raised her hand to turn a page and two silver bracelets jingled together then came back to rest against a thin gold watch. Her blue bathing suit wrapped around her hip with some white skin showing at the edges. A white bow held her hair back.

"How's the book?"

"Good," she murmured without stopping her reading.

She put her arm back up. The bracelets clinked as she moved her hand around in the air.

"Do you have a cramp in your hand?"

"No."

"Then why are you moving it around?"

"Are you trying to disturb me?" she asked, leaning her head back.

"Yes."

I kissed her lips and smelled the faint scent of talcum or faded perfume.

"Now let me finish my book."

I reached over and she squeezed my hand lightly, holding it till she had to turn a page. I pulled out my own book and heard someone walk behind the umbrella. I looked up just as Christian came into the shade.

"Hey, Brenton," he said, his grin under the image of myself in his sunglasses.

"—Christian."

He sat down in a chair and pushed his sunglasses up onto his head. It had been a hot day at Christian's beach stand when I'd told him I was seeing Jane. He had just nodded and said "Good luck." After that I was careful to juggle things so I wouldn't have to tell him what nights I saw her, but I did lose track of Christian and Calamitous for a few weeks. I would tell Christian I was working, or just not tell him anything and not go to his beach stand during the day. Sometimes I felt guilty about the way things had ended up, but mostly Jane gave me no chance to think of anything.

"Christian, this is Jane—"

"Hi Jane," Christian nodded, glancing at her.

"Hello Christian," Jane said, holding her book in her lap.

She kept her sunglasses on. I looked at Christian.

"I wasn't sure if you two had actually met—"

"I don't know if we ever really have — I think I saw you at a couple of parties," Jane answered smoothly.

Christian took off his sunglasses and ran his hand through his hair.

"I think that must have been it."

My chair was next to Jane's, and Christian was sitting across from us. Nobody spoke for a few seconds that seemed like minutes. I squinted down the beach.

"Pretty hot out."

Christian looked down the beach. I glanced at Jane and could see her watching him behind her sunglasses.

"Looks like you got some people on your beach today, Brenton."

I cleared my throat and nodded.

"I think the weather helped me."

Jane's hand was next to mine and I thought about holding it. There was a loud, long silence.

"Brenton says you have a beach stand on Tenth Street, Christian."

He looked at Jane and something flickered behind his green eyes.

"Yup," he nodded, looking away and tapping the arm of the chair.

Heated wind came across the sand and ruffled the pages of the paperback at my feet. The surf and a child's occasional scream wafted up from the beach. I cleared my throat several times. Christian dug his feet into the sand and he turned to me.

"Calamitous and I are going out tonight—I didn't know if you were doing anything."

I shrugged and shifted in my chair.

"I think we're going to the Tanqueray Club," I said, looking at Jane. "A guy I met handles the door there."

Christian nodded, tapping the armchair faster.

"Sure . . . maybe another night."

We sat for a few long minutes, then Christian stood up.

"Well, I better get back to my beach stand."

I nodded quickly.

"Maybe tomorrow night, Christian . . ."

"Yeah, maybe—nice meeting you, Jane."

"You too, Christian."

He ducked out from the umbrella and ran for the boardwalk. I turned to Jane and she was already reading her book again. I looked back to where Christian had gone and considered running after him, but then I didn't really know what I would say. He was mad because I was spending so much time with Jane . . . maybe jealous. I looked at Jane and knew I would be jealous if things were reversed. A surge of confidence went through me and I decided to go to his stand tomorrow. Things would be all right then; he'd just have to accept that some things had changed.

Jane and I walked to the Tanqueray Club that night. The club was just down the highway from my apartment. Jane was quiet as I apologized for my lack of transportation. She picked her way carefully along the sidewalk in a Hawaiian dress that wrapped tightly around her small waist, then flared out over blue high heels. Two dangling stones moved under her ears as she walked.

We reached the lights of the club and I flashed the card Duke had given me at the door. We walked into a wall of music and moved to the bar through swirling lights and small tables with glass candles. I saw a Stetson and recognized Duke.

He turned to me and a big smile cracked across his brown face.

"Hey, partner!" he said, with a strong, wild handshake.

"Hi Duke." I relaxed a moment in his aura. "Duke! — this is Jane Paisley."

Duke's face softened and his tone notched down.

"Well ma'am . . . I have seen some pretty ladies, but I have never seen such fetching beauty as I did when I looked at you," he said, taking her hand and kissing it lightly.

Jane smiled faintly and took her hand back, deftly rubbing it against her dress.

Duke turned back to me.

"What'll it be, partner? It's on me."

"I thought you'd be working the door, Duke."

Jane turned toward the dance floor where a lone couple tried to wrestle some dignity from the disco beat.

Duke shrugged.

"Aw hell, I told you, I practically run this place. If I feel like working the door — I do it. If I feel like bartending, I do it!"

Jane was still gazing at the lone couple. Duke pushed his hat back on his forehead and raised his eyebrows toward her.

"So, what'll it be, pard?"

"Jane, you want a daiquiri? . . . I'll take a beer."

"Comin' right up," he nodded, walking down the bar.

I looked at Jane who had turned around and was staring straight ahead.

"Do you like the place?"

She raised her eyebrows.

"It's all right."

"Not many people," I said, looking around.

The lone couple finally gave up.

"No, there aren't really."

Duke put the drinks in front of us.

"Here you go!"

I started to reach into my pocket and he put up his hand.

"Tonight's on me, partner. I don't want to see any money on the bar."

I looked at him.

"Are you sure, Duke?"

"I told you . . . I run the place, buddy — if I want to give someone VIP treatment, I *will*. How's that daiquiri, little lady? I made it from my own recipe," he said, winking.

Jane sipped the drink and nodded.

"It's fine."

"Well good! I make that drink for all my ladies." Duke raised his eyebrows and grinned at me. "Now, just call if you need anything."

He sauntered down the bar to some other people. Jane leaned over and put her head against mine.

"Tack-y," she whispered.

I didn't ask if she meant Duke or the bar, but we kissed and I didn't really care.

"Hey — none of that!"

Duke came back down in front of us. Jane laughed and I thought maybe the evening would come off.

"Let me get you another round, so you have them waiting!"

Jane laughed again. I knew she liked the idea of having daiquiris lined up and waiting for her. Duke set the new round of drinks up on the bar.

"There you go buddy, now y'all—"

"Duke, could I speak to you a moment?" a fat, baldheaded man called behind him.

He had squinty eyes and a striped shirt that hung out in the back. Duke was taller and had to lean down as the man talked. He looked angry and I could hear parts of their conversation.

"Giving goddamn drinks away. . .I don't care where he works. . . pay up. . .you make good—don't be doing that shit again. . . warning you . . ."

The man turned away and went down the bar. Duke concentrated on the cash register. I turned to Jane to say something, but she was staring at Duke and I knew she had heard it all. Jane slowly shook her head and pushed the drinks away.

Duke came over and the old smile was back on his face.

"Hey, how the drinks?"

"Uh, listen Duke," I said quietly. "Why don't you let me leave you some money for these drinks —"

"Hell no!" Real anger flared in his eyes before he remembered himself. "I bought you the drinks—don't worry about it," he said, with a wave toward the fat man.

"Duke—no really, I'd feel better. . .I'll just—"

"No buddy—I can't let you do that," he said, shaking his head. "It's the principal of the thing."

I put a twenty on the bar. Duke picked it up and put it in my shirt pocket. He stared at me, his eyes glittering.

"Don't do that, partner—you'll make me look bad."

For a moment I wished I had never seen Duke before. I held up my hands and surrendered.

"All right, all right."

Duke nodded and moved off down the bar. I glanced at Jane. She looked away and I realized what a terrible mistake it was to have brought Jane to the bar. Her drinks sat on the bar and slowly melted. I considered leaving the twenty, but I didn't want another scene with Duke. We hurried out, and Jane was silent the whole walk home.

Then I tried to explain what had happened.

"Oh, let's just forget about it!" she snapped.

I lapsed into silence and the only sound was Jane's quick steps on the sidewalk. We finally reached my apartment. Jane said she was tired and laid down on the bed. Her breathing was soft and rhythmic by the time I had my clothes off. I laid down quietly.

I was asleep and there was a loud knocking. It came and went and I didn't want to open my eyes. It stopped, and then came so loudly I thought the door was going to break down. I jumped out of the bed.

"Who is it?" Jane asked, sitting up sleepily.

"BRENTON! WAKE UP—GET OUT OF BED!"

There was laughing. I recognized Christian's voice.

I unlocked the door and opened it slowly. The blue street light poured into the room. Christian and Calamitous stood in the wet parking lot between reflecting puddles that had formed from an earlier rain. They stood unsteadily with their shorts and shirt sleeves outlined by the light behind them.

I faced them in my underwear with the light in my eyes. It was quiet; I couldn't even hear the ocean. I squinted into the light.

"Hey guys, little late?"

"It's only about four!" Calamitous shrieked, laughing stupidly.

"We've come to say hello to the happy couple," Christian slurred.

"Hey Brenton—how's *Jane?*"

I stepped outside and pulled the door shut behind me. I glared at Calamitous.

"She's fine."

Christian stared at me in the darkness. He swayed and then hiccupped.

"Hey. . . Brenton . . . you *giving* it to her?"

I had my arms crossed against the morning coolness, and brought them down to my sides.

"Why don't you shut up, Christian!"

I looked back to make sure the door was shut. My face felt hot and I wished I at least had some pants on. Calamitous joined in.

"Yeah! You *screwing* her, Brenton?"

"I would shut my mouth if I were you."

"Ha!" Christian scoffed. "Did we interrupt the screwing couple?"

He let out a short laugh that was followed by more laughter from Calamitous. My heart thumped against my chest.

"Christian, why don't you shut up and go home."

I took a step forward away from the door. He smiled.

"Why don't you make me, Brenton?"

I stopped and felt suddenly cold.

"Come on, Brenton. . .do something about it."

Wind rustled the trees behind the parking lot and rolled a paper cup into a puddle. I looked down the steps that went into the lot. A trickle of cold sweat moved down my side.

"Come down into the parking lot, Brenton."

I stared at Christian and the wind died back down.

"I'll see you guys in the morning."

He shook his head. "You're a coward, Brenton."

I turned back to the apartment and went inside and shut the door. Christian's voice came into the room.

"YOU COWARD BRENTON!"

I picked up the covers and Jane was staring at the wall. I got in the bed and started to say something, but she had already closed her eyes. I laid awake and didn't fall asleep till it was light out.

8

The ocean swelled onto the beach with an exhausted whoosh. The sound floated across the airy heat to my chair as I stared down the wavering sand and tried to understand what had happened the night before. Christian had wanted to fight because he was jealous. I knew that. He was jealous and wanted me to look bad in front of Jane. She had left in the morning with a quick, dry kiss. She was going to visit some friends in Baltimore and I wouldn't see her for a week. I wondered if she would even call when she came back. I decided not to see Christian again till he apologized to me. I even considered leaving Ocean City.

I calmed down slowly and started wondering what to do for the next week. I could work at the bar, but I felt like going out and doing something. I slid down in the chair and shut my eyes against the sun. The merry-go-round started up — its plaintive tune carried away by the summer wafting down the long beach.

I took walks on the beach the first few nights, then Duke came to my rescue. He had made a habit of stopping by a couple of times a week to talk. I didn't know how long Duke had worked in Ocean City, but he hated the people and the work.

"Broken-down, bloodsucking greenhorns!" he called them one night outside the disco. "The west is where this cowboy's headed!"

He leaned back against his luminous car. I looked at him.

"What are you going to do when you get there?"

"*Shoot!* There's a thousand things for a man to do out west," he said, moving a hand across the glittering lights of Ocean City behind him. "But this cowboy is going to ranch!"

"Ranching — doesn't that take a lot of money to get started in?"

"Aw — hell!" He waved his hand. "If you got the know how, a little thing like money ain't going to get in your way. And Brenton?" He tipped his hat to me and cocked an eyebrow. "I got the know-how, boy!" He yelped and nodded. "Soon as I got enough money I'm packing this little wagon up and heading out for the range," he said, hooking his thumbs in his belt and looking off into the parking lot.

That was Duke.

The shadow of the club was long on the parking lot when Duke pulled up and sauntered over to my post. It was slow for a Wednesday night.

"Haven't seen you around for a few days, Duke — what have you been up to?"

"You know me — always busy," he said, tipping his hat back. "I'm working right now, so I'm gonna have to get back soon . . . just thought I'd see what was happening around here tonight."

I shrugged.

"Not much."

"What time you get off?" he asked, popping a wooden match into his mouth.

"About three."

He moved the match with his tongue.

"Want to go for a drink, pard?"

"Sure!"

He nodded.

"All right, I'll see you around three."

He jumped back in his car and roared off.

Duke and I didn't end up going out for a drink till four. I was just about to go into my apartment when I heard a low rumble. His white Sting Ray throttled down and leapt into the parking lot, the lights flying around the lot in a circle before coming to a stop next to me.

"Sorry I'm late, pard—got held up," he called out the window.

"No problem," I said, glad he showed up at all.

I sat down into the low car. Duke screeched out of the parking lot onto the empty streets. We hit Ocean Highway and he ran through the gears mercilessly as the car bucked and lunged down the street. The wind whistled around the open top and Duke pulled his hat down low. He throttled back the engine and all I could hear was the airy roar of the salty night air.

Duke reached into the glove box and handed me a silver flask.

"What's in it?"

"Coca-Cola," he cracked with a grin. "What the hell do you think is in there? *Whiskey*—good ol' American, knock your socks off whiskey, now drink up!" he commanded, pushing down on the accelerator and whipping the car forward.

I held the flask up to my nose and the smell made me want to put it right back down. I took a deep breath and drank quickly.

"God!—" I choked. "How long has it been in there?...twenty years?"

He yelped.

"Tastes good, huh?"

He took a big drink and then put it back into my hand.

"Where're we headed?"

"Don't know—just thought we'd cruise around," he shrugged.

"Whooh!" I shook my head again to get rid of the taste of the whiskey in my mouth.

"Shoot, boy," Duke scoffed, taking the flask again.

It was past five when the flask was finally empty, and I didn't care if we drove around forever. I was drunk. Duke hadn't been saying much or maybe I hadn't been saying much. He abruptly swung the car around on the highway, the engine roaring to life again and pushing the wind away.

"I know a place we can go—you ever seen the gulls, boy?"

He stomped down on the accelerator.

"Of course I've seen gulls."

"I mean have you ever really seen the gulls?" he asked, looking at me from under the brim of his hat.

"Yes—I think so. . .I mean, what do you mean?"

"You'll see," was all he said, the car going faster.

The sky was a beginning pink in the east when he pulled up to a deserted sand dune on the far side of the island.

"Right over that dune are the gulls," he said, getting out of the car. "Don't make any noise."

We shut the car doors quietly. Duke started climbing up the sand dune and I followed. I was amazed at how fast he could move in cowboy boots in the sand. We finally got to the top of the dune and the ocean rose out of the night. The horizon was giving way to a strong, deep red.

"Shhh, be quiet now, we don't want to disturb them," he whispered.

He sat down on the top of the dune facing the ocean.

"Where are they?. . .I don't see anything."

I looked over the weeds growing out of the sand. An old wood-slatted storm fence ran across the top of the dune. He pulled me down.

"Sit down and shut up—you'll see them."

He lit a cigarette and I borrowed one. We smoked in silence for a while. I looked at him.

"How come you want to go west so bad, Duke?"

"I told you."

"Yeah, I know, to ranch and all . . . is there anything else?"

I was feeling the boldness of the whiskey. The ground swayed a few times. He took a deep breath.

"There's something else," he said, squinting in a way that made me regret having asked the question. "—A woman."

I nodded.

"Oh!—you have a *girlfriend* out there!"

He turned with a faint smile.

"Yeah, I got a girlfriend out there." He paused, holding the cigarette in front of his face. "My wife."

The ash flared in front of him. I opened my mouth.

"You're married?"

He grinned.

"I don't know how else to get a wife."

"Well?—what happened? . . . I mean, where is she?" I asked, knowing I shouldn't be asking, but I was tired and drunk and didn't care.

"—west." He looked down. "She left me."

"Oh—"

He was quiet, then he shrugged.

"She said I wasn't going to amount to anything and that all my dreams were just a lot of talk . . . and she wanted some security . . . wanted someone to take care of her—the way her daddy did, not someone who was going to be a bar bum all his life." He paused; a long, luminous stream of smoke came out from under his hat. "I told her to wait a little longer and I'd have enough money to go west." His voice became hard. "She got tired of waiting I guess—said that

I was lousy with money and we'd never have enough." Duke paused and stubbed his cigarette in the sand. He laughed, shaking his head. "Hell! — I guess she was right. I'm still here, and I haven't saved enough money yet — so, she left. . . went with a trucker going west. I think she's in Wyoming now — that's what her sister said."

He took out his pack of cigarettes and handed me one.

"Shoot, Duke. . . it was her loss."

"Yeah. . . I know — that's what I kept telling myself for a while. But you know —" He lit a wooden match with his thumbnail and cupped it for me. "It comes back to haunt you at the damndest times — just when you think you're getting over it." He lit his cigarette and took it out of his mouth. "I tell you too," he added, cocking an eyebrow. "I know it's over — I ain't foolin' myself. . . but the good times are what you remember — always the good times."

I nodded slowly.

"I think my own good times are ending with Jane."

Duke glanced over.

"That little filly you brought in?"

I nodded and told Duke the story of the night before.

"I think it's over. . . Christian was right — I can't handle her."

Duke was silent for a moment.

"If she loves you for who you are, then what happened won't matter."

"You don't understand. . . she's a debutante — she has all this money. . ." I shook my head. "I probably should have never tried to take her out."

Duke tipped his luminous hat back on his head, resting his hands on his knees.

"That's what I used to say — but only cowards never take a chance, Brenton."

The surf came back and we sat smoking among the weeds. I listened to the lulling surf, feeling sleepy, then Duke said it was time to look at the gulls.

We looked up over the fence. I began to see the gulls — thousands of them. Dawn illuminated the beach and it was covered with the birds. I couldn't believe they all came to one beach.

"It's the first time I've come out here and looked at these damn gulls since she left . . . she showed me this beach. We used to come out here to look at them in the morning."

I shook my head.

"Well, it's something."

He nodded.

"She used to say, 'Duke, the gulls know about life,' and I'd say, 'What the hell do you mean?' " he said, frowning with his eyes. "And she'd say, 'Look at them, at their eyes — they know.' I never knew what she meant . . . but I liked coming out here."

I nodded, looking out at the spreading dawn and the pink gulls on the beach.

We drove back in the early morning. We were still on the south part of the island when Duke squinted down the highway and hit the brakes.

"What the hell is that?"

There was something laying in the road. Duke pulled the car over and got out. I followed him to the dark mass in front of the car.

"I'll be damned — a deer!" Duke shook his head. "What the hell is a deer doing in Ocean City?"

He squatted down and the deer moved.

"She's still alive — looks like somebody hit it."

The animal looked at us with frightened eyes. A trickle of blood was coming out of one nostril, and her short brown fur moved up and down quickly. I petted the deer's neck.

"What should we do?"

He took a deep breath and scratched his forehead.

"Well—she's dying. . .got to put her out of her misery."

I looked at the deer's wide eyes.

"Wait a minute, Duke. . .we can do something!"

"No we can't, Brenton—look at it, the neck's broke!"

The deer's neck was too far back to be normal.

"But—but what about a veterinarian. . .they can do *something!*"

Duke shook his head and walked back to his car. I followed him.

"Now hold on, Duke. . .you can't just kill it!"

He glanced at me with bloodshot eyes.

"What the hell you want me to do? It's dying," he muttered, opening the trunk and pulling out a gun in a leather holster.

I looked back at the deer. Her ears twitched. He couldn't just kill her.

"Don't do it, Duke!. . .let it live. . .we can take it into town — it'll be all right!"

I grabbed his arm. He turned and faced me.

"What do you want me to do, Brenton? Take it down there so they can put it to sleep? Her goddamn neck is broke! There's not shit anyone can do for it. . . ."

Duke broke away and walked over to the deer. I followed him and pleaded incoherently. It all seemed so terrible. I knew that the deer was dying, but it was way back behind some sort of panic. Duke drew the gun from its holster and clicked the safety off.

"Wait a minute, *wait a minute!*"

"What?"

I shook my head and held up my hand.

"Just hold on. . . ."

It was quiet. I knelt down by the deer and looked into the eyes shining with the first light of day. Dark spots appeared on the deer's fur and I realized they were my own tears. What a terrible thing it all was—no one should have to die. . .not alone. I knelt with my head down.

"Good-bye," I whispered, and the deer blinked.

I petted her neck and smoothed my tears into the brown fur.

"C'mon, Brenton," Duke said, putting a hand on my shoulder.

I got up slowly and went back to the car. I sat, just gazing out the window and seeing the sun on the weeds in the sand till I jumped and knew the deer was dead. I heard Duke pick up the animal and carry it off into the weeds. He threw his gun in the trunk and jumped in.

Duke had his hat pulled low over his eyes as he gunned the car to life. We took off. He didn't say a word and neither could I.

9

"Take the ski, Brenton. That's right—now put it on your foot."

"I can't! It keeps falling off."

"Hold your breath and go underwater!"

"I'm drowning!"

"That's what the life jacket is for, stupid—if you drown, it keeps your body afloat."

"Comforting, very comforting. O.K., I got one ski on—where's the other one?"

"It floated away while you were busy drowning."

Christian grabbed my other ski, which had floated over to the boat, and threw it at me. The ski slid across the sparkling green water and stopped about an inch away from my face. I grabbed it.

"You trying to kill me or what?"

"You can do it, Brenton," Jane called out from the boat, holding up a beer.

I smiled back, struggling with the ski. Christian and Jane had water-skied before. I had not.

Jane had come back from Baltimore on Sunday. She appeared at my beach stand the next day and told me about her trip. She seemed to have forgotten about our bad night altogether. I dismissed the night too, and eventually stopped by Christian's beach stand.

"Where ya been?. . .I was just thinking of coming down to see you," he had offered as I approached his stand.

I took this as a concession and we both avoided the subject of Jane and that night.

"I do stupid things when I drink," he admitted, and that was as close to an apology as I needed.

It was several weeks later when he offered to take Jane and me skiing on his father's powerboat. At first I thought he was kidding, but then I took this as an acceptance of my going out with her. I excitedly told Jane and after a hesitation she said that it sounded fun.

Jane and I had careened on through the weeks. There were perfect moments together next to nights where my calls went unanswered. I lay in the darkness—the air conditioner clattering through the night—certain I would never see her again. But a flip of her hair and a careless, whispered "With my friends, silly" was enough, and the summer continued.

We arranged to have some people look after our stands for the day while we were skiing. The morning came so crisp and clear that it didn't seem like summer. We drove over to the sound where Christian's father kept the boat.

The sound was green and muddy. On one side was Ocean City; on the other was a line of green trees that leaned out over the water in thick, leafy abundance. Jane was quiet behind a pair of sunglasses and a white bathing suit that made her look even more tan. We jumped aboard the red boat that nudged a rickety, bleached, wooden dock. Jane and I sat down as Christian commanded the boat. The engine sputtered briefly then roared into the morning stillness, causing several gulls to abandon the dock. There was a wet-sour smell around the shore and I looked for fish floating in the sun-mirrored water.

Christian unhooked the mooring line and put the boat in gear with a clunk, moving it away from the dock. The bubbling engine asserted itself and the boat lifted out of the water as we slipped across the morning quiet.

"Brenton, put on the ski already — by the time you start skiing, it's going to be dark!"

Christian maneuvered the boat so the rope would pass by me.

"O.K.—I got the other ski on . . . now what?"

"Put your skis together and grab the tow rope," Jane called.

I grabbed the tow rope and then the bar it was connected to.

"All set!"

I gripped the rubber bar tightly. Christian started the boat forward and the rope grew taut.

"Here we go," Christian yelled, throttling the motor.

I braced my arms and started to move. The water pushed heavily against my body as I fought with the rope. The bar pulled out of my hands and I sank back into the sound. I bobbed back up in the water with my skis off.

"You have to hang on to the tow rope, Brenton," Christian yelled, bringing the boat back around.

"My skis came off!"

"That's what happens when you fall — just put them back on."

I went through the process of drowning all over again and finally got my skis back on.

"You can do it, Brenton," Jane shouted from the back of the boat.

"Ready?" Christian called.

I grabbed the tow rope and lifted the tips of my skis out of the water and into position.

"Yeah!"

He started the boat forward again. I stiffened my arms against the pressure. This time I came up sideways and did a half belly flop back into the water. The skis came off again. Christian brought the boat back.

"What happened?"

"I don't know — maybe I'm not cut out to water-ski."

Christian shook his head

"Brenton, put the skis back on — anyone can water-ski."

I started struggling with the skis. I readied myself and told Christian to take off. The line tightened. I started moving through the water — one of my skis popped off and I did a right-sided cartwheel into the water.

"Forget it! . . . Forget this sport!"

Not skiing was better than being embarrassed in front of Jane like this. I swam toward the boat, pushing the skis in front of me. Christian revved the boat and moved away. I thought he was going to circle around but he stopped.

"Hey! Bring the boat over!"

Christian shook his head slowly.

"You're going to water-ski first!"

"What are you talking about? Bring the boat over!"

Christian shook his head calmly.

"You can do it — just try again."

"Christian, he wants to come in," I heard Jane say.

Christian waved her away. She said something else, then he turned and spoke quickly. They stared at each other.

"Christian — bring the boat over here!"

"Nope, not till you water-ski," he said, moving away more.

Jane glared at Christian, then looked at me and shook her head. I considered that Christian had gotten me out here to show me up again in front of Jane. I hit the water angrily with my hand.

"I'll swim to shore!"

I looked at the shore in the distance and thought this might not be such a good idea. Christian reclined in a chair on the boat.

"Fine — have a nice swim."

I bobbed around in the warm, green water. I looked down and wondered what was below me. The sound was full of crabs and jellyfish. I splashed around some more and decided the only thing to do was put the skis back on.

"You bastard!" I yelled, swimming to get the skis.

He nodded and just grinned.

"You'll thank me for this later."

I struggled with the skis and took the tow rope. Christian brought the boat to life and I went down just as quickly.

"Christian, let me in the damn boat!"

"Nope, not till you water-ski," he said, shaking his head.

Jane stood up.

"Christian, I can't believe you're doing this!"

He looked at her and smiled, standing with the muscles of his stomach moving slowly in the harsh, overhead sun. Jane sat down sulkily, looking out at me.

"What's it to *you* if I ski or not?"

"I don't like quitters," he shrugged, looking over the side of the boat at me.

"Let me in!"

He shook his head.

"Can't do it."

I called him everything I could think of, then went and put the skis back on. I grabbed the tow rope, fell down again, and decided to just wait him out.

"I JUST CAN'T WATER-SKI!"

"Yes you can," Christian said, turning the boat around.

"Don't *you* want to water-ski?"

"Nope, not till you have."

He hesitated and leaned over the side of the boat.

"Brenton, keep your ankles stiff and your legs even — I guarantee you will rise up."

"But that's how I have been doing it!"

Christian shook his head.

"You're only keeping your legs even in the beginning. Keep them even and steady all the time."

I looked at him. "If I don't get up this time, bring the boat over — I'm not going to try again!"

He brought the rope by and I grasped it securely.

"All right . . . *go!*"

The rope tightened as the crossbar pulled against my fingers. I squeezed the bar, moving through the water and using every muscle to keep my legs rigid and tense. I pulled the bar to my chest for more control. The water poured into my face, pushing on my body to keep it down. I tensed my legs and arms even more, hanging on to the rope with all my strength. The water left my back and then, as if something had released me, I was up.

The wind whistled around me and blew my hair straight back. The cool water started drying on my body. I didn't release any of my tense muscles, but crouched down to take the waves that my skis bounced over. I was moving! The trees on the shore ran by quickly. I glanced down at my skis going over the white water beneath. Christian looked back from his driving and held a fist up in the air. Jane waved. I couldn't help but grin: I was water-skiing.

"You can come in the boat now, Brenton," Christian offered after I had grown tired and fallen in.

I grabbed the rope again.

"Forget it! Just shut up and drive."

I did finally get back in the boat after skiing a few more times.

"I'm glad you're back — I think Jane wants to hit me in the back of the head with the anchor," Christian said, taking the dripping skis and setting them down.

I glanced at Jane. She sat unmoving, gazing at something toward shore. Christian had gotten me to water-ski, and in some way he was right for making me do it, but I still suspected that he was trying again for an upper hand.

"Listen Christian, I know you wanted me to water-ski, but —" Jane turned.

"Oh forget it, Brenton! You water-skied, what's the difference?"

I stood stupidly, then started to say something but Jane started laughing. She stood up and pulled off her sunglasses.

"I did want to hit you with an anchor," she said, staring at Christian. "But I think I'll just settle for pushing you over the side!"

She pushed Christian, but he grabbed her arm and they both fell into the warm sound. They came up out of the water with their hair smoothed back and water streaming off. Jane and Christian stared at each other, the sun coming off the water in designs that played across their cheeks.

"I'll get you for this!" Jane splashed him.

"I'll get you for this," Christian mimicked and dove under.

He reappeared behind her and pushed her under.

"I hate you!"

She splashed Christian while he dove underwater and came up behind her again. I stared at the two of them. Christian kept splashing Jane while she shrieked in protest, but she was laughing, too. All I could do was watch.

It was late in the day when we started back to shore. The sun was low over the trees and the bay was a dying orange. Cottages dotted the shore with yellow porch lights and the warm smell of the distant ocean blew over us. A white gull flew low across the bow.

I sat on the front of the boat as we moved slowly through the sound.

Jane leaned back against my chest, the wind-blown smell of her hair slipping over me. Christian drove silently with the motor gurgling behind us. The boat nosed through the still water, making ripples that spread out from us toward shore before fading slowly away.

10

I led a dual life in some respects that summer. Christian, Jane, and Calamitous were on one side with Duke and King on the other. The two sides of my life were separate, but as the summer progressed they melted together, until one side became a compass for the other.

"I'll tell you — life is quick!" King said into the brooding darkness on one of his breaks from behind the bar. "You gotta reach out and snatch it — before you know it, twenty years have gone by. . . then thirty."

He hunched down on one leg and flicked his cigarette on the step below. Some dark strands of hair fell onto his forehead. He pulled on his cigarette, looking to the running lights of the highway. King blew the smoke out tiredly.

"Life is composed of three phases, as I see it. . . . First part is preparing to shoot your wad — that's the part you're in," he said, motioning to me. "Second phase is shooting your wad, and the third phase is helping other people shoot theirs," he finished, sparking his cigarette again by hitting it with his middle finger.

I nodded and looked at him.

"What phase are you in, King?"

He looked down to his dying cigarette. King had come to work late again with his eyes bloodshot and puffy. He spent a lot of time out on the porch, smoking with a trembling hand and shaking off the effects of a bad drunk from the night before.

"Well. . . I guess I shot my wad a while back—but I'm not to the third phase, 'cause I ain't completely done. . . ." He looked up, staring. "I got a little bit left, and I want to be careful how I use it—" He turned away and I felt as if a flame had just been turned down. He smoked quietly, still hunched down, then nodded slowly. "—'cause I'm gonna need all of it when the time comes."

King and I worked the early shift one Saturday night. I found myself walking out to the parking lot after work with nothing to do. Christian and Calamitous were off somewhere and Jane was out with her girlfriends. King was walking to his car with his leather jacket slung over his shoulder and a cigarette dangling from his mouth.

"Hey—kid!" I called.

He always called me that. He looked as he got his car keys out.

"Hey, kid," he nodded.

"Where're you headed, King?"

He opened the car door.

"Out drinking—'bout yourself?"

I shrugged.

"Don't know. . . maybe I'll just go to bed."

He threw his jacket in the car, pulled the cigarette out of his mouth, and looked at me with his T-shirt glowing eerily.

"You got nothing to do?"

"Oh sure—I could go out to the bars if I wanted. . ."

"I said, do you have anything to do?"

"Well . . . no—not really, but I—"

"Get in the car," he said, throwing a thumb over his shoulder. I shook my head.

"Nah—I don't want to impose—"

"Shut up and get in the car!"

"O.K.!"

I ran over and jumped in the other side of the car. He just shook his head. It was the first time I had been in his car. The white leather seats gleamed in the blue night and reflected the twinkling, chromed dashboard. King slapped in a tape: "Baby love, my baby love. . ."

"Where're we going?"

"To a place where I hang out—doubt if you've been there before," he said, lighting another cigarette from a lighter in the dashboard.

We headed for the far side of the island and sped past ghostly trailers that gleamed in pale fields of sand and high weeds. The trailers did not pull in for the summer—these rusting, silver missiles weathered all the seasons. Ocean City's transients occupied this corner of the island. King pulled off the highway onto a dirt road camouflaged by tall trees.

"Where are we?"

"In the twilight zone—don't worry, trust Uncle King."

We came to a parking lot of cars. I was amazed. All the cars were like King's: beautiful restorations of classics that had cruised the streets years ago. The bar's neon sign gleamed in the mirrored paint of the chariots. I stared at the cars drenched in the blue light.

"This is it," King announced, getting out of the car.

"These cars are incredible!"

"Yeah . . . come on—you going to sit in the parking lot all night and stare?"

I ran to catch up with him as we made our way to a loud building. We stopped at the door for King to run a comb through his hair. He opened the door and the noise rushed out.

The room was smoky; low-hanging lamps dropped columns of hazy light onto tables. A rough bar occupied one corner, and directly across from that was a plywood stage with a band playing late-fifties and early sixties songs. Everyone was dressed similarly to King: black leather jackets, T-shirts, and boots. King was mobbed with people he knew.

"Hey, King—what's up boy?"

"King, you old dog! Where you been hiding?"

"Hey ladies! The pretty boy is here!"

These people loved King. I was introduced as Brent—King told me he thought it would be easier to remember than Brenton. The band belted out songs one after another. "Let's go to the hop, oh baby. . ."

The beers were coming fast and I tried to keep up with King as we stood against the wall. Every woman in the place stopped by to talk to him. King was polite, but showed no real interest. A cigarette dangled from my lips while I talked to the ones he passed on.

"Having a good time, kid?"

"Yeah!" I shouted, sloshing beer on the floor.

The band stopped and the singer stepped to the microphone.

"We have an added treat tonight for everybody—a friend of mine is here and he's going to do a few songs for us. . .let's here it for King!"

I nearly dropped my beer. King looked surprised and started shaking his head, but the crowd wasn't to be put off. Four large, leather-jacketed men came over, picked King up, and carried him to the stage. He tried to get down, but they wouldn't let him leave. He had to give the audience what they wanted.

He put on a guitar and everyone quieted down. King launched into some old rock classics in a rich baritone voice and I started to realize why they called him King. He did one song that he had written, a hauntingly slow song with just King on the guitar. I remember one verse.

> "Well I don't know how to take it—
> things have changed so very much.
> The cards are stacked against me
> and there's so little I now trust.
> I don't know how to take it—
> they went and changed it all.
> I don't know how to take it—
> feel I'm heading for a fall."

After King finished singing, we drank till late into the morning. There were only a few cars left in the lot when we pulled out.

"I had a great time. Thanks a lot, King."

He just nodded and gunned the car down the highway. We stopped at a red light. A white Corvette pulled up next to us and revved its engine. For a moment I thought it was Duke. King turned his head and looked over at the driver.

"Young punks," he muttered, shifting into first gear and revving his engine.

The light stayed red for an instant, then blinked green. I was slammed back against the seat as the engine roared and the tires squealed down the highway.

"Hang on, Brenton!"

We stayed up with the Corvette. King slammed through the gears, the tires screeching with every shift. I watched the speedometer go past one hundred.

"King!—there're cars up ahead!" I yelled above the screaming engine, gripping the armrest of the door so hard my hand ached.

"I can beat him, I can beat him!"

I glanced into the side mirror and saw flashing red lights behind us.

"King, stop for chrissake!—the *cops* are behind us!"

"I can beat him! I can beat him!"

The car was winding out with the speedometer now useless. A pack of cars appeared in front of us—the Corvette shot into our lane. King swerved into the oncoming lanes. Headlights came straight at us and horns blared. I lunged over to turn the motor off, and there was a deafening screech that was more in the car than out. We went off the road sideways. King spun the wheel one way then back, as the car fish-tailed to the right and left. The world whizzed around and around and I was pinned to my seat. We stopped in the weeds.

It was quiet and the air was full of dust. King hit the steering wheel. Sirens screamed and red beams played through the dust. King took a deep breath and looked at me.

"You O.K.?"

I was numb and nodded dumbly. Spotlights lit the car and blue uniforms floated toward us.

"I think we're in for some shit now," King muttered.

The police took us to the station. We had to come up with bail for drag racing. King called a friend who said he would come down with the money. The police put us in a gray cell; even if it had been another color, I would have sworn it was gray. A broken porcelain toilet smelled of urine. Chains anchored the cots to a wall covered with desperate philosophies and crass humor.

King stood with his hands on the bars. He stared at the square window of light that came in through a heavy metal door. The door separated the holding tanks from the police administration. I laid down on the low bench with the moth-ball smelling blanket. King smoked quietly, then started talking to the steel bars that kept us.

"Did you know I was going to get married?" he asked, his voice echoing off the cement in front of us.

"No."

"Oh yeah. . . . I went out with this girl all through high school and we were going to get married."

Something in his voice made me feel I was being offered a confession. He paused. I could hear the squeaky suction noise of his cigarette. A cloud moved above him into the light.

"Her name was Betty. . . it was when I lived in Salisbury — from the moment I saw her, I knew she and I belonged together."

I was only half listening because I was wondering how I'd ended up staring at the bottom of a steel cot in a jail cell. King reached as high as he could on the steel bars in front of him.

"We went out for three years and decided to get married." He breathed in heavily and I looked over at his stretched figure against the bars. "I went out on a spree the week before — you know, the final fling. . . . I was out drinking all night — there was this brunette, I was with a bunch of guys. . . . She didn't mean anything to me," he said, his voice metallic against the cement walls. He slid his hands down the bars in front of him. ". . . It turned out she knew a girl who knew Betty and she broke off the wedding. . . . She wouldn't even talk to me. I was busted up real bad — that's why I enlisted."

I looked at him.

"You were in the army?"

He dropped his cigarette next to him — a feeble glow on the concrete.

"Yeah man . . . in the army — did a tour in 'Nam, too."

"What was Vietnam like?"

King paused and shrugged.

"It was a bad scene. . . ."

He paused again, leaning his head against the bars.

"By the time I came back, Betty had married some rich college guy. I moved to Ocean City. . . . I tried to see her but she wouldn't even talk to me . . . but I never forgot about her — I knew she married that guy only 'cause I was gone. I started writing her letters and they came back unopened, but I just kept writing . . . then finally she wrote back." He shifted his weight. "She wrote this letter and told me she wasn't happy with the guy she'd married. I wrote her and told her to leave him, but she quit writing . . . nothing — just like that, and then I get a call about a year ago and it's Betty." He lit another cigarette. "The moment I talked to her. . . I knew it was still good."

He gestured with a smoky hand as if I were standing in front of him.

"She starts calling me on a regular basis. This guy has been mistreating her and she wants to leave him — so we started to see each other again." King slid his hands back up the bars, his cigarette topping his reach. "Betty says she wants a divorce and says she's going to tell him before the summer's out."

King turned to the side and acknowledged my presence for the first time.

"I know now I can make what happened . . . right."

Light from the hallway outlined the edge of his face. I didn't know what to say, and really was too tired to think. King turned back in silence and rested against the steel bars, just smoking and waiting.

His buddy came and got us out. It turned out the police couldn't charge me with anything since I wasn't driving. I went home in the morning light and fell into the merciful darkness of sleep.

11

I woke with the steel bars in front of me and sat up in the darkness looking for King in a smoky square of light. A dull clatter and the outline of a surfboard came to me. I fell back into bed with a descending relief, and listened to the reassuring shudder of the air conditioner going through its cycle once again. Thin bars of light seeped into the room from the sides of the door. I groped for the clock — it was only a little past nine.

I walked down the boardwalk with my hangover and decided to stop at Christian's beach stand. The morning glared off the beach and sparkled on the green ocean. Children rode their bikes down the boardwalk, the planks clunking up to me and then away like keys on a piano.

I thought of the night before. King had said nothing about my turning his car off. I wasn't even sure he knew I had done it. I thought about his story in jail. That was what he had talked about before:

"I'm not to the third phase, 'cause I ain't completely done. . .I got a little bit left, and I want to be careful how I use it." His voice moved through my mind like a ghost. "I know now I can make what happened. . .right." Maybe if this Betty left her husband, King's long vigil might be rewarded. . .but I wondered if even this would satisfy him. My head throbbed. I pushed the night from my mind and watched the heat shimmer up the beach in waves of melted glass.

I squinted to make out the blue box that marked Christian's beach stand. It wavered for a moment, then came clear. Christian was sitting next to the box. I shook off my mood and quickened my pace. I looked up again and saw someone seated next to Christian. It was Calamitous—no, it was a girl. One hand came up and flicked back a wave of hair. I stopped.

Jane leaned her head back. She turned to Christian and placed her hand on his arm—it could just as easily have been a kiss. A warmth flushed my face. She took her hand off his arm and then laughed, laughed the way she did with me. I stood in the middle of the boardwalk just staring. I couldn't move, but I had to do something. I went quickly down one of the avenues, getting away from the beach.

I walked fast, my heart beating.

"You'll never be able to handle her, Brenton. You'll never be able to handle her, Brenton. . . ." Because he would take her if I tried! Christian knew all along he would get Jane because he got everything he wanted. I cut into an alley.

I tried to calm down. He and Jane did know each other from before. Jane had lots of friends. What had I actually seen? Jane had put her arm on his—that was it—so what? This wasn't anything . . .but Christian had been making himself look good to her while showing my weaknesses—he wanted her and now he was going to get her.

I stopped and grabbed a whiskey bottle laying in the alley. There was whiskey in the bottom. I saw a brick wall and threw the bottle so hard I fell forward, the bottle smashing into tiny shards. The whiskey came out when I threw it and the smell was all over me. The sour, rotten odor of hot trash cans in the alley came with the wind and my head throbbed more. I sat down against a building. Everything spun around and I leaned over to spit. I waited on my knees, my eyes watering . . . it felt like a cough, but it was deeper. I gagged — then felt the unreality of liquid coming out of my mouth into the alley.

I stayed on my knees and took some deep breaths. The nausea left. I unbuttoned my shirt and wiped myself off. The world slowed down and the spinning stopped. I sat down and looked around. The backs of all the stores along the boardwalk faced the alley; old, weathered brick that showed the age of the buildings. In front, the stores had the new look of neon and plastic. Old boxes and greasy dumpsters lay scattered on the sides of the alley.

I stood up unsteadily and started walking down the alley. Slowly, a new determination came to me. Christian thought I would give in without a fight — after all, that's the way it had always been — but I knew him now. I would wage my own private war. I would win this time.

I turned out of the alley toward the beach. I would say nothing of what I had seen until I had the advantage over Christian. He would lose this time.

A week later we were at Calamitous's father's cottage. We bought two fifths of whiskey to drink before we headed out to the bars. Calamitous was drinking Coca-Cola. The cottage had the feel of belonging to someone from a different time. The tables were made from the planks of shipwrecks with pegs of steel sticking out. Bamboo chairs squeaked when we sat down or got up. The sliding glass door was open to the warm air that came in with the slap of the surf.

A telescope pointed out to a low-slung moon dripping silver into the sea night. The glazed wood of the cottage subdued the light to a warm sepia that sheened dully on a mounted blue and white sword-fish. The bottles were soon half empty.

"It's hard to believe it's already August!" Calamitous said, pushing his long hair from his eyes.

"I know — the summer's flown by," I agreed.

Christian looked through the telescope.

"We still have about three weeks."

"Yeah," Calamitous nodded. "But you and Brenton are going canoeing the last week, aren't you?"

"Uh-huh," Christian nodded, turning from the telescope. "Going to take it all the way to the ocean."

I nodded slowly and looked at Christian and Calamitous. Christian had on some light-blue shorts with a yellow surfer shirt. He put a brown, calloused foot up on the edge of the table in front of us. I glanced at my own dark arms and felt my eyebrows that were now blond. Calamitous was sunburnt, but his pale skin resisted tanning. He had on blue jeans and a button-down shirt. Unless he was on the beach, he always wore long sleeves and pants. Christian said too much sun made Calamitous dizzy.

Jane had been visiting during the day as before, and when we went out things were the same. I watched her closely, but being with her pushed suspicion from my mind and at times I thought maybe the whole thing with Christian was just my imagination.

"I can't believe you guys are going to finish that whiskey," Calamitous said, shaking his head.

"Hey, Calamitous — why don't you drink?" I asked, motioning toward him with my half-empty fifth.

He shrugged and flipped his hair out of his eyes.

"I don't know — guess I just don't."

Calamitous had been this hovering third wheel through the summer. He didn't drink much, didn't talk much, just hung on what Christian was doing or saying.

"Why don't you drink with us? C'mon . . . I'm not going to be here forever, you know."

He blinked rapidly and shook his head.

"No. . .I can't."

I jumped up and held my bottle out to him.

"C'mon and drink with us, Calamitous. Jesus! You can't go through life not drinking!"

He shook his head and blinked quickly. Christian moved between us and pushed the bottle back toward me.

"Knock it off, Brenton."

I stared at him.

"What do you mean? Let's get him to drink!"

"Just what I said — he doesn't have to drink if he doesn't want to."

"If it was anybody else, they would have to drink! What the hell is so special about him?"

I looked at Calamitous, then pushed the bottle into his face.

"Here, Calamitous! DRINK THE GODDAMN WHISKEY!"

He reared back and made a noise in his throat. Christian knocked the bottle out of my hand and the whiskey poured out onto the wood floor.

"I told you to knock it off!"

Christian stood in front of me. There was a tingling in my legs. He stared, then shook his head.

"Don't know when to quit, do you Brenton?"

I swallowed, my heart racing.

"Jesus! . . . I just wanted him to have a drink."

Christian picked up the bottle with some whiskey left in it and handed it to me. He went to get a towel. Calamitous sat on the couch and looked down. I stared at him and took another drink of my whiskey.

Christian came back in and wiped up the spill. He walked over to me and held out his hand for my bottle.

"What?"

"Give me your bottle."

"Why?"

"Just give it to me."

I handed the bottle to him reluctantly. He held it up to his bottle and then poured some of his whiskey into mine.

"There. . . we're even."

He handed me back my bottle.

There was silence. I was still standing in the middle of the room, although I was swaying a bit.

"A toast!" I proposed, feeling I should try and make up for something. "To next summer!"

I held up my fifth. Christian raised his bottle and Calamitous his Coke. We clinked our bottles and Calamitous smiled sheepishly.

"I wonder who will be back?"

"I should be," I nodded.

Christian grinned.

"If you aren't married by then."

Calamitous sat up.

"Married! Who's getting married?"

Christian pointed to me.

"Brenton is, to Paisley."

"No!. . ."

I looked at Christian, but he just laughed.

"I'm not marrying anybody," I muttered.

Christian shrugged.

"Could have fooled me — seems like she's in love with you."

I looked at him again.

"Well — can you blame her?"

He shrugged and glanced at me.

"No—guess I can't."

Christian took a drink, looking at me without expression; then oddly, his eyes laughed. I opened my mouth to say something, but then it was gone from his eyes and I wasn't sure what I had seen.

"Calamitous will probably be the first to get married. Some dark Latin beauty will sweep him off his feet at college and that'll be it," Christian laughed.

"Yeah, you think so? You're probably right," Calamitous said, blinking his eyes.

Christian started laughing.

"What's so funny? You don't think that could happen?" Calamitous became more indignant. "Just you wait—it might just happen!"

We finished the bottles and went to The Outlet. I was drunk and one moment slid into the next in a general haze of indifference. Christian and Calamitous were somewhere in the bar, but I couldn't muster the energy to go find them. I was in a fog, wondering what to do next, when someone kissed my cheek.

I turned into Jane's blue eyes and a faint mist of Chanel. I stared at her from a distance and she reminded me of an ad for a prep school: the pink ribbon in the pony tail, the crisp yellow polo shirt. . . what was that ad?. . .

"Brenton!. . .Oh, you are drunk! How did you get so drunk?"

I weaved a little.

". . .whiskey!"

A wave of annoyance passed through her eyes.

"Well. . .I hope you don't get sick."

I squinted at her through slitted eyes. She sniffed as she looked around the bar. Christian's laughing eyes appeared in front of me again. I leaned forward.

"Are?. . .are you in love with Christian?"

133

Jane turned from the bar, her eyebrows coming together.

"Am I what?"

The music and the noise rushed up and then away again. I steadied myself against the wall.

"—are you in love with Christian?" I repeated, in what I thought was a very calm voice.

Even in my stupor I saw some level of control go out of her, then come back again.

"Of course not!" she cried. "Why would you ask such a thing?"

I shrugged and looked around.

"I know. . .don't try and talk your way out of it—*I know!*. . . He's good looking—got money. . . Hawthorne Man and—"

"Brenton—you're drunk! I don't know what you heard or why you would think such a thing, but if you make a scene here you can forget about me," she hissed.

I wavered, opened my mouth to apologize, then stopped. There was her arm again on Christian in the shimmering heat. I closed my eyes—some form of conviction, or maybe it was just rebellion at her control, came to me.

"That's O.K.," I said, holding up an unsteady hand. "I can take it. . . he's probably better than me at *everything*—which ought to make you happy, if you know what I mean. . . ."

I winked at her, grinning.

A rage came into her eyes, then a look that reminded me of someone who was about to swat a pesky fly. I really didn't feel the slap so much as hear it. It had that sharp sound that makes people look. There was a stinging warmness on my cheek—things had somehow gotten out of control.

"You're disgusting!"

Her eyes were hard, but there were tears in the corner.

I felt as if I had made some colossal mistake. She moved away and disappeared. I stood against the wall, aware that some people were staring at me. Christian walked up.

"What happened? I saw Jane leave the bar—"

I shook my head; he sounded far away.

"Ah, nothing," I waved. "She had to go. . .where's Calamitous?"

"Don't know. . .maybe he left. . . ."

I nodded and tried to focus, but people and things were moving too much. Christian wasn't standing, but leaning and rocking. I needed air.

"You ready to leave?" I shouted.

Christian replied by dropping his beer on the floor and walking out the door. I staggered out from the heat of too many people into the cool night. The ocean was quiet and rhythmical after the noise of the bar. I looked for Christian on the boardwalk, then saw him kneeling in the sand on the beach.

"Hey Christian!. . .Ya getting sick?" I shouted at him, falling off the boardwalk into the sand.

I got up to see him running for the ocean.

"Heeey—Christian. . .wait for me!"

I started a running stumble down the beach, keeping my eyes on him as he headed for the ocean. The surf roared out and a wave knocked him down. I came running up. He was laying on his back in the water. The waves washed up over him, moving him closer to the ocean each time.

"You nut. . .what the hell. . .trying to do?" I gasped, falling down onto the wet sand.

He laid silently with the moon water washing over him.

"Did. . .you want to go for a swim?"

"Don't know—just felt like running for the ocean," he murmured, his eyes glistening.

I shook my head.

"—thought you were going for a swim and I was going to have to rescue you."

I kicked off my deck shoes and laid back, letting the water rush over my feet. I gazed up at the speckled universe. Some of the detachment of the alcohol started to fade and I felt my cheek where Jane had slapped me. What had made me accuse her?. . .I was going to fight for her, but I had just given in. . . .

"You want to go to college, Brenton?"

I sat up and looked at Christian, one reality fading for another.

"Do I want to go to college?"

He was still laying on his back. I looked out at the dark ocean for a moment.

"Yes. . .I guess I do, I mean, yeah, I do."

Christian sat up. I looked at him.

"Do *you* want to go?"

He hesitated, then shrugged.

" . . .course — everyone goes to college."

I nodded and tried to think clearly.

"Yeah — but what do you want to do?"

He blinked and looked away.

"It's not that I don't want to go — I do. . .I mean . . .really, I have to."

I nodded and shut my eyes against the spins that were starting. I felt as if he wanted me to say something.

"I just wondered," he said, laying back down in the water.

College. . .I was going to college. Why would Christian not want to go? He would do well . . .like he did in everything. He didn't want to go, but he would. Even if I told him he didn't have to go, he would. He's taking Jane away from me. . .why should I care what he does? . . .but maybe he wasn't. . . .

I put up my hand.

"Christian, I—" A large wave crashed on us, running over him and soaking me.

We moved further up the beach and by the time we were settled again, I had forgotten whatever it was I was going to say to Christian.

I must have fallen asleep or passed out. I woke up with Christian dripping on me in his wet clothes.

"Wake up, Brenton."

"— what."

I put my hands up to my face.

"Come on! — we're going to see the old man tonight."

"What old man?" I sat up and rubbed my eyes. "What time is it?"

Christian was already walking down the beach.

"Come on, Brenton. We're going to see the sand sculptor," he called from the dark beach.

"Wait up!" I groaned.

I stood and could see the blue light far down the beach in the late mist. I staggered after Christian.

I felt we had walked miles down the beach. The blue light was always in the distance, never growing closer. I trudged heavily between alcohol and fatigue. Christian's stride just seemed to get stronger as we got closer. Finally, we reached the large mound of sand. We walked to the side and looked around quietly, almost reverently. The night was so quiet I couldn't even hear the ocean. Mist ran past the blue light and not one person could be seen.

The sand sculptor had left Christ on the Cross. He was perfectly formed out of sand. His beard flowed down in rivulets onto His chest. His hair was of a darker sand, flowing into the hill He was formed from. The sand was so compressed that the cross looked solid. Pieces of real wood were used for tiny stakes through His hands and feet. On His face were little balls of sand coming from His eyes.

The bucket of money was inside a roped-off section which went around the entire scene. It was overflowing with money at Christ's feet. I looked down the deserted boardwalk and saw a clock . . . it was four in the morning.

"That's something, huh?"

"It is," I said, sitting down in the sand.

Christian stared at the figure on the cross.

"We'll find out who this guy is, Brenton. This time we'll know."

"Is it the same guy as before?"

Christian stared at me.

"Of course! The sand sculptor doesn't change."

I nodded and looked at the eroding figure of sand. Soon we were both passed out in the sand, and then Christian woke me, motioning to come up on the boardwalk. I jumped up. The bucket of money was gone. Christian pointed down a side street with the expression of a child at Christmas.

"Look, Brenton—it's *him!*"

I looked down the dark avenue and could see a hunched-over figure. Christian waved me on.

"Come on—let's follow him and see where he goes!"

We ran through the mist after the sand sculptor. I was soon gasping for air, trying to keep up with Christian. We didn't seem to be gaining on him. The hunched silhouette rounded the corner of a street and disappeared. We sprinted after him. I was exhausted and still drunk and I wondered why we were running after this old man and why we couldn't catch him. We came around the corner of a building. The old man was much closer this time—I could see the glint of the bucket he carried and his tattered clothes.

"Come on, Brenton! We can catch him," Christian called back.

I couldn't keep up the pace. Just before the sculptor turned the next corner, he paused and looked back at us. Sweat poured off me as my feet pounded the pavement. I pumped my arms to go faster, but by the time we got to the corner he was gone.

We stopped on the sidewalk trying to catch our breath.

"Where'd he go?" Christian demanded.

I shook my head. Drops of rain started to darken the sidewalk. Christian looked up at the rain, then stared at me.

"What?"

"The sand sculpture!"

He took off running toward the boardwalk and I lagged after him. The rain was heavy by the time I reached the darkened planks and I was soaked. The rain hissed on the wood around me. Christian sat next to the soft hill of sand that had been Christ on the Cross. I jumped into the sand. He turned to me with his hands up in despair, not speaking, but motioning to where the sculpture had been and crying in the loud rain.

The rain had stopped by the time we reached Christian's car. He started driving and I was glad the night was finally over. Christian had sat by the soggy hill of sand staring at it for ten minutes, then muttered, "Nothing lasts. . . ." I had sat on the edge of the board-walk not knowing what to say.

I leaned against the car door and closed my eyes.

"Let's go to the lighthouse, Brenton!"

I looked at him.

"What?"

"Let's go to the lighthouse — like before."

"I'm tired."

"C'mon, you don't have to go up in it if you don't want to."

"Haven't we done enough in one night?"

Christian shrugged and paused.

"If you're scared of going there. . ."

I glared at him.

"I'm not scared. . .let's go," I said, feeling I now had to go.

Christian started driving toward the other side of the island. I was never going to sleep. I shifted uncomfortably in the seat. The tall gray tower floated through my mind. I would have to jump across that hole. But maybe if I could do this, I could keep Jane. It would show Christian that things were different now. One success would lead to another. Maybe it was all connected.

The last beach house fell away and there was only the highway and sand running alongside the headlights. It seemed we hadn't driven very long when Christian pulled to the side of the road.

"Here we are."

He turned off the motor. We sat among the high weeds that swished from a noiseless wind. Christian's car creaked and made soft, tinny popping noises. The ocean rumbled in the background and a thin line of light on the horizon had become wide, pushing away the fading stars.

Christian got out of the car. We started off toward the long ridge of sand that ran between the highway and the ocean. The gray lighthouse emerged against the dawn. Christian reached the top of the ridge and disappeared. I walked slowly up the hill, watching the dark shape become larger, then the wide open beach spread out of the half light and the ocean wind blurred my eyes.

"Come on, Brenton! Let's climb the lighthouse and watch the sunrise," Christian called from the shadows.

I ran down the hill, my heart quickening as the ocean became louder. Christian stood at the bottom of the lighthouse, his eyes burning with a queer light.

The same faded NO TRESPASSING signs were there. Christian stared at the door.

"Someone put a new lock on the door. . ."

"I guess we can't go in," I shrugged.

Christian abruptly leaned back and kicked the door. The hasp tore out of the wood and the door flew open just as it had before.

"No problem," he grinned.

I was going into the lighthouse.

Christian went into the dampness and I followed. The same musty smell came to me from years before. The small table was still there with the chair. We started up the spiral stairwell. Our steps echoed in the cement tower like before and I wasn't sure any time had passed at all. We moved up through the darkness, the years slipping behind with each step until we were left with only this lighthouse. Our shoes tapped against the metal as we got closer to the summit. Far below, the light of the door had become just a faint glimmer. We were headed back to where Christian wanted to go.

"Brenton, there's the platform!" Christian called from the darkness.

I felt the steps end and walked onto the metal grating.

"Here's the ladder," he whispered next to me. "I'll climb first."

He went up the ladder and pushed open the trap door. Morning light came down on us. He hoisted himself up and turned around.

"All right, come on."

I climbed the ladder silently up into the lighthouse. I looked around at the machinery. Everything was dark in the dawn light. The dust-covered cables were bigger than I remembered and more dark and sinewy. The glass that housed the large filament reflected the dawn and held all the colors of the sunrise in it. Everything was waiting for the sun.

I looked at the door to the outside. In front of it was the dark opening in the floor. It was larger somehow. I had hoped it would be smaller, less ominous. Christian stood on the small space of flooring before the hole.

"Brenton, you don't have to go outside. . . but it's going to be a great sunrise."

"It looks bigger," I observed.

"What does?"

"The hole."

He looked at me and nodded.

"You don't—"

"I'm going," I said, staring at him.

Christian shrugged and stepped back, flattening himself against the wall. He paused, crouched down, and then jumped across. He landed on the other side and turned around.

"See?—same as before. Go ahead."

I climbed up and stood against the wall on the space of flooring. I looked at the hole. A vibration moved up from my stomach as I got in a low stance and tried to see myself leaping over the hole to the other side.

"Come on, Brenton!—we're going to miss the sunrise."

There was no saliva in my mouth. I looked at the ground, gritted my teeth, and commanded my feet to move. I crouched down again, took a deep breath. . .it was no use. I would fall if I tried.

"I can't do it."

Christian stared at me.

"Sure you can, just do it!"

"I can't—I'll fall," I said, hating him for bringing me here again.

"Look at it!" Christian commanded. "It's not that bad."

I edged up toward the hole and looked down. There was a wrenching, cracking noise, then the flooring left me. I turned and lunged for what was left of the floor against the wall.

"Brenton!"

My feet dangled in the nothingness.

"Jesus Christ!"

I tried to pull myself up.

". . .hang on, Brenton!"

Christian jumped back across, landing in the doorway and on the ladder. I managed to get one foot up on the ledge by swinging my leg. Christian grabbed my ankle.

"Can you work your way over to me?"

"No. . .I'm afraid to move my hands."

"You can't move them at all?"

"No!"

"Then let go—I'll pull you up by your leg."

I glanced at him.

"Jesus! You can't do that!"

"Yes I can—I'll tie my belt to these cables behind me and then I'll just pull you up hand over hand," he said steadily.

"God!...do it! I can't hold on much longer!"

The strength was leaving my hands and the rotten flooring looked like it could give way altogether.

"I'm going to let your foot go for a second—can you swing it back up?"

"Yes...I think so."

Christian let my foot go and took off his belt, running it through the cables behind him and back around his waist.

"All right—swing your leg up!"

I swung my foot back up and he grabbed my ankle and calf.

"All right, Brenton...just let go."

"Jesus, Christian! DON'T LET ME FALL!"

"I won't just let go."

"God!...Here I go!"

"Do it!"

"I can't—I'll fall!"

"Let *go,* Brenton!"

I let my hands go and fell back, looking straight down into the darkness. I swung upside down, then felt hands moving methodically up my leg. I came back into the light. Christian set me on the ladder and I crawled down to the metal platform. He came down next to me.

"You all right?" he asked, breathing hard.

I nodded.

"—I think so."

"I wouldn't have thought that floor would give way like that."

Christian stood on the ladder and looked at the place where the boards used to be.

"I don't think we'll get across that again," I said, rubbing my knee.
Christian shrugged.

"I can still get across."

I looked at him.

"Why would you want to?"

"See the sunrise."

I nodded and he glanced down.

"You sure you're O.K.?"

"Yeah . . ."

"O.K. . . . I'm going across."

I shook my head. He crouched down above me and I heard him
land on the other side.

"You're nuts!" I hollered.

"I'll meet you at the bottom," he called. "I'll be down right after
the sunrise."

I went down the steps and out of the lighthouse. I walked slowly
across the beach to the water. The surf washed over my shoes.
Christian had made it plain again—nothing had changed. Even if
the floor hadn't broken, I wouldn't have gone across. How stupid
I was to think I had somehow changed. Things were the same and
Christian knew it.

The glow over the ocean was a burning red and soon the sun would
peak over the Atlantic. I waited for the moment when the first rays
would streak across the water. I looked down at the water, then there
was a brightness as the sun moved over the horizon. I turned and
looked up to the lighthouse. Christian was standing on the platform
with both hands on the railing, watching the sunrise.

12

I slipped in and out of dreams all day at the beach stand. There was a long fall into the darkness of the lighthouse, then an old man with a bucket of money in a white mist. The worst was Jane and Christian laying in the surf under the moonlight. The beach was in shadow when I woke up.

A descending remorse washed over me as I replayed the scene with Jane. I was still in love with her and had less than two weeks left in Ocean City. Maybe she would forgive me. I felt my cheek and saw the look of hate in her eyes. I had made a terrible mistake — there was nothing between her and Christian. She would probably never talk to me again and I would go back to Chicago. I had to see her again and explain that I was drunk and didn't know what I was saying. I sighed loudly. The summer was roaring to a close and I could only follow events to wherever they would lead.

I called up Jane and she promptly hung up on me. After more tries she finally listened to my apology, and then began with "I don't know what kind of girls they have in Chicago. . . ," followed by threats of never seeing me again, and then the more rational "Maybe it would be better if we didn't see each other." She finally gave in to going somewhere nice for dinner the following night. I hung up relieved, then panicked at the thought of taking her somewhere nice without a car.

Duke pulled up to the disco that night. He asked the reason for my preoccupied silence after my lack of enthusiasm to his latest story. I breathed in sharply and told him about the whole night.

He nodded when I finished and looked at me.

"Sounds to me like you popped off at the mouth, boy. . . .Well, is it true?"

"What?"

"Is she in love with your buddy?"

I shrugged.

"I don't know—I was drunk or I wouldn't have said it. Even if it is true. . .I still want to see her."

"Most people say what they usually wouldn't when they're drunk," he said, pushing his hat back and fishing a match out of his pocket. "But that don't mean it ain't any less true."

"I suppose—but it could all just be me."

"I'm not saying nothin'. . .look," he said, changing his tone. "Take her to that nice lobster place by the bay—she'll love it."

". . .I'd like to, but I'd need a car," I said, thinking out loud.

Duke glanced at me, then smiled.

"You got one, partner!" he announced, pointing to his shimmering white car.

I was silent, not believing him.

"No. . .I couldn't do that—"

"Now you listen, boy— when I offer something I expect it to be taken. . .or you better be prepared to whip me!"

I looked at his size.

"I'll be real careful," I promised.

"I know you will—I'm not worried."

Duke brought his car over the next night and I drove him back to the Tanqueray Club. He showed me how the gears worked, and pointed out various idiosyncrasies that I should know.

"Now boy, don't you wreck her," he said, with a laugh and a slap on the back fender as I took off.

I drove over to Jane's apartment in the evening light. I rang the buzzer, looking at the glowing white machine. It was my ticket to make up for the night at the bar. The door opened and Jane looked more defiantly beautiful than I had ever seen her. Her blue eyes glittered with the same icy magnificence as her diamonds. A silk dress came up from white high heels and wrapped around her waist before melting into soft curves. Thin straps reached over her brown shoulders. She clutched a black purse in her hands.

"Hello, Brenton," she said with a quick smile.

"—you look beautiful!"

"Thank you."

"Ready?"

She nodded and I went to the car and held the door open. Jane stopped and stared.

"This is our car?"

"Sure is. . . what do you think?"

She slipped in and I shut the door. Jane looked up, smiling.

"It's nice."

I jumped in and started the car and felt better about the night. The wind blew around the open top of the car as we drove along the ocean. Jane stared straight ahead.

"Jane, about the other night. . ." She glanced at me quickly, her eyes cool. "I'd just like to apologize again. . . ."

"Oh let's just forget about it," she said quickly.

Jane smiled and I forgot about it. I nodded and pressed down on the accelerator.

We sat in a corner booth at the restaurant. Jane slipped in behind the table and looked out upon the whole restaurant. I faced her. Waiters clustered around her with ice water, bread, matches, wine — they were all there for her. Jane smoked and looked about remotely. I stirred the ice around in my drink and tried to talk to her. She sat back and nodded or answered in short sentences. She was slipping away and I wanted to grab her before it was too late.

"Jane. . .the summer is going to be over in a couple of weeks," I began again.

She looked at me with distant eyes.

"And Christian and I are going canoeing the last part of next week, and then I head back to Chicago, and—"

"Oh—I'll have to give you my address at Princeton," she said quickly.

"—I was thinking maybe we could even get together and maybe I could visit you at Princeton—or you could come up to Chicago."

"Oh certainly," she said, putting her hand on mine as the food came. "That sounds *fine.*"

She took her hand back and the cool feel of her skin stayed with me.

Jane barely spoke all during dinner, just nodding as I talked. I finally went to bring the car around to the door, feeling there was no one to blame but myself. I fumbled with the keys in the dark, turned on the interior light, and started the car. I saw a black book on the floor in front of Jane's seat.

I picked it up and flipped through the pages. Jane's careful writing was on every page. It was her address book. I stopped. Christian's name was on a page with his telephone number. I stared at the page, feeling the engine vibrating through me.

I had been right! Everything I'd suspected was true. I sat feeling the hotness in my face, seeing Jane's arm on Christian, his laughing eyes, and the look of hate in her eyes when I accused her in the bar. It had all been true. I put the book inside my jacket and jerked the car into gear.

The ride to Jane's apartment was silent. She looked out the window while I raced down the highway with the address book inside my sport coat. I pulled into the driveway of her apartment and jammed on the brakes. It had started to sprinkle.

Jane looked at me.

"Well. . .thank you," she said, opening the door.

"Let me get the door for you, Jane."

"Oh, that's all right—"

I went around the car and pulled opened the door as she stood up.

"You dropped this, Jane."

I held the black book in front of her.

"Oh—"

She put her hand on the book.

"Why do you have Christian's number in there, Jane?"

She pulled her hand away as if the book were hot.

"You aren't starting *that* again?"

"Why do you have his number Jane?"

The sky rumbled distantly.

"I don't know what you're talking about," she said, her eyes harder, more like blue ice.

The rain started to fall and made dark spots on the white silk of her dress.

"You've always had his number, Jane!"

Lightning touched down somewhere.

"So what? It doesn't mean anything."

She wiped her face and streaked her make-up. My shirt was sticking to my body.

"You don't care anymore, do you, Jane?"

The rain became heavier.

"This is ridiculous! I'm getting soaked!"

Jane started walking toward her apartment. I grabbed her arm.

"Answer me, Jane."

"Let go of me!"

I hung on tighter.

"Not till you answer me—you don't care anymore, do you?"

Two inky rivulets started down her face.

"Let me go!"

She twisted out of my hand and ran toward her apartment. I came up behind her and pulled her around to face me.

"You dirty bastard—"

She struggled to get free.

"Did you ever care about me, Jane!"

She struggled more.

"Let go!"

"DID YOU JANE?"

She paused, the rain loud around us, wet on her face and on mine. Her eyes were just hard now. She looked at me steadily, almost a smile on her lips.

"No—now let me go."

She kept her eyes on mine and I had to look away. I took my hand off her wrist and heard her run away from me and out of the rain. I drove back home in Duke's car and everything was wet.

13

The heavy storm clouds rolled in and turned the hood from blue to black. There was no rain yet, but there was a quiet "listen" in the air. The sun hid behind the clouds, the car turning so dark in the parking lot it looked wet. The white seats kept their color along with the red chromed dashboard; only outside was there no color. The rain didn't come. Autumnal light broke through as the sun came out, and the car turned back to blue.

I was watching the storm pass over King's car when he came out. He lit his customary cigarette and claimed what was his from the evening. I motioned out to the parking lot.

"Your car is pretty clean."

"Have to keep it clean — gonna be making that trip soon and she's gotta be ready."

I nodded and watched the distant cars on the highway. A woman walked by and I glanced over. The evenings were when I thought of Jane most. I tried to keep her out of my mind by staying busy, but our evening swims and strolls down the boardwalk always came back to me in the warm air of the day passed. I thought about calling her, but the thought that she was with Christian kept me from doing it. She could even be with him right now. The evenings were the worst.

I stood up and looked at King.

"King?"

"Yeah."

I paused.

"If you had a friend . . . let's say your best friend."

"Yeah? . . ."

"—and you had a girlfriend . . ."

He turned to me and leaned with one foot on the supporting column.

"And you started to think that maybe your girlfriend and your friend had something going." I held up my hands as if to square it all up for him. "Then things started to go bad between this girl and you—but you still aren't completely sure that anything is really going on . . . what would you do?"

King smiled and looked down. He took the cigarette out of his mouth and wiped the corner of his eye with his thumb.

"It would depend on my reasons for thinking it."

I nodded.

"The reasons?"

"Sure—you seen anything going on between your buddy and your girl?"

I paused.

"She's not my girl anymore."

"Well—had you seen anything?"

"No . . . not exactly."

"What have you seen?"

I looked out to the highway and shrugged.

"I saw her talking to him at his beach stand..."

"And?"

"I saw his number in her address book."

King nodded.

"What else?"

He took a final pull on his cigarette and flicked it into the parking lot.

"I don't know, I guess that's it...it's more of a feeling I get sometimes."

King was silent.

"Well, sounds to me like none of that stuff is very concrete...but it also sounds to me like it's the girl that's doing the pursuing — not the other way around," he said with a nod.

I looked at him.

"Think so?"

"From what you've told me I do. Sounds to me like it's more the woman than your buddy — it might not be anything," he added, shrugging his shoulders. "You ever think of that?"

I nodded.

"I guess that's what kept me from saying anything."

He pulled out a comb and started running it through his hair.

"I'd give your buddy the benefit of the doubt — at least till you really know something. You aren't going out with this girl anymore?"

I shook my head. He shrugged.

"Wouldn't worry about it much."

King was silent and looked out into the dusk. He glanced at me.

"Last night working, huh?"

"Yeah."

"Not bad....I don't think I'll be here much longer myself — going to be taking a little trip back to Salisbury." He hunched down on one leg and lit another cigarette. "She said she's going to ask him

153

for a divorce...then I'm going to bring her back with me," he nodded, rubbing the dark stubble on his jaw.

"What will you do then?"

"I figure we'll move down south—get the hell out of this town." He paused. "This place really shuts down for the winter," he muttered, looking out to the highway.

"I'll bet it does," I said, seeing a lonely gray winter of snow and ice.

"But it's time," he said, standing up. "It's time to make it right."

I remembered those words from before. King took another puff from his cigarette and then did something very unlike him: he held out his hand.

"So long, Brenton," he said, smiling in a way that made him look very young.

I shook his hand and was sorry that I was leaving.

"'Bye, King."

He flicked his cigarette into the creeping darkness and went inside. I looked out into the parking lot. The orange glow lay next to his dark breathless vision.

I read a lot my last week at the beach stand and tried to get some grasp on the fleeting summer. I thought about Jane—finally walking over to a pay phone and calling her. Her roommate answered the phone.

"May I speak to Jane?"

A long pause.

"Who's calling?"

"—Brenton."

There was another long pause, whispering, then a thinly disguised "She's not here right now," followed by a bright "May I take a message?"

I hung up.

I walked slowly back down the boardwalk to my beach stand. I sat down and looked across the hot beach and watched the summer roll into the treasured past.

We went out with Calamitous the night before our canoe trip. It was unseasonably cool, glimmering the coming fall where shorts and bare feet would have no place. We drank in the bar and tried to drive away whatever had come in with the brisk air. Even Calamitous was drinking.

We ended up back at Christian's beach stand with a bottle. A soft rain had started. Christian set up a couple of umbrellas and we sat down in beach chairs. The rain speckled the sand with tiny craters in front of us. The ocean collapsed and white surf rushed up out of the darkness. We dug our feet under the consoling sand and there was only the rain-swept ocean in front of us. We were safe again.

"This is it! The summer is coming to an end," Calamitous nodded to the rainy darkness.

The muffled plunking against the umbrella was slowing down as the rain moved out into the ocean.

"To the terrible threesome and the summer," Christian said, standing up and raising the bottle in toast.

"Hear! Hear!" we called out.

"I want to know, when are we all going to get married?" Calamitous asked loudly.

"Not that again . . . ," I groaned, waving him away. "Well, I'm not going to marry Jane Paisley."

Christian glanced at me. I had told him we broke up. He just nodded and said the summer was ending anyway so it was probably for the best. I watched him closely now, but couldn't tell anything.

"Speaking of getting married, what time is it, Calamitous?"

Calamitous was never without his oversized diving watch. He made a large gesture with his hand as he brought his wrist up.

"It's ten thirty—why, do ya have a date or something?"

Christian handed him the bottle.

"As a matter of fact, I do have a date later."

"Ohhh, gonna get a little before you go," Calamitous snickered, bobbing his head up and down. "Your parents in Baltimore?"

"Yeah—are you going to drink out of that bottle or just hold it all night?"

"I'll hold it all night if I want to," Calamitous said loudly, flicking the hair out of his eyes and blinking more than I had ever seen him.

"Someone new?" I asked.

Christian shook his head and looked at me.

"Nah...someone old."

I nodded and felt my heart beat faster. It might be Jane, but then he wouldn't say he had a date if it was with her. I shook my head. No, it wasn't with Jane.

Calamitous leered at Christian.

"Who—Debbie?"

Christian smiled.

"Yeah—Debbie...."

I watched some lightning flash way out over the ocean. A distant rumbling made its way to the mainland.

"She's not bad," Calamitous slurred.

He upended the bottle and I reached out to take it from him. Calamitous looked at me, his eyes bulged, and he dropped the bottle into the sand. The veins on his neck stood out, his face turning red as he choked, saliva coming out of his mouth. His face went down into the sand so quickly it looked like someone pushed the back of his head. Calamitous's body scissored together, then opened, then jerked back together again. He looked like a puppet with a madman at the strings.

I jumped up.

"What's he doing?"

Christian dove on him and wrestled toward his face.

"He's having a seizure! Jump on his legs!"

I fell down onto his kicking legs and was thrown off. I jumped on his legs again. Christian tried to pry open his mouth. Calamitous was gagging.

"We gotta get his mouth open . . . he'll suffocate on his tongue!"

He pulled harder on Calamitous' locked jaw. Christian worked his hands in to his teeth and pried his mouth open.

"Give me your wallet Brenton, *quick!*"

I couldn't get my wallet out, pulling it against my pocket and ripping my shorts to get it free. Christian stuck it in Calamitous' mouth. The gagging noise stopped and he took deep breaths. His legs started to calm down.

"He'll stop . . . just hold on."

Calamitous' breathing became steady and his body relaxed completely.

"He'll sleep for a while now."

Christian stood up and I sat back on my legs.

"What—"

"He has epilepsy." He dragged a chair over by Calamitous. "Help me put him in the chair."

We picked him up and placed him in the reclining chair.

"How come you never told me?"

"He didn't want anybody to know," Christian shrugged, sitting down. "I'm one of the few people that know — he shouldn't have been drinking."

I sat down slowly and looked at Calamitous. The ocean sounded small.

"—how'd you meet him?"

Christian leaned his chair back.

"At Hawthorne — soon after you moved. He managed the equipment for the lacrosse team and was in a couple of my classes.

Calamitous is smart and I was doing lousy in chemistry and math."

"Did he tutor you?"

"He got me through those classes: did my assignments, stayed up all night with me cramming for the tests — that was the first time I saw him have a seizure. We had stayed up late and he just started convulsing. I remembered from one of those first-aid classes that you have to get their mouth open."

I nodded slowly.

"He's on all these drugs for the epilepsy — that's why he moves so slow and is always pale. I set it up so he could manage the football and wrestling teams. We just started hanging around, and then we both came to Ocean City — he doesn't have many friends."

I looked at Calamitous sleeping in the chair. Epilepsy. That's what it was with him. I felt bad about the way I had treated him.

Christian sat up and looked down the boardwalk at the clock.

"There goes my date."

"Go ahead — I'll take care of Calamitous."

He looked at me.

"Are you sure?"

"Yeah — when should I wake him?"

Christian stood up and stretched.

"Give him another hour. . .he'll probably just wake up on his own."

Christian started for the boardwalk.

"See ya in the morning," I called.

He waved back as he jogged down the wet boardwalk. I put a raft over me for warmth and fell asleep listening to the surf. It was one o'clock when Calamitous woke me up.

"Hey. . .Brenton."

I looked over and he was sitting up in the beach chair. His eyes were squinty.

"What happened — did we all pass out?"

I stared at him, then nodded.

"You passed dead away."

Calamitous shook his head.

"I must have. . .I feel real weak," he said, holding his stomach.

"Are you going to get sick?"

He shook his head.

"No, I don't think so — I just got cramps."

I sat up and looked at the clock. A foghorn brooded out on the ocean.

"Come on, Calamitous. . .I'll help you get home."

I held on to his arm as he stood up unsteadily.

"Nah, I'm O.K.," he said, walking slowly.

"I'll just walk with you — you drank a lot."

He smiled.

"I did. . .didn't I?"

"You sure did."

It was when we were going past Christian's building that Calamitous remembered he had left his keys inside the apartment.

"I ought to get them — otherwise I'll have to wake up my parents."

He was still hunched over holding his stomach.

"All right, stay here — I'll go get them." I guided Calamitous to a bench on the boardwalk. "I'll be right back."

I ran into the lobby of Christian's building and rode the elevator up to his parents' place on the fifth floor. The building was designed so each apartment faced to the outside. A concrete walkway ran in front of the apartments with a long railing. Globe lights hovered next to the tropical-orange apartment doors. The lights of Ocean City spread out for miles with the airy sound of traffic in the distance.

The apartment was at the end of the hallway across from a fire escape door. I approached Christian's bedroom window. The pulled white curtains tufted from the ocean breeze. I put my fist up to knock on the door — the sound of someone breathing came out of the window. There was a rustle of sheets, then the squeaky groan of a bed. Quick breaths came through the dark, screened window. I stepped quietly to the side. The breathing was heavier.

"Oh, Christian!"

I didn't move.

I listened to Jane breathe heavier and could picture her face as she let out one final lusting sigh. The movement stopped. I still didn't move. A piece of paper scraped along the concrete walkway. There was only silence from the dark screen and then a giggle.

I walked to the red door of the fire escape steps and opened it. It was cool in the concrete passageway. My feet echoed down the steps. I lightly touched the firehoses that were coiled on the landing of each floor. The concrete work was crude; even the black railing was rough to the touch. Trash lay on some of the landings. It was dank and smelled of urine at the bottom. I pushed on the black door and went back out into the night.

A slow steady burn moved up from my neck. Everything I had suspected rushed up to me, then passed through with a visceral pain. Christian was not fair. I had always told myself that he had a sense of fairness, but this was no longer true. He didn't care about Jane — she was like Debbie to him. It was just another game; a contest to show himself and me that he would always triumph. He had won, but he had lost me.

I walked up to the boardwalk. Calamitous was still sitting on the bench.

"You get my keys?"

"Christian couldn't find them — I guess you'll have to wake your parents."

"Oh no," he groaned.

"You'll live," I muttered as we started down the boardwalk.

Duke's car was parked in front of my apartment. He was snoring with his hat pulled down over his eyes. I considered just walking into my apartment, but I went over and nudged him anyway. He stopped snoring, coughed, and looked out from under his hat.

"There you are," he growled, sitting up and pushing his hat back.

He opened the car door and stepped out, stretching. His hat glowed above his dark face. He ran a large hand over his jaw and stretched again.

"Goddamn!. . .that buggy is uncomfortable for sleeping." He looked at me. "What the hell is the matter with you?"

"Nothing. . ."

He watched me, then nodded, and his face became serious.

"I came to show you something, Brenton."

"Can't it wait till some other time?"

I didn't want to go on some wild adventure with Duke.

He shook his head.

"Nope. . .it can't," he said, raising his chin and peering down his nose.

I started toward my apartment door.

"Not tonight, Duke—I just want to go to bed."

"Brenton!—you better come with me."

"No, I'm going to bed!"

I took out my keys.

"It's about your buddy. . .King."

I turned around slowly.

"What about him?"

Duke nodded to the car and got in. The engine cussed once, then rumbled to life. He revved the motor, the sound echoing off the walls around the parking lot. I walked over and got in the car silently. Duke jammed it into gear and we screeched into the darkness.

We went to the other side of the island where I had gone with King. We flew through the deserted streets till Duke pulled into what looked like a closed service station. His car lights hummed as they hid back under the hood. The crickets were loud in the weeds that bordered the back of the station. There were a couple of tow trucks parked in front. I made out a dilapidated sign, TONY'S WRECKER SERVICE.

"Come on," Duke motioned, getting out of the car.

I got out and followed him around to the back of the building. Little squares of glass crunched under my shoes. We went through a gate and came upon hundreds of wrecked cars among the weeds. The crickets were louder. Duke walked slowly, the weeds swishing against his pants, and then he stopped. There were just the low, steady crickets now.

I looked at him, feeling shaky, my mouth dry.

"Well . . . so why are we here?"

Duke looked at me, and nodded with his hat to a corner of the fence that ran around the junkyard.

"Look over there."

I turned my head slowly. A wrecked car glittered in the blue-white glow. It was King's car. Nothing moved. A dog barked at something far away.

"I knew you and him were kind of buddies — my friend drives one of these wreckers. He gave me a call after he brought it in." Duke was quiet. "Hell — everybody knew him and that car. . . I guess he was doing close to ninety when he hit the tree."

A breeze rustled across the field of wrecks.

"He was on the highway, coming back from Salisbury. There was nothing anyone could do for him. . . ."

I just stood there, looking at the twisted metal in the weeds. I didn't want to look closer, thinking King was laying dead in that twisted metal, but I couldn't not look. I walked through the swaying weeds. They had put King's car in the corner of the junkyard. The moon shone on the broken glass and jagged metal. The front of the car was pushed into the shape of a large U. The restored interior was still perfect, except for the broken glass and a dark stain on the dashboard where King's head must have lain. There was a quietness about the car now, as if it had never been anything but this wreck.

I saw a square piece of paper beneath the steering wheel. I leaned carefully through the window and picked it up off the floor. The picture was of King and a pretty blond-haired girl leaning against a car. The car was white. It was the same one. I turned the picture over. On the back there was some writing in a faded script, "I'll love you forever, King — Betty, 1966."

There it was. I stared at the picture, the faces oddly clear in the half light. I knew he loved her and she loved him. It was all in this picture. I wondered what she had told him on his final trip into the past. I put the picture up on the dash, leaning it against the broken windshield and facing the stain on the dashboard. Now King was forever. I took one last look at the car, then said good-bye to King and his part of me.

We drove back in silence for a while, then I slowly began to tell him about the night.

"You sure it was her?"

"No doubt," I nodded.

Duke pulled out a wooden match and chewed on it.

"That's some tough shit, buddy," he drawled, shaking his head.

"I'm just glad the summer's over and I'm leaving."

He glanced over.

"When?"

"Tomorrow. . .and that's not quick enough."

"Aren't you supposed to go on a canoe trip with your buddy?" he asked, taking the match out of his mouth.

I stared at him.

"He betrayed me!"

Duke was silent, then shook his head.

"You can't just leave, Brenton."

"Why the hell not?"

"Because. . . you guys have been friends all these years, and it sounds to me like this confrontation's been comin' , " he said, looking at me. "The way you looked up to him and all when you were younger, and now you goin' out with this girl. . . him maybe jealous of you, and you not so sure he's somebody to look up to anymore—"

"*Look up to him!*. . . How the hell could anybody look up to him?"

"You did— for a lot of years," Duke answered quietly.

"I was wrong, *all right?* It's all about winning. He thinks he won!"

Duke nodded slowly.

"That's why you can't just leave, Brenton. . . you gotta have it out with him. The thing I think that's gettin' you most is he ain't what you thought he was," he said, taking the match out of his mouth. "And that's what you gotta find out." He hesitated. "Otherwise you'll end up like King."

I looked at him.

"Like King?"

"Everybody knew he'd been pining after that girl in Salisbury for years, ever since he came back from Vietnam. He'd drive around, all drunked up lookin' for those days gone. . . spent all his time lookin' backwards— and it finally killed him."

I glared at Duke.

"Well at least he went after his dream! What the hell are *you* doing? You talk about going west— I wonder if you have the *guts!* At least he went for it, instead of talking about something he would never do!"

I was so mad my voice was shaking.

Duke glanced at me with steady eyes and pulled into the parking lot. He put the car in neutral and looked out the window. He spoke quietly.

"You might have something there. . . but I'm lookin' to the future

—King looked back," he said, pinning me to the door with his eyes. "And you don't want to be lookin' back at something you never settled, Brenton. . . . I wouldn't just leave town. I'd go on that trip and you and he have it out—once and for all."

I sat for a moment, feeling the car engine vibrating, then slowly got out. I walked to my apartment and opened the door with the low throaty breathing of Duke's car still behind me. He screeched away as I went into my room in the morning light.

14

The river meandered between walls of rock formations and reflected the sky and trees. The bow of the canoe moved gently through the water, cutting a swath of ripples on both sides which folded back for the mirror to return. The silence was broken by the cry of a gliding hawk, then a spring running down a sheer molten slab for a three-foot fall into the river. A breeze dipped down into the valley and chastised the trees with an echoing rustle. Just when the fugue started to become loud, the silence came back and there was just the rythmic splash of our paddles again.

I dipped my paddle into the water and looked at the white haze in the trees along the edge of the river. Birds called out in the forest with shrieks and whistles that came from all around us. Dragonflies danced in front of the canoe, then skittered off. Turtles and fish splashed by the shore. A locust started up—the buzzing growing at an even tempo, and then slowly decreasing to a final halt. The sun was in the tall, leafy branches that hung over the east side of the river. It was getting warmer.

We had canoed for two hours. I watched the green water move by the canoe. The ride in the car had been quiet and Christian just thought I was tired. We arrived and packed our provisions for an overnight camp. Christian was tying the cooler, the tent, and our sleeping bags into the cross struts of the canoe. He first tied the handles of the cooler with the rope, then pulled it across the other gear. It was cool for the morning.

"I don't think I would use the same piece of rope," I said, watching him work in the shallow mud along the river.

"Why not?" he asked, not stopping.

"If we tip, that rope won't hold everything in."

Christian shrugged and finished tying the gear to the canoe, then looked up and wiped his brow.

"It'll hold...besides, we won't tip," he said, his face red and swollen from being bent over.

I let it go. We pushed the canoe into the water and Christian held the back, the water up to his knees.

"You get in first, Brenton."

I looked at him.

"Are you taking the back?"

"Sure," he nodded, smiling.

"Why don't I take the back?"

His eyes became dull. They were a darker green above the water. The warm current slid around my legs as I stood hanging on to the canoe. His eyes became sharp again.

"Because I'm better at steering."

"Really?"

"Yeah, now get in, Brenton — we don't have all day."

I looked at him and the smile faded from his face.

That was how we had started. I had lain awake most of the night after Duke dropped me off. My decision to leave Ocean City stayed with me till sometime in the morning when I realized what Duke had said was true: "You don't want to be lookin' back at something you never settled, Brenton." I would have to find out at last if the river did lead to the ocean.

The sun glared up from the river as midday passed. We were deep in the forest and slowly, almost imperceptibly, the river was picking up speed. The sun was hot on our backs and sweat slid down my chest to my stomach, then made a wet spot on my shorts. I pulled on the paddle. The aluminum canoe reflected the sun onto my face with a slow, steady burn.

"Sure is nice."

"Sure is," I said without turning around.

He paused.

"If you want to take the back . . . I don't care."

"No, that's all right." I put my paddle down onto a dead leaf. "—how was last night?"

His paddle splashed.

"Fine . . . good time."

I looked at the glistening sweat on my arm.

"I'll bet."

I put my paddle back in and pushed against the water. We were getting further and further away from civilization. The river narrowed. Rock walls came up on both sides and squeezed the water into small passages. Mossy green water leaked out of the walls — we passed so close I touched the slippery rockface. Trees had fallen over the top of the narrow passage and only sporadic light found its way down to the inky water. A cool dampness hovered between the rocks. The sun had found one open spot between the trees and beamed onto a flat boulder. The top of the rock was bright. Taking in the warmth on the rock was a mass of thick, dark rope. The snakes moved and slithered in the sunlight. As we passed, a few coils fell into the water.

"Jesus! Did you see that, Brenton?"

I nodded silently and looked ahead to where the river opened back up. We came back into the sunlight. All the passages of the river squeezed into one final venturi. I could hear the fast current, and then I saw white water. The water ran between two walls of granite with a force that dominated the middle. On the sides it was calmer, but large underwater boulders tipped the surface.

"I'm going to steer for the middle," Christian called out.

I nodded and started to take long strokes with my paddle to get the canoe over to the center. There was a drop that added to the speed of the current. The smooth surface broke into rushing water just as the front of our canoe came to the center. A rock scraped along the bottom. I tried to straighten the canoe with my paddle, but the back stayed crooked.

"Christian—paddle and get the back end over!"

"I am!"

The back end came around and the canoe picked up speed. A breeze dried the sweat on my face and chest as water sprayed up around the front. Directly in front of us there was an explosion of white foam.

"There's a rock!" I shouted, putting my paddle in the water, trying to steer the front of the canoe away from it.

"Where?"

The aluminum bottom scraped the rock and we just stopped. The back then swung around while the rock held the front and water hit the side turning us over into the swift current.

"SHIT!"

"Here we go!" I shouted, cold water rushing up to my neck.

The current took me along; rocks bruised and scraped my legs till the river became wide and the current slowed. I stood up in the waist-deep water. Christian came down holding on to his paddle while I grabbed the canoe and pulled it over to shore. The rope that had held the provisions was floating in the shallow water. The cooler was still in the canoe, but was now full of green river water. The tent and sleeping bags were gone.

Christian came over and stared at the water-filled canoe. He stood, pushing his wet, matted hair up off his forehead, and looked again. Water dripped down his forehead onto the tip of his sunburnt nose. His eyelashes were wet. He blinked in disbelief.

"Goddamnit! . . . I can't believe we turned over!"

He slapped the water with his paddle. I pulled the canoe to shore where there was a clearing of smooth, flat stones. The sun was already drying my back.

"I lost my damn shoes," Christian said, still standing in the water.

"Me too."

I dragged the canoe up on shore and pushed up one side as the water ran out in a waterfall. Christian just watched. His face looked red and flushed in the midday sun. His stomach muscles moved in and out slowly. I finished emptying out the canoe.

"Where's your paddle?"

"With everything else," I said, not looking up.

"You didn't hold on to your paddle?"

I looked up at him — he had his paddle over his shoulder.

"Nope."

He let out a loud breath.

"Oh that's just great! No paddle — how the hell do you expect us to get down the river?"

I took the cooler out of the canoe. He kept staring at me.

"I can't believe you were stupid enough to let your paddle go!"

I walked back into the shallow water and picked up the piece of rope from the canoe. The end was bent where the knot had been. I threw the rope onto the water in front of him.

"Why? You were stupid enough to use one piece of rope."

He looked at the rope and then at me. I walked back to the canoe and picked up the cooler lid.

"I think I can use the top of the cooler as a makeshift paddle."

I felt something slap me on the back as the wet rope fell down between my legs. I turned around, a tightness coming into my chest. Christian stood in the water with a taunting smirk. He still had the paddle over his shoulder. I stared at him.

"Don't be an asshole, Christian . . . you're the one who didn't tie it right."

Christian grinned and shook his head.

"We don't need that stuff—we'll just canoe till we get there."

"Canoe night and day, without rest?"

He shrugged.

"Can't you take it?"

I looked at him and nodded slowly.

"Sure I can."

The water had dried on our skin. The sun was in the west just enough to begin the hottest part of the day. Sweat stung my eyes as I kneeled and tried to paddle with the cooler top. The underside of my arms burned on the rim of the canoe, leaving drops of perspiration that evaporated quickly on the hot aluminum. We had lost our water jugs when the cooler opened and had not yet come to drinking the water of the river. Nothing moved and the current barely pushed us at times. Only the insects that buzzed back and forth across the river broke the heated silence.

We moved around a bend. A large tree had fallen across the river and branches extended up the river, acting like a dam and catching any debris that came down. The river slipped under two narrow openings at the base of the tree. There was no way to go past.

"Looks like we'll have to portage. I think there's a place we can get around over there," I said, pointing to a clearing on the right.

Christian steered the canoe toward the shore. I jumped out and pulled the front toward the muddy bank. Tall reeds swished the sides of the canoe in the shallow water. Christian got out and slipped in the mud on shore.

"Damn it!"

"I'll hand the canoe to you to pull up on shore," I said, still standing in the water.

Christian stared into the woods, then looked at the tree in the river.

"There might be a road out of here someplace. . . ." He peered back into the forest, then looked at me. "We could get some more supplies then."

"I don't think there's a road this far in the woods."

He looked back at the woods.

"Let's just check around before we lug the canoe over that tree."

"We ought to at least pull the canoe up so it doesn't go anywhere."

Christian cocked his head back.

"Why? It's not going anywhere," he said, motioning to the tree. I shrugged.

"Sure."

Christian found a path and we went into the close woods. The mosquitoes attacked us viciously. The woods were swampy and mud streaks ran up our legs. Flies bit our backs, legs, and arms. Christian sweated and cursed as the trail ended in undergrowth. He took off in a different direction, thinking some landmark or road would appear to show him the way, but we were deep in the woods and there would be no roads.

Christian stopped and looked around. His face was scratched from branches. Sweat streamed from his matted hair onto his face and dripped off his chin. He arched his back and slapped at a mosquito. Christian squinted for something in the thick woods and crossed his arms.

"There's no road, Christian."

I wiped the sweat off my face with the edge of my hand. He turned to another part of the woods.

"I'll bet there's a road around here somewhere. I'll bet up over that hill there might be something that will get us out."

He pointed to a marshy area where the light fell in spots on the wet green bottom of the forest.

"I don't think so, Christian."

"What the hell do you know?" he snapped, and started toward the hill.

Christian's foot caught on a vine running across the floor of the woods. He fell down to one knee in the mud and put his hands down in the muck to get up.

"Goddamnit!"

I heard a hawk cry out high above.

"Must have been that long night with Jane."

Christian stopped.

He stood with his back to me. I watched him breathe. He turned around slowly and looked at me with no emotion in his eyes. He just stared. A drop of sweat was on the end of his nose. My heart thudded against my chest. The forest was very quiet. His eyes crinkled in a smile.

"Oh, is *that* what all this is about?. . .I thought you were acting strange." He laughed shortly. "I'm gonna straighten you out once and for all on this whole Jane thing, Brenton," he said, pointing a shaky finger at me. "I *told* you to stay away from her—but you wouldn't listen," he said, shaking his head quickly.

"You can go to hell, Christian!"

I started walking away.

He ran up and grabbed my arm, turning me around.

"I told you about her—she used you just like I knew she would . . .*I went out with Jane Paisley last summer."* He swallowed and continued, his voice shaking. "I went out with her and I dumped her. . .she got mad and never got over it—she wanted to burn me and here you come along and she used you to get at me!"

I shook loose from his grip, turning away.

"Go to hell, you bastard!"

He smiled oddly, then let out a forced laugh.

"You were a fool, Brenton! She screwed you and *acted* like she was in love with you—the whole time she just wanted to get back at me," he said, pointing to himself. "She never really gave a *damn* about you!" He pointed at me with a strange, uncomfortable smile on his face. "That's why I screwed her—"

I turned and hit him hard.

I heard his teeth clap together. He staggered back, grabbing his mouth as a long stream of saliva and blood came from his hand. I tackled him and we fell down, sliding in the mud.

"You goddamn dirty bastard!"

I swung wildly at his face, feeling my fist connect again. Christian turned and climbed on all fours to get away. I jumped on his back and knocked him down on the ground, grabbing the back of his head by the hair and pushing his face down in the mud.

"YOU BASTARD!"

I drove his face into the mud with all my strength. My hand slid off. He turned with his face covered in black muck and drove his fist directly into my nose. I heard a series of quick cracks inside my head. I couldn't see and fell back. I held my hands up to my face and cried out as warm blood flowed down from my nose. He fell on top of me and swung again, hitting my jaw so squarely I felt faint. He grabbed my neck and started choking me.

"I OUGHT TO KILL YOU!"

His mud-covered face was an inch from mine. He tightened his hands. I grabbed at them weakly.

"How's it feel to choke, Brenton?"

He was cutting off my air and spitting saliva and blood into my face. I gagged and looked up at his green eyes peering out of the mud. I couldn't get him off and the air wouldn't come into my lungs. He was going to kill me. He was going to kill me and there was the golf course again and we had just finished playing football. "I'm going to kill you," he screamed far away, and I saw the two of us years before — he was jumping up and laughing at how he had fooled me, how I had believed him. . . .Christian wasn't going to kill me. He never would.

I opened my eyes and saw his muddy face on top of me. I lifted his body with my arms, just enough to bring my knee into his crotch. He raised up, grunting as the air went out of him, his eyes getting wide. His hands fell off as he rolled to the side, holding his crotch and groaning.

My breath came back, but I could still feel his hands on my throat. He lay there groaning in the mud. I touched my nose and tried to slow the blood. The sun moved into evening.

15

The heat had subsided and the amber dusk fell through the trees in bits of twilight. The sky was between the branches that reached over me. A driving ache crossed my head, then centered in my nose. I came up from some sleepy, unconscious world and I moved my mouth, feeling something pull at my skin and down my neck. Dried blood had formed two paths down the sides of my mouth. I sat up slowly and my neck muscles protested with tightening pain. I stood up and began to make my way out of the woods.

The river had turned to a pink and gold mirror. I fell down in the shallow water among the reeds and washed the blood and dirt from my face and neck. I stopped and touched my nose. It felt oddly flat. I pushed gingerly and a sharp pain went through my nose. I got to my feet, turned back to shore, and that was when I saw Christian.

He was sitting among some weeds with the low sun behind him. I thought he had come back to the river when I didn't see him in the woods. I shaded my eyes against the sun. He had cleaned himself up; the only sign of our fight was a swelling on one side of his mouth and a cut that wrapped around to the outside of his lip. He stared at me from the weeds, then quickly looked to the river.

"Canoe's gone. It's down under that big tree," he said, motioning with his head. "I guess the current caught it somehow and wedged it under there."

A tip of aluminum flashed above the water where it went under the tree. The sky was in deep twilight and it would be getting dark soon. I went above the mud of the bank and sat down.

"I think we have a couple hours before it gets dark." I heard the nasal sound of my voice for the first time. "We're going to have to sleep in the woods tonight, but there might be something on the other side of the river. Even if there's not, we can always follow the river and eventually we'll get to some pick-up point, or maybe we can hit a road."

I didn't really care if he was listening or not. I would figure my own way out. He could come along if he wanted, but I was really on my own either way.

Christian just nodded as he stared down the river.

We swam across to the other side and started following the river. I tried to find some sort of trail by keeping close to the shore. Rocks cut our feet and bushes made long scrapes on our legs. We moved quickly as the light left the woods and the crickets were already becoming loud. I found a path that led into the woods but roughly followed the course of the river. It was close to dark when I heard something ahead of us and stopped.

I held up my hand and Christian halted behind me. The night had come and the forest breathed with insect life. Fireflies flickered yellow around us, dying back into the dark woods. I heard the sound again. It was a voice.

I crept up and saw light coming through some bushes. I peered through. There was a lantern on the ground. A man sat in a chair holding a fishing rod across his knees in the circle of yellow light. His hair flowed out of his worn hat to a scraggly dark beard. He was leaning back and snoring. A little boy with long hair wearing a pair of dirty shorts played in the mud next to the man's feet and the lantern. A pit smoldered from an earlier fire. Above the pit was a grill thrown over cinder blocks. The river gurgled softly on the edge of the clearing, glowing with falling light from the horizon. Behind the man and the boy and across the clearing was a shack. A dim light came out of the doorway.

"I guess we should see if we can get some food, or better yet a ride," I whispered, as Christian came up and peered into the opening.

He nodded silently.

We came through the bushes and the child stopped playing in the dirt. The man stirred, looked over, and stood up. He was a giant. His dark eyes flickered. I wished I had on something more than my shorts. Our skin was very white against the dark. I cleared my throat.

"Uh — we were canoeing. . .and had an accident and lost our canoe. . . ."

His eyes didn't move.

"We aren't really sure where we are. . .and I was wondering if we could use your telephone. . .or get a ride — we'd really appreciate it."

The man stood, then gnashed his teeth on a wad of tobacco and spat in the dirt. His dark eyes were black in the lantern light — just two spots glimmering under his hat. The fishing pole looked small in his hand. He and the child stared as a wind fanned the coals in the pit. His breathing was a heavy, growling wheeze.

"Ain't got no phone," he said, in a voice that sounded like it came from underground. "Truck broke down. . ."

I wanted to cover my ears.

"Couple of miles next town."

He was silent and there was the gurgle of the river. He spat and a stream of juice landed in the dry dirt in front of us. I tried again.

"— do you think we might borrow a little food and some blankets?"

He breathed out. At first I thought he groaned, but it had more of a wheezing noise to it.

"Eat supper 'bout an hour — sleep here tonight."

He spat again and the smoldering pit hissed back a puff of steam. The man picked up the lantern and headed to the shack. The child followed him. We went down to sit by the river and wait for whatever would happen. I watched the night turn the water silver under the moon. We sat in silence watching the luminosity pass by. It was the child that came back.

He had dirty long hair and a scared, haunted look to his face. He was dirty from head to toe and the only whiteness was around his eyes.

"Y'all come on." He motioned weakly, holding the lantern.

We got up and followed him into the darkness toward the dimly lit shack. The lantern floated ahead of us and at times the little boy disappeared into the night. The light flew up and landed on a table in front of the shack where the giant was sitting.

The giant's wife was a squat woman with her hair pulled back in a single braid that went down her back. The original color must have been brown, but some dying had given it an off-red quality. She smiled in the lantern light, showing decaying brown teeth. There were marks all over her face. A black eye ran down to the top of her cheek and various cuts and scars gave her the look of having a bad skin disease.

She greeted us with a quick "How do," then ladeled out some sort of meat. The dark man picked up the meat and ate it with his hands. He tore the meat with a flash of sharp teeth, grunting as grease oozed down his hands and shined in his beard.

"Y'all canoeing, and it tipped over?" the woman asked, putting some meat on plates in front of us.

The meat smelled rotten, like hamburger that had been left out too long.

"Well—I reckon we seen more canoes come down this ol' river with no ones in 'em. I seen 'em and I wonder where the people are and I wonder if they lost in the woods. And I says, 'Chester Lee, do you know wheres all them people go without their canoes?' I believe God takes some of 'em," she whispered, looking at us with eyes too small for her face. "God gits 'em—or the *devil,* an' there's both in these woods. I seen 'em! I seen God an' I seen the devil— he comes an' gives me a terrible beatin' sometimes. Y'all keep an eye out for the devil tonight an' in the mornin' God will come an' save your souls. . .but watch out for the devil," she said, looking into the hissing darkness.

The giant growled and threw what was left of his meat from the table into the woods.

After we ate we went down by the river. The man sat at the table, dark and smoldering, breaking the silence with a rumbling that came from somewhere deep inside him. The child went into the shack with the woman. I looked back and the man sat by himself at the table in the yellow light of the lamp. He had a bottle in front of him.

We laid down in the damp grass and I shivered. The night was getting cooler and the mosquitoes were bad. My nose was throbbing. The boy came out of the night.

"Here some blankets," he said, putting two coarse wool blankets down on the ground and running back toward the shack.

"Thanks," I called after the sound of his bare feet running across the ground.

I handed Christian a blanket. We took off our damp shorts and laid them beside us. I cocooned myself in the blanket.

"I guess we'll take off at first light," I said sleepily.

Christian was sitting up with the blanket wrapped around him. He nodded quietly and stared at the pale, moon river flowing next to us. I looked over to the table in the distance and the man was still facing his bottle. I looked at Christian and watched the light of the river in his eyes until sleep came.

There was a screaming in my dream. It was far away, but it was becoming louder. It was a woman and she was coming toward me. I opened my eyes and the scream echoed through the quiet woods, then all I heard was the quiet pulse of the crickets. The river came into the night—the darkness was broken again by an agonizing scream that started strong and went down to a whimper.

I jumped up and looked to the kerosene-lit shack. Christian was already sitting up, peering into the dull shadows that played inside the shack.

"What the hell was that?"

Christian shook his head.

"I don't know—"

A terrible, desperate scream came out of the shack, then a dark shadow passed across the door, like a cloak someone pulled in front of a candle.

"DON'T DEVIL!...DON'T!...PLEASE!"

There was the sound of breaking glass and two steady thumping noises followed by another long scream. I stood up. A shadow moved into the door and then something in white went past the shadow out of the shack. The woman was running toward us with blood streaming down her face and holding the little boy by the hand.

"Help me!...Please help me! It's the *devil—help me!*"

The man stood in the doorway. He was barechested and held a piece of wood in his hand. He came out with giant steps, advancing on the woman who fell directly in front of us in the dirt. Christian and I stood naked, watching in horror.

"STAY AWAY DEVIL!"

The giant advanced toward her and us with the wood held in his hand, his black eyes glittering.

"Christian, let's get out of here!"

We grabbed our shorts and started running for the woods and the river. The woman screamed again. Christian turned and looked at her. She was bent over protecting the little boy. The man raised the piece of wood. The woman held up her hands.

"Come on, Christian!"

I pulled at him again. He took a step toward the woman.

"Christian!"

He looked at me in terror—just then the little boy ran out from the woman and toward the woods. The giant watched the small figure disappear into the darkness as the woman lay on the ground whimpering. The man didn't seem interested in the woman anymore; he kept looking to where the little boy had gone. He dropped the wood and staggered back toward the shack. The woman slowly got up and walked back to where the man had gone. The little boy was nowhere to be seen.

"Come on!"

I pulled Christian and we stumbled to the river, diving in and swimming to the middle. We rode with the current, the moon-drenched water taking us downstream into the pale morning.

We finally found a road out to a highway and hitched a ride back to Christian's car. Neither of us spoke during the drive back to the beach. It wasn't until we had come in on the far side of Ocean City that Christian slowed the car down and pulled off the road. He turned off the motor. The foghorn of a lighthouse came across the swirling dunes and high weeds tipped with twilight.

I looked at him.

"What are you doing?"

Christian got out of the car.

"Where're you going, Christian?"

He looked at me, not really seeing me.

"I'm going to the lighthouse to watch the sunrise."

I stared at him.

"What—are you crazy?"

He crossed the highway toward the beach.

"Forget the lighthouse, Christian. . . .WHAT ARE YOU TRYING TO PROVE?"

He started jogging across the sand.

"Shit!"

I sat and looked down the highway and considered hitching a ride home. I glanced to the beach and Christian was climbing the sea wall. I shook my head disgustedly and looked down the deserted highway again, then back at him just as he came to the crest of the dune before the beach. I knew what his ritual meant.

"Shit!"

I jumped out of the car and went after him. He looked back once at the sound of the car door. I caught up to him just as he pushed open the door of the lighthouse.

"I know. . .what you're doing," I panted as he started to climb the steps. I called up to him in the spiraling darkness. "It's not going to work, Christian!. . .This doesn't matter. . .*this doesn't change anything!*"

There was only the sound of his shoes on the iron ladder. I climbed up after him. The metallic echoing of his footsteps increased above me. I was near the top when light poured down onto the steps from the trap door. I reached the bottom of the ladder just as he pulled himself through the opening.

"I'm right here, Christian. . . ," I gasped.

He looked down at me.

"—I'm calling your bluff. . .you can't change it, Christian—"

He disappeared from view. I started climbing the ladder and reached the top as he stood against the wall with the blue ocean at his back. He looked at me calmly.

"Going to jump across, Brenton?"

I nodded.

"Yes—goddamnit. . .if you can, I know I can. There's nothing special about you."

I got off the ladder and stood next to him.

Christian smiled and motioned to the other side.

"I'll go first."

"Fine. . .go ahead!"

He crouched down and spanned the opening with the same effortlessness, stopping himself against the lighthouse wall. He turned around.

I licked my dry lips, looking at the hole. It didn't look so big. If he could do it, I could. It was just another one of his bluffs. He was always bluffing. It was very easy to get across this hole, only Christian had me thinking it was hard. I would show him. I would show him now. I could jump over this hole.

"You going to jump, Brenton?"

"Of course! This doesn't prove anything, but I'm going to do it."

I looked at the hole and crouched down. There was nothing to it. Just a jump and I was across. The other side was right there. Nothing to it. All right, here we go. Here we go. I took a deep breath.

"—Brenton, you don't have to."

I stared at him. Now I knew he was bluffing.

"You'd like that. . .you know I'm going to do it now!"

I set myself again. Christian shook his head.

"Brenton, don't be stupid."

I stood up.

"I can't believe you . . . you have got to win, don't you, Christian?

I'm jumping and you can't stop me."

Christian stared at me for a moment, then shook his head.

"Forget it, I'm coming back across," he said, waving me out of the way and crouching down on the edge of the floor.

I glared at him.

"No you're not!"

"Yes I am, Brenton—move! I'm coming back across—*move!* I'm coming back across—"

He moved closer to the edge.

"Screw you, Christian! I'm going—"

The crack was sharp. It was the single board that Christian stood on. He stared at me as the board broke from under him. He made one grab back for the side, then disappeared into the darkness below. I heard several noises that sounded like a heavy bag of clothes bumping down a long laundry chute. I stared down into the darkness. He had fallen onto the stairwell near the bottom. I ran down the steps, not believing what I was doing at all. I ran and ran around in the circling darkness and reached Christian laying on the stairs. The metal steps were slippery wet under him. Blood was coming out from the back of his head.

"Jesus Christ, Christian!"

I kneeled down next to him on the steps. The blood was running down the black step in little streams. I felt the back of his head and blood came out between my fingers. He was breathing lightly. I tried to slow the flow of blood. His eyes opened faintly.

"Christian!—can you hear me?" I whispered, holding his head.

There was a tiny light reflected in his eyes. His head moved slightly.

"You're going to be all right," I said, speaking rapidly. "I'm going for help. . . just hold on—you're going to be all right!"

I tried to keep a steady, even pressure on his head. Christian moved his head. His eyes were slits of light. His lips moved.

"What?. . . what did you say, Christian?"

I put my ear down to his mouth and listened very closely.

"Cold. . .don't leave," he whispered in this faint, small voice.

"Cold?"

I looked into the light of his eyes. His head moved slightly.

"—all right. . .I'll warm you up first. . .then I'll go."

I laid down next to Christian on the steps, putting my arm across him and my body next to his. I was careful not to move him in any way. I held myself close to him and we laid there for a few minutes with his blood running on me. Then he spoke once more, very softly.

"What?" I asked, putting my head next to his.

His eyes opened some. I leaned closer and heard him.

"—warm. . ."

I pulled myself closer, and then the light slowly faded from his eyes like a candle burning down to just the wick, then smoke, then nothing. And that was all.

16

The flashing lights and questions all blended together into a nightmare of lost time and reality. I watched the ambulance carry Christian's body away. His parents and the police questioned me and then it all finally ended that night with an Ocean City policeman dropping me off at my apartment. I went in and fell into a deep, dreamless sleep.

I slept till noon the next day and woke up to hear the rain pattering against the metal housing of the air conditioner. I called my parents and told them what had happened and that I was coming home. Nobody knew yet when the funeral would be in Baltimore, and I was scheduled to leave anyway. We decided I would fly back for the funeral. I started going through the mechanics of getting packed to leave. The surfboard was gone from the room. There was a hurried note from Sheldon on the dresser saying his good-byes and wishing me well in college. He had been the roommate I never saw anyway. I opened the door and let the sound of the rain and thunder into the room as I finished packing.

I went over to see Calamitous and tell him what had happened. We sat on his screened-in porch with the rain coming down and misty wet breezes passing over us. He just sat through the whole story of the fight, then the river people, then of Christian dying. I told the story as if it had happened to someone else. His eyes blinked several times, then silent tears rolled down his face.

I looked down at my hands and feet while he cried.

"You know, he really did go out with Jane last summer," he said, wiping his eyes and blinking rapidly.

"It doesn't matter, Calamitous."

"I know — but you don't understand . . . *she broke up with him.*"

I looked at him.

He sniffled loudly and continued.

"He was in love with her, Brenton . . . I hardly saw him. He was always with her and he even wanted to get engaged — but she started seeing other guys while she was going out with him . . . he didn't even care . . . he still wanted her."

I stared at Calamitous.

"But he said he broke up with her. . . ."

Calamitous nodded.

"All during the year he tried to get back with her — then you came down and he saw you talking to her . . . it would kill him if she started going out with you . . . but she did."

I opened my mouth and had a bad moment.

"He didn't want to tell you — I told him he should have, but he said that would have been unfair to you. . . ."

Calamitous wiped his eyes on his shirt sleeve.

"It hurt him to see you two together . . . and when you broke up — she called him. I didn't know he was going to see her that last night . . . but he was in love with her. . . ."

I started tapping my foot. Christian had been in love with Jane all the time. She had thrown him over. . .the way she had thrown me over. Yet he never told me. . .because that would be unfair. *I had hurt him.* He had been with her because he loved her. I put my head down into my hands and the world blurred in front of me.

"I just wanted you to know. . . ."

I looked at Calamitous and nodded. Calamitous blinked and new tears slid down his cheeks while the rain fell all around us.

I went back to my apartment at some point. I lined my suitcases up next to the door and wondered what to do next. There was a gnawing inside me that made me feel weighted down. The bus would leave at six for the train and it was only three o'clock. I laid down on the bed and shut my eyes. I thought of Chicago. It didn't seem to exist. It was like I was moving there again for the first time. I remembered the day my father had taken off work to show me around. It was January, the first year we had moved there. A storm off Lake Michigan had cleaned the air the night before. We rode a bus down Michigan Avenue with the white buildings sparkling in the bracing air. The bus rolled past the Tribune and Wrigley buildings and then over the frozen Chicago River. My father pointed out various buildings to me, and told me the history of the city that was once the last trading post before the frontier. . . .

The low roar of a car pulled up to the open door. The nose of Duke's white car appeared in the doorway. I stood up. The car door slammed and Duke ran in from the rain.

"Hey, pard! I thought that was you — you're back early." He wiped the rain off the brim of his white hat with one sweeping finger.

" — Hi, Duke."

"How was the trip? Damn, boy — what happened to your nose?"

I sat down and went through my mechanical recitation. He sat on the bed holding his hat. I finished and he shook his head slowly and put his hat back on.

"I feel for you, Brenton," he said with honest pain in his eyes.

We sat for a few minutes with the gray light coming in the open door. He looked down to the floor and held his brown hands in front of him.

"Well—I'll tell ya what I came over for...although after what you been through, I don't think you'll give a damn," he said, still looking down.

"—what is it?"

I wanted something else to think about.

"I did a lot of thinking," he said slowly. "I thought about what you said the other night—about me talking and never really doin' what I say I am..."

"I don't—"

"Let me finish now....I thought about that and I think in a way you were right...and I did a lot more thinking and figured I could sit around waiting for some time to come that maybe never will." He looked out the door, then at me. "You see...I'm from this town, Brenton—I've never even seen the West—shoot, I thought the army would get me there, but they don't want somebody with a bum back...so I started working at these bars and been doing it ever since."

I nodded slowly and he adjusted the tip of his hat.

"But I gave my notice at the club—packed my car with everything I could and sold everything else." He looked down at his hands, nodding. "And this cowboy's goin' west."

I stared at him.

"When?"

"Right now—that's why I came to say good-bye. I'm leavin', buddy."

"Congratulations, Duke—I knew you'd do it."

"Thanks, Brenton...I appreciate it." And for the first time, just for a moment, his accent had fallen away.

We sat for a few more minutes and then walked to the door. The rain had dissipated to a drizzle that pattered on the tin gutters. We stood and looked at his car. He turned to me.

"You know. . . I'm gonna get that ranch, one way or another."

I nodded.

"I know you will, Duke."

He hooked his thumbs on his belt, squinting up to the sky.

"She's gonna clear up soon," he murmured, then he looked down. "—well, buddy, I guess this is it."

I followed him to his car, moving through the clean, rain-swept air. He opened the car door with his head tilted down and the long white brim of his hat hiding his face. Duke paused.

"I thought of something last night my wife had said to me a long time ago. She said, 'You know, Duke, you talk about your dreams so much—'" He looked up at me. "'—how do you know that your dreams aren't real, and that they're really what's happening, and it's your life that's just the fantasy?'" Duke smiled and shook his head. "I guess I'll find out."

He held out his hand.

"So long, Brenton. Don't give up the fight, boy."

I shook his hand.

"Good luck, Duke."

He got in his car and fired it up. He drove around the parking lot once and came back to where I was standing. Duke stopped and looked at me—pointed out to the highway, his white Stetson filling his stagecoach.

Some of the heaviness left and I saw clearly.

"GO FIND HER, BOY!"

A wide smile broke across his face. He gave me a nod and screeched out of the parking lot. I watched his white car go down the road till it was out of sight.

I decided to walk to the beach and look at the ocean one last time. Not many people were out in the cold, damp drizzle. Ocean City already had the feel of closing down for the season.

I stood on the wet planks of the boardwalk. There was a fog on the ocean and the wood path disappeared into white mist in both directions. I jumped onto the wet sand and headed for the ocean. The wind made my eyes water and the sand was heavy on my shoes. The beach was deserted except for a fisherman standing in the distant surf.

The ocean was going through its ritual of rising and falling. The beach stands were now just blue boxes, locked up against the storm. I stood and the numb feeling I'd had since the previous night started to fade. Slow realizations crept up over my mind.

My cheek felt wet and it came on suddenly. I must have stood a good hour staring at the ocean, scarcely moving, just feeling. I walked down the beach and sat in a chair someone had left out from one of the stands. I stared out to the wide, gray ocean. I leaned my head back and sleep came on like a welcome stranger.

A figure approached out of a mist. He was coming very slowly down the beach. He was hunched over and using a great walking stick to insure his progress. As the distance closed, I could make out a very old man with a long gray beard. His clothes hung in strips that dragged on the ground and his feet were wrapped in the same cloth. I watched the ocean as he walked up to me and stopped. He stared at the sea.

"Magnificent, isn't it?"

I turned to him.

"Beg your pardon?"

He looked at me. His gray hair looked as if it hadn't been washed or combed for years. The old man's eyes were sunken in, watery, and bloodshot. There were streams that ran down both cheeks as if he had cried a million tears. He leaned against his walking stick.

"The ocean—it's magnificent, isn't it? I'm very proud of it," he said, looking back out.

I nodded.

"Christian loved the ocean."

The old man's eyebrows went up and he turned to me.

"Yes he did."

"You knew Christian?"

"Oh yes!" he said, moving his head slowly. "He was always trying to find me...always looking, and in the end he found his answer," he said, surveying the water again.

I stared at him.

"What do you mean he found his answer—he's dead!"

"Oh yes—but everyone will die. I meant before he died." He paused. "He found it."

The wind blew his gray beard up and his bushy eyebrows moved around. I stared at him.

"What answer?"

He was silent.

"I've got to get moving. If I stay in one place too long, I get very stiff," he said, planting his walking stick and moving down the beach.

"Wait a minute!"

"Come...walk with me."

I came up next to him and walked.

"—well?" he asked.

"How do you know so much about Christian?"

"Oh, never mind that—the important thing was the answer to his question."

"What was his question?"

"What does one do with one's self?"

I shook my head.

"He knew what to do with himself. . ."

"Did he?" he said, looking over at me. "You knew what to do with yourself. . .but Christian didn't."

"But I was a bad friend. . .I hurt him."

The old man paused, walking steadily.

"You always thought Christian had the answers, and then you found out he was only human."

"But he lied to me! I didn't want to hurt him and now he's dead!. . .He should have told me he didn't have all the answers!"

"Maybe he did," the old man nodded. "Even when you held him up as your crutch against the world, he was watching you also."

I wiped my eyes. He kept his slow, steady pace.

"Christian was scared of the unknown—that's what he depended on you for. You could think for yourself; he couldn't."

I held my head, shaking it.

"But I didn't help him. . .and now it's too late!"

"You did help him—you were a good friend."

I shook my head again.

"No. . .I should have known he was like me. . . .I wasn't fair to him!"

He stopped and turned.

"You had faith in him—that helped him."

"Not in the end. . . ."

"The end is up to each of us. . .the answer was within him—he found it and even left you an answer."

He turned toward a large wall of fog that hovered on the beach.

"To what?"

"To your fear," he said, moving away. "I must be going. Really, I have stayed too long."

"What fear is that?"

He turned next to the fog and the wind blew his clothes around him. He planted his stick in the sand.

"Why. . .the fear of what is known."

He stepped into the fog and vanished.

I blinked and opened my eyes in the beach chair. The beach was gray and deserted. I stood up and felt dizzy from the rush of blood. I started to walk, then looked down the beach to the south part of the island where the lighthouse blinked in the mist. I stood hearing the old man in my dream and watching the lighthouse. Then I was running for the highway.

I caught a bus and rode the creaking machine to the other side of the island. I got off at the last stop and started walking. I put my thumb out and a car pulled over.

"Need a lift, young fella?" an older man asked as I opened the car door.

"Yeah."

I jumped in and he started driving. He looked down the highway through thick, black-framed glasses. His hands shook even as he held the wheel.

"Where're you headed, young man?"

"I'm not really sure. . .I'll know it when I see it," I said, watching the weeds go by in the sand dunes.

"Well, that's as good a policy as any," he chuckled. "When you get to be my age, that's the only policy you can have — know it when you see it."

I looked at him.

"Have you lived here long?"

"Oh yes, all my life. Good long life it was too, but the missus died and I'm ready for whatever comes next," he said, slapping the steering wheel lightly.

The tires hummed with a steady splattering noise on the highway. I nodded.

"I'm sure it'll be something good."

"Hmmm."

We rode down the highway for a while in silence.

"Are you religious?" he asked, ducking his head and peering through the windshield that had fogged over.

I paused.

"Not really."

"I used to go to church myself, but after the wife died — I don't know, just doesn't seem the same without her."

I nodded slowly.

"I can see that."

"I don't think God will mind — I think he knows me by now," he said, laughing lightly.

There was just the sound of the car again. He looked over at me.

"You believe there's anything after you die?"

I looked straight down the highway.

"I think so," I said slowly, looking over at him.

He smiled and tapped the steering wheel.

"Me too," he said, tapping it again.

I saw the signs that I recognized and told him he could let me off.

"Well, I hope your life is a happy one," he said out the car door.

"Yours too."

"It has been. I'll be moving on soon."

I nodded and he called out through the window.

"Good luck to you, young man!"

I made my way from the highway and ran over the sand dune. The red and white lighthouse stood against the ocean. I ran across the rain-flattened beach, my shoes making perfect tracks. I came to the old wooden door. There was a new lock on the door with signs forbidding entry by order of the Ocean City police. I pushed on the door and it wouldn't budge. I pushed again, then hammered and smashed against it with a piece of wood — nothing happened. I stared at the door in amazement. It had always opened before, and now when I needed to make that climb most of all, there was to be no climb; no moment of truth. I would never know if I was capable of making the jump. I sat down slowly at the foot of the door with tears of frustration rolling down my cheeks.

I sat for a good hour staring at the ocean. I just stared and thought. I thought about Christian and the answer the old man in the dream had talked about. The answer was here outside the door. I wasn't meant to make the jump, Christian was. I had always tried to be like him, while he was trying to be like someone else. We both had run after something we could never have or be. . . we were, after all, only ourselves. Christian would have realized that if he were alive.

I stood up and walked to the edge of the water. It was cool and the evening was red along the shoreline. It had cleared up like Duke said it would. The lights from the cottages dotted the coast and moved across the ocean with the ships of promise. The summer paraded past me. I thought of King and his search for some past magic, and Duke looking forward to the same magic in the future. Then there was Calamitous, who only wanted the magic that exists in some type of normalcy. Finally I thought of Christian, who had been sure the perfect moment could only be held by some dominance of will.

They were lighthouses — all of them: beacons that break the night with only the effort of their illumination to guide them. Christian's lighthouse was never mine. I could only follow him to the edge, but never jump.

But another lighthouse will be mine, just as others will find theirs. And when the time comes. . . I too will leap to the other side.

William Elliot Hazelgrove was born in Richmond, Virginia in 1959. He grew up in Baltimore, Maryland, spending his summers in Ocean City, then moved to Chicago where he now lives with his wife, Kitty Lynn. He is the author of several novels and many short stories and has worked an assortment of different jobs supporting himself while writing. RIPPLES is his first novel.

Author photograph by Thomas Gallagher

Bertrand Puard

Musique
de nuit

LIBRAIRIE DES CHAMPS-ÉLYSÉES

Pour Georges, tout naturellement.

Le spectacle de ce soir sera l'un des plus merveilleux jamais donné dans cette ville, et a nécessité plusieurs jours de préparation.

Slogan de l'affiche présentant le célèbre numéro de cirque de MM. Kite et Henderson (1843).

Mercredi 24 décembre 1997

1

Lucy Chambers, assise derrière la caisse, guettait avec impatience les derniers clients. En cette veille de Noël, elle s'attendait à être submergée de travail et avait donc décidé de ne fermer sa bijouterie qu'une fois les trottoirs déserts. Elle aurait ensuite bien le temps de rentrer chez elle à Woodford pour réveillonner en compagnie de ses parents. Elle avait eu raison : les clients se succédaient un à un dans sa petite boutique.

Idéalement placée, sur Lumley Street, une rue perpendiculaire à Oxford Street, la plus importante artère commerciale de la capitale britannique, la petite bijouterie de Lucy commençait à avoir ses habitués, attirés autant par la compétence de la propriétaire que par son charmant sourire.

Les bijoux : l'éternelle passion de Lucy. Toute petite déjà, elle tirait la manche de sa maman à chaque fois qu'elle passait devant la vitrine d'une bijouterie. Sa mère s'arrêtait alors et lui apprenait le nom des pierres précieuses en les lui montrant du doigt. Alors tout naturellement, elle avait voulu en faire son métier.

— Mais tu es folle ! l'avait prévenue son père à de nombreuses reprises. Tu n'imagines pas quelle somme il te faudrait pour t'installer !

13

Elle ne répondait jamais et préférait le fixer tendrement de ses yeux vert émeraude, lui sourire et lui tapoter affectueusement la joue en lui répétant de ne pas s'inquiéter. Oh, certes ! Ce ne sont pas ses parents qui auraient pu lui offrir le fonds de commerce tant espéré. Un électricien proche de la retraite et une mère au foyer !

Elle n'avait pourtant jamais douté de sa réussite. Ses *A-levels* en poche, elle arrêta ses études et occupa différents petits boulots sous-payés, dont elle gardait scrupuleusement le moindre *penny*. Et puis, au bout de quatre dures années, où elle ne s'accordait qu'un seul jour de congé par semaine et deux semaines de vacances par an, elle parvint à réunir la moitié de l'apport personnel nécessaire à l'achat du fonds.

Sa grand-mère maternelle, dont elle était l'unique petite-fille, lui prêta le reste. Et c'est âgée de 24 ans seulement, avec une simple expérience de vendeuse, mais animée d'une forte motivation, que Lucy entama sa carrière de bijoutière. Elle savait que ses amies l'enviaient. La plupart d'entre elles étaient encore en études et dépendaient financièrement de leurs parents...

Lucy jeta un bref regard à travers sa vitrine. La lumière des lampadaires se reflétait sur le trottoir rendu humide par la petite bruine de ce début de soirée. Elle cligna des yeux et reporta son attention sur l'intérieur de sa boutique. Son nouvel agencement permettait aux passants de voir ses trois vitrines scintillantes depuis la rue.

Début décembre, en prévision des fêtes, elle avait décoré la vitrine « or » et la vitrine « montres » avec deux magnifiques guirlandes argentées. Pour celle des pierres précieuses, la sobriété s'imposait : l'éclat des nombreux bril-

14

lants et des quelques diamants donnait naturellement à l'ensemble un air de fête permanent.

L'horloge au-dessus de la porte indiquait 18 h 45. Un bon quart d'heure s'était écoulé depuis la venue du dernier client. Il avait acheté un petit pendentif en or représentant la silhouette d'un chien. Lucy sourit en repensant au visage juvénile de ce visiteur. Il devait avoir dans les quinze-seize ans et n'arrivait vraiment pas à se décider. Lucy l'avait poussé à la conversation pour l'aider dans son choix. Elle connaissait maintenant quasiment tout de sa petite amie : ses goûts vestimentaires, ses couleurs préférées. Une chose était sûre : si l'amour n'existait pas, Lucy serait au chômage technique ! À cette pensée, elle haussa les épaules. Cela lui rappelait la réflexion idiote d'un de ses oncles : « Tu ouvres une bijouterie, Lucy ? C'est parce que personne ne veut t'offrir de bijoux ? »

Lucy ne relevait jamais les provocations familières de son oncle Charles. Tout le monde le savait dans la famille : elle n'avait jamais eu de relations durables avec une personne du sexe opposé. Et même si ses quelques amies étaient toutes en ménage ou en passe de l'être, elle n'éprouvait aucune honte à être encore célibataire. Ce n'était pas qu'elle manquait de charme : grande d'un mètre soixante-sept, une jolie frimousse, de longs cheveux qui lui descendaient jusqu'au bas du dos et un sourire ravissant qui avait, d'après elle, joué un grand rôle lors de son entretien avec le banquier au sujet du prêt pour la boutique.

Parfois, elle se demandait si son caractère déterminé, sa capacité de travail ou même ses lourdes responsabilités de propriétaire n'effrayaient pas ses partenaires occasionnels.

Était-elle si impressionnante ? Pas assez insouciante ? Trop exigeante ? Non, c'était plutôt une question de disponibilité. Pas le temps de chercher l'homme idéal pour l'instant... Mais il n'y avait qu'à voir Hugh Grant dans *Quatre mariages et un enterrement*. Tout vient à point pour qui sait attendre !

Plus que quelques minutes et elle fermerait le rideau de fer automatique. Elle activerait l'alarme reliée directement à une société de surveillance privée et se dirigerait tranquillement vers la station de métro de Bond Street, direction Woodford par la Central Line. Elle se voyait déjà chez elle, à table, partageant avec ses parents non pas la sacro-sainte dinde de Noël (Lucy était végétarienne), mais le non moins célèbre *Christmas pudding*, préparé six mois à l'avance par sa mère et attendant le 24 décembre près du faux sapin saupoudré de coton dans la cave du pavillon.

Lucy entreprit de ranger le tiroir situé sous la caisse. Tout au fond, elle aperçut l'éclat métallique et rassurant de son pistolet d'alarme. Elle se savait bien incapable de s'en servir, mais sa seule présence suffisait à dissoudre les quelques crises d'angoisse qui l'assaillaient parfois. Elle descendit de son tabouret et déplissa sa jupe. *Capital Radio* passait en ce moment le dernier tube de The Verve, *Bitter Sweet Symphony*. Une chanson qu'elle trouvait envoûtante... Elle se rassit, referma le tiroir et augmenta le volume de son radiocassette. Le petit grelot de la porte retentit au même moment. Un client. Lucy regarda sa montre : il était 7 heures moins cinq. Probablement le dernier de la journée. Elle ne se donna pas la peine de baisser la musique. Si envoûtante...

L'homme jeta un dernier regard dans la rue avant de pousser la porte de la bijouterie. Excepté un vendeur de la dernière édition de l'*Evening Standard* à plus de cent mètres et un jeune garçon assis sur un perron, visiblement absorbé par la musique tonitruante sortant de son baladeur, la rue était déserte. L'homme était à nouveau seul, face à son destin.

Il n'était pas là pour acheter des bijoux. Ni même une montre. Il était là pour accomplir sa tâche. Une tâche qui le remplissait d'une joie intense. Sexuelle. Il enleva son chapeau et afficha son plus beau sourire. La bijoutière, une charmante jeune femme, lui répondit par un sourire plus commercial que sincère, mais il en aurait presque rougi. Elle lui demanda ce qu'il désirait. L'homme ne désirait rien. Juste la tuer.

Il répondit d'un ton suave qu'il voulait offrir une bague sertie d'un diamant à sa femme, pour son anniversaire. La belle bijoutière sortit une clef de la poche de son petit gilet vert (comme ses yeux, nota-t-il) et l'introduisit dans la serrure d'une des vitrines. L'homme s'avança alors vers elle. Il sentit son odeur. Son parfum. *Calvin Klein*, le parfum androgyne, un choix plein de distinction.

Elle sortit de la vitrine une bague sertie d'un petit diamant. L'homme pensa au temps qu'elle avait dû passer à faire ces minuscules nœuds avec ce petit fil rouge si fin où était accrochée une étiquette de prix. La bague valait deux cent quinze livres. Toujours ce même sourire enchanteur dévoilant des dents d'une blancheur éclatante. Et elle ne fumait pas !

L'homme prit la bague entre ses doigts. En attendant mieux. Elle s'étonna qu'il n'enlève pas ses gants pour examiner le bijou. Il remarqua son étonnement et la rassura d'un simple plissement des yeux. Il tourna lentement la bague entre ses doigts de cuir, l'approchant de ses yeux, de sa bouche. Il aurait voulu que ces instants durent une éternité, mais la jeune femme à la poitrine si bien soutenue et aux reins si fermes semblait impatiente... voire inquiète. Son sourire se figea.

L'homme venait de faire tomber la bague sur la moquette. Il l'écrasa d'un coup de talon. Les mains maintenant libres, il fit un pas vers elle. La jeune bijoutière, tétanisée par la peur, appela à l'aide. Mais sa voix se perdit au milieu de la symphonie. L'homme était de plus en plus rouge. Son front luisait bien plus que tout à l'heure. Il posa ses mains autour du cou de la jeune femme.

L'instinct : elle essaya de lui échapper et de se diriger vers la caisse. L'homme serra plus fort. Elle se débattit violemment. « Elle veut rejoindre la caisse... Probablement a-t-elle planqué là-bas un pistolet d'alarme », pensa-t-il. Elle n'y arrivera pas. L'homme serra de plus en plus fort. Elle suffoquait de douleur. Lui de plaisir. Puis il sentit qu'elle abandonnait tout espoir. Ses jambes bougèrent de moins en moins vite. Elle cherchait de moins en moins d'air.

C'était fini. Les derniers spasmes de la condamnée et le silence. La libération. L'homme desserra lentement ses mains gantées. Une brève sensation d'humidité lui chatouilla l'intérieur des cuisses. Il allongea délicatement la jeune femme au milieu de la boutique, entre la vitrine des diamants, ouverte, et celle des montres. Il la contempla quelques secondes et ébaucha un sourire.

Son cou était zébré de larges marques rouges. Sa jupe était légèrement relevée. D'un geste élégant, il se pencha et la remit impeccablement en place. Après un bref regard à travers la vitrine pour s'assurer que personne ne l'observait, il se mit à l'œuvre.

L'homme n'avait pas mis longtemps pour la tuer. Une minute, peut-être même un peu moins. Il sortit de la poche droite de son imperméable vert foncé une pince à glaçon chromée. Il se baissa alors vers son visage et entreprit d'extraire l'œil droit de son orbite. Après quelques tentatives maladroites, il sectionna le nerf optique, proprement, avec une paire de ciseaux qu'il sortit de la poche gauche de son imperméable. Il procéda de même pour l'autre œil. Il déposa les deux globes par terre. Puis, il rangea la paire de ciseaux et la pince à glaçon dans la poche intérieure de son imperméable après en avoir sorti ce qu'il considérait comme le clou de son spectacle.

L'homme inspecta une dernière fois son matériel : les deux ampoules miniatures avaient l'air intactes, la pile également. Il relia donc l'ensemble grâce à deux minces fils gainés. Les ampoules s'allumèrent dans la seconde. L'homme posa le boîtier à terre et enfonça ensuite les ampoules dans les orbites vides de Lucy. La pile tiendrait jusqu'à l'arrivée de la police. Il en était sûr.

Il frotta machinalement ses gants contre son imperméable et jeta un coup d'œil vers la vitrine. Personne. Il commença alors à vider la vitrine ouverte en prenant bien soin de disposer méticuleusement les bijoux tout autour du cadavre de la jeune fille et ce, à intervalles réguliers. Puis, pour achever sa mise en scène, il posa sur le pubis de Lucy un triangle de percussionniste.

L'homme regarda son œuvre. Admirable ! Il était fier de lui. Et tout cela en à peine cinq minutes. Il se dirigea vers la porte, se retourna vers le cadavre et lui adressa un dernier sourire. Il pressa ensuite l'interrupteur près de la porte d'entrée et plongea la pièce dans une douce pénombre, seulement troublée par l'éclat des petites ampoules et des nombreux diamants. Puis, il poussa la porte et s'engouffra dans Lumley Street. Le vendeur de journaux était encore là, mais cent mètres plus loin, le jeune homme au baladeur avait disparu. Il remit son chapeau, fourra ses mains dans les poches et se dirigea vers Oxford Street en sifflotant...

Au même moment, dans la petite bijouterie de feu Lucy Chambers, The Verve, à la radio, venaient de finir leur symphonie douce-amère...

2

L'inspecteur Paul Kite, du New Scotland Yard, tapotait avec impatience le toit cabossé de sa vieille Rover. Il attendait depuis bientôt cinq minutes le sergent Nancy Kelling, qui discutait encore avec le pasteur de l'église de Savoy Row. L'inspecteur ne pouvait plus voir la façade de cette petite chapelle et la tête du jeune prêtre.

Depuis hier, jour du meurtre de cette vieille femme, il avait passé le plus clair de son temps ici avec le sergent Kelling et les très rares fois où elle venait sur les lieux d'un crime, Kelling s'en donnait à cœur joie et tenait à interroger tous les gens du quartier.

Kite regarda sa montre. Bientôt 8 heures. L'Eurostar de son jeune stagiaire n'allait pas tarder à arriver et si Kelling ne venait pas tout de suite, ils allaient le rater.

— Seigneur Dieu, bougonna Kite en prenant place derrière le volant. Il faut qu'elle nous fasse le même numéro à chaque coup !

Il regarda à travers la vitre la silhouette du sergent, debout avec le pasteur sous un lampadaire. Son uniforme la boudinait de partout et ses cheveux mi-longs étaient toujours aussi mal peignés. Kite soupira et actionna son klaxon. Kelling se retourna et adressa un geste d'apaisement à l'intention de son supérieur qui, du coup, klaxonna une seconde fois. Il s'apprêtait à sortir de la Rover lorsque sa subordonnée mit fin à l'entretien et vint rejoindre en courant la voiture banalisée. Elle était en nage.

— Du calme, Paul ! Pourquoi êtes-vous si énervé ?

Kite, pour toute réponse, lui tendit un Klee-nex et tourna la clef de contact. Il ne supportait pas la façon de travailler du sergent Kelling. Depuis une semaine, depuis que son jeune ins-pecteur stagiaire était rentré à Paris pour les congés, il vivait dans l'ennui. La présence de Nancy Kelling l'incommodait plus que toute autre chose.

Ce n'était pas spécialement l'attitude de la jeune femme qui le mettait dans un pareil état de lassitude : l'inspecteur n'éprouvait plus de grande joie dans la routine du New Yard et ses collègues ne l'intéressaient plus. Cela faisait combien de temps qu'il n'avait pas déjeuné dans la salle de repos pour papoter avec ses collaborateurs ?

Tout cela était bien fini. Kite avait tourné la page. Maintenant, il se consacrait exclusivement à la formation de Clément, le jeune inspecteur français qui avait débarqué de Paris en septembre dernier dans le cadre du programme d'échange des polices anglaise et française. Il l'avait rapidement adopté et aidé. C'était un ami de l'inspecteur qui avait loué pour une bouchée de pain un appartement spacieux au jeune homme. Et pour ses premières soirées londoniennes, Kite avait invité à de nombreuses reprises Clément à dîner avec sa petite famille. Il fallait faciliter l'acclimatation du jeune *froggie* et lui faire travailler son anglais déjà d'excellente facture. Kite tenta de sourire. Sa femme et sa fille parlaient couramment le français et elles ne manquaient jamais de se moquer de son niveau lorsqu'ils entamaient une discussion dans la langue de Molière.

Mais ensuite ? Quand sa mission serait terminée, l'inspecteur Kite ne savait pas encore de quoi son avenir serait fait... Et puis si, il le savait... C'était cela le plus insupportable... Il resterait encore au Yard à remplir des rapports et à mener l'enquête sur des affaires toutes plus banales les unes que les autres. Il était en rage alors qu'il tentait de faufiler sa Rover entre les dizaines de voitures qui embouteillaient le Waterloo Bridge.

Nancy Kelling remarqua la teinte pourpre du visage de l'inspecteur et lui demanda ce qui n'allait pas. Kite lui répondit vertement que cela ne la regardait pas.

— Bon ! se renfrogna le sergent. Eh bien, puisque c'est comme ça que vous avez décidé de vous comporter avec moi, Paul, je ne vous raconterai rien de mon entretien avec le pasteur !

Kite ricana.

— Vous le lirez demain dans mon rapport...

Kelling avait l'air satisfaite de sa punition.

— Nancy, je suis au regret de vous dire que demain, nous ne formerons plus équipe...

— Le jeune Français revient ?

— Précisément, ma chère, et nous allons le chercher par cette route longue et sinueuse...

— Mais je n'ai pas le temps d'attendre son arrivée ! s'offusqua le sergent de son ton strident. Je réveillonne avec mon ami ce soir...

C'en était trop pour Kite. Tout le monde au Yard lui reprochait son naturel irascible. Il allait donner une nouvelle occasion de se gausser de lui à tous ses détracteurs. Il freina avec violence. Le cri de Kelling couvrit les crissements des pneus sur l'asphalte. D'un coup de volant calculé, il braqua sa Rover vers la file de gauche et fit un demi-tour de toute beauté en évitant les pare-chocs d'une dizaine de voitures.

Il stoppa net au feu rouge et en profita pour hisser le gyrophare sur le toit. Au vert, il passa la première. Un vrombissement inouï se fit entendre et une odeur de caoutchouc brûlé arriva à ses narines. Il jeta un bref coup d'œil vers Kelling, qui s'agrippait comme une forcenée à son siège, et lâcha la pédale d'embrayage. La Rover partit comme une bombe sur Embankment. Un savant braquage leur permit

23

de ne pas s'emplafonner dans une camionnette en stationnement.

Kelling comprit la manœuvre de Kite : il allait la reconduire au Yard vitesse grand V. Elle ferma les yeux durant le trajet.

3

Il reposa délicatement la tasse sur sa soucoupe et ramassa ses gants posés sur le comptoir du pub. L'homme salua l'assistance d'un geste de la main et se dirigea vers la porte. Il s'attendait à ce qu'il fasse froid dehors, mais il ne sentit pas la différence de température à travers son imperméable. Il éprouvait en ce moment une sensation de pouvoir intense. Rien ne l'aurait arrêté à cet instant. Cette bijoutière était vraiment magnifique. Cela lui avait semblé bien plus excitant — non, ce n'était pas le mot qu'il désirait — bien plus vivifiant que son premier meurtre, cette vieille femme dans l'église. Ah ! Le contact de ses gants sur le cou de ces femmes ! Ce glissement du cuir sur leur peau parfumée... Comme il aimerait le faire plus souvent... Deux fois, ça n'était pas suffisant. Mais il se devait de suivre son chemin. Vers ce but qu'il s'était fixé. Et qu'il atteindrait coûte que coûte. Il en était sûr.

Il pouvait regagner sa voiture garée dans Green Street. Tranquillement, sans se presser. Son petit monde attendrait. Il glissa la clef dans la serrure et actionna la poignée. Il sifflotait encore et toujours, ce même air, si entêtant...

4

Clément Bellanger, 22 ans, stagiaire au New Scotland Yard depuis trois mois, chercha l'inspecteur Kite des yeux immédiatement après le passage des douanes. Il aperçut très vite le petit bonhomme, coincé entre une femme qui n'arrêtait pas de remuer la tête à droite à gauche et un grand chauve tenant à la main une pile de livres. Clément détailla sa silhouette coincée dans ce strict imperméable noir dont le col laissait entrevoir une cravate impeccablement nouée, son visage, rond, avec quelques rides lui donnant un air de réflexion permanente, des yeux marron sous de fins sourcils et puis enfin ses cheveux, poivre et sel, légèrement bouclés.

— Bonjour, mon jeune ami..., commença Kite après avoir rejoint Clément. As-tu fait un bon voyage ?

— Excellent, lui répondit le jeune Français.

— OK, s'enthousiasma Kite en déchargeant Clément de son sac. Ne perdons pas de temps. Tu vas venir passer le réveillon avec nous. Mary et Michelle ont préparé un bon repas !

Clément ne trouva rien à redire à cette invitation. Ils s'engouffrèrent tous deux dans la voiture. Clément remarqua une vague odeur de plastique brûlé dans l'habitacle, mais s'abstint de tout commentaire. Il se doutait que l'inspecteur n'avait pas dû être tendre avec les pneus de la vieille Rover. Kite prit l'initiative de la conversation quand la circulation se raréfia.

— Sans te mentir, il ne s'est pas passé grandchose entre ton départ et l'affaire de lundi. Rien de bien palpitant en fait : les paperasses, les réunions, les conneries quoi... Avant lundi... Car

25

lundi, les affaires ont repris sur les chapeaux de roue !

Kite marqua une pause. Sur leur gauche on pouvait apercevoir le cimetière de Hampstead.

— Ce lundi 22 décembre est à marquer d'une croix noire sur ma vie de couple. Pour la première fois depuis vingt ans, nous n'avons pu fêter, ma femme et moi, la date anniversaire de notre premier flirt. Et pour cause...

Kite continua sans se faire prier. Il aimait ménager ses effets.

— J'étais revenu comme de coutume un peu plus tôt dans la soirée, aux alentours de 19 heures, pour que nous puissions arriver à temps à notre restaurant fétiche. Et à peine entré dans la maison, ce putain de téléphone portable se met à carillonner de tous les diables... Quel bruit ça peut faire, ces bordels-là !

— Vous me le passerez. Je réglerai le volume pour qu'il sonne moins fort..., proposa Clément.

Kite secoua la tête.

— Il n'y aura pas de prochaine fois. Je n'arrivais pas à prendre la communication et ce foutu téléphone n'arrêtait pas de sonner. J'ai ouvert la porte donnant sur la rue et je l'ai balancé de rage sur la route...

C'était tout Kite.

— Au même moment, le téléphone de la maison s'est mis à sonner. Michelle, ma femme, a décroché et c'était, bien entendu, cette chère Nancy. On venait de retrouver, dans la petite chapelle de Savoy Row, pas loin de Waterloo Station, le cadavre d'une vieille femme. C'est le pasteur du coin qui avait donné l'alerte une demi-heure plus tôt. Il avait trouvé la porte de la chapelle, habituellement fermée, légèrement

26

entrouverte. Enfin, bref... J'ai bien entendu repris la voiture et il m'a fallu plus d'une heure à cause du trafic pour arriver jusqu'à la chapelle. Une ambulance, Nancy et le légiste étaient déjà sur place. C'est drôle, mais quand je suis arrivé dans Savoy Row, j'avais du mal à croire qu'un cadavre puisse s'y trouver. C'était une toute petite allée avec, au fond, une chapelle au mur recouvert de lierre et de mousse. Il y régnait une atmosphère de calme sans pareil. J'aurais bien aimé garder cette image de l'endroit. Mais après avoir pénétré à l'intérieur de l'église...

Kite reprit son souffle. Clément resta silencieux.

— Le légiste m'avait prévenu que ça n'était pas beau à voir... Je suis entré dans la chapelle au bras de Nancy, si je puis dire, et la première chose que j'ai vue c'était une forme ovale étendue sur le sol, au milieu de la nef. Une espèce de tas de terre ou quelque chose comme ça... En fait, il s'agissait bien de terreau. On avait recouvert le cadavre de cette vieille femme de terreau... Comme pour lui offrir une sépulture. La victime avait été étranglée. Le légiste situait sa mort aux alentours de 14 heures. Aucune trace de lutte. Pas la moindre empreinte digitale sur son cou. Pas de sévices sexuels, ni de viol... Mais un acte *post mortem* surprenant. On avait... Non, mais, regardez-moi cet imbécile heureux qui se rabat sous mon nez...

Kite ne supportait pas les mauvais conducteurs. Il baissa sa vitre tout en continuant à accélérer pour coller au train du chauffard. D'un geste calculé, il se saisit du gyrophare bleu et le brancha pendant cinq secondes. À bout de bras, il porta le gyrophare à la hauteur du toit.

Le conducteur fautif ralentit immédiatement et permit ainsi à Kite de lui rendre la pareille. Fier de lui, il rangea le gyrophare et reprit :

— Donc... Je continue... Le meurtrier avait voulu nous laisser également sa « carte de visite ». Il avait gravé maladroitement à l'aide d'un cutter, sur le visage de la victime, « Eleanor Stout, O.P.D. [1] » et avait enroulé autour de son poignet droit quatre cordes de guitare. (Kite marqua une pause.) Pour l'inscription sur le visage, « Eleanor Stout » était bien entendu le prénom et le nom de cette retraitée des postes, préposée à l'entretien de la chapelle. Quant aux cordes de guitare, je ne sais absolument pas, pour l'instant, quelle signification leur donner... Maintenant, tente d'imaginer la scène, Clément... Dans cette petite chapelle glaciale, miss Stout est en train de nettoyer ce qu'elle peut. Le meurtrier arrive. Il l'étrangle. Ça ne devait pas être bien difficile vu l'état physique de la victime. Puis il la recouvre de terreau dont il a probablement apporté les sacs avec lui. Alors, il lui dépoussière le visage et lui grave l'inscription sur la figure... Il roule ses sacs de terreau vides et s'en va tranquillement.

— Et personne n'a rien vu ? interrogea Clément.

— Ah ! Pour ce qui est de l'enquête de voisinage, tu sais bien que c'est la spécialité du sergent Kelling. Son rapport est attendu demain.

Clément acquiesça.

— Et pour le moment ?

— Pas grand-chose. Apparemment, miss Stout était chargée de l'entretien de cette chapelle depuis vingt ans et d'après le pasteur elle

1. Officially Pronounced Dead.

n'avait aucune relation susceptible de commettre un tel crime. Selon lui, c'est un acte purement gratuit et qui n'a pas été commis par un de ses paroissiens... Pour ce qui est de la vie privée de la victime, rien à signaler de ce côté-là. Elle habitait un petit appartement dans Covent Garden et ses voisines m'ont dit qu'elle menait une vie paisible de vieille fille, jamais mariée et sans enfant... Bon, tout ça n'a pas l'air trop clair, mais vous aurez quelque chose de plus complet pour demain...

— Et sur les motivations du tueur ? enchaîna Clément.

— Rien pour l'instant. Probablement un cinglé.

Kite s'arrêta au feu rouge marquant la fin de Finchley Road et le début de Ballards Lane. La Rover prit la direction du 151, Etchingham Park Road, le domicile de Kite.

— On reparlera de tout ça après-demain, déclara Kite. En attendant, pas un mot sur cette affaire à table...

Clément soupira. Comme s'il n'existait pas d'autres sujets de conversation. Une brune aux yeux bleus répondant au charmant prénom de Mary par exemple...

5

Mary guettait par la fenêtre en ovale de sa chambre l'arrivée de la vieille Rover. Sa mère était en train de lire le journal du soir confortablement assise devant le coin repas de la cuisine. Médecin au Finchley Memorial Hospital, elle n'avait pu se libérer ce soir avant 19 heures. C'était sa fille qui avait admirablement mis la table et préparé le repas de Noël.

Michelle Kite était contente que Clément se joigne à eux pour le repas. Elle appréciait beaucoup le jeune Français. Au tout début, elle n'avait pas bien compris ce que faisait Clément dans la police et puis Mary lui avait raconté toute l'histoire : ses espoirs déçus, ses galères... Michelle avait un peu compris maintenant, mais ne s'expliquait pas tout.

Il y avait toujours une lueur dans les yeux du jeune homme. Cette lueur qui avait disparu depuis longtemps des yeux de son mari. « Les flics ont tous les yeux éteints. Leur esprit meurt à petit feu », lui avait un jour confié un de ses collègues psychologues. « On pourrait croire que c'est la routine qui les tue, mais c'est justement l'inverse : les grosses affaires, le sang répandu, les corps déchiquetés, les médias envahissants... » Michelle se prit à sourire malgré tout. Était-ce cette lueur qui attirait sa fille vers Clément ?

Malgré tous les efforts que faisaient Mary et le jeune Français pour cacher leur liaison, Mrs Kite n'avait jamais été dupe. Il fallait voir comment Mary parlait de Clément : un mélange de crainte et de respect. C'était à peu de chose près les paroles qu'avait utilisées Michelle pour exprimer à sa mère son amour pour Paul au tout début de leur relation. Sa mère l'avait alors sermonnée, lui conseillant d'épouser un médecin plutôt qu'un policier. Mais il y avait cette attraction... Irrémédiable... Une attirance juvénile... Inexplicable...

Michelle ferma son journal. Mary n'était pas

aussi emballée qu'elle l'avait été. Il faut dire que la jeune fille avait des raisons pour... Malgré lui, Kite avait à de nombreuses reprises fait souffrir son entourage. Qu'y pouvait-il ? Était-ce de sa faute ? Fallait-il lui lancer la pierre ? Non, bien sûr... Il était déjà assez malheureux pour cela... Du reste, Michelle ne comprenait toujours pas pourquoi il n'avait pas encore quitté le Yard... Il semblait avait perdu toute sa motivation pour le métier... Ou peut-être attendait-il sa vengeance sur le destin ? Une autre grosse affaire qu'il pourrait mener à bien et ainsi décrocher toutes ces casseroles qui traînaient derrière lui ?

Un bruit de sonnette. Michelle se leva. Elle entendit Mary dévaler l'escalier. Ils n'avaient maintenant plus qu'à passer une bonne soirée... Loin de tous ces problèmes...

Paul Kite était assis près de sa femme sur le canapé, un verre à liqueur vide à portée de main. Les yeux fermés, il tirait sur un mince cigarillo. Le dîner avait été excellent, les conversations bon enfant. On parla de Paris, de la Côte d'Azur, de Monaco, de Menton, de Saint-Raphaël. Cela l'avait détendu après cette journée atrocement longue...

Lui qui rêvait, en entrant au Yard après ses études de droit, à une grande carrière au sein de la brigade criminelle... Son quotidien était tout autre : dépouiller rapport sur rapport entre deux enquêtes peu palpitantes, et tout cela à cause de cette terrible affaire de juin 1987, dont il fut l'un des principaux protagonistes... Certains de ses collègues avaient été carrément limogés. Kite y avait échappé, mais il savait pertinemment que sa carrière était définitivement gelée. Ces mauvaises pensées lui firent oublier son cigarillo et quelques cendres tombèrent sur son pull jaune. Il les chassa d'un revers de main tout en se demandant ce que pouvaient bien se dire Mary et Clément dans la cuisine.

— Alors, tout va bien ? chuchota Clément en français, tout en remplissant le lave-vaisselle.

— Bien sûr, tout va bien...

Clément se demanda si Mary classait sa question dans les « interrogations idiotes du couple ». Une de ses expressions favorites.

— Depuis lundi, j'ai bien essayé de t'appeler sur le portable de ton père, mais je crois que le pauvre téléphone a été victime de ses foudres...

Mary rigola enfin. Ils entendirent les premières mesures de *Sultans of Swing* des Dire Straits venant du salon. Clément jeta un coup d'œil circulaire sur la salle de séjour avec sa cuisine intégrée dans le coin à droite. Et à gauche, cette table où il s'était assis tant de fois avec Mary, alors que ses parents étaient tous les deux au boulot.

— Et toi ? interrogea Mary. Le fils prodigue était de retour dans la famille...

— C'était un peu ça, oui ! Mes grand-mères en ont presque pleuré ! Quant à mes parents, ils avaient invité tous mes amis pour le soir de mon retour ! La surprise, quoi...

— Tu as revu Sébastien ?

— Oui, mais pas ce soir-là. Il joue en ce moment. J'ai été le voir à l'œuvre dimanche soir.

— Et c'était bien ?

Mary était appuyée contre le mur. Pour toute réponse, il la rejoignit et lui donna un long baiser en posant ses mains sur les hanches de la jeune fille. Mary lui répondit avec fougue.

— C'est toujours d'accord pour vendredi

soir ? demanda Clément, ne voulant visiblement pas s'étendre sur ce sujet.

— Bien sûr ! Tu passes me prendre à 6 heures et demie à la danse. Je t'appellerai demain pour confirmer.

— On dîne au restaurant et tu viens coucher à l'appartement...

Mary sembla réfléchir.

— C'est d'accord, répondit-elle enfin. Je dirai à mes parents que je couche chez Anna.

Ils s'embrassèrent une dernière fois et regagnèrent le salon.

Il était plus de 23 heures lorsque Kite décida qu'il était temps pour Clément de rentrer chez lui.

Lorsque Clément débarqua à Londres, Scotland Yard lui octroya une petite somme pour le logement, somme qui se révéla bien insuffisante pour louer quelque chose proche du centre de la capitale. Mais Kite lui obtint un petit appartement très bien situé pour un prix modique ; le propriétaire n'était autre que Robert Pungent, le meilleur ami de Kite, un homme d'affaires influent de la City. Il devait bien posséder une douzaine d'appartements dans la capitale et ses alentours, plus un hôtel particulier dans St John's Wood, un quartier très chic de Londres dans lequel il vivait.

— Il est tard, Clément... Et demain tu commences à 9 heures...

— Vous n'êtes pas de service demain, inspecteur ?

— Non, je suis en congé. Mais s'il y a le moindre problème, n'hésite pas à m'appeler. Et puis tu ne seras pas seul, Kelling est de garde !

Clément acquiesça et enfila le blouson que

Mrs Kite lui tendait. Ils se dirent au revoir. Il faisait très froid dehors et la pluie recommençait à tomber. Kite frissonna dans son pull et se reprocha de ne pas avoir pris plus de précautions. Clément et Kite se dirigèrent vers la voiture.

— Tiens, dit Kite en tendant les clefs de la Rover. Mais vas-y mollo, mon petit Clément... Je tiens à ma voiture de fonction. Et à en croire Alexander, tu as plutôt la conduite fougueuse ! Clément : l'arme fatale ! (Il adopta une voix grave.) N'oublie jamais ça : moi seul ai le physique de Mel Gibson, donc moi seul suis habilité à conduire comme lui.

Clément sourit et ouvrit la portière arrière. Il s'empara d'un paquet qu'il sortit de son sac à dos et le tendit à Kite qui le remercia d'un clin d'œil. Puis il contourna la voiture et ouvrit le coffre avec la clef. Il jeta un rapide coup d'œil à l'intérieur et le ferma d'un air malicieux.

— Et au moindre problème, n'hésite pas à m'appeler, ajouta Kite.

Ils se serrèrent la main et se séparèrent. Clément prit place dans la voiture et Kite se réfugia sur le perron. Une douce lumière éclairait ses fines bouclettes argentées. Il se frotta le ventre tout en regardant la Rover s'éloigner, puis rentra.

6

L'homme revint chez lui, l'estomac plein. Il avait passé une très agréable soirée. Et il se promit de tout faire pour en passer d'autres comme celle-là. Il était visiblement content de retrouver la chaleur et le silence de son foyer. Pas un bruit. Seulement quelques sons en dessous de lui, à la cave. Comme d'habitude, du reste. Rien de bien méchant. Il se dirigea vers la cuisine d'un pas assuré. Une fois sur place, l'homme remplit sa bouilloire électrique avec cette eau qu'il filtrait régulièrement grâce au broc équipé d'un système à base de charbon naturel. Le matin, avant de partir, il versait l'eau du robinet dans le réservoir du broc. Durant toute la journée, l'eau était filtrée en passant dans le charbon, puis retombait dans la partie basse de l'appareil. Depuis qu'il avait découvert ce système, il pouvait enfin boire un thé à sa convenance, avec une eau pure et sans aucune trace de tartre, ni de calcaire. Il pressa le bouton MARCHE de sa bouilloire et le témoin orange de fonctionnement se mit à luire dans l'obscurité de la cuisine. L'homme s'assit derrière la table, alluma la lumière et déplia le journal qui devait traîner là depuis hier. Il décida également de croquer une pomme. Tous les soirs depuis peu, il s'offrait une pomme bien verte, bien brillante. Le radiateur électrique lui chauffait agréablement le dos. Il retira son pull et soupira d'aise. Décidément, quand arrivait enfin votre heure, la vie semblait d'une douceur si intense...

L'homme entendit le clac de la bouilloire alors qu'il finissait de lire l'article de journal concernant le meurtre de cette vieille femme, Eleanor Stout, retrouvée assassinée, enterrée et défigurée au fond de cette petite chapelle plus guère fréquentée. Cela faisait beaucoup pour une seule femme, pensa l'homme. Puis il tira la langue et se leva pour aller chercher dans le placard au-dessus de l'évier son mug favori. Et tout en versant l'eau bouillante sur le sachet de thé extra-fort, il se mit à siffloter doucement. Puis il se rassit à la table et attendit que son thé infuse.

Au bout de trois minutes trente, l'homme enleva le sachet à l'aide d'une pince prévue à cet usage exclusif et le jeta dans la poubelle. Puis, il se leva à nouveau pour gagner le réfrigérateur d'où il sortit une petite bouteille de lait frais. Il en versa quelques gouttes dans son mug et rangea la bouteille. Tout à coup, il repensa à ces pas au-dessous de lui. Il sortit alors un yogourt de son réfrigérateur et une tranche de cheddar emballée dans un plastique transparent. Il déposa sa collecte sur un petit plateau rose qui traînait sur la table. L'homme alla ensuite vers l'évier pour remplir un verre d'eau au robinet, qu'il posa près de la tranche de cheddar. Il se demanda ensuite s'il devait également sortir une petite cuillère pour le yogourt. Mais il se ravisa et empoigna fermement le plateau. Il poussa la porte de la cuisine avec son pied et ouvrit celle de la cave grâce à un bouton situé tout à côté des interrupteurs. La gâche se fit entendre et l'homme descendit le long escalier froid et humide.

Lorsqu'il arriva devant cette porte blanche fichée entre deux murs de brique, il entendit comme un grattement, ponctué de brefs soupirs. Il posa le plateau sur une petite table et se dirigea vers un curieux boîtier fixé au mur. Il s'agissait en fait d'un simple Interphone communiquant avec l'intérieur de la pièce. L'homme marmonna quelques mots en insistant sur le fait qu'il ne désirait, à partir de maintenant, plus aucun bruit. Il annonça son intention d'ouvrir la porte pour apporter le plateau-repas du jour. Un glissement silencieux, semblant s'éloigner de la porte, se fit entendre à l'intérieur de la pièce. L'homme sortit un trousseau de clefs de la poche de son pantalon et commença à déverrouiller la première des trois serrures.

Il tourna la poignée et entrebâilla la porte au minimum, juste pour y laisser passer le plateau. Une bouffée de chaleur vint lui gifler la face, accompagnée d'une odeur infecte, à la limite du supportable. Il sentit son estomac faire un bond jusqu'à sa poitrine. Il ferma précipitamment la porte et verrouilla les trois serrures une par une. Avant de remonter, il se dirigea vers un thermostat fixé près de l'Interphone. Il baissa la température de deux degrés. Vingt-quatre degrés étaient une température amplement suffisante pour cet hiver somme toute pluvieux, mais pas réellement glacial. Il se dirigea vers l'escalier.

De la lumière ! De la lumière ! Oh, merci mon Dieu ! Et de l'air frais et pur ! Et puis de l'eau, et puis mon yaourt, et puis mon morceau de fromage ! Oh, merci mon Dieu ! Comment pourrais-je jamais vous remercier ?

Le lait s'était maintenant complètement mélangé à son thé. Il porta le mug à ses lèvres et décida que son breuvage était à la bonne température. Il le but en une seule gorgée, n'en laissant pas une seule goutte au fond. La pendule murale indiquait 23 h 30. Allait-il déjà se coucher ? Non, décida-t-il. Il avait envie de faire une séance de sauna. Il porta son mug dans le lave-vaisselle plein et monta à l'étage en faisant bien

attention de ne pas faire craquer les marches. Il
s'enferma alors dans son immense salle de
bains, tout de suite à droite après l'escalier. Il
était fier de cette pièce dont il avait lui-même
supervisé l'installation. À l'origine, avant qu'il
ne rachète la maison, la salle de bains était bien
plus vétuste que cela. Il y avait fait installer un
jacuzzi et un mini-sauna. Et maintenant, il
aimait ces instants parfaits, de calme, de silence
et de recueillement.

Il enleva sa chemise bleu clair et son maillot
de corps blanc. Le miroir lui renvoyait l'image
d'un homme à la poitrine quasiment imberbe.
Puis, il retira son pantalon de toile et son caleçon. Il était maintenant nu dans sa salle de
bains. Il se tourna face au miroir et observa son
corps avec une attention soutenue. Des mains
passaient le long de sa tête puis descendaient
vers ses pectoraux qu'elles massèrent de longs
instants. Elles entreprirent de descendre encore
plus bas, vers son nombril, son pubis et son sexe
qu'elles caressèrent avec une parfaite habileté.
Ces mains étaient les siennes. Et encore plus
que sur son corps, l'homme imaginait ces mains
autour du cou de ces femmes, de ces femmes
dont il avait décidé la mort. Pour la bonne
cause.

L'homme alluma la chaîne hi-fi encastrée
dans le mur, au-dessus du panier à linge. Puis il
se glissa dans le mini-sauna, après avoir allumé
la résistance délivrant la chaleur à l'intérieur de
la petite maison de bois. Il ferma la porte et
posa ses fesses nues sur le bois dur et froid. Il
attendit que la chaleur vienne. Il l'attendit en
écoutant son disque préféré. Il avait dosé admirablement le volume de sa chaîne pour pouvoir
entendre de l'intérieur du sauna tout en ne

dérangeant pas les personnes présentes dans la maison. Il les avait croisées dans l'escalier. C'était une sensation bien étrange que de croiser les esprits de ces lieux... Des esprits si vivants. Depuis que l'homme leur avait confié son plan, ils sortaient souvent pendant la nuit. Il en était sûr : lorsque tout serait terminé, lorsqu'il leur aurait rendu un tel hommage, alors ils le féliciteraient. Pour l'instant, ces personnes ne faisaient que passer de pièce en pièce, ou réveiller l'homme en pleine nuit pour le faire participer à une de leurs séances si spéciales... Mais bientôt, dans quelques jours maintenant, ils l'embrasseraient ! De cela, l'homme était sûr. En y pensant, il se mit à entonner une chanson à pleine voix. Définitivement heureux.

Jeudi 25 décembre 1997

7

Clément se retourna une énième fois dans son lit et, tout en soupirant, envoya valdinguer la couette au-dessus de lui. Il faisait bien trop chaud dans cet appartement. Clément tapa sur son oreiller pour tenter de lui redonner sa forme originale et y reposa sa tête. Il n'arrivait pas à trouver le sommeil. Il pensait et repensait à Mary. Pourquoi son amie était-elle si distante avec lui parfois ? Pour en avoir parlé avec elle à de nombreuses reprises, la même réponse revenait toujours : « Je ne veux pas tomber amoureuse d'un flic. Si tu deviens un clone de mon père, je ne deviendrai sûrement pas un clone de ma mère... » Là était tout l'ennui de leur relation, qui glissait peu à peu, au fur et à mesure des jours et des mois, vers une routine purement sexuelle. Mary avait été catégorique, elle refusait de venir partager l'appartement du jeune homme. « Il faudrait déjà l'annoncer à tes parents », avait constaté Clément. « Et puis quoi ? Tu veux peut-être qu'on se fiance aussi ? » avait-elle répondu d'un ton cinglant.

Au tout début, alors que le sexe n'avait pas encore pourri leur histoire, il prenait Mary pour une partie intégrante de sa reconstruction, une pièce nécessaire à l'édifice du nouveau Clément

43

qu'il voulait bâtir loin de Paris... Il avait pris la décision de partir un an à l'étranger, laissant derrière lui son cocon familial et tous ses amis, pour tenter de se construire un nouvel avenir, après avoir dynamité d'un simple coup de tête le destin qu'il s'imaginait depuis si longtemps.

Lors de son arrivée en Angleterre, le dépaysement avait eu lieu. Les journées d'investigation en compagnie de Kite ou d'Alexander lui emplissaient suffisamment l'esprit pour qu'il ne pense pas à son échec. Il devait meubler son cerveau par quelque chose de neuf, susceptible de faire palpiter son cœur comme auparavant. Un vrai amour, teinté d'une certaine maturité. Un amour qu'il vivait non plus simplement à travers lui, mais à travers l'autre également, était quelque chose de neuf pour lui.

Mary était là pour l'aider, mais la jeune fille refusait formellement ce rôle. Ou bien elle ne voulait absolument pas le montrer et dressait la peur du flic, la peur du père, comme une armure. C'était ce doute qui faisait chavirer Clément. Il tourna la tête vers le mur beige. Son pyjama lui collait littéralement à la peau, et cette humidité forcée, cette transpiration, commençait à l'énerver prodigieusement. Il se demanda s'il n'allait pas se lever, marcher silencieusement vers la salle de séjour et allumer la console de jeux. Mais il savait que ce mouvement tirerait les pans de son pyjama, qui collerait encore plus à sa peau. Et il ne voulait pas avoir à le supporter. Il ferma les yeux. Rideau sur le mur beige.

À 7 heures, le réveil sonna. Clément se leva, ouvrit en grand la fenêtre de sa chambre avec vue sur le cimetière de Fulham et prit, au radar, la direction de la salle de bains. En une heure, Clément avait eu le temps de se laver, de s'habiller, de déjeuner et de finir les derniers chapitres d'*American Psycho*, un excellent bouquin que lui avait conseillé un ami parisien. À 8 heures précises, il descendit donc ses trois étages à pied et se dirigea vers la voiture de Kite, qu'il avait garée tant bien que mal dans une petite rue perpendiculaire à Bronsart Road, là où se situait son appartement. Une fois monté dans la voiture, il enleva son gros blouson. Le temps n'était plus à la pluie, mais au froid. Clément tourna le bouton du chauffage à fond et alluma le ventilateur. Une traînée d'air glacial lui sauta au visage. Il fit une moue de circonstance et démarra tout en réglant l'inclinaison des aérateurs.

Il aurait pu conduire les yeux fermés de chez lui à l'immeuble du New Yard Bronsart Road — Victoria Street, sans arrêt, ni hésitation. À chaque fois que Kite était venu le chercher, il s'était amusé à retenir tous les noms de rue jusqu'au siège de la police.

Il arriva jusqu'au bâtiment du New Scotland Yard sans le moindre problème. Là, il présenta sa carte de stagiaire et accéda ainsi au parking. C'était bien plus pratique, même si Londres, en ce jour de Noël, ne connaissait pas son encombrement habituel. Clément entra dans le hall de l'immeuble et croisa l'agent Alexander.

— Alors, Clément ! Joyeux Noël ! Tu es de garde aujourd'hui !

— Joyeux Noël, Greg ! Ouais. Je vais avoir le bureau de Kite pour moi tout seul...

Le bureau de Kite était minuscule. Il avait dû installer lui-même une planche de bois et des tréteaux pour que son stagiaire puisse bénéficier d'un minimum d'espace de travail. Clément se rappelait ce jour mémorable où Kite avait failli perdre la moitié d'un doigt en descendant simplement les tréteaux de son coffre. Il s'était ensuite broyé un orteil en montant la grosse planche à son bureau et, pour finir, une écharde de cinq centimètres s'était enfilée malencontreusement dans son avant-bras alors qu'il disposait la planche sur les tréteaux.

Clément, dès le premier incident, avait, bien sûr, proposé son aide. Mais Kite, borné comme à son habitude, avait tenu à finir seul le travail. Ce petit rappel de cette grande page de l'histoire de Scotland Yard occupa les pensées du jeune stagiaire jusqu'à son arrivée au bureau de Kite, situé au second étage. Il se dévêtit et s'installa derrière le bureau, lorgnant avec malice la planche de bois.

Il n'avait plus qu'à attendre que Nancy vienne le déranger. C'était bien tout ce qu'il pouvait escompter de cette journée de Noël. Pour patienter, il ouvrit un manuel de droit pénal britannique tout poussiéreux qui traînait sur le bureau en désordre et commença sa lecture.

« Allô ? Allô ? Scotland Yard ? Pouvez-vous me passer un inspecteur, s'il vous plaît ? J'ai quelque chose de très important à dire [...]. Ah, vous êtes inspectrice... Oh, pardonnez-moi [...] Voilà, j'habite non loin de Lumley Street et en rentrant chez moi hier soir, j'ai aperçu une chose bien étrange qui se passait devant la bijouterie *My Kingdom for a jewel* : un homme semblait charger un corps sur la banquette arrière de sa voiture [...] Oui [...] Non, je ne sais pas, il faisait nuit noire [...] 11 h environ [...] Hier soir, je n'ai pas réagi sur le coup. Mais je viens de repasser à l'instant devant la bijouterie. Je vous appelle d'une cabine toute proche [...] Elle n'est pas fermée, cette boutique ! Je veux dire : pas de rideau de fer. Et j'ai jeté un coup d'œil à l'intérieur [...] Non, non, ne vous inquiétez pas, j'ai juste regardé à travers la vitrine. Quel bazar ! Des bijoux sens dessus dessous ! Des vitrines ouvertes, des... [...] Oui [...] Très bien [...] D'accord [...] Mon nom ? Euh... (Clic) »

Le sergent Nancy Kelling reposa le téléphone sur son socle en émettant un énorme soupir d'énervement. C'était à chaque fois la même chose lorsqu'elle était de permanence un jour férié. On lui renvoyait tous les appels reçus.

Un jour, folle de rage, elle s'en était plainte à son supérieur hiérarchique. Ce dernier, misogyne au possible, lui avait répondu qu'il était normal, pour une ancienne standardiste comme Nancy, d'assurer la réception des appels les jours où le standard ne fonctionnait pas. Sur quoi, Nancy avait argué du fait que son métier de standardiste était maintenant bien fini et que, comme tout sergent du Royaume, elle devait recevoir le même traitement. Son chef l'avait fixée avec de grands yeux étonnés pendant quelques instants, puis lui avait ordonné de se mettre au garde-à-vous et de déguerpir en vitesse.

Depuis cette charmante entrevue, Nancy continuait à recevoir les appels. Et à chaque sonnerie, elle décrochait, autant par dépit que par conscience professionnelle. La plupart du temps, elle devait écouter les élucubrations de pauvres gens qui profitaient de leur journée chômée pour s'amuser au téléphone. Cet appel-là ne semblait pas échapper à la règle. La personne ne laissait même pas son nom et, qui plus est, avait appelé d'une cabine publique. Nancy relut les informations notées sur son petit calepin. Elle n'avait vraiment pas envie de se déplacer aujourd'hui... Soudain, elle pensa à Clément, le jeune stagiaire de l'inspecteur Kite qui, justement, était de garde aujourd'hui. En voilà un boulot de stagiaire... Vérifier les dires d'un anonyme.

Elle prit la direction du bureau de Kite.

Clément vit entrer le sergent Kelling, une feuille à la main. Elle le salua d'un petit signe.

— *Bonsoir*, Clément.

— *Bonjour*, sergent Kelling, comment allez-vous ?

— Bien, bien... J'ai quelque chose pour toi.

Clément ferma le manuel de droit et se leva. Kelling lui tendit la feuille et entreprit de résumer l'appel téléphonique.

— Donc, je t'ai marqué le nom et l'adresse de la bijouterie. Tu jettes simplement un coup d'œil. Si vraiment ce que m'a raconté ce cinglé est vrai, que la bijouterie a été dévastée par exemple, alors tu m'appelles.

« Tu peux toujours compter là-dessus », pensa Clément en hochant la tête pour approuver les recommandations du sergent Kelling. Elle reprit :

— Et surtout ne touche à rien...

— OK, sergent. Est-ce que je peux demander à un agent de m'accompagner ? On ne sait jamais. Un uniforme peut souvent débloquer les situations...

— Bon... Demande à Alexander si tu veux. Il n'a rien à faire jusqu'à 3 heures.

Elle s'en alla enfin. Clément décrocha le téléphone et composa le numéro de la salle des agents. Il demanda l'agent Alexander.

— Greg ? Rebonjour, c'est Clément.

— Ouais...

— Es-tu disponible ? J'aurais besoin de tes services pour ce matin... Une visite de bijouterie.

— Hold-up ?

— On sait pas encore... Tu es partant ?

— OK, j'arrive.

Clément soupira d'aise. Il était content que son ami Greg l'accompagne.

L'agent Greg Alexander avait le même âge que lui, mais n'était encore que sergent. Clément avait tout de suite sympathisé avec l'un des rares jeunes que comptait le quartier général de Victoria Street. Mais ils ne se voyaient que très rarement, car Greg était souvent appelé pour la sortie des écoles ou la surveillance des stations de métro. Clément lui avait conseillé de tenter le concours d'inspecteur. Greg avait été réticent au début, « prestige de l'uniforme oblige ». Pour le convaincre, Clément lui avait fait un exposé sur le côté palpitant de son quotidien, et ce dernier s'était enfin laissé séduire. Il avait promis de se présenter à la prochaine session d'examens.

Depuis son arrivée au Yard, Clément n'avait pas passé une soirée avec Greg en dehors du boulot. L'agent prétextait toujours quelque chose d'imprévu. Kite avait expliqué à Clément que la mère du jeune homme était très possessive et l'empêchait de sortir le soir.

Clément et Alexander trouvèrent facilement une place dans Lumley Street. Ils se garèrent quasiment en face de la petite bijouterie *My*

Kingdom for a jewel. Elle ne payait pas de mine, cette boutique ! Deux petites vitrines séparées par une porte en bois peinte en blanc. Et une enseigne minuscule, à l'ancienne, accrochée comme un drapeau, ballottait dans le faible vent de la matinée. Clément s'approcha de la vitrine. Alexander, lui, resta près de la voiture et inspecta les alentours.

Lumley Street était une rue étroite. Pas bien passante, quoique très proche d'Oxford Street. Composée principalement de petits immeubles et de quelques maisons individuelles. La bijouterie en était le seul commerce.

Greg rejoignit son ami.

— Tu as un mouchoir ou quelque chose dans le genre ? demanda Clément.

— Tiens, répondit Greg en lui tendant un Kleenex propre, mais négligemment plié.

Clément posa le mouchoir sur la poignée et la poussa. La porte s'ouvrit sans un grincement, mais avec un bruit de clochette, qui poussa l'agent Alexander à porter la main sur son ventre, à la recherche d'un revolver qu'il n'avait pas. Clément lui fit un signe pour le rassurer et pénétra à l'intérieur.

Ils contemplèrent la scène tout en dégrafant leur blouson, car il faisait extrêmement chaud dans la boutique. Ils avaient immédiatement compris que le coup de téléphone reçu par Kelling n'était pas l'idée saugrenue d'un plaisantin. Il s'était bien passé quelque chose là.

— Regarde-moi ce bazar ! s'exclama Greg. Et dire que n'importe qui pouvait entrer et se servir !

Clément ne répondit pas, tournant autour des vitrines. Il remarqua que seule celle contenant les pierres précieuses avait été ouverte. Et que, malgré les nombreux bijoux par terre, elle n'était pas tout à fait vide. Alexander entreprit à son tour l'étude de la pièce. Il remarqua bientôt la présence d'un triangle en fer dont se servaient les percussionnistes. Il s'étonna de l'incongruité d'un tel objet à cet endroit.

— Les diamants sont tous par terre, il me semble, fit constater Clément. Regarde, Greg... dans la vitrine, il ne reste plus que les pierres précieuses de couleur...

— Oui, tu as probablement raison. Tu as remarqué le triangle posé contre la vitrine des montres ?

— Non, répondit Clément tout en se dirigeant vers la vitrine désignée.

— C'est fou... On appelle Kelling ou pas ?

— Pas.

— Pendant que tu continues à farfouiller ici, je vais aller faire un petit tour derrière la caisse.

— Hum, hum, marmonna Clément, à quatre pattes sur la moquette. Nom de Dieu ! Greg, viens voir !

L'agent accourut.

— Regarde ça, près du triangle. Regarde, on dirait un de ces petits montages électriques qu'on réalise au collège en Technologie.

Alexander examina à son tour le curieux appareil. Il s'agissait en fait de deux ampoules éteintes reliées à un boîtier contenant une pile. Clément déploya le mouchoir autour du boîtier et le prit dans sa main. Il contenait bien une pile. Il reposa l'objet et s'empara des deux ampoules avec le mouchoir. Elles étaient froides. Leurs filaments avaient l'air encore intacts.

— Attends ! dit Clément. Je vais essayer de faire marcher le truc.

Il sortit le mouchoir de sa poche et brancha les cosses partant des ampoules sur le boîtier. Les ampoules s'allumèrent faiblement à travers le mouchoir.

— Qu'est-ce que ça peut bien être, cette connerie ? lâcha le jeune inspecteur en décrochant les fils.

— Je ne sais absolument pas... Ça et le triangle...

Clément allait ranger le mouchoir dans sa poche lorsqu'il vit de minuscules taches à l'endroit où il avait tenu le culot des ampoules. Il rapprocha le mouchoir de ses yeux. De petites mouchetures rouges le maculaient. Il regarda alors le culot des ampoules. Même couleur. Et la moquette près de l'endroit où il avait trouvé ce curieux objet. Mêmes taches.

Il se leva et cligna des yeux. Du sang ? Alors le coup de téléphone disait vrai. Un meurtre ou un vol avait bien eu lieu ici et on avait transporté le blessé ou le cadavre hors de la bijouterie.

Clément rejoignit son collègue qui était en train de fouiller soigneusement le tiroir au-dessous de la caisse.

— La propriétaire de cette bijouterie s'appelle Lucy Chambers, commença Alexander. Elle a 24 ans. Elle est ici depuis bientôt six mois. C'est du moins ce que précise le contrat du bail. Il y a aussi un pistolet d'alarme dans le tiroir. Et apparemment, on n'a rien volé dans la caisse. Les chèques et les billets y sont encore.

— Il y a de minuscules traces rouges sur le culot des ampoules et sur la moquette, enchaîna Clément. Là-bas, entre les deux colliers au sol...

— Bordel...

— On va appeler Kite, proposa Clément.

— Mais Kelling va s'inquiéter et va se pointer.

— Kite la calmera par téléphone.

Greg approuva.

— Continue ta recherche dans le tiroir. Je vais dans la réserve, ajouta le jeune inspecteur. Elle doit bien avoir de la famille, cette Lucy Chambers.

C'est Alexander qui, au bout de quelques secondes, obtint le renseignement. Au dos d'une des cartes de visite traînant dans le tiroir, il lut : « *En cas d'urgence, prévenez SVP Mr Mrs Alan Chambers, Prospect Road, 94. Woodford. Tél. ... »*

Ils étaient en possession de ce que Kite leur demanderait certainement. Ils pouvaient l'appeler maintenant.

Ils avaient envie de mener l'investigation euxmêmes. Mais un enlèvement ! Il vaut mieux avoir l'aval de l'inspecteur.

Clément entra le premier dans la cabine téléphonique la plus proche, située au coin de la jonction Lumley Street/Oxford Street. Comme dans toutes les cabines de Londres, une multitude de numéros érotiques recouvraient presque entièrement les parois. Alexander y entra à son tour. Ils étaient serrés à l'intérieur, mais aucun des deux ne voulait manquer une bribe de la conversation avec Kite. C'est Clément qui décrocha le combiné et régla le volume de l'écouteur au maximum pour que son camarade puisse profiter de leur dialogue. Puis, il glissa une pièce de vingt pence dans l'appareil et composa le numéro.

— Tu le connais par cœur ? s'étonna Alexander.

— Ouais, mais j'ai de bonnes raisons pour ça...

Il adressa un joyeux sourire à son ami, visiblement perplexe.

8

Paul Kite s'était levé d'excellente humeur ce matin. Il avait embrassé sa femme dès son lever, ce qui était fort rare, et avait insisté pour descendre préparer le petit déjeuner. Il voulait le prendre au lit. Cela faisait longtemps qu'il ne l'avait pas fait. Mais autant profiter au maximum de cette matinée !

Toute la famille était en effet conviée au sacro-saint repas de Noël chez la mère de Michelle. Kite, qui n'aimait pas trop ce genre de déjeuner-retrouvailles, acceptait néanmoins de s'y rendre tous les ans, essayant par tous les moyens de repousser l'heure du départ.

L'année dernière, il avait caché les clefs de la voiture familiale dans le panier à linge. Idée qui s'était révélée bien fumeuse : non seulement sa femme possédait un double (ce que Kite ignorait) et l'heure du départ ne fut pas décalée d'une minute, mais, comble de l'histoire, Kite oublia de retirer les clefs du panier le soir en rentrant, ce qui leur coûta l'achat d'un nouveau lave-linge. Cette année, Kite avait décidé de ne rien tenter et de combattre vaillamment. Debout.

À midi pile, alors que Kite s'apprêtait à rejoindre Mary et sa femme dans la voiture, le téléphone se mit à sonner. Kite brandit le combiné devant la fenêtre à l'intention de sa petite famille en y rajoutant une « moue maison ». Au fond de lui, il exultait.

— Kite.

— Inspecteur ? Ici Clément.

— Où es-tu ?

— Sur Oxford Street. Inspecteur, je suis avec l'agent Alexander et nous avons un problème...

— C'est sérieux ?

— Je crois.

Le ton de la réponse ne laissa aucun doute à Kite.

— Je t'écoute.

Kite ressentit un léger picotement vers le bas du dos au fur et à mesure du résumé de son jeune stagiaire bilingue. C'était une sensation dont il n'arrivait jamais à définir la nature.

— Tiens ! C'est en effet bien étrange. Mais plus étrange encore, constata Kite, c'est que tu n'aies pas eu la présence d'esprit de donner l'ordre à Alexander de surveiller la bijouterie ! (Le ton était monté d'un cran.) Tu ne crois pas que le « libre accès » a assez duré ? C'est déjà a priori un miracle si rien n'a disparu...

Kite entendit la porte de la cabine téléphonique claquer. Alexander devait avoir regagné les lieux. Il continua, en baissant le ton :

— Reprenons, tu as le nom du ou de la propriétaire ?

Kite entendit un grognement d'approbation.

— Son adresse ?

Le même grognement.

— Tu as appelé le labo pour les traces ?

— C'est-à-dire que j'attendais votre autorisation, répondit Clément, seul survivant de l'en-gueulade de Kite. En fait, nous avions pour consigne de contacter Kelling à la moindre complication...

Kite réprima un juron.

— Qu'elle reste le cul collé sur sa chaise ! Non, mais des fois ! (Il prit l'intonation caracté-ristique de Nancy Kelling.) Vous comprenez, Paul, on ne me confie jamais rien de bien important... Alors si un jour, j'ai l'occasion de vous couper amicalement l'herbe sous le pied, je n'hésiterai pas... (Il reprit sa voix normale.) Oh, la garce ! Faire ça à mon stagiaire par-des-sus le marché ! Qu'elle se mette une bonne fois pour toutes dans la tête qu'*elle* dépend de moi et non pas l'inverse.

— Et nous ? questionna Clément.

— Vous continuez... Visite au domicile de la bijoutière. Entretien avec elle. Voir si elle est au courant. Voir déjà si elle est chez elle. Et puis retour au New Yard. J'essaierai d'être là-bas en fin d'après-midi, ça me permettra d'échapper un tant soit peu au calvaire du jour.

— Et pour le labo ?

— Je m'en occupe. Je téléphone de chez moi. Pas de problème. En attendant, n'oubliez pas de bouffer quelque chose ! (Il haussa le ton une nouvelle fois pour bien se faire comprendre.) Ce n'est pas parce que l'on roule dans une voiture de police avec sirène et gyrophare qu'il faut entièrement se prendre pour un de ces flics débiles des séries télévisées américaines qui ne dorment, ni ne mangent pendant des jours entiers... À bon entendeur, salut.

— Message reçu, inspecteur. À ce soir.

Kite raccrocha aussi sec.

Si Clément était un véritable adorateur de la civilisation anglaise, il était aussi le premier à admettre que les Anglais possédaient un sens culinaire bien étrange. C'est pourquoi il avait décidé d'adopter la tactique McDonald's tous les midis de la semaine. Pendant que Kite déjeunait avec ses sandwiches au concombre ou à la mayonnaise sucrée, il préférait s'empiffrer de hamburgers bien huileux et dégoulinants de sauce. Le jour de Noël n'échappait pas à la règle. Et c'est d'un pas décidé que Clément et Alexander se dirigèrent vers les caisses du McDonald's de Marble Arch. L'attente ne fut pas longue.

— Tu penses que nous allons trouver la bijoutière chez elle, tout à l'heure ? demanda Clément qui se battait comme un beau diable pour ouvrir la boîte contenant son troisième hamburger.

— Je ne sais pas vraiment... Mais je suis étonné que Kite te confie l'affaire pour aujourd'hui. C'est une sacrée marque de confiance venant de lui. On le dit si solitaire... Certains l'appellent même *Clint* dans l'immeuble...

Une feuille de salade tomba sur le sweat-shirt de Clément. Il la ramassa et la replaça à l'intérieur du sandwich. C'était bien la première fois que Clément entendait parler de ce surnom. Kite n'avait pourtant pas grand-chose à voir avec l'inspecteur Harry. À moins qu'il s'agisse d'une odieuse référence à la terrible affaire de juin 87...

— Ce qui me paraît le plus étrange dans tout ça, reprit Clément, c'est le petit appareil avec

les deux ampoules... C'est complètement fou...
Franchement...

— Hum.

— T'es pas d'accord ?

— Hum.

Greg était déjà en train de savourer son milk-shake.

— Si Kite te voyait, mon vieux... Avec cette traînée de sauce sur ta barbe de trois jours...

— Quatre jours. Et puis je ne risque pas de croiser Kite ici ! Il est bien trop attaché à ses *fish and chips* emballés dans un bon vieux papier journal...

Il s'essuyait maintenant les mains tout en regardant son ami Greg aspirant avec sa paille les dernières gouttes de son milk-shake. C'était amusant de voir ce jeune homme engoncé dans un uniforme strict déjeunant au McDonald's.

— C'est vrai ce que raconte Kite au Yard à ton sujet ?

Alexander avait lâché cette phrase en fixant la paille sortant du gobelet.

— À mon sujet ? s'étonna Clément, vivement interloqué.

— Oui... Il raconte à qui veut bien l'entendre que tu as joué dans des pubs en France.

Clément voyait sur quel terrain Greg voulait l'entraîner.

— J'avais 13 ans...

— Il paraît qu'il y en a une où tu jouais les James Bond pour une marque de jouets.

— Kite raconte ça ?

Clément avait confié ses diverses expériences de comédien à Kite, mais lui avait fait jurer de ne rien répéter. Néanmoins, il sembla éprouver un sentiment de fierté plus fort encore que son malaise habituel inhérent à ce sujet. Il aimait se

58

dire que les autres faisaient attention à lui et Paul Kite plus qu'un autre.

— Faut dire que tu as le physique ! reprit Greg.

Alexander aurait voulu avoir l'assurance de son ami français, sa contenance et cette sorte d'aura qui faisait converger bon nombre de regards sur lui. Sa haute taille et sa carrure digne d'un rugbyman n'empêchaient pas Clément de conserver un charme adolescent, dont son visage surmonté d'une tignasse blonde souvent décoiffée parachevait la représentation. Les traits fins de sa figure faisaient habilement ressortir deux petits yeux marron très clair qui, d'un simple plissement de la paupière, passaient du rire à la mélancolie. Des yeux d'acteur qui avaient toujours quelque chose à exprimer.

— Un physique ! Mais je n'étais pas mannequin, sembla s'offusquer Clément. J'étais comédien ! Au collège, je devais jouer dans une petite pièce de théâtre qu'on avait travaillée avec un metteur en scène venu spécialement pour ça. Je m'étais engueulé avec lui car je n'étais pas d'accord sur ce qu'il voulait me faire jouer. D'abord, j'ai été puni et privé de représentation, mais il s'est vite lassé de mon entêtement et m'a donné carte blanche en me reléguant à la toute fin du spectacle. J'ai fait un truc délirant avec de la musique, des danses et tout et tout, alors que je devais simplement réciter un monologue ! Et toute la salle a applaudi comme jamais... Le metteur en scène aussi, en coulisse... Ça lui avait bien plu ! Plus tard, il m'accompagnait pour les castings...

Greg semblait étonné.

— Tu veux dire que tu avais abandonné tes études pour ne faire que ça ?

— Plus ou moins... Disons moins que plus, en fait. Ça me prenait beaucoup de temps tout ça, alors mes parents ont voulu que j'assure quand même le minimum. C'était étrange, ils étaient à la fois contents de ma réussite — papa est comédien amateur —, et à la fois inquiets. Au lycée, je faisais partie d'un club en plus des cours et des castings que je tentais. Pendant mes années de fac, je suis resté dans cette petite troupe, j'étais l'aîné de la bande.

— Mais pourquoi alors tu n'as pas continué dans cette voie ? Pourquoi es-tu entré dans la police ?

Clément fit une grimace et commença à empiler les emballages vides sur le plateau. C'était étrange, mais depuis son retour de Paris, depuis qu'il avait vu Sébastien, son ami qui tentait de faire du théâtre son gagne-pain, il sentait que toutes les questions dont il s'était forcé à refouler les réponses resurgissaient de plus belle. Si en plus Alexander et Kite se mettaient à la tâche !

— J'ai laissé tomber pour plusieurs raisons... Tu sais, c'est dur pour moi d'en parler. Je suis même étonné d'avoir réussi à te raconter tout ça en anglais ! (Il se donna un répit.) Remarque bien, c'est peut-être ainsi que j'y suis arrivé...

Greg posa une main sous son menton et lui sourit.

— Mais tu es content de travailler dans la police ?

— Ouais... C'est toujours mieux que de rester toute la journée assis derrière un bureau. Après ma licence, je me suis dit que cette voie serait la plus dépaysante...

Alexander n'avait pas trouvé le ton de la réponse très convaincant. Décidément, Kite ne pouvait que s'entendre avec son jeune acolyte. Ils semblaient tous les deux si nostalgiques de leur passé... L'agent se demanda si l'assurance et l'humour de Clément étaient bien réels ou s'il s'en servait comme d'une façade pour cacher aux autres et à lui-même un profond vague à l'âme. Mais, même ainsi, Greg aurait aimé ressembler à son ami. Clément était de ces personnages dont on ne cernera jamais complètement la personnalité. Lui était trop basique ou tout du moins s'estimait ainsi.

Le jeune inspecteur stagiaire jeta un coup d'œil à sa montre. Il était déjà 1 heure moins le quart.

Ils mirent trois quarts d'heure pour atteindre Prospect Lane, 94, le lieu de résidence de Lucy Chambers et de ses parents. Ils avaient pris la direction de Stratford, remontant ensuite vers le nord pour atteindre Woodford Green. Ils stoppèrent exactement devant le numéro 94, une petite maison toute en briques, avec sur le devant un jardinet composé principalement d'une pelouse mal entretenue et de quelques fleurs plus en attente de la faucheuse que du printemps. Une Vauxhall grise stationnait devant le portail de l'entrée. La maison ne semblait pas avoir de garage.

Clément sortit sa grande carcasse de la voiture et jeta un coup d'œil sur les fenêtres de la maison. Les volets n'étaient pas fermés. Mais aucun signe d'une présence quelconque. Clément et son compère attendirent encore trois bonnes minutes pour être fixés mais, ne notant aucune variation, ils décidèrent de forcer le sort et de sonner au portail. Une, deux, trois, quatre, cinq, six, sept, huit, neuf... Clément s'imaginait déjà en train d'interroger les voisins... treize, quatorze, quinze... Un bruit de porte. Et la silhouette d'un homme sortant sur le perron.

— C'est pour quoi ?

L'homme avait un physique en accord avec sa voix. Brut de décoffrage.

— Nous sommes les adjoints de l'inspecteur Kite de Scotland Yard..., déclara Clément.

Il brandit sa carte en direction de l'homme. Alexander fit de même avec son insigne.

— Nous aimerions parler à miss Lucy Chambers. C'est au sujet de sa bijouterie...

— Ma fille n'est pas là... Allez-vous-en maintenant ou j'appelle les flics.

— Je crois qu'il y a erreur, Mr Chambers. Nous sommes de la police.

— Foutez-moi le camp !

Le silence retomba. À ce moment, Clément et Greg entendirent comme des sanglots filtrant à travers la porte. Les pleurs redoublèrent. Clément réussit à saisir quelques mots entre deux sanglots :

— À quoi bon, Damon... À quoi bon !

L'homme consentit enfin à ouvrir la porte en grand.

À l'intérieur, Clément et Greg virent, assise sur un canapé, une petite femme toute frêle secouée par de violents spasmes. Elle serrait dans la main un petit mouchoir blanc. Cette femme, qui devait être la mère de Lucy, était habillée très simplement, un chemisier blanc brodé sortant de son tailleur rouge complètement froissé.

Les parents de Lucy avaient tous deux de gros cernes sous les yeux. La nuit avait dû être courte. Il était arrivé malheur à Lucy Chambers. C'était bien la seule chose dont Clément et

Alexander étaient convaincus lorsqu'ils pénétrè-
rent à la suite de Mr Chambers dans le hall de
la petite maison. Il était décoré avec un manque
évident de goût. À droite, on pouvait apercevoir
l'escalier menant à l'étage et au rez-de-chaussée, plusieurs portes.

— Je suis désolé pour tout à l'heure, s'excusa
l'homme. Mais nous sommes à bout de nerfs
depuis hier soir.

Greg pensa immédiatement à l'hypothèse du
kidnapping. On devait avoir enlevé Lucy à la
bijouterie et on demandait maintenant aux
parents de payer. Mais pourquoi ? Ces gens ne
roulaient visiblement pas sur l'or... Et il y avait
beaucoup de fric dans la boutique...

— Ce n'est rien, Mr Chambers, le rassura Clément. Permettez-moi de me présenter : je suis
l'inspecteur stagiaire Clément Bellanger et voici
l'agent Greg Alexander du New Scotland Yard.

Les parents de Lucy restèrent parfaitement
immobiles.

— Si nous venons vous importuner en ce jour
de Noël, c'est pour la simple et bonne raison
que nous désirons parler à votre fille. Ce matin,
on a trouvé sa bijouterie saccagée. Et nous
sommes venus pour la prévenir. À moins qu'elle
ne le soit déjà, bien entendu...

La mère de Lucy se blottit un peu plus dans
les bras de son mari.

— Lucy est ici.

— Pouvons-nous la voir ?

— Elle est morte.

La réponse claqua comme un coup de fouet.
Clément vit les lèvres de l'homme trembler de
plus en plus. Les muscles de ses joues et de son
cou se contractaient. Il était au bord des larmes.
Sa femme les laissait déjà couler.

— Venez, suivez-moi. (Il chuchota à l'adresse de sa femme :) Reste là, ma chérie. Tout va bien se passer. Tout ça va bientôt finir.

Cette scène avait vraiment quelque chose de difficilement supportable. À 22 ans, est-on suffisamment blindé pour accueillir en soi la détresse des gens ? Peut-on, ne serait-ce que trouver les mots qu'il faut pour rassurer en de pareils moments ? Clément et Greg s'en sentaient bien incapables. Ils contenaient leur émotion. C'est le meilleur moyen pour garder une distance souvent nécessaire — cruel dilemme de jeune flic.

Ils montèrent doucement l'escalier moquetté qui menait à l'étage. Conduits par Mr Chambers, ils longèrent le petit couloir. Le père de Lucy stoppa net devant une porte sur laquelle était fixée une petite plaque en porcelaine représentant un chat jouant avec une balle accrochée entre ses pieds. « Lucy » était inscrit au-dessus du chat. Le père passa la main sur l'inscription et la descendit vers la poignée.

De la porte entrouverte, une lumière d'église filtrait et éclairait le sombre couloir. Clément et Alexander entrèrent. Lucy Chambers était étendue sur son lit, vêtue d'une petite jupe et d'un pull assorti. Elle avait les mains croisées au niveau du nombril. De nombreux cierges disposés sur la table de nuit et sur le bureau répandaient leur lumière dans toute la pièce. Ils virent les yeux fermés de Lucy et ses paupières abîmées toutes plates. Ils remarquèrent ensuite sur la table de nuit deux globes oculaires posés côte à côte. Clément et Alexander réprimèrent un haut-le-cœur.

— Je n'ai pas pu les jeter, répétait à voix

basse Mr Chambers en désignant timidement la table de nuit. Je n'ai pas pu les jeter...

La première chose que fit Clément fut de prévenir la police locale. Il leur expliqua calmement la situation. L'inspecteur du coin décida de venir superviser l'affaire sur-le-champ. Ils se mirent d'accord pour que la police locale se charge de l'enlèvement du corps et le mette le plus tôt possible à la disposition de la brigade criminelle, en prenant contact avec l'inspecteur Kite. Alexander, qui tardait à retrouver ses esprits, restait silencieux, visiblement ému. Ils rejoignirent ensuite le père de Lucy Chambers dans la salle de séjour pour écouter attentivement son témoignage.

— Notre fille devait venir réveillonner avec nous hier soir après la fermeture de sa petite bijouterie...

La pauvre mère sanglotait encore et toujours. Elle tentait de faire le moins de bruit possible en se cachant la tête dans un coussin.

— Elle avait décidé de rester ouverte plus tard hier soir en raison des fêtes. Elle devait fermer vers 7 heures, je crois bien. Et puisqu'il faut un peu plus d'une demi-heure pour faire le trajet de Bond Street, nous nous attendions à ce qu'elle revienne pour 8 heures grand maximum. Et comme elle n'arrivait pas, nous avons essayé de téléphoner à la bijouterie. Mais personne n'a répondu. Ça sonnait dans le vide...

— Vous n'avez pas pensé à appeler ses voisins ?

C'était la première intervention de l'agent Alexander.

— C'est que ça faisait pas longtemps que Lucy (sa voix vibra subitement) était installée.

Et elle n'avait pas encore de relations avec le voisinage. Donc je me suis dit que j'irais voir ce qui pouvait bien se passer. J'ai pris ma voiture et j'ai fait le chemin d'ici à la station de métro de Woodford, mais elle n'était pas sur la route. Alors, j'ai été jusqu'à Londres et jusqu'à sa boutique...

Clément se frotta les yeux doucement pour ne pas abîmer ses lentilles de contact. L'homme semblait à bout de forces.

— J'ai pu garer ma voiture juste en face de la vitrine et déjà je me suis dit que quelque chose tournait mal. Le rideau de fer n'était pas descendu alors qu'il était tard. Et puis je suis entré dans la bijouterie...

Il marqua une longue pause. Ses yeux devenaient de plus en plus rouges. La mère de Lucy se boucha les oreilles, la tête encore figée dans le coussin.

— J'ai d'abord allumé car il faisait tout noir à l'intérieur. Lucy était étendue par terre. Il y avait plein de bijoux autour d'elle. Elle avait des traces rouges sur le cou. Mais le plus horrible, c'était qu'elle n'avait plus d'yeux. On les lui avait enlevés. Et à la place... à la place...

La mère de Lucy se mit à pousser de grands cris aigus. Clément et Greg écoutaient, incrédules, le récit de Mr Chambers. Ils n'avaient plus aucune notion du temps ni de l'espace.

— À la place de ses yeux, poursuivit le père, on avait mis des ampoules allumées. Elle avait comme deux lumières à la place des yeux. C'était terrible. J'ai couru vers elle et je l'ai secouée tant que j'ai pu. Les ampoules ont glissé le long de ses tempes et sont tombées sur la moquette. Et puis il y a ce triangle en fer qui est tombé aussi. Alors j'ai compris qu'elle était morte, ma Lucy. J'ai pas bien réfléchi sur l'instant, mais je voulais pas que l'on trouve son corps comme ça et qu'on tourne autour et qu'on le touche. J'ai chargé ma fille dans la voiture et l'ai ramenée jusqu'ici. Pendant le trajet, quand je regardais sur la banquette arrière et que je voyais Lucy allongée là, son visage caché par un appui-tête, je me disais qu'elle s'était juste endormie...

Un reniflement et un bruit de déglutition.

— Ma femme et moi, on l'a installée dans ce qui était toujours sa chambre et on l'a veillée jusqu'à ce midi. Mais on allait appeler la police. Soyez-en sûrs... On allait le faire...

— Je n'en doute pas, répondit Clément.

L'inspecteur de la police locale, un certain Owen, accompagné d'un médecin, arriva cinq minutes après la fin du pénible récit de Mr Chambers. Clément et Alexander prirent aussitôt congé des deux époux en leur présentant leurs sincères condoléances. Puis Clément informa l'inspecteur que Kite prendrait rapidement contact avec lui. Il n'avait en fait qu'une envie : partager ce terrible moment avec l'inspecteur Kite. Pour tenter de comprendre. D'appréhender la tragédie.

Ce ne serait qu'après une telle discussion qu'il pourrait évacuer tout le stress et toute la peine emmagasinés durant cette heure. Clément et Greg n'échangèrent pas un mot pendant le trajet du retour.

10

L'homme ouvrit en grand la fenêtre de son immense chambre bleue. Un vent glacial pénétra aussitôt dans la pièce et fouetta son torse nu. Comme un défi, il resta de longues minutes dans la même position. Les quelques poils de son torse se hérissèrent peu à peu et sa peau, sur les bras et sur son cou, laissa apparaître de minuscules granulés. L'homme avait très froid. Mais il garda les dents serrées. Encore quelques instants.

Puis il se retira de l'embrasure de la fenêtre et vint ramasser sa robe de chambre qui traînait négligemment par terre. L'homme l'enfila calmement et cette protection le remplit d'un plaisir nouveau. Il se dirigea vers la porte de sa chambre et éteignit sur son passage le rétroprojecteur ultramoderne qu'il s'était fait installer il y a peu. L'image disparut immédiatement de l'immense écran situé sur le mur opposé à son lit. L'homme était fier de son système. Il se passait tous les soirs des cassettes vidéo depuis cette acquisition. Du moins presque tous les soirs... Les soirs où il ne tuait pas.

L'horloge de la cuisine lui indiqua l'heure : il était bientôt midi. Midi, le jour de Noël, tradition oblige, c'était le repas de fête ! Mais l'homme n'avait pas envie de faire la fête de cette façon. Il n'aimait pas manger. Certes, il devait obligatoirement se nourrir, mais n'éprouvait aucun plaisir ni dans l'ingestion ni dans l'excrétion. Lui, ce qu'il lui fallait, c'était sentir le parfum d'une femme en écoutant une douce mélodie... et puis la serrer fort dans ses mains... entendre sa respiration s'accélérer... se ralentir...

L'homme sourit, en pensant qu'il était un grand romantique ! Il n'était pas de ces salauds qui violent atrocement leurs victimes après leur avoir coupé le bout des seins. Ses crimes ne répondaient pas à de simples pulsions sexuelles. Ils étaient savamment organisés, planifiés et préparés dans les moindres détails. S'enchaînant avec une logique implacable. L'homme se félicita d'être aussi intelligent. Cela ne devait pas être donné à tout le monde ! Et certainement pas à ces idiots du Yard qui n'étaient pas près de retrouver sa trace. Ça, l'homme en était sûr et certain. Il avait pris ses précautions.

Il alluma le petit récepteur FM de la cuisine et écouta attentivement le bulletin des informations régionales de Londres et sa banlieue. On ne parlait même pas du meurtre de la bijoutière. Pas un mot sur cette pauvre Lucy. Il remua la tête plusieurs fois et soupira longuement. Qu'allait-il bien pouvoir faire pour occuper cette journée de repos ? Se promener peut-être ? Marcher lui ferait le plus grand bien. Il décida donc de partir vers 3 heures de l'après-midi.

En attendant, il devait ranger un peu sa chambre et nettoyer ses vêtements de la veille. Et puis, il s'occuperait de la petite pièce au fond de la cave. D'ailleurs, il n'avait encore rien entendu venant de là ce matin. Cela lui sembla bien étrange. Mais, peu importe. Il lui fallait faire son devoir. Comme un rituel, il disposa sur le plateau la tranche de cheddar habituelle et le verre d'eau. Mais quelque chose le tourmentait. C'était Noël aujourd'hui et il se sentait obligé de marquer le coup, de faire un petit geste. Grand seigneur, il retourna vers le frigo et s'empara d'une tranche de bacon crue qu'il déposa près du verre d'eau. Il se dirigea ensuite vers l'escalier de la cave, s'assurant bien que les pans de sa robe de chambre ne laissaient pas à découvert un seul centimètre carré de sa peau.

Un silence religieux planait sur la demeure tout entière. Il n'avait croisé personne ce matin, ni dans la cuisine ni même à l'étage. Ses hôtes devaient être encore enfouis sous leurs draps. Après une nuit entière de création, c'était bien légitime. Au tout début, l'homme dormait peu lui aussi, les regardant travailler, les yeux écarquillés de bonheur, le souffle court... Mais depuis le début de son hommage avec ces femmes, ils n'osaient plus le déranger la nuit. Ils avaient compris. Du reste, c'était tant mieux. L'homme avait besoin de calme, de sommeil, et de silence.

Au moment où il déposa son pied droit sur la première marche, il entendit enfin des bruits sourds venant de la pièce. Comme si l'on tapait sur ses épaisses parois. Il éprouva un soulagement légitime. Tout était redevenu normal. Dieu merci, pas de contrariété cette semaine... Dans quelques minutes, ils viendraient prendre leur breakfast, voilà tout... Et la vie continuerait... En posant son deuxième pied, il se mit à chantonner un de ses airs favoris.

11

Il était 6 heures moins le quart quand Clément, qui guettait Kite par la fenêtre de son bureau, le vit sortir du *cab*, devant la façade du

New Scotland Yard. Cela faisait maintenant plus d'une heure et demie que Clément et Alexander s'étaient séparés. Greg avait dû retourner à ses occupations habituelles. Personne n'était venu déranger le jeune inspecteur, sauf bien sûr le sergent Kelling, qui avait demandé le récit détaillé de sa journée. Si Clément n'avait aucune envie de le lui raconter, il se sentit obligé devant l'insistance du sergent. Il avait ensuite continué la lecture du manuel de droit, mais n'arrivait vraiment pas à se concentrer. Il ne parvenait pas à enlever de son esprit l'image du cadavre énucléé de la jeune fille allongé sur son lit. Et ses paupières abîmées. Il entendait toujours la lancinante mélodie des sanglots parentaux, qui résonnait dans sa tête depuis un peu plus de deux heures. Et pourtant, il devait en reparler. Alexander n'avait pas voulu. Il raconterait à Kite l'affaire dans ses moindres détails. Sans rien omettre. Aussi paradoxal que Clément pût le penser, c'était pourtant la seule manière d'évacuer ces images : les partager avec le sage inspecteur Kite et son expérience en la matière. Lui qui se plaignait encore ce matin d'une certaine routine dans son travail...

La porte s'ouvrit brusquement. Kite fit son entrée dans le bureau. En fan inconditionnel de Sean Connery, il jeta un chapeau imaginaire sur un portemanteau qui ne l'était pas moins et gratifia Clément, en prenant un monstrueux accent écossais, d'un « Good Evening, Miss Moneypenny ». Même dans les moments importants, Kite se devait à son public. Il arracha difficilement un sourire à Clément. Il fronça alors les sourcils et, reprenant son véritable accent de Liverpool, enchaîna :

— Eh ben ! Ça n'a pas l'air d'être la grande forme !

— C'est le moins que l'on puisse dire..., répondit Clément.

— Des complications ? demanda Kite tout en prenant place derrière son bureau à la place que Clément venait de libérer.

— Oh, non... Trois fois rien.

— Bon, raconte-moi tout depuis le début... Du moins, depuis ton départ de la bijouterie ce matin.

Clément lui fit un récit de ses découvertes en regrettant que Greg ne soit pas présent pour compléter ses lacunes. Il lui parla donc de la visite des parents Chambers à Woodford, des pleurs de la mère, des sanglots du père. Il s'attarda un peu plus longuement sur la découverte du corps de Lucy. Et de son état. Et de ses yeux. Il pensait aux siens, bien présents, qui tournaient en ce moment dans ses orbites. Il portait la main sous sa paupière inférieure et sentait son squelette. Clément termina le récit en parlant de leur triste retour vers Londres. Kite n'interrompit pas une seule fois son adjoint. Il écoutait, les yeux mi-clos et les mains posées à plat sur le bureau.

— Je vais en premier lieu appeler l'inspecteur Owen de Woodford... Puis, on reparlera de tout ça après. Si tu le veux, bien entendu... (Clément approuva d'un signe de tête.) De toute façon, il faut absolument que nous parlions de ce meurtre et de celui de miss Stout. Ils se ressemblent curieusement et on peut sans doute trouver quelques similitudes...

Le jeune Français fronça les sourcils. Kite reprit, évasif :

— Nous en reparlerons bien assez tôt. En attendant, il faut que j'appelle l'inspecteur de garde à Woodford. Tu as son numéro ?

Clément hocha la tête et le dicta à l'inspecteur.

— Inspecteur Owen, j'écoute.

Kite, qui avait posé le combiné sur son bureau en attendant la communication, s'empressa de saisir le téléphone.

— Bonsoir, inspecteur... Je suis l'inspecteur Kite de la brigade criminelle... New Scotland Yard.

— Bonsoir, inspecteur.

Le ton était fatigué.

— Je crois que nous avons une affaire en commun, reprit Kite. Vous avez été en contact avec mon jeune adjoint et un agent du Yard tout à l'heure, car je m'étais accordé ce jour de repos, mais devant l'urgence de la situation, j'ai préféré revenir au bureau ce soir.

— Et vous avez fort bien fait. Car il faut absolument que nous prenions une décision pour le cadavre de cette jeune femme. Nous l'avons déposé pour le moment à l'Holly House Hospital de Woodford Wells, mais il ne pourra pas y rester indéfiniment. Et si vous désirez pratiquer une autopsie...

— Bien entendu, coupa Kite. Mais cette décision ne peut pas me revenir seul. Il faut attendre demain qu'un de mes supérieurs me donne son aval...

L'inspecteur Owen grogna.

— Demain, c'est bien le grand maximum. Vous savez, inspecteur, les parents de cette

73

Lucy Chambers ont été extrêmement choqués par ce qui vient de leur arriver. Et le psy que nous leur avons envoyé nous a bien fait comprendre que plus vite le corps leur serait rendu, plus vite ils sortiraient de ce cauchemar.

« Si tant est que l'on puisse en sortir », pensa Kite.

— Je vous comprends parfaitement, inspecteur, et je désire ardemment que l'on épargne aux parents Chambers tous les tracas possibles, mais si nous voulons faire avancer l'enquête, il faut pratiquer cette autopsie.

— Bien sûr... Bien sûr... Si je vous dis cela, ce n'est évidemment pas pour vous jeter la pierre, mais parce que les parents ont vraiment été secoués par tout ça. Tout à l'heure, le psy a cru bien faire en disant aux parents que nous allions peut-être pratiquer une autopsie. Il voulait créer un « électrochoc », a-t-il dit. Eh bien, les parents ont très mal réagi, vous vous en doutez...

Il marqua une pause. Clément en profita pour approcher l'oreille encore un peu plus près du haut-parleur. Owen continua :

— Le père a carrément menacé le psychologue de ses poings en lui disant qu'il ne tenait pas à ce que sa fille se fasse charcuter. Quant à la mère, elle a prétexté un besoin pressant pour se rendre dans la salle de bains et avaler plus de la moitié d'un tube de somnifères...

Clément jura à voix basse. Kite le fit plus bruyamment.

— Comme vous dites, lui répondit l'inspecteur Owen. Mais fort heureusement ses jours ne sont pas en danger. Nous l'avons tout de suite transférée à l'Holly House Hospital, elle aussi, et son mari est resté pour la veiller cette nuit.

Après un court blanc, Kite reprit :

— Vous transmettrez de ma part, et de celle de mon stagiaire, un prompt rétablissement à cette dame. Nous nous recontacterons demain pour la suite à donner à cette affaire.

— Le plus tôt possible, inspecteur... N'oubliez pas.

-— Ne vous en faites pas. À demain, inspecteur Owen.

— À demain, inspecteur Kite.

Ils raccrochèrent presque simultanément.

Il était bientôt 6 heures et demie. Kite et Clément décidèrent de sortir du bureau et de se rendre dans un endroit plus convivial et surtout moins étroit pour évoquer le sujet de ces deux meurtres. Pas la peine d'attendre au bureau : Kite ne recevrait pas les conclusions du labo aujourd'hui. D'abord parce que le labo travaille en effectif réduit le 25 décembre ; ensuite parce qu'il n'était pas censé être présent au Yard ce soir ; et enfin parce que Nancy Kelling se ferait un plaisir de les garder pour elle jusqu'à ce que Kite les lui demande. Clément proposa donc de se rendre dans le West End, le quartier de Londres où se trouvaient bon nombre de théâtres, de cinémas et de pubs. Kite approuva cette idée.

— Allons-y à pied ! proposa Clément. Ce n'est vraiment pas loin de là.

Kite lui tapa amicalement sur l'épaule.

— Non, je dois reprendre la voiture pour rentrer ce soir à Finchley. Donc autant que je la prenne tout de suite.

Kite gara sa voiture à cheval sur un trottoir marqué des deux bandes jaunes signifiant « Interdiction absolue de stationner ». Mais c'était

une des seules places disponibles à ce momen'.
de la soirée près de Leicester Square. La nuit
était bien noire et un vent horriblement froid
soufflait sur Londres. Kite voulait trouver un
pub relativement accueillant avec surtout de
bons fauteuils et naturellement de la Guiness,
sa bière irlandaise préférée. Et ils trouvèrent
justement un spécimen du pub recherché juste
en face du plus grand cinéma londonien *Odeon
Leicester Sq.* Clément jeta rapidement un coup
d'œil aux films programmés. *The Full Monty*
passait en ce moment, et si ce soir le cinéma
était la meilleure façon d'éclipser les images de
cette journée et celle de Mary, seule dans sa
chambre ?

Paul Kite et Clément étaient tous deux assis
autour d'une table, dans un coin relativement
sombre de l'immense salle du pub. C'est Kite en
personne qui alla chercher les bières. De retour,
il posa les deux pintes face à lui, puis les répartit
avec le sourire en prenant bien soin de garder
la plus remplie pour lui.

— Ça peut te sembler bizarre que je t'em-
mène dans un pub pour parler de cette affaire...

Son jeune stagiaire fixa Kite droit dans les
yeux.

— Mais ce soir, dis-toi bien que cette discussion est informelle. Aucune décision n'a été
prise concernant le meurtre d'hier soir. Et s'il
est vrai que j'ai été désigné pour enquêter sur le
meurtre de miss Stout dans la chapelle, il est
peu probable que je sois aussi chargé des suites
du meurtre de la bijouterie...

— À moins que nous puissions établir un lien
entre les deux, déclara Clément d'une voix sûre.
Car deux meurtres aussi étranges en trois jours,

ça reste tout de même assez inhabituel, même pour une ville comme Londres...

Kite reposa sa bière et essuya d'un revers de main la mousse laissée sur ses lèvres.

— Je suis assez d'accord avec toi, Clément, répondit-il. Mais si vraiment ces deux meurtres ont un rapport et que nous avons affaire à des meurtres, disons « en série », les grands pontes du Yard prendront probablement la responsabilité de l'enquête... Procédons méthodiquement, reprit Kite après une courte pause. Tentons d'établir une liste des similitudes possibles entre les deux meurtres. Je vois au moins trois similitudes.

— Combien ? s'étonna Clément.

— Trois. Allez... Un peu de perspicacité... Je vais aller me payer une autre Guiness.

Le verre de Kite était déjà vide. Clément réfléchit en attendant le retour de Kite, puis commença :

— D'abord, on peut dire sans trop se mouiller que les deux meurtres ont été suivis d'une sacrée mise en scène de la part du tueur. La terre sur le cadavre de miss Stout, les ampoules dans les... yeux de Lucy Chambers.

— Tu vas un peu vite en besogne, lui reprocha Kite. On ne sait pas encore si les mises en scène ont suivi ou précédé les meurtres...

— Vous voulez dire qu'on aurait pu énucléer Lucy avant même de la tuer ?

— Et pourquoi pas ? Pour ça, il faudra attendre le rapport du légiste. Mais admettons donc : premier élément, les mises en scène macabres. Soit la terre et les ampoules... Et puis ?

Clément réfléchit à nouveau. Le niveau de sa

bière n'était quasiment pas descendu depuis le début de la discussion. Kite le mit sur la voie :

— Des cordes de guitare et un triangle de percussionniste par exemple ?

Clément sursauta.

— Des instruments de musique. Ou une partie de l'un d'eux...

— Bravo ! Il ne te reste plus qu'à trouver le dernier lien possible... Cherche par rapport aux victimes...

— Des femmes..., fit Clément. D'âges bien différents... Peut-être leur appartenance à un même groupe... ou bien quelque chose sur leur naissance, leurs études...

— Et tu connais tout ça, toi ? le gronda Kite.

— Non, mais leur situation familiale, oui ! se réjouit Clément. Il s'agissait bien de miss Eleanor Stout et de miss Lucy Chambers... Deux demoiselles. Une vieille et une jeune, toutes deux célibataires...

Kite approuva d'un hochement de tête.

— Ce qui nous donne le portrait d'un tueur aimant les femmes seules, adorant la musique et mettant en scène ses meurtres d'après un schéma bien précis. C'est facile de jouer au détective, non ? On se croirait presque dans un film, hein ?

Il porta le verre de bière à ses lèvres.

— Il ne nous reste plus qu'à savoir si le meurtrier de la bijouterie a agi seul, s'il n'a pas violé cette pauvre Lucy Chambers et s'il portait bien des gants de cuir noir.

— Ce sont les éléments rapportés par le labo sur l'assassinat de miss Stout ? s'enquit Clément.

— Exactement. Et si cela s'avère juste, alors

il existera peut-être réellement un lien entre les deux meurtres. Et nous aurions bien affaire à un tueur en série. Série qu'il faudrait alors rapidement écourter...

Ça y était enfin ! Kite avait réussi une fois de plus à remonter le moral de son stagiaire. Il venait de définir un but précis à atteindre. En synthétisant les aspects connus des deux meurtres, Kite était arrivé, un peu à la manière d'un jeu des différences, à dresser un premier bilan. Clément n'attendait que ça, de l'activité en perspective...

Kite regarda sa montre. Il était plus de 20 heures. Il vida le fond de sa troisième pinte.

— Il va falloir que je rentre. Michelle et Mary m'attendent, car nous n'avons pas eu le temps ce matin d'ouvrir nos cadeaux... Mary s'est levée bien trop tard.

Inexplicablement, Clément se mit à rougir.

Ça ne te dérange pas de rentrer en bus à Fulham ?

— Bien sûr que non.

— Ou en *cab*, si ça ne te fait pas peur d'attendre plusieurs mois l'hypothétique remboursement de ta course ! Bon et bien alors, bonne soirée ! Et essaye de te changer les idées ce soir...

Kite se leva tandis que Clément restait assis. Il ne savait pas encore quoi faire. Une seconde pinte de Guiness l'aiderait sûrement à réfléchir.

— Demain à 8 heures au Yard, lui lança Kite sans se retourner. Huit heures... On aura probablement pas mal de boulot...

Clément en était, à l'avance, ravi.

Une fois Kite parti, il se paya une seconde mousse, puis opta pour le cinéma d'en face, l'*Odeon Leicester Sq*, et sa séance de 20 h 15. *The Full Monty* lui viderait peut-être la tête...

12

L'homme avait sorti sa voiture pour se rendre dans le quartier de Chelsea. Il était 3 h 30 de l'après-midi lorsqu'il gara sa Mercedes sur le parking quasiment vide du Chelsea Village, non loin de la station de métro Fulham Broadway. Il aimait retrouver ce quartier qui l'avait vu grandir, regarder à nouveau ces petites maisons si charmantes, ce grand stade de football de Stamford Bridge, où, enfant, avec son père et étudiant avec ses amis, il assistait aux matchs du Chelsea Football Club. Il coupa le contact de sa voiture et regarda le ciel. Tout gris.

Une fois hors de sa voiture, il se dirigea vers la sortie du parking et prit à gauche, remontant vers le stade qu'il regardait avec attention. Apparemment, il était en travaux. L'homme remarqua la présence d'une grue et de quelques bulldozers autour de l'enceinte. Il avait lu, l'autre jour, dans le journal, que l'on construisait un nouveau centre commercial qui accueillerait, en plus de l'immense boutique du Chelsea FC, un grand nombre de commerces et de restaurants. L'homme marmonna quelque chose, visiblement mécontent des travaux en cours. Il avait l'impression que l'on défigurait le paysage du quartier de ses premières années.

Il ne s'arrêta pas devant le stade, continuant

sa route sur le trottoir de la grande rue principale. Il passa devant le King's College où il avait failli faire une partie de ses études. Puis devant l'immense cimetière de Brompton dont il n'apercevait que l'enceinte. Il poursuivit sa route calmement, marchant à pas lents, le visage et le cou fouettés par un vent glacial. Il se reprocha de ne pas avoir pensé à emmener une écharpe. S'il attrapait aujourd'hui une bronchite, il ne pourrait plus continuer son chef-d'œuvre. Il n'osait même pas y penser... Rater l'exécution d'un plan qu'il peaufinait depuis si longtemps...

Il arriva en plein cœur du quartier de Chelsea. Non loin de Gilston Road, la rue qu'il avait habitée en compagnie de ses parents jusqu'à l'âge de 18 ans, puis seul avec sa mère par la suite. « La troisième à gauche après le Chelsea & Westminster Hospital lorsque vous remontez la rue en direction de Knightsbridge », annonçait-il fièrement à ses copains et copines lorsqu'il les invitait chez lui. C'est vrai que l'appartement que ses parents possédaient dans cette rue était immense. Et si bien décoré. Sa mère avait eu le cœur ravagé lorsqu'elle l'avait abandonné pour partir s'installer avec son fils, plus au nord.

L'homme passa enfin devant l'hôpital et compta les rues, comme un vieux réflexe qui l'amusait toujours autant. Il changea de trottoir et monta sur celui de gauche. Peu de voitures roulaient en ce moment dans le quartier. Ils se posta à l'angle de Fulham Road et Gilston Road pendant quelques instants et épia les quelques personnes marchant dans le quartier. Il respira un grand coup, garda l'air le plus longtemps possible dans ses poumons, puis expira bruyamment.

Visiblement, ce petit périple le remuait beaucoup. L'homme apercevait au loin le clocher de l'église St Mary, enclavée dans son petit espace vert. Il s'en rapprocha petit à petit, mais n'alla pas jusqu'à elle. Il s'arrêta devant le numéro 11 de la rue. C'était un petit immeuble à la façade blanche un peu vieillotte composé de deux appartements. Il se trouvait juste en face de son ancien logement. Il ne se retourna même pas pour voir à nouveau ce porche qu'il avait tant de fois franchi pendant son enfance et son adolescence. L'homme se concentra plutôt sur le numéro 11, sa porte d'entrée et ses fenêtres.

Un air lui venait à l'esprit en regardant cet immeuble. Un air qu'il aimait beaucoup. Et qu'il se mit immédiatement à chantonner. Et tout le long du chemin du retour pour retrouver sa voiture, il chantonna, siffla, récita. Même dans l'église St Mary de son enfance, lorsqu'il entreprit ce petit détour pour prier, il ne put s'empêcher de marmonner les paroles de cette chanson. Il avait hâte. Hâte d'être à demain soir.

Dès son retour chez lui, à 18 heures, l'homme se coucha. Il avait monté un peu le chauffage de sa chambre pour ne pas avoir froid, nu, sous son large drap bleu. Il éteignit toutes les lampes sans fermer les volets. La nuit était déjà bien noire dehors et les lumières de la rue ne parvenaient pas à percer le mur formé par les nombreux arbres bordant la façade de son pavillon.

Si l'homme avait écouté les informations à la radio ce soir, il aurait appris qu'on avait enfin découvert le cadavre de Lucy. Il aurait aussi entendu une interview du sergent Nancy Kelling qui informait les auditeurs que la section de la brigade criminelle de Scotland Yard, dirigée par Andrew Barlow et Paul Kite, n'allait pas tarder à éclaircir toute cette affaire.

L'homme n'avait pas allumé sa radio, mais il aurait éprouvé une grande fierté d'apprendre que le tristement célèbre inspecteur Kite allait s'occuper de lui. Mais l'homme avait le casque de son Discman sur les oreilles. Il savourait la version originale de la chanson qu'il avait fredonnée devant le numéro 11 de Gilston Road. Et après... Mais il devait l'écouter avec des écouteurs car il ne fallait pas faire de bruit... « Chut ! Ils devaient probablement travailler... »

Plus bas, dans la cave, derrière cette porte blanche fichée entre deux murs, quelqu'un pleurait, tout doucement.

13

Kite klaxonna plusieurs fois afin que quelqu'un vienne lui ouvrir le portail, mais personne n'entendit, sauf Mrs Jenkins, sa concierge de voisine, qui colla son vieux visage à la fenêtre de sa cuisine. Kite lui fit un amical et hypocrite salut de la main, puis se résolut à descendre de sa voiture afin d'ouvrir lui-même le portail. Il remonta ensuite et manœuvra pour rentrer dans la petite cour. La Rover correctement garée, il coupa enfin le moteur. Il entendit, malgré les fenêtres fermées, un rythme, comme une chanson... Kite comprit maintenant pourquoi sa femme et sa fille ne l'avaient pas entendu. Elles devaient encore être en train de se faire un de leurs « délires musicaux ».

Une fois par semaine, souvent le dimanche, Mary appelait sa mère, qui s'empressait de la rejoindre dans sa chambre. Elles écoutaient alors, sur la chaîne hi-fi de Mary, n'importe quelle musique, du moment que le bouton de volume était bloqué au maximum. Leurs goûts étaient bien éclectiques. De l'adolescence franco-anglaise de Michelle avec les Beatles (une de ses grandes passions de jeunesse) ou encore Eddy Mitchell, à l'époque contemporaine de Mary avec REM ou Blur, Kite reconnut cette fois-ci, bien que difficilement, *Wonderwall* du groupe Oasis. Tout en déposant son imperméable sur le portemanteau, il reprit la chanson à pleins poumons « *And all the roads we have to walk are winding. And all the lights that lead us there are blinding...* [1] » En rythme, il se dirigea vers la cuisine, pour se préparer une tasse de café.

Au moment de se coucher, Kite et Michelle fredonnaient ensemble le refrain de *Wonderwall*. Mais un autre air, moins gai celui-là, se faisait entendre dans la conscience de Kite. Celui de ces meurtres atroces perpétrés à seulement deux jours d'écart. Une vilaine musique résonnait dans ses oreilles. Cette même musique qu'il entendit un soir de juin, dix ans auparavant. Symbole de cette terrible affaire qui lui avait coûté sa carrière, à lui et à tant

1. Et toutes les routes que nous devons emprunter sont sinueuses. Et toutes les lumières qui nous guident sont aveuglantes.

d'autres. Michelle remarqua l'air préoccupé de son mari.

— Quelque chose ne va pas, Paul ?

— C'est-à-dire... oui.

— Ce pourquoi tu es retourné au Yard ce soir ?

— Oui.

— Le meurtre de la bijouterie ?

Kite se retourna vers sa femme, torse nu, le haut de pyjama à la main. Il bredouilla sur un ton étonné :

— Comment le sais-tu ?

— Je l'ai entendu à la radio tout à l'heure.

— Mais enfin, comment ces fouille-merdes de journalistes ont-ils bien pu apprendre la nouvelle ? (Il soupira.) Eh bien, on peut être sûr que demain, ça va faire la une des torche-cul...

Extrait du dictionnaire Anglo-Kite : *Torche-cul* désigne les journaux populaires racoleurs.

— S'ils apprennent que l'on m'a chargé de l'enquête sur le premier meurtre, ils vont bien trouver à nous ressortir quelque chose sur juin 87...

Michelle fit la moue et s'approcha de son mari pour lui passer les bras autour du cou.

— Tu sais bien que je n'aime pas que tu reparles de cette histoire...

Kite embrassa sa femme sur le front.

— Je sais bien, Michelle, mais si la presse s'en mêle... C'est inévitable... (Il marqua une pause et desserra son étreinte.) Si je tenais l'abruti qui a bien pu vendre ces informations à la presse...

Michelle voulait absolument relativiser l'affaire. Elle aussi avait été durement éprouvée par cet odieux mois de juin 1987. Mary était heureusement bien trop jeune à l'époque, elle n'avait que 8 ans. Kite se glissa entre ses draps encore froids. Michelle l'imita quelques minutes après, une fois récupéré le tome III des œuvres complètes de Céline dans La Pléiade que son mari lui avait offert pour Noël, chargeant Clément de le ramener de Paris. Elle commençait juste le premier chapitre de *Guignol's band*, merveilleuse fresque sur la capitale britannique, lorsque Mary vint frapper à leur porte.

— Entre, ma chérie...

— Vous êtes déjà au lit ?

Kite tourna la tête sur son oreiller et regarda le réveil digital posé sur sa table de nuit.

— Il n'est pas loin de 11 heures, Mary, et demain, je risque d'avoir une journée sacrément chargée, alors...

— Oh, je ne vous dérange pas longtemps... Simplement pour vous dire que demain, après la danse, je vais directement chez Anna.

— Et tu dors là-bas ? s'enquit Kite.

— Oui, je rentrerai samedi dans la matinée... Mary les embrassa puis sortit.

— Qu'on veuille bien me pendre s'il n'y a que Anna demain soir pendant la soirée, maugréa Kite. À mon humble avis, Michelle, Mary fréquente... Tous ces cours de danse où elle joue les prolongations...

— Je te rappelle, mon cher Paul, que Mary a 18 ans.

Michelle adressa une petite tape sur la couverture, à l'endroit où se dessinait le derrière de son mari.

— Je crois donc que tu peux la laisser vivre sa vie...

Kite, pour toute réponse, fit passer le drap au-dessus de sa tête.

— Eh bien voilà, ajouta sa femme sur le ton

86

de la plaisanterie. À chaque fois que nous parlons sérieusement, tu te drapes la face !

Mrs Kite éteignit la lampe après quelques pages. Son mari semblait être plongé dans un profond sommeil.

Te rappelles-tu, Kite, ce terrible mois de juin ? Te rappelles-tu l'odeur cuivrée du sang que tu as tant de fois sentie à l'époque ? Oh, ne mens pas ! Je sais que tu te souviens de tous les détails de cette affaire. Mais tu ne veux pas les faire remonter à la surface. C'est un tort : je m'amuserais bien si tu le voulais... Allez, Kite, fais un petit effort. La lune était magnifique ce soir-là. Tu étais encore jeune. Tout juste 30 ans, si je ne m'abuse. Promis à une carrière épatante, tu attendais ta promotion d'inspecteur principal. Le coup de téléphone que tu as reçu ce jour-là a scellé à jamais ta carrière. C'était ton chef, l'inspecteur principal Simon Aysgarth, et il voulait que tu te rendes avec deux de tes collègues près du Rectory Field à Charlton. Il était bien 3 heures du matin. Tu avais des cernes sous les yeux, je me rappelle bien ce détail... On avait retrouvé le corps d'un petit garçon de 5 ans nu et affreusement mutilé. Te souviens-tu précisément du rapport d'autopsie, Paul ? Mort par étouffement, hématomes importants sur le dos et le torse, brûlures au deuxième degré sur le visage, viol post-mortem aggravé par la pénétration de multiples objets et j'en passe, Paul, j'en passe...

Tu es arrivé sur les lieux en moins d'une demi-heure, flanqué de tes deux collègues habituels. C'étaient les parents du jeune garçon (tu te rappelles le nom ? moi, ce détail m'échappe) qui avaient eux-mêmes appelé la police. Tu as alors discuté avec la police de Charlton présente sur place. Ils t'ont raconté ce que les parents étaient bien incapables de te dire, étouffés par leur chagrin probablement définitif : leur fils avait disparu le mercredi matin sur le trajet de l'école. Dès sa disparition, la mère avait reçu un coup de téléphone à la maison l'informant du kidnapping de son petit garçon et lui demandant une rançon de plus de cinquante mille livres. Au cas où elle parlerait de quoi que ce soit à la police, la voix du téléphone lui avait promis la mort pour son enfant. Alors elle et son mari avaient réuni la somme, sans problèmes majeurs — c'était une famille aisée. Et ils se rendirent seuls au rendez-vous du vendredi soir, au Rectory Field de Charlton. Mais ils ne trouvèrent personne et durent attendre plus d'une heure, le sac rempli de billets de banque à la main.

Ils n'avaient pas remarqué ce gros paquet enveloppé d'un drap blanc posé près de la poubelle la plus proche du lieu du rendez-vous. Cela les intrigua peu à peu. Jusqu'à ce que le père décide d'entrouvrir le voile blanc. Par curiosité. Par nervosité. Il reconnut d'abord la couleur des cheveux de son fils. Puis la forme de son nez, qui avait été partiellement épargné par la brûlure. Sa femme, penchée par-dessus son épaule, s'évanouit aussitôt. Lui, serra fort le corps encore enveloppé et poussa un râle profond. Et il pleura. Et il balança la mallette sur la chaussée qui s'ouvrit sous le choc. Et il se dirigea avec un sang-froid retrouvé vers la cabine la plus proche pour contacter le 999...

Le corps fut embarqué par l'ambulance sous tes propres yeux, Kite. Tu faisais une drôle de mine. Tu peux bien me croire, je t'observais de l'autre côté de la rue, dans ma camionnette. Une fois toutes les procédures d'usage respectées, tu *as regagné ta voiture avec tes collègues. Direction le New Scotland Yard, où, le reste de la nuit, vous avez planché sur cette terrible découverte. Sans attendre le rapport du légiste. Ni les témoignages précis des parents.*

Ah, au fait ! J'ai oublié de te préciser un élément du rapport d'autopsie : la mort du jeune garçon datait du jeudi matin. Soit un jour avant le rendez-vous. Le meurtrier semblait prendre un plaisir malsain à faire espérer les parents et à suivre leur désespoir. Il avait dû déposer le corps un peu avant l'heure du rendez-vous puis se cacher quelque part pour épier les parents. De ça, tu en étais quasiment sûr. Et tes collègues aussi. Mais cela ne te donnait bien évidemment pas le nom du meurtrier. Tant mieux...

Je n'aurais jamais pu tuer cette charmante petite jeune fille de 6 ans, Pamela, si tu m'avais arrêté dès le début. Ses parents non plus n'avaient pas prévenu la police. Malgré les appels que des grandes pointures de Scotland Yard avaient passés. Et eux aussi, ils ont retrouvé le corps de leur petite fille empaqueté dans un drap blanc. Je m'étais bien moins amusé avec elle. Tu avais dû bien moins vomir, Paul, en lisant le rapport du légiste. Je lui avais simplement roué le corps méthodiquement, de la tête au talon, à l'aide d'un simple tisonnier. Pas de viol. Ni rien de sexuel. Ce n'était pas de la mauvaise volonté, mais elle ne me faisait vraiment pas envie.

Par contre, Paul, la réaction des parents devant le corps, et ces têtes que vous faisiez, toi, tes collègues et le si-propre-sur-lui Simon Aysgarth qui avait daigné se déplacer ce soir-là... Mon Dieu, quelle jouissance ! J'étais toujours dans ma camionnette, garée cette fois-ci en face du Lewisham Park, non loin du mémorial de guerre.

Oh, n'aie aucun remords, Paul, de ne pas avoir reconnu ma camionnette : je l'avais repeinte. Ne culpabilise pas tout de suite... Attends un peu que je te remette en mémoire ce samedi soir de la fin juin. C'était un peu moins d'un mois après le premier meurtre. L'opinion publique commençait à trouver sa police franchement incompétente. Un député travailliste avait même posé une question à ce sujet à la Chambre des Communes. Il attaquait le gouvernement de l'époque en lui reprochant son laisser-aller sur cette affaire. Il est vrai que je courais toujours, Paul... Et ton chef, Aysgarth, avait le cul posé sur un siège éjectable. Tout comme d'autres encore plus haut placés... Alors que toi, consciencieux, tu délaissais ta femme et ta fille — déjà trop âgée à l'époque et c'est bien dommage — pour courir nuit et jour avec tes collègues et ratisser les réseaux de pédophiles.

Peine perdue. Le dernier vendredi de juin, j'ai enlevé d'une façon magistrale Mark Thomson, le petit-fils âgé de 4 ans d'un éminent ministre de sa très Gracieuse Majesté. Te rappelles-tu, Paul, le branle-bas de combat à Scotland Yard ? Le quadrillage de Londres et d'une partie de sa banlieue. Car le vieux ministre et son fils, brillant médecin et père du gosse, n'ont même pas respecté mes consignes. La police était on ne peut plus prévenue. C'était l'occasion pour moi d'exécuter mon bouquet final. Mon dernier pied de nez. J'ai appelé le père en lui donnant l'heure et le lieu du rendez-vous ainsi que le montant de la rançon : « Devant la gare de Cannon Street, samedi soir à 3 heures et demie, avec un million de livres. »

J'ai fait celui qui ne savait pas que la police allait être invitée au rendez-vous. Car il fallait absolument qu'elle vienne. Et que tu viennes, mon brave Paul, toi qui me cherchais depuis si longtemps... Je suis arrivé dans ma camionnette rouge à 20 h 30 précises. J'ai facilement trouvé une place dans Bush Lane et tranquillement attendu l'heure de notre rencontre en observant de temps en temps les mouvements des policiers en civil dans la rue, des tireurs sur les toits, des voitures banalisées. Je m'en délectais.

Et enfin l'heure du rendez-vous arriva. Je suis sorti tranquillement de ma camionnette en portant sur mon dos le corps du petit Mark. J'ai ensuite obliqué vers la gauche pour remonter Cannon Street sur quelques dizaines de mètres. Je voyais la silhouette d'une personne, figée sous un lampadaire puissant, tenant à la main une mallette en acier brillant. Plus je me rapprochais et plus je voyais cette personne au sombre costume : c'était bien le père de Mark. Et il me regardait avec des yeux tristes, épouvantablement tristes. Il savait que son fils était mort et qu'il n'avait pas réussi à le sauver.

Certes, il aura contribué à mon arrestation, car je n'avais objectivement aucune chance de m'en sortir, mais lui, qu'a-t-il vraiment gagné dans cette histoire ? Je m'approchais de plus en plus de lui. Il semblait pâlir à vue d'œil et jetait de grands regards inquiets sur le sac que je portais sur mon dos et qui commençait à me peser. Lorsque j'arrivai à moins de deux mètres de lui, il laissa tomber sa mallette. Le bruit métallique, c'était votre signal. Une bonne trentaine de flics, revolver à la main, sortirent de la gare, de la station de métro dont les grilles avaient été laissées *ouvertes pour l'occasion, et de quelques porches d'immeubles.*

Et tu étais là, Paul... Juste devant moi. Tu sortais de la gare et n'étais qu'à quelques mètres de moi. Te souviens-tu de mon visage ? De mes fines moustaches qui me conféraient cet air si distingué ? De mes cheveux blancs coupés court ? Et mon corps ? T'en souviens-tu de ma grande taille et de ma petite bedaine ? Peu importe d'ailleurs, je ne sais même pas si tu as eu le temps de me regarder. Vous avez tous crié votre « Freeze ! » habituel et j'ai porté la main qui ne tenait pas le sac par-dessus mon épaule, dans ma poche. Et tu as tiré. Toi et les autres.

Je ne sais pas qui a commencé à tirer. Ce dont je me souviens, Paul, c'est que ta balle m'a atteint en pleine tête. Juste au milieu de mon beau front bien lisse. Tes collègues, eux, ont visé au hasard, les jambes, les bras, le torse... Mon corps se brisait peu à peu sous l'impact des balles. Le sac, que je tenais d'une main, tomba, entièrement déchiqueté. La dernière chose qu'il m'ait été donné d'entendre sur cette terre fut, non pas le bruit d'une balle rentrant dans ma chair, mais les sanglots du père de Mark en voyant dépasser de la toile blanche une petite main où coulait un filament rouge.

Bravo, Paul, bravo ! Bravo à vous tous ! Vous avez réussi à m'arrêter définitivement. Vous avez vous-même rendu justice ; économisé à l'État un procès. Pauvres ignares que vous étiez ! Et cela s'adresse aussi à toi, Paul ! Si vous n'aviez pas tiré sur moi alors que je portais simplement la main à la poche pour vous provoquer, vous auriez pu simplement m'arrêter et me passer les menottes. Alors, vous vous seriez aperçu que

Mark, dans le sac, dormait simplement, drogué
par mes soins.

Il n'était en aucun cas mort. Simplement
endormi. Je suis presque sûr que tu te rappelles
ce rapport du légiste qui avait fait la une de tous
les journaux à l'époque : « Le décès est survenu
à la suite d'une grave hémorragie généralisée
consécutive à vingt-quatre blessures par balle.
On a retrouvé également dans le sang du sujet
des traces d'un somnifère assez puissant. Le sujet
est mort dans son sommeil, etc. »

Cela explique bien des choses au sujet du lyn-
chage médiatique et politique qui suivit. Et sur
la fin de tes espérances concernant ta carrière. Et
sur tes crises d'angoisse la nuit quand tu es sur
une affaire similaire. Mais ne t'inquiète pas,
Paul... Tu n'es pas le seul à qui je remémore ce
cauchemar. Vous êtes plusieurs... Peut-être une
bonne trentaine... Non, Paul, non... Ne te réveille
pas... Je n'ai pas tout à fait terminé... Non,
Paul... Laisse-moi continuer ton cauchemar...
Laisse-moi continuer mon rêve... Ne te...

Kite se réveilla, le dos couvert de sueur. Et
cette voix encore présente dans sa tête. Il reprit
lentement ses esprits, cherchant de sa main le
corps de sa femme comme pour trouver un lien
vers la réalité. Sa paume tâtonna tout autour de
lui, mais ne rencontra que le vide. Le vide ? Pas
même le drap... Ses yeux s'habituèrent peu à
peu à l'obscurité. Sa main battait l'air, il n'était
pas allongé, mais assis. Comment... ?

Devant lui, des diodes multicolores cligno-
taient : il reconnut la façade de leur chaîne-hifi.
Son cœur se mit à battre fort, il sentit la sueur
envahir son front. Ses aisselles devenaient
humides. Il n'était plus dans son lit, mais affalé

dans le confortable fauteuil du salon... Il devait s'être levé... Seul... Tel un somnambule. Kite imagina sa silhouette pataude descendant les marches de l'escalier les bras tendus vers l'avant, à moitié défroquée... Se pourrait-il qu'il soit atteint de somnambulisme ? Cette pensée lui fit peur. Il ne se rappelait pas avoir déjà été la victime d'une telle manifestation.

Les circonstances du moment, son malaise devant l'enquête en cours, son rêve étaient révélateurs de son mal-être... Kite sentit qu'il avait besoin de lumière. Pour se rassurer. Il se leva et alla actionner l'interrupteur le plus proche. La lumière lui fit l'effet d'un flash. Mais avant de fermer les yeux d'instinct, il eut le temps d'apercevoir le sol de la pièce. Des CD étaient éparpillés par terre, certains ouverts à côté d'une tâche foncée sur la moquette.

Les yeux de l'inspecteur s'acclimatèrent à la luminosité du salon. Il se rassit, abasourdi, dans le fauteuil. Ainsi, dans son sommeil, il s'était emparé de disques pour les écouter... C'était inimaginable... Et pire encore... Il avait uriné sur la moquette. La tâche ne faisait pas de doute et Kite ne prit pas la peine d'aller s'assurer de son origine. Médusé, anxieux, il resta le regard scotché sur le désordre de la pièce. Maintenant, il se savait condamné à trouver rapidement une solution à ces crimes s'ils se révélaient liés. S'ils se révélaient commis par le même homme. Par un autre de ces foutus tueurs en série. Et même si on le déchargeait de l'affaire, il chercherait... Seul. Pour lui. Pour Michelle. Pour Mary. Et surtout, pour sa propre conscience.

Vendredi 26 décembre 1997

14

Jude Parlour claqua la porte du 11, Gilston Road. Elle était affreusement en retard pour prendre son service au Chelsea & Westminster Hospital. Sa chef de service allait encore copieusement l'engueuler : « Maintenant, tu habites tout près de l'hôpital et tu trouves encore le moyen d'arriver en retard ! » Elle anticipait la réaction de cette vieille garce frustrée. C'est vrai, pensa Jude, que cela devait faire pas mal de temps qu'un interne n'avait pas dû peloter la vieille ! Elle reprochait assez à Jude ses relations sans lendemain avec les jeunes internes du service Cardiologie. Mais Jude s'en fichait pas mal et cela ne l'empêchait pas d'être considérée comme une excellente infirmière au sein même de tout l'hôpital. Et puis c'était bien pratique ce petit appart tout près : les internes arrivaient tout chauds.

Jude marcha à grandes enjambées vers Fulham Road. Le jour n'était pas encore levé et la jeune femme suivit le trottoir grâce aux lampadaires disposés à intervalles réguliers tout au long de la rue. Elle regarda sa montre plusieurs fois en chemin. Et dire qu'elle n'avait même pas eu le temps de prendre son bol de cornflakes habituel ! Elle avait rapidement pris une douche et passé un jean, un tee-shirt et un sweat rouge, sa couleur préférée. Attrapant sa veste d'hiver et son écharpe au passage, elle s'empressait de sortir lorsqu'elle avait entendu le téléphone sonner. Elle n'avait même pas pris la peine de décrocher. La vieille était sûrement au bout du fil. Pas la peine de se retarder encore un peu plus...

Arrivée dans l'hôpital, Jude emprunta directement l'ascenseur jusqu'au troisième sans même s'arrêter pour embrasser son amie Dorothy à l'accueil. Elle se dirigea immédiatement vers le local des infirmières. Ouf ! La vieille n'y était pas. Elle enfila sa blouse et jeta un coup d'œil sur le planning fixé au mur ainsi que sur les nouvelles fiches d'admission posées sur leur table commune. Elle prenait son métier très au sérieux. Jude rajusta sa petite coiffe, qu'elle prenait plaisir à porter, et se dirigea vers la porte.

L'homme entra dans le local des infirmières du troisième étage. Sa première vision fut celle d'une Jude étonnée qui marchait en direction de la porte. Elle s'arrêta net. L'homme fit de même et referma la porte. À clef. Jude ne sourit que quelques instants encore. Jusqu'à ce qu'il se rapproche d'elle. Elle ferma alors les yeux. L'homme prit son geste pour une invitation muette. Il la colla à la table et entreprit de passer ses mains dans l'échancrure de sa blouse. Il voulait toucher son soutien-gorge.

Jude ne dit rien et enroula ses bras autour du cou de l'homme, lui caressant les cheveux qui tombaient sur sa nuque. Elle rentra alors sa main à l'arrière du col de la blouse de l'homme, lui touchant le haut de la colonne vertébrale. Le désir de l'homme s'en trouva décuplé. Il l'embrassa fougueusement ; elle lui répondit avec la même intensité.

Décidément, elle s'entendait vraiment bien avec David Ball, ce jeune interne. À 7 heures et demie du matin, pensez-vous ! Il fallait vraiment qu'elle soit amoureuse ! Et si le jeune David, 23 ans, son cadet de quatre ans, lui faisait réfléchir sérieusement à son statut de femme farouchement opposée au concubinage... Depuis trois semaines, elle semblait vivre une aventure passionnée avec lui. Allait-elle enfin consentir à partager son appartement de Gilston Road ? Mais dans l'instant présent, elle ne voulait pas répondre. Juste s'abandonner.

Profites-en bien, jeune David... Prends bien ton temps. Car ce soir, c'est un autre que toi qui tiendra Jude dans ses bras.

15

Paul Kite gara sa Rover dans le parking du New Scotland Yard. Il avait plus d'une demi-heure de retard sur l'horaire fixé à son jeune stagiaire. Cette nuit, après s'être réveillé et avoir repris ses esprits, il avait rangé le salon en remettant les CD à leur place, puis épongé tant bien que mal la moquette. Exténué autant par son activité physique que par les pensées noires qui lui transperçaient la tête, il s'était rassis dans le fauteuil et avait terminé sa nuit ainsi.

C'était sa femme qui l'avait réveillé. Elle croyait que Kite était déjà levé et parti. L'inspecteur ne devait son salut qu'à un oubli de Michelle qui voulait récupérer un livre dans le salon. Sans cela, il aurait probablement continué sa nuit jusqu'au déjeuner ! Cela le mit tout de même bien en retard et il était de très méchante humeur. Dire que Clément devait l'attendre depuis 8 heures !

Kite emprunta l'escalier de secours pour rejoindre son bureau. Il ne voulait discuter avec personne dans les couloirs ce matin. Arrivé devant son bureau, Kite passa machinalement ses doigts sur les larges cernes qui bordaient ses yeux, comme pour tenter de les faire disparaître en les poussant à droite et à gauche. Mais c'était peine perdue. C'est avec eux qu'il fit son entrée à la « James Bond exténué » dans un bureau vide. Vide si l'on exceptait la belle cocotte en papier qui siégeait au milieu de son bureau.

Un crachin typiquement britannique tombait sur Londres depuis ce matin. Clément avait pris ses précautions en s'emparant d'un parapluie qui traînait ouvert au beau milieu de l'entrée de son appartement depuis une bonne dizaine de jours. La soirée s'était rudement bien passée après sa discussion avec l'inspecteur Kite. *The Full Monty* l'avait fait rire aux éclats, même si certains dialogues lui avaient échappé à cause de la dureté de l'accent des acteurs. Mais quelle jubilation ! Sur le trajet du retour, il s'était plu à imaginer Kite dans le rôle d'un de ces hommes s'essayant au strip-tease. « *You can leave your hat on...* », fredonnait-il dans la rame de métro vide.

Il avait ainsi réussi à vaincre pour la soirée les

images de Lucy sur son lit. Mais il avait néanmoins envié Kite, qui devait être avec sa femme et sa fille, en compagnie et non pas seul... Ce devait être plus facile d'oublier. L'heure de son arrivée à Fulham l'avait dissuadé de passer un coup de fil à Mary. Toutefois, il y avait un bémol : lorsqu'il jouait encore, Clément éprouvait toujours une frustration à la sortie d'un film qu'il avait aimé, la frustration de ne pas apparaître au générique certainement... Puis cette sensation s'était estompée... Tout doucement... Pour revenir l'assaillir hier soir... Tout doucement... Quelque chose était-il en train de changer à nouveau ?

Il regardait la bruine se coller sur les vitres. Il faisait sombre dans cette salle vide. Clément jeta un coup d'œil à sa montre. Neuf heures cinq ! Cela faisait plus de quarante minutes qu'il poireautait dans la salle. Il se leva.

Lorsqu'il passa la porte du bureau de Kite, ce dernier lui intima l'ordre de se taire d'un geste sec de la main. Il s'assit près de ses tréteaux en espérant que l'inspecteur était de bonne humeur ce matin. Mais apparemment, il était très énervé. Il était au téléphone avec l'inspecteur Owen de Woodford, auquel il confirmait l'autopsie à effectuer. Ses phrases étaient courtes et sèches, le ton employé sans aucune équivoque. Il raccrocha violemment.

— Pauvre con !

— Un problème ? s'enquit Clément, tout en s'asseyant.

— Non, une bonne dizaine de problèmes ! (Kite colla son dos au dossier du fauteuil.) D'abord, j'arrive en retard au boulot, et je te prie de m'en excuser. Ensuite, je trouve sur mon bureau cette feuille de journal. C'est un article de *Metro*, qui n'a rien trouvé de mieux que d'interviewer cette imbécile de Kelling. Elle raconte dans ce truc un tas de conneries.

Il tapa avec le bout de son doigt sur la feuille.

— Je vais aller mettre les points sur les i avec elle ! Bon, heureusement, Giggs n'est pas là et c'est Barlow qui prend en charge les affaires aujourd'hui. (Giggs et Barlow étaient les noms des inspecteurs-chefs dont Kite dépendait.) Et il m'a fallu un bon bout de temps pour le convaincre de me mettre sur l'affaire Chambers en plus de celle de lundi. Il m'a dit qu'il attendait le rapport du labo avant de prendre sa décision et que je n'avais qu'à continuer l'investigation du meurtre de miss Stout. Du coup, ni une ni deux, j'ai appelé Owen pour lui donner le feu vert pour l'autopsie. Et ce con me réclame l'accord écrit de mon supérieur ! Ah, ces inspecteurs de banlieue ! Heureusement, il a fini par céder. On devrait avoir le rapport en fin de soirée ou demain au plus tard...

— Et en attendant ? demanda Clément.

— En attendant, tu n'as qu'à te tourner les pouces...

— Et vous, qu'allez-vous faire ?

— Moi, je dois m'occuper jusqu'à tard ce soir, je suis de garde... Au fait, tu restes avec moi ?

— Eh non ! Je ne peux pas... J'ai un cours d'anglais à 7 heures, mentit le jeune stagiaire en tentant de dissimuler tant bien que mal le rose qui lui recouvrait peu à peu les joues.

— Eh bien, avec tous ces cours, tu vas bientôt savoir mieux parler anglais que moi ! rigola Kite.

— Disons que je m'améliore, inspecteur. J'arrive maintenant à comprendre la quasi-totalité de vos jurons.

Kite gloussa. Il se détendait peu à peu.

— Je vais aller rendre une petite visite au père de Lucy ce matin pour essayer d'évoquer plus précisément avec lui l'entourage, disons... « affectif » de sa fille. Pendant ce temps, tu peux jeter un coup d'œil sur le rapport du meurtre de l'église... C'est le dossier rouge, là-bas...

— OK, répondit Clément.

Kite se leva.

— Mais avant cela, je vais aller dire quelques mots gentils à Nancy. Tiens, Clément, si tu veux encore enrichir ton vocabulaire, tu n'as qu'à venir avec moi...

Clément déclina l'invitation.

16

Paul Kite stoppa la voiture devant la petite maison des Chambers, à Woodford, un peu avant 11 heures. Il espérait bien y trouver le père de Lucy, si ce dernier n'était pas encore retenu à l'hôpital par la tentative de suicide de sa femme. Ce serait de toute façon bon signe que l'inspecteur trouve Mr Chambers chez lui, cela signifierait au moins que Mrs Chambers allait mieux. Kite ferma à clef la porte droite de sa Rover et se dirigea vers le petit portail.

Jetant un rapide coup d'œil à la maison, il sonna et attendit patiemment une bonne trentaine de secondes, les jambes légèrement écartées, les mains enfouies dans les larges poches de son imperméable, luttant comme il pouvait contre le froid et la pluie. Kite avait une sainte horreur des parapluies. Il n'en avait jamais avec lui. Cela datait de ses années fac, où il les oubliait tout le temps dans les salles de cours et ne les retrouvait jamais. Poste budgétaire important de sa vie estudiantine, les parapluies avaient fait l'objet du caractère bougon et teigneux de Kite, qui s'était juré de ne plus jamais en acheter une fois ses études terminées.

Il attendait donc la tête découverte, sans protection, devant le portail des Chambers, lorsqu'un homme, que Kite identifia comme étant probablement le père de Lucy, ouvrit la porte de la maison et passa sa tête dans l'embrasure. L'homme ne dit pas un mot, laissant à Kite l'initiative.

— Pardonnez-moi de vous déranger, cher monsieur. Je me présente : je suis l'inspecteur Paul Kite, du New Scotland Yard. Mr Chambers, je présume... Pourrions-nous avoir une petite conversation concernant cette terrible affaire ?

Damon Chambers n'ouvrit pas plus la porte et lança à l'attention de l'inspecteur :

— J'ai déjà eu la visite de vos collègues hier après-midi et je n'ai rien d'autre à vous dire.

— Mr Chambers, s'il vous plaît, il faudrait absolument que nous évoquions un tant soit peu la vie de votre fille. C'est une procédure habituelle et primordiale pour retrouver la personne qui a fait cela.

Le père de Lucy sembla réfléchir quelques instants et entrouvrit un peu plus la porte.

— La personne ? cria-t-il. L'enfant de putain, plutôt, vous voulez dire !

Il ouvrit la porte en grand et Kite, prenant ce geste comme une invitation, tourna la poignée du portail et pénétra à l'intérieur du minuscule jardinet. Ses cheveux étaient tout humides et ses petites frisures gonflées d'eau. Il y passa machinalement une main comme pour chasser d'un coup toute cette pluie accumulée. Puis, après s'être essuyé la main avec un mouchoir, il la tendit à Mr Chambers.

— Merci beaucoup, monsieur. Je tiens d'abord à vous exprimer tout mon soutien en ces pénibles heures.

Kite détailla un peu mieux le père de Lucy. Il était vêtu négligemment d'un pantalon et d'une veste de survêtement aux couleurs du club de football d'Arsenal. Ses yeux étaient à moitié ouverts et remplis de petits filaments rouges. Visiblement, l'homme n'avait que peu dormi.

— À propos, comment va votre femme ? questionna Kite.

— Mieux, fit Chambers avec une moue. Le lavage d'estomac s'est bien passé. Mais elle reste très fatiguée.

Sortant un paquet de cigarettes de sa poche, il en porta une à sa bouche, perdue dans son immense barbe, et l'alluma. Puis il fixa le paquet.

— Ça faisait bientôt six mois que j'avais arrêté... Six putains de mois... C'était comme ma fierté à moi. Les collègues de boulot en étaient verts de jalousie...

Kite compatit d'un hochement de tête. Il était vraiment touché par l'émotion manifeste de cet homme. Il avait le même masque de douleur que les parents des jeunes enfants dans les souvenirs de Kite. Le même masque que dans ses rêves. La détresse est bien universelle, pensa-t-il.

— Venez vous asseoir, monsieur l'inspecteur...

Mr Chambers guida Kite dans le salon-salle à manger, puis lui indiqua une chaise posée contre le mur. Lui choisit plutôt de s'asseoir sur le canapé, près d'une serviette qui recouvrait la moitié des coussins. À peine passé le seuil de la pièce, une forte odeur âcre assaillit les narines de l'inspecteur.

— Je ne vous propose pas de venir à côté de moi. Le médecin a tout de suite fait vomir ma femme hier et j'ai pas eu le temps de nettoyer...

Kite, tout en s'asseyant, avait la gorge de plus en plus serrée. Il détailla la pièce en quelques secondes avant de commencer son entretien. D'un tout petit volume, cette salle avait été décorée avec un mauvais goût certain. Des tentures d'un rouge passé semblaient miraculeusement collées au mur et certains pans s'en détachaient. Le plafond, peint en blanc, était peut-être la seule partie propre de la pièce. Le canapé et les différents fauteuils devaient avoir dépassé de loin leur âge limite. Une table en bois peint et un meuble sur lequel était posée une vieille télévision des années 80 finissaient de constituer l'ameublement sommaire de l'endroit.

— Si vous le voulez bien, Mr Chambers, commença Kite, évoquons les relations de votre fille. Avait-elle un petit ami ?

— Non, pas que je sache. Vous savez, Lucy s'était jetée à corps perdu dans sa bijouterie. Je crois que c'est d'elle qu'elle était amoureuse.

— Et des amies proches ?

— Bien sûr, des camarades de classe qu'elle voyait encore de temps en temps, mais rien de bien sérieux. En fait, Lucy a arrêté ses études après les *A-levels* et puis elle a tout de suite travaillé pour obtenir de l'argent dans l'idée d'acheter sa bijouterie. Et ça signifiait pas de vacances et même pas beaucoup de week-ends.

Damon Chambers tirait de plus en plus vite sur sa cigarette. Il mordillait de temps en temps le bout du filtre.

— Ses petits boulots ont suffi pour acheter la bijouterie ? demanda Kite, étonné.

— Bien sûr que non ! Ma belle-mère l'a aidée dans la mesure de ses moyens. C'est pas qu'elle est riche, elle non plus, mais il y a de cela cinq ans, alors qu'elle sortait comme à son habitude pour faire quelques courses, un camion l'a renversée et lui a tué les deux jambes... Alors vous pensez bien qu'elle a touché le pactole pour ça... Et puis vu qu'elle ne pouvait plus rien faire, eh ben, elle en a fait profiter notre Lucy. C'était sa seule petite-fille, vous savez, elle y était très attachée... Si elle était encore vivante aujourd'hui, je crois qu'elle en mourrait, la pauvre !

Les yeux du père de Lucy semblaient rougir de plus en plus. Kite décida de revenir sur la personnalité de sa fille.

— Avait-elle de quelconques ennuis dont elle vous aurait fait part ?

— Vous savez, inspecteur, je ne sais pas ce que Lucy a fait pour mériter ça. Probablement rien. Elle ne faisait pas de politique, elle ne faisait partie d'aucune association, elle n'avait pas d'ennemis, peut-être même pas de vrais amis, alors vous voyez bien... Elle n'avait vraiment que nous, Lucy...

— Je suppose qu'elle ne prenait pas de substances interdites ?

— Hein ?

— De substances interdites, de la drogue par exemple...

— Sûr que non.

— Mr Chambers, je vais être franc avec vous. Je crois que Lucy a eu le seul tort de se trouver dans sa bijouterie au mauvais moment. Ce meurtre est atroce, Mr Chambers. Et si votre fille était une personne sans histoire, comme vous semblez le laisser entendre, le meurtrier devait lui être totalement inconnu... Il devait être tout au plus client. Et encore... (Il marqua une longue pause.) Je ne vais pas vous embêter plus longtemps, Mr Chambers, cette situation est déjà assez pénible pour vous...

— Pensez-vous pouvoir retrouver le tueur de ma fille ? questionna le père de Lucy.

— Je l'espère de tout cœur, Mr Chambers, je l'espère énormément. D'autant plus que Lucy n'est peut-être pas...

Kite s'arrêta net. Il pensait dire à Mr Chambers que l'homme n'en était peut-être pas à son coup d'essai avec Lucy. Mais quel idiot aurait-il été ! Dire cela signifierait pour le père que le meurtre de sa fille aurait pu être évité. Quoique de toutes les façons, il ne tarderait pas à l'apprendre par les journaux. Alors il maudirait la police, et Kite.

— Mr Chambers, reprit-il, puis-je jeter un coup d'œil dans la chambre de votre fille ?

Sans un mot, le père de Lucy se leva et se dirigea vers l'escalier.

Kite ne resta pas longtemps dans l'ancienne chambre de Lucy. D'une part parce que cela faisait visiblement beaucoup de mal au père, qui grillait cigarette sur cigarette, laissant même parfois tomber des cendres sur le sol moquetté ; d'autre part parce qu'il était persuadé qu'il ne trouverait aucun indice réel dans la pièce. Il devait attendre l'autopsie et le rapport du labo pour en être sûr, mais la piste du tueur en série semblait de plus en plus probable. Et d'ailleurs, était-il vraisemblable de penser à quelqu'un d'autre qu'à un fou devant ce cadavre énucléé autour de ces bijoux ?

Kite se sépara du père de Lucy en lui serrant une nouvelle fois la main. Ce dernier, avant de refermer la porte, demanda son avis à Kite. L'inspecteur Owen, hier soir, avait prévenu Mr Chambers des poursuites qui pourraient être entreprises à son encontre pour le déplacement du corps de sa fille. Mais Kite le rassura en lui expliquant que dans un cas comme celui-là, la police ne porterait sûrement pas plainte, et quand bien même elle le ferait, il bénéficierait de circonstances hautement atténuantes.

Avant de regagner sa voiture, Kite s'arrêta sous le petit auvent devant la porte refermée. Il entendit derrière la porte un toussotement de Mr Chambers. Il regarda la pluie tomber sur le petit bout de pelouse, sur le trottoir et sur sa Rover. Il la sentit ensuite tomber toute droite sur sa tête alors qu'il empruntait la petite allée qui descendait vers le portail. Triste, il boutonna rapidement son imperméable, un bouton sur deux.

17

L'homme déboutonna son manteau délicatement, prudemment, ne voulant pas découdre un seul bouton. La dernière fois que cela lui était arrivé, il avait été obligé d'aller en racheter un chez *Hackett*, son tailleur préféré. Il ne pouvait supporter les choses rapiécées. Il lui fallait du neuf, du net, du beau. Et puis l'imperméable qu'il portait actuellement avait un fort côté affectif : il avait été son compagnon pour les deux premiers meurtres. Et, l'homme en était sûr, il le serait pour les trois prochains. C'est pourquoi, une fois déboutonné, il l'accrocha au portemanteau, derrière la porte et le plus près possible du radiateur pour qu'il sèche vite.

Il se dirigea alors vers son immense bureau près de la verrière. Quelle vue magnifique ! se félicita-t-il. Même quand le ciel était gris, il pouvait voir le dôme de la cathédrale St Paul et sa lanterne. Ça n'était pas dû au hasard : il avait demandé son bureau au dix-septième étage, alors que les neuf autres associés du cabinet d'avocats se partageaient les étages douze et treize. Comme ils lui avaient dit : « Tu as vraiment la folie des grandeurs ! » Les imbéciles.

L'homme détourna son regard de la fenêtre et vint s'asseoir dans son fauteuil en cuir noir, qu'il trouvait extrêmement confortable. Il aimait s'y blottir et sentir pendant les premières secondes son contact froid à travers sa veste et son pantalon. Posant devant lui un petit sac de sa chaîne de sandwiches préférée, *Prêt-à-manger*, il appuya sur un des boutons de son téléphone multifonctions. Une voix féminine aux accents graves lui répondit immédiatement. L'homme demanda gentiment une tasse de thé à son assistante pour accompagner son déjeuner du midi.

Il s'était acheté un paquet de sandwiches en triangle aux crevettes et à la mayonnaise, ainsi qu'un minuscule paquet de chips aromatisées au poivre vert. C'était son menu quotidien.

Jamais, depuis qu'il se fournissait dans ce même magasin, il ne s'était aventuré à goûter autre chose. Même les jours comme aujourd'hui où il devait être au maximum de ses capacités physiques pour accomplir ce qui, depuis son lever, lui donnait ce sourire qu'il ne portait que très rarement. Il n'attendit pas l'arrivée de son thé pour commencer à avaler ses sandwiches. Il avait pour habitude de manger les chips bien à part et de les laisser une à une dans sa bouche pour que sa salive les ramollisse doucement et que les petits grains de poivre recouvrent son palais.

Tenant un triangle de pain d'une main, il s'empara avec dextérité de l'édition du jour du *Times* que son assistante avait déposée ce matin dans son trieur. Ce midi, il ne fit pas comme à son habitude et ne se rendit pas directement à la page *Law Report*. Il s'arrêta à la rubrique *News*. Un petit article attira son regard

UNE JEUNE BIJOUTIÈRE ÉTRANGLÉE ET ÉNUCLÉÉE LA VEILLE DE NOËL.

Il sourit et commença sa lecture :

Un terrible drame a secoué une famille londonienne en cette veille de Noël. Lucy C., jeune femme de 24 ans, a trouvé la mort dans sa petite bijouterie de Lumley Street, dans le quartier de Mayfair, hier matin. La victime aurait été tuée dans sa bijouterie le soir du réveillon. Le meurtrier aurait bénéficié de l'heure tardive de fermeture pour commettre son atroce forfait. Le corps de la jeune femme portait des marques visibles de strangulation et de coups. Elle aurait également été victime d'abus sexuels. La brigade criminelle centrale de Scotland Yard a immédiatement ordonné une autopsie pour déterminer l'heure et les causes exactes du décès. D'après les informations livrées à la presse par le sergent Nancy Kelling, on aurait retrouvé un triangle de percussionniste sur les lieux du crime.

L'inspecteur de la brigade criminelle du New Scotland Yard, Paul Kite, un des principaux protagonistes de l'affreuse mort du petit Mark Thomson en juin 1987, aurait été chargé de mener les investigations. Rappelons que l'inspecteur Kite a déjà été dépêché en début de semaine sur le meurtre d'Eleanor Stout, retrouvée morte dans une chapelle du quartier de Covent Garden (notre édition du mardi 23 décembre.) Il ne serait pas étonnant de trouver un quelconque lien entre ces deux crimes.

L'homme avait fini ses sandwiches. Il saisit le journal et le roula en boule en froissant le papier si fort que ses doigts le transpercèrent. Direction la corbeille à papier. Il avait maintenant les doigts tachés d'encre, mais il s'en fichait bien.

Il fulminait en lui-même contre cette garce de sergent Kelling et ces abrutis de journalistes. Insinuer qu'il avait pratiqué des abus sexuels sur la petite Lucy. Elle était si belle. Si frêle, avec de si beaux yeux. Comme si cela lui était venu à l'idée de lui déchirer sa petite jupe verte qu'il avait à l'inverse ramenée sur ses genoux ! Comme s'il avait imaginé se déshabiller devant son cadavre et se pencher sur elle et... L'homme en avait presque des nausées et il sentit son estomac fragile se contracter plusieurs fois. Rester calme, respirer, fermer les yeux... Et comble de tout, ils n'avaient même pas évoqué ce dont il était le plus fier : les ampoules allumées qu'il avait délicatement enfoncées dans les orbites de la jeune fille.

112

L'homme avait besoin d'un thé. Rapidement. Et cette satanée bonne femme qui n'arrivait pas ! Il s'apprêtait à réappuyer sur son téléphone lorsqu'il entendit des coups répétés à la porte. Il donna l'autorisation d'entrer et son assistante lui posa son mug sur le bureau avec son sourire habituel, que l'homme appréciait modérément. Il la remercia d'un grognement et lui fit signe de partir. Ce qu'elle fit. Alors, il porta le mug à ses lèvres, se rejeta dans son fauteuil et ferma les yeux.

Le calme revenait peu à peu. Il ne devait plus penser négativement. Pour l'instant, la police était sans indice. Et puis, c'était le fameux Paul Kite qui allait s'occuper de lui. L'homme s'en faisait une joie. « Mais oui, réfléchis bien... Tout est positif. Ce soir, tu vas t'amuser, n'est-ce pas ? Et tu peux rentrer à l'heure que tu veux, puisque tu as donné double ration ce matin dans la cave. Sage homme... » Il but son thé à petites gorgées. Le breuvage le rasséréna.

Bien à l'abri derrière son bureau, il regardait le ciel gris pluvieux et souriait. Content de penser à sa voiture qui l'attendait sagement sur sa place de parking. Content de penser au contenu du coffre qu'il avait rempli tôt ce matin. Il s'imaginait déjà débarquant avec son sac au 11, Gilston Road. Le sac qu'il aurait préalablement rempli avec les objets contenus dans sa voiture. Il tenta de se représenter leur disposition méthodique. L'archet de violon au fond à droite. Juste en dessous, la sphère gonflable toute plate, qui ressemblait plutôt à un planisphère. Mais une fois gonflée ! Ils allaient voir ce qu'ils allaient voir ! Et puis, à gauche, le sac de sport et le long couteau bien aiguisé. Tout semblait normal. Vivement ce soir !

Il allait vite régler le dossier de cette histoire de droit maritime et pourrait ainsi sortir avant 7 heures. Et quand bien même ! Il n'avait de comptes à rendre à personne. S'il avait envie de s'en aller tout de suite, il pouvait le faire. Mais c'était bien trop tôt. Elle attendrait encore un peu. Le sursis. Dieu ce qu'il était heureux ! S'il s'était écouté, l'homme se serait même mis à pleurer.

18

L'inspecteur principal Andrew Barlow reposa dans le tiroir le crayon qu'il tenait à la main et jeta un dernier coup d'œil sur la grille de mots croisés qu'il venait de terminer. Il ne connaissait que ce remède pour arriver à se calmer rapidement. Et ce matin, il en avait bien besoin.

Depuis son arrivée dans les bureaux du New Yard, il était assailli de toutes parts. D'abord Paul Kite, qui lui demandait de lui confier l'enquête sur le meurtre de Lucy Chambers, car un lien était peut-être envisageable avec le meurtre de lundi. Puis, il avait été convoqué par trois de ses supérieurs à propos de l'affaire des « deux meurtres tout de même un peu étranges ». Il revoyait le vieux Forbes susurrer cette expression entre ses lèvres complètement desséchées.

C'est que la presse n'avait pas tardé à s'emparer des crimes et il devenait donc urgent pour le Yard de montrer de forts signes d'implication dans cette enquête. En d'autres termes, les inspecteurs actuellement sur cette affaire étaient déchargés de toute enquête. Exit l'inspecteur Kite et ses éventuels collègues que Barlow s'apprêtait à nommer. Le public voulait du neuf, du frais ! Plus de ces pâles inspecteurs réchauffés et traînant derrière eux une sombre et sale affaire ! Place aux jeunes cons, à leurs études de psychologie et à leur haute opinion de leur personne. Le public aimait ça.

Barlow repoussa la feuille de journal contenant la grille de mots croisés et se leva de son fauteuil pour se dégourdir les jambes. Il était bien content de prendre sa retraite dans un an et demi. Ce ne serait pas lui qui aurait le symptôme « déprime-retraite », si courant chez les flics en manque d'activité. Il passerait des journées entières avec sa femme et son petit jardinet. Plus besoin de grilles de mots croisés, il ne serait jamais plus énervé.

Il chassa ces sympathiques pensées de son esprit et se concentra sur le point qui le préoccupait. Il fallait qu'il annonce à son ami Paul Kite que l'affaire ne lui incombait plus. Ça n'allait pas être une partie de plaisir ! Barlow connaissait le personnage... Il imaginait facilement la réaction de son ami, qui semblait si motivé ce matin.

Il était midi. Il devait agir. Barlow décrocha le téléphone et appela le bureau de Kite pour s'enquérir de sa présence. Un homme avec un curieux accent anglais décrocha :

— Bureau de Kite.

— L'inspecteur Kite est là ? demanda-t-il.

— Qui le demande ?

C'était un accent avec de faibles intonations françaises. Il y était ! Ce devait être le jeune stagiaire que Kite avait bien voulu accueillir dans le cadre du programme d'échange habituel.

Mon Dieu ! Quel courage et quelle abnégation, pensa Barlow.

Il y a quatre ans de cela, lui-même avait accueilli un stagiaire allemand. Il n'avait pas tenu plus de trois semaines. Le jeune Germain avait, en plus d'un niveau d'anglais déplorable, une capacité de travail plutôt limitée, voire nulle. Barlow l'avait donc rendu à la police de Francfort rapidement. Alors que Kite supportait son jeune *froggie* depuis trois mois déjà !

Barlow pensa pendant un moment continuer la conversation en français, langue qu'il maîtrisait plutôt bien depuis qu'il passait ses vacances d'été en Dordogne. Mais il s'abstint.

— Dites-lui que, si ça ne le dérange pas, Andrew va venir lui rendre une petite visite...

— OK. Il doit rentrer vers midi et demi.

Barlow approuva et raccrocha. Il aurait aimé pouvoir ralentir le temps. Repousser le moment d'affronter Kite... L'inspecteur principal Andrew Barlow chercha bien, mais ne trouva pas une seule grille de mots croisés vierge dans les tiroirs de son bureau. Il se mit alors à grincer des dents.

Clément raccrocha le téléphone avec force et fracas, son large sourire favori aux lèvres alors que plusieurs coups étaient frappés à la porte. Le sergent Nancy Kelling ouvrit sans même attendre de réponse et balaya la pièce du regard. Elle tenait dans sa main boudinée un dossier jaune en carton épais, d'où dépassaient quelques feuilles blanches.

— Kite est là ?

— Non, répondit Clément. Comme les grandes stars, il se fait attendre...

116

Kelling ne sembla pas prêter une quelconque attention à la phrase du jeune inspecteur.

— Quand il rentrera, donne-lui ça. (Elle tendit le dossier jaune à Clément.) Il y a le rapport du labo concernant la bijouterie et l'autopsie de Lucy Chambers, tout du moins le fax de l'original qui est encore à Woodford. Mais c'est déjà un vrai miracle que le légiste ait pu pratiquer l'examen si vite ! Et encore plus miraculeux qu'Owen ait pensé à nous faxer le rapport. Pour une fois qu'il ne rechigne pas à collaborer avec nous ! Paul avait dû lui mettre une sacrée pression...

Elle claqua la porte si fort que la vitre opaque où était indiqué le nom de l'inspecteur vibra pendant de longues secondes. Clément commença la lecture du rapport.

Lorsque la porte du bureau s'ouvrit dans un immense fracas, Clément ne releva même pas la tête tout de suite et attendit d'avoir fini sa phrase. C'était Kite, accompagné de Greg Alexander, portant à la main un sac aux couleurs de McDonald's. L'inspecteur esquissa son geste de l'envoi du chapeau sur le portemanteau et se dirigea en vitesse vers son bureau.

— Rebonjour, Clément, dit-il. J'ai croisé l'agent Alexander et je l'ai envoyé chercher la bouffe... Il paraît qu'on a déjà procédé à l'autopsie ? C'est incroyable !

— Rebonjour inspecteur ; bonjour Greg, répondit Clément de son habituel ton calme. Encore une petite minute de patience et j'en aurai fini...

— Dépêche-toi...

Kite se laissa tomber dans un fauteuil sans même prendre le temps de retirer son imperméable. Ses cheveux étaient luisants. On avait l'impression qu'il s'était renversé un pot de gomina sur la tête. Cela fit sourire Alexander qui avait pris place autour des tréteaux pour déballer les victuailles. S'il avait su, il aurait été acheter un *fish & chips* pour Kite. Il s'excusa :

— Inspecteur, je ne vous ai rien pris à manger...

— Ce n'est pas grave, répondit celui-ci en se levant pour aller accrocher son imperméable. Je n'ai pas bien faim ce midi. Je sors d'une entrevue avec le pauvre Mr Chambers. Il est défait. Heureusement, sa femme va mieux.

L'inspecteur se rassit en ayant bien pris soin de passer sa main sur le tissu du fauteuil pour déterminer son niveau d'humidité relatif au contact prolongé avec son imperméable dégoulinant. Kite détestait avoir les fesses humides.

— Du nouveau sur Lucy ? s'enquit Clément.

— Rien du tout à première vue... De toute façon, j'ai de plus en plus l'impression que l'assassin ne connaissait pas *vraiment* ses victimes. Même s'il ne doit pas les choisir au hasard, je ne pense pas qu'il les connaisse personnellement.

C'est alors que Clément leva la tête et referma le dossier dans un geste théâtral. Ses yeux marron contenaient une expression pleine d'espoir.

— Le lien existe bien, inspecteur. Sans le moindre doute.

— Un lien ? Quel lien ? interrogea Alexander.

Clément glissa le dossier entre le pouce et l'index de l'inspecteur et résuma à son ami les conclusions du rapport.

L'atmosphère du bureau était redevenue calme. Seuls le murmure de la voix de Clément et les bruits de gargouillis venant de l'estomac

118

à jeun de Kite troublaient un silence apaisant. Clément commença ainsi son résumé :

— Prenons d'abord le rapport du laboratoire concernant la bijouterie. Le crime a bien eu lieu là. Les minuscules traces rouges sur le sol sont des traces de sang. Groupe A, rhésus positif, le même que Lucy. Ce même sang a été retrouvé sur le culot des petites ampoules. Le labo a pu mettre en évidence quelques minuscules plaques de sang séché. Il a aussi retrouvé, à plusieurs endroits sur l'ampoule, de minuscules morceaux de tissu conjonctif.

Clément fit une pause et s'empara d'un gobelet de coca. Il en aspira une goulée avec la paille et plissa les yeux. La boisson était bien trop fraîche. Il reprit :

— Ça prouve donc la version des faits de Mr Chambers : on avait bien enfoncé dans l'orbite des yeux de Lucy les deux ampoules. Pas profondément, et surtout avec douceur, car elle n'a aucune autre plaie aux yeux.

Alexander écoutait attentivement, une main sous le menton.

— En ce qui concerne la pile, elle était encore chargée au maximum. Mais bon, c'est tout à fait normal dans la mesure où le père de Lucy a « débranché » le mécanisme en emportant le corps de sa fille. Le labo dit que la pile aurait bien tenu une journée entière sans le moindre problème. Rien de plus sur le montage électrique, modèle et marque des fils, des ampoules et de la pile couramment employés, disponibles partout...

Nouvelle pause.

— Bon, pour les empreintes, il faudra repasser : rien de chez rien ! Pas une seule si ce n'est, bien sûr, celles de Lucy un peu partout et un enchevêtrement logique sur les poignées intérieures et extérieures de la porte. Rien de bien spécial sur les empreintes de chaussures. La moquette était légèrement tachée à plusieurs endroits ; un peu de boue, de saleté, la conséquence du petit crachin qu'il devait faire à ce moment-là...

— Justement, l'interrompit Greg. À quelle heure a eu lieu le meurtre ?

Clément l'apaisa d'un geste de la main.

— Attends, je finis sur le labo et après tu auras le droit à l'autopsie.

L'agent du Yard marqua son contentement en avalant une dizaine de frites en même temps. Il s'attendait à un récit bien plus âpre.

— Donc, en résumé, le meurtrier devait porter des gants. Sur le triangle en fer, il n'y a rien non plus. Ce n'est donc pas l'élément qui nous aidera dans l'enquête. Maintenant, je te parle vite fait de la bijouterie. La porte n'a pas été forcée, ce qui pousserait donc à croire que le meurtrier a agi pendant les heures d'ouverture et probablement vers la fin de la journée, si aucun client n'a découvert le corps avant Mr Chambers. (Clément s'arrêta et observa la réaction de son ami.) Les bijoux, placés autour du corps comme le laisse supposer leur disposition par rapport aux taches de sang, contiennent tous un ou plusieurs diamants. Tous sont en parfait état sauf une bague qui a...

Un grognement sourd interrompit le récit de Clément. Les deux jeunes fixèrent Kite. Ce dernier était toujours en train de lire le dossier. Il avait le visage rouge vif.

— Je disais donc, reprit Clément en se retournant vers son ami qui fixait encore Kite d'un œil inquiet, que les bijoux étaient intacts sauf une

120

petite bague en apparence sans pierre précieuse. Mais un diamant desserti a été retrouvé au pied d'une des vitrines. Le labo en a donc déduit que la bague avait dû être mise à terre et écrasée. Le diamant se serait desserti. Je ne sais pas si c'est un élément important, mais, bon... Je crois que je n'ai rien oublié...

Clément s'empara d'un beignet de poulet, le trempa dans une sauce à la couleur plus que douteuse et le fourra dans sa bouche. Il attendit quelques instants et continua :

— Le rapport d'autopsie, maintenant. D'abord, les éléments les plus importants. Primo, Lucy est décédée des suites d'une forte strangulation sur la base du cou. Elle a dû suffoquer pendant trente ou quarante secondes tout au plus. L'assassin devait avoir une sacrée force, car elle ne s'est même pas débattue. Il n'y a aucune trace de lutte et aucun coup sur le corps. Ça se rapproche bien de la méthode employée pour miss Stout. Simple strangulation dans les deux cas. Maintenant, le plus important peut-être : le légiste a procédé à une analyse microscopique sur plaquette d'un bout de tissu épidermique prélevé sur le cou de Lucy. Eh bien, le meurtrier, ou la meurtrière, portait des gants... des gants noirs en cuir, comme ceux utilisés pour le meurtre d'Eleanor Stout. La simple coïncidence serait étrange, tu ne trouves pas ? Ensuite, autre élément important, Lucy n'a été victime ni de viol ni d'aucun autre abus sexuel. Elle était encore vierge. Donc, il ne commet pas ses crimes pour des mobiles sexuels...

L'agent Alexander fronça les yeux.

— En apparence, du moins. Secundo...

— Tertio, corrigea l'agent.

— Oui, tertio, les yeux de Lucy ont été enlevés juste *après* le meurtre. Je n'ai pas compris comment le légiste l'a déduit, mais c'est un fait certain. Le sadique a extrait les globes oculaires avec une sorte de pince.

Heureusement, les deux jeunes venaient de finir leur déjeuner. L'image du cadavre énucléé de la jeune fille allongé sur son lit leur revenait en mémoire.

— Il a ensuite sectionné le nerf optique à l'aide d'un scalpel ou peut-être d'une simple paire de ciseaux bien aiguisée. La coupe est nette. Voilà pour le rapport d'autopsie. Du moins ce qu'on peut en lire sur les fax dégueulasses que nous avons reçus, et ce que j'ai pu comprendre grâce à mon anglais que je n'ai évidemment pas appris dans un manuel médico-légal...

Alexander remua légèrement les fesses sur sa chaise.

— Et l'heure de la mort ?

— Selon le légiste, entre 6 et 8 heures du soir. Lucy devait fermer sa bijouterie à 7 heures selon son père. Le meurtrier a dû arriver un peu avant pour que personne ne puisse le déranger. Mettons, 7 heures moins dix. Ça coïnciderait bien.

— Oui, à ce détail près qu'une personne aurait pu débarquer à l'improviste, sans connaître l'heure de fermeture, à 7 heures ou un peu après, l'interrompit Kite qui avait posé le dossier sur son bureau. Ce qui me ferait plutôt penser qu'il est venu à l'heure limite pour que personne ne trouve le cadavre avant le lendemain. Cela expliquerait qu'il ait pris soin d'éteindre les lumières en partant. Mr Chambers vous a bien parlé des deux seules ampoules

122

allumées dans l'obscurité de la bijouterie lorsqu'il est arrivé ?

— Oui.

— En plus, la pile pouvait facilement tenir
jusqu'au lendemain.

— Mais pourquoi ?

— Parce qu'il est tout à fait possible que ce
sadique ait voulu attendre le lendemain pour
que l'on découvre le corps. Le jour de Noël,
peut-être... Mais il ignorait que la jeune fille
réveillonnait en compagnie de ses parents... En
réfléchissant, c'est bien la même chose avec
miss Stout : il n'y avait pas d'office à la chapelle
le lundi soir. Si le pasteur n'était pas venu ce
jour-là...

Les deux jeunes approuvèrent d'un hochement de tête simultané. C'est alors qu'on frappa
à la porte. L'inspecteur-chef Andrew Barlow
pénétra à l'intérieur du bureau sans même
attendre de réponse. Kite se leva immédiatement et invita son supérieur à s'asseoir. Il
remarqua le costume toujours aussi triste de
son ami, et son visage d'une pâleur laiteuse où
sa petite moustache d'un noir encore très foncé
pour son âge paraissait factice. Andrew n'avait
pas l'air très à l'aise. Il adressa un petit signe
de la main à Clément et à l'agent Alexander et
répondit à l'invitation de Kite en s'effondrant
littéralement dans le fauteuil désigné.

— Paul..., commença-t-il d'une voix enrouée.

— Non, écoute plutôt, nous avons reçu les
rapports concernant le meurtre de Lucy Chambers, tu le savais, au fait ?

— Oui, Kelling me l'a dit.

— Bon, eh bien, le lien entre le meurtre
d'avant-hier et celui de lundi ne fait plus aucun
doute, déclara Kite en mettant le ton.

Barlow n'essaya même pas d'interrompre son ami inspecteur et écouta, l'air plus triste que jamais, tous les éléments importants des rapport d'autopsie et du laboratoire. Quand Kite eut enfin fini, il prit la parole :

— Paul, je suis désolé de te l'apprendre comme ça, mais ce n'est plus moi qui m'occupe de l'affaire de ces deux meurtres...

Kite marqua le coup et écarquilla ses petits yeux.

— Tu veux dire que tu as été déchargé par... Mais alors, moi aussi je...

— Hélas, Paul...

Kite avança outrageusement sa mâchoire en avant tout en serrant les dents. Les salauds ! Les pourris ! Il en avait tant besoin de cette affaire. Et ils la lui enlevaient probablement pour la confier à ces jeunes peigne-culs psychologues. Il demanda la confirmation de sa supposition à Barlow, qui la lui donna. Forbes, le vieux manitou, avait dû subir tant de pressions qu'il déchargeait la criminelle « classique » de l'enquête.

Kite fulminait. Il était hors de lui, fou de rage, rouge d'aigreur. Les deux jeunes craignaient le pire. Giggs aurait annoncé la nouvelle à la place de Barlow, l'ami de Kite, il lui aurait probablement décoché une bonne droite à travers la figure. Mais Kite n'était pas le seul à être contrarié. Clément avait l'air vraiment dépité. Il voulait vraiment s'investir dans cette affaire, la plus importante dont ils auraient eu conjointement la charge à ce jour.

— Forbes a été intraitable, reprit Barlow alors que Kite semblait se calmer légèrement. Il n'a rien écouté de ce que je disais.

124

— Je suppose qu'ils veulent que je leur apporte le dossier en main propre ?

Le ton de Kite était glacial.

— C'est-à-dire que...

— Qu'ils aillent se faire mettre ! Je vais aller balancer les feuilles dans les chiottes...

— Paul... raisonne-toi, lui adjura Barlow. Cela n'arrangera rien.

— Ça me défoulera...

— Et ça ne changera rien, ajouta l'inspecteur-chef. Kelling, avant de te confier le dossier, a fait une copie qu'elle s'est empressée de transmettre à Forbes.

— La garce !

— Ne lui en tiens pas rigueur, tenta de relativiser Barlow. Elle n'a fait qu'obéir aux ordres...

— On se ligue, marmonna Kite. On se ligue contre moi.

Il avait la mine plus grave que jamais. Et il se sentait étrangement léger. Il tenait là le moyen de se racheter, de conjurer ses atroces souvenirs, et on le lui ôtait des mains. Il regarda machinalement son bracelet-montre. Il était 13 h 30. Maintenant, les journées allaient lui paraître longues. Bien longues. Trop longues. Mais il n'allait pas abandonner comme ça. Pas son style.

— Forbes, reprit Barlow sur un ton hésitant, m'a conseillé de te mettre sur une autre enquête pour t'occuper... Il sait que ce n'est pas une partie de plaisir d'être déchargé d'une mission... Bref, il m'a dit de te mettre sur le meurtre-suicide de Tottenham Court Road.

Clément avait lu effectivement un entrefilet dans *Metro* ce matin à propos de ce fait divers. Il s'agissait d'un homme qui s'était jeté sous le métro la veille dans la soirée. Suicide banal en

125

apparence si l'on n'avait pas retrouvé un petit stylet planté dans le dos de l'homme.

— Il peut toujours aller se faire foutre ! Il n'en est pas question...

— Écoute, Paul, répondit son supérieur tout en se levant de son fauteuil, réfléchis bien, mais ne fais pas le con... Et puis cela intéresse peut-être ton jeune stagiaire français...

— Ce qui intéressait mon jeune stagiaire français, Andrew, c'était de continuer cette putain d'enquête. C'est lui qui a découvert le corps chez les parents Chambers, avec l'agent Alexander. Et il se faisait un devoir de mener l'enquête. Alors ton affaire de merde... Tu peux dire à la vieille momie de Forbes qu'il se la carre au cul !

Clément était bien triste. Alexander, qui devait regagner son poste, s'excusa et salua les trois hommes. Il tapota amicalement l'épaule de Clément. Ça promettait pour lui qui rêvait de réussir le concours d'inspecteur ! Mais Kite avait eu raison de réagir ainsi. Clément connaissait la terrible affaire de juin 87 qui hantait les nuits de l'inspecteur et ce pourquoi il voulait boucler cette enquête.

— Bon, je te laisse Paul. Quand tu le désires, tu passes au bureau prendre le dossier pour le meurtre de Tottenham. À tout à l'heure, Paul...

Barlow sortit et ferma délicatement la porte.

Paul Kite et son jeune collègue restèrent seuls dans le bureau. L'estomac de Kite ne faisait plus aucun bruit. Il n'y avait que le bruit de la pluie sur l'unique vitre du bureau qui troublait un silence bien pesant.

19

Clément sortit du grand immeuble du New Scotland Yard sous une pluie battante et se dirigea vers la station de métro de St James's Park pour rejoindre celle de Tottenham Court Road. Une fois à l'abri, il replia le parapluie et le secoua énergiquement de bas en haut. Une grosse flaque apparut immédiatement à ses pieds. Un homme portant l'uniforme du *London Transport* le regarda d'un air sévère. On ne rigolait pas avec la discipline dans le métro de Londres. Il arrêta immédiatement son manège et sourit à l'intention de l'homme, qui détourna immédiatement le regard et continua à écrire sur un tableau Velleda l'état actuel des lignes *Circle* et *District*. Le jeune Français sortit alors sa *travelcard* de la poche et passa les portillons.

Kite, calmé, assis derrière son bureau, fixait le plafond d'un regard vide en pensant au pacte qu'il venait de passer avec Clément. Cela n'avait pas été chose facile pour lui d'accepter cette pauvre enquête de meurtre-suicide. Néanmoins, il s'était résigné à la considérer et, après une longue discussion avec son stagiaire, était monté chercher le dossier chez Andrew Barlow. Ce dernier, heureux de voir son ami reprendre du poil de la bête, l'avait accueilli avec moult sourires et compliments, allant même jusqu'à lui offrir un cigarillo. C'était plutôt inhabituel de la part de son supérieur, qui était célèbre dans toute la criminelle pour son avarice. Kite redescendit donc avec le fameux dossier à la main pour le confier à Clément.

L'inspecteur et son jeune stagiaire avaient en effet mis en place une stratégie pour, comme le disait Kite avec un cruel sourire aux lèvres, « faire la nique au vieux Forbes ». Ils étaient tous deux partis d'un constat : l'inadmissible prise en charge du dossier des meurtres de Lucy et miss Stout par une autre unité que la leur. Il en résultait donc une certitude : ils se devaient de continuer l'enquête, officieusement, parallèlement, pour eux. D'où cette tactique qui consistait à ne pas se faire remarquer : Clément allait donc instruire pendant l'après-midi l'enquête sur le meurtre-suicide du métro ; pendant ce temps-là, Kite aurait les mains libres et retournerait sur les lieux des crimes, pour tenter de récolter d'autres informations.

Barlow et Forbes n'y verraient que du feu. Et ça, ça faisait sourire l'inspecteur Kite pour la première fois de la journée. Il regarda sa montre et estima que ça n'était pas encore l'heure de passer à l'action. Il repensa plutôt à l'entretien de ce matin avec le père de Lucy. Il se reprochait d'avoir été trop peu indiscret avec lui. Plus il y repensait, plus il se disait que cet entretien n'avait servi à rien. C'était une terrible impression : avoir remué les souvenirs de ce pauvre homme pour rien. Kite ne s'en félicitait pas.

Il se leva et se dirigea vers le placard près de l'entrée. Il commençait à avoir un peu faim. D'un geste précis, il introduisit la petite clef dans la serrure et les portes de l'armoire s'ouvrirent. Retirant sa veste et la posant sur le dossier de la chaise dévolue habituellement à Clément, il tenta de hisser sa main sur la dernière étagère. Difficilement, il l'atteignit du bout des doigts et commença à farfouiller à droite et à gauche. Puis ses doigts rencontrèrent une résistance. Kite poussa un petit grognement de satisfaction. Il venait de mettre la main sur son paquet de Crunchie, sa confiserie préférée, des barres de chocolat fourrées au miel. Ça n'était pas bien nourrissant, mais ça le ferait déjà patienter. Il en prit trois et referma l'armoire.

Le métro rentra à toute vitesse dans la station de Tottenham Court Road. Clément descendit du wagon. Il s'épongea le front à l'aide d'un mouchoir en papier. La chaleur était incroyable. Il se dirigea vers la sortie, tout du moins vers le haut de cette station très profonde, où il devait prendre contact avec Mr Evans, le chef de la station, et le seul nom dont faisait référence le très mince rapport existant sur cette affaire.

Vraiment, cet après-midi s'annonçait infect. Il avait beaucoup de mal à trouver la motivation après avoir subi ce véritable revers de se voir déchargé d'une affaire qu'il n'avait pourtant pas si mal menée toute la journée d'hier. Mais plus que sa propre frustration, Clément tentait de comprendre celle de l'inspecteur Kite. Il ne fallait pourtant pas être bien clairvoyant pour comprendre que Kite était aussi capable qu'un autre de mener à bien cette enquête. Peut-être même encore plus compétent, car son terrible échec passé l'avait au final servi et aujourd'hui il n'en était que plus fort. C'était tout du moins l'analyse a posteriori que l'inspecteur avait délivrée à son jeune adjoint. Mais les raisons « politiques » passent avant les autres... Et il valait mieux pour tous les petits chefs le cul assis derrière leur bureau que les casseroles de Kite ne bringuebalent pas trop bruyamment à sa suite.

Clément serra très fort les poings pendant toute la montée de l'escalator. Le milieu artistique l'avait déçu. Et Hicks pourrait bien le dégoûter de la police... Déjà ? Il avait mis dix ans à désenchanter du théâtre. Clément se dirigea vers le guichet de l'entrée. La soirée avec Mary serait-elle suffisante pour faire passer le goût de l'injustice ? Il pensait à cela, mais ne voulait pas l'évoquer : chaque chose à sa place. Ne rien mélanger.

L'inspecteur Kite trouva miraculeusement une place dans Savoy Street et put ainsi garer sa Rover très près de la petite chapelle de Savoy Row. C'était la première fois qu'il voyait le quartier de jour. Il se dirigea paisiblement vers la chapelle après avoir pris soin de fermer à clef les portes de sa voiture. La pluie battante du midi n'était plus qu'une toute petite bruine que Kite trouvait même agréable. Que c'était frustrant pour lui de se rendre sur les lieux d'un meurtre sans pouvoir réellement se réclamer du Yard ! Il ne pourrait pas montrer sa carte car, officiellement, il devait se trouver à deux kilomètres de là, sous terre, à mener l'enquête sur ce meurtre du métro.

Il distinguait de loin les bandes habituelles en cas de scellés. En se rapprochant, il remarqua la présence d'un placard punaisé sur la lourde porte en bois. Le pasteur s'excusait de la gêne occasionnée par « le terrible drame qui a frappé notre brave Eleanor Stout et, par elle, la paroisse tout entière ».

Kite cligna des yeux et laissa l'affichette pour se concentrer sur les alentours de cette charmante petite chapelle. Il y avait cette ruelle qui longeait sa façade. Kite voyait bien le meurtrier se garer ici. Ou sans doute un peu plus loin pour ne pas éveiller l'attention. Et dire que les voisins des immeubles environnants n'avaient rien vu du tout ! Ça ne risquait pas d'arriver chez lui, pensa Kite. Avec la vieille bignole de Jenkins, il n'y avait aucun souci à se faire... Elle aurait noté le numéro d'immatriculation de la voiture et tout le reste... Kite sortit les mains des poches de son imperméable et se lissa les sourcils tout en réfléchissant à mi-voix. « Voyons, il a dû se garer non loin car il fallait se les transporter, ces gros sacs de terreau... Et il avait intérêt à être sûr de la présence de miss Stout... Bref, il entre dans l'église une première fois pour la tuer. »

Une jeune femme aux cheveux orange et au jean déchiré à plusieurs endroits passa devant Kite et lui ricana doucement au nez. Kite haussa les épaules et se tourna de nouveau vers la façade de l'église. Il tentait d'imaginer l'homme en train de franchir la petite porte. « Il n'a pas dû avoir beaucoup de mal à étrangler cette pauvre miss Stout. Puis il l'a étendue par terre et a gravé maladroitement avec un cutter l'inscription sur son front. » Kite revoyait le cadavre tel qu'il l'avait trouvé. « Il est alors ressorti et a donc pris un risque considérable en faisant ça... Si quelqu'un entrait à ce moment-là dans la chapelle ? Mais personne n'était venu. Alors il a recouvert le corps de terreau. Pourquoi ? Et il est reparti, probablement avec le sentiment du devoir accompli... »

Kite avait, lui, le sentiment du devoir non accompli. Était-ce une si bonne idée que ça de revenir sur les lieux des meurtres ? Cela l'aiderait-il à mieux comprendre les motivations de l'assassin, son mobile, sa façon de procéder ? Il décida que oui. Comme cela. Sans argumenter. Il avait un peu l'impression de jouer le personnage principal de cette série médiocre dont sa fille ne ratait d'ailleurs jamais un épisode : *Millenium*. Sauf que lui n'avait pas une perception extrasensorielle des événements. Méthode classique. Kite sourit en imaginant sa fille devant un épisode d'une série dont il serait le héros. « Même un pauvre auteur raté en mal d'inspiration n'oserait me prendre en tant que personnage principal de son futur torchon... », pensa-t-il.

Et sur ces pensées, il regagna sa Rover. Une fois à l'intérieur, il tourna le rétroviseur en guise de miroir et regarda l'état de son visage. Fatigué, cernes, bouclettes humides... Il n'avait pourtant rien à envier à la classe d'un Indiana Jones affrontant les rats dans les égouts de Venise. Mais pourquoi pensait-il tout d'un coup à jouer l'acteur de cinéma ? Ses vieilles prétentions artistiques, datant de son adolescence, ressortiraient-elles ? Michelle s'amusait parfois à trouver des ressemblances entre Clément et lui. Eh bien, en voilà une de plus, ces prétentions artistiques datant de leur jeunesse... Le jeune Français lui en avait fait la confidence un soir de garde.

Kite tenta un sourire charmeur dans le rétroviseur pour voir s'il ressemblait vraiment à Harisson Ford et, devant le peu de succès qu'il s'accorda, tourna la clef de contact et accéléra pour lancer le moteur. Il alluma son autoradio, dont le tuner était bloqué sur *Capital Radio*. C'était une chanson de Simply Red, *Stars*. Kite adorait. Il reprit en même temps que la voix « *IIIIIIIIIIIIIIIII wanna fall from the stars, Straight into your arms, IIIIIIIIIIIIIIIII, I feel*

132

you, I hope you comprehend. » La voiture s'ébroua avant même le troisième couplet.

Il régnait une activité intense dans la station, jonction entre deux des lignes les plus fréquentées de Londres. Clément se présenta au guichet de renseignements et demanda Mr Evans, en exhibant sa carte devant la vitre légèrement teintée qui protégeait la guichetière. La jeune femme se leva. Le jeune inspecteur attendit au moins cinq minutes avant qu'Evans veuille montrer le bout de son nez. Cela ne le mit pas dans les meilleures dispositions, d'autant plus qu'une chaleur épouvantable régnait dans la station. La chaleur, le bruit digne d'un stade de Wembley bondé et différentes odeurs allant d'une transpiration âcre à celle, piquante, du soufre achevaient le tableau.

— Monsieur...

John Evans venait à l'instant de sortir du « bocal ». Il tendit sa main à Clément. C'était un Black d'une quarantaine d'années, avec des cheveux frisés très courts, dont certains tiraient déjà sur le blanc. Il avait de gros yeux striés de veines d'un rouge écarlate. Ni trop grand ni trop petit, probablement de la même taille que Clément, John Evans portait avec distinction une superbe veste vert pâle sur une impeccable chemise blanche, assortie d'une cravate jaune sable du meilleur effet, et un pantalon beige. Clément prenait là une véritable leçon d'élégance.

— Je vous remercie d'être venu si vite, dit-il d'un ton vaguement ironique.

— Je vous en prie, lui répondit Clément. Vous avez déjà dû recevoir la visite de deux inspecteurs hier pour les premières constatations, si je ne m'abuse...

— Oui, du moins je le suppose... Je n'étais pas ici hier. Jour férié. C'est mon adjoint qui a reçu vos collègues ainsi que les ambulanciers et tout le bastringue... (Il marqua une pause et rajusta sa cravate qui n'en avait pas besoin.) Mais je suis à même de vous guider dans votre enquête.

— C'est-à-dire... Je préférerais que votre adjoint s'en charge si vous n'y voyez pas d'inconvénient.

John Evans fit une moue d'excuse anticipée :

— Moi, je n'y vois aucun inconvénient, mais il est en congé et est parti voir sa famille dans le Wessex...

— Je comprends, conclut Clément. Bon, eh bien, je vous suis, Mr Evans, pouvez-vous m'emmener sur les lieux du drame ?

— Bien sûr, fit Evans avec un sourire.

Le chef de station semblait visiblement bien s'amuser. Cela le changeait de la routine. Après avoir ouvert la porte du bocal et marmonné quelques mots à son employée, il se dirigea vers les escalators, Clément sur ses talons.

Oxford Street était fermée à la circulation en ce lendemain de Noël. Seuls les bus et les taxis étaient autorisés à emprunter la grande rue. Bien sûr, les véhicules de police pouvaient faire de même, mais Kite ne voulait surtout pas attirer l'attention sur lui. Devant la bijouterie, il voulait passer pour un simple passant, un curieux, voire un fouille-merde de journaliste si vraiment il le fallait. Mais pas pour un flic.

Il tourna de longues minutes autour du Roosevelt Memorial à la recherche d'une place et finit par en dégotter une sur Grosvenor Square. Il regarda sa montre. Déjà 5 heures ! Lui qui croyait que la journée lui paraîtrait longue. En fait, évoluer dans cette sorte de demi-illégalité l'excitait beaucoup ! Il devenait aussi gamin que pouvait l'être parfois Clément.

Il éteignit la radio d'un geste sec et ouvrit sa portière. Au même instant, un *cab* noir avec à son bord deux vieilles dames remontait à vive allure la rue en roulant très près du trottoir. Le chauffeur, visiblement absorbé par ses pensées, anticipa mal la distance nécessaire, entre son *cab* et la file de voitures en stationnement, pour éviter la portière de Kite. Trop tard. Elle vola littéralement en éclats après un dur impact avec la carrosserie avant du taxi. La Rover tangua un grand coup à gauche puis revint dans sa position initiale. Le chauffeur du *cab* arriva tant bien que mal à garder le contrôle de son véhicule, qui finit sa course en travers de la chaussée, évitant par bonheur une autre collision. Il régnait une pagaille incroyable dans la rue. Tout le monde se précipitait pour assister à l'agonie des victimes. Peine perdue. Le chauffeur du *cab* aida les deux vieilles femmes, hilares, à sortir du taxi. Une forte odeur de gomme assaillit les narines des spectateurs.

Kite ne s'était pas tout de suite rendu compte de l'accident. Penché vers sa boîte à gants pour en extraire sa petite bouteille d'eau pétillante habituelle, il avait juste entendu le bruit infernal de la porte éclatant sous l'impact et senti les secousses de sa voiture. Néanmoins choqué, il s'extirpa de sa voiture pour avoir une vue d'ensemble sur la scène. Et merde ! Il allait être obligé de sortir sa carte de flic. Merde, merde et merde ! Lui qui était ici incognito, c'était réussi ! Il prétexterait une course dans le quartier, mais ça paraîtrait bien louche. Heureusement que l'accident ne s'était pas déroulé précisément dans Lumley Street.

Se dirigeant vers le chauffeur du *cab*, les jambes légèrement chancelantes, Kite pensa qu'il n'était peut-être pas passé loin de la mo... Non, il ne voulait pas y penser. Le chauffeur, visiblement choqué lui aussi, était en train de contempler l'étendue des dégâts sur la carrosserie de son *cab* lorsque Kite lui tapa fermement sur l'épaule.

— Inspecteur Paul Kite, Scotland Yard. (Il sortit à regret sa carte.) Dites-moi, vous transportiez des passagers ?

L'homme fixa Kite avec deux yeux grands ouverts.

— Déjà la police ! Quelle rapidité !

— C'est-à-dire que je suis l'homme de la portière.

Il désigna la Rover dont on pouvait maintenant voir l'intérieur.

— Oh ! Euh... J'avais deux personnes âgées, mais l'accident les a fait plus rire qu'autre chose. Elles sont assises là-bas...

— Je vois. Avant que nous ayons une discussion sérieuse concernant, par exemple, la vitesse excessive de votre véhicule, je vous prierais de bien vouloir ranger votre *cab* sur le côté de la route. Vous ne vous rendez pas compte du bordel que vous provoquez dans le quartier !

Pour toute réponse, une multitude de klaxons se firent entendre. Des jurons plurent sur Kite et le chauffeur de *cab* plantés juste en plein milieu de la rue. Trois conducteurs, très énervés, sortirent de leur voiture, l'écume aux lèvres. Ils voulaient visiblement avoir une petite discussion, voire plus si affinités, avec ces deux chauffards. Kite, sentant l'urgence de la situa-

136

tion, les calma comme par magie en brandissant bien haut sa carte de police à l'attention des trois hommes, puis vers la foule.

— POLICE, messieurs-dames, POLICE. Allez, foutez tous le camp, il n'y a vraiment rien à voir... Dégagez ou j'appelle les collègues et je vous fais à tous un prix de gros sur la garde à vue... Allez...

La foule se dispersa aussitôt et les trois énergumènes regagnèrent leur voiture rapidement en ravalant leur colère. Tout proche, on entendait le bruit caractéristique d'une sirène de police. Les collègues, pensa Kite. Ouf ! Il allait pouvoir partir. De toute façon, il n'avait plus le temps, ni même l'envie d'aller à la bijouterie. Il allait rentrer au Yard. La nuit était maintenant tombée sur Londres. Et avec elle, le froid. Kite pensa au bonheur de la climatisation... Option dont sa Rover n'était pas équipée, c'était maintenant le moins que l'on puisse dire...

Clément avait la rage au ventre. Passer deux heures de son temps entre le quai de la *Northern Line*, où le meurtre avait eu lieu, et le bureau d'Evans l'avait rendu d'une humeur exécrable. Sur le quai, lors du speech du chef de station, un courant d'air tiède leur giflait la figure à chaque fois qu'une rame de métro pénétrait dans la station. C'était une sensation qui, répétée des dizaines de fois, avait vraiment le don de vous énerver. Ensuite, cette discussion interminable et stérile dans le bureau d'Evans avait fini d'achever le jeune stagiaire. À 6 heures et demie, Clément s'excusa auprès du chef de station et prit congé. Une fois hors du bureau, il sortit à l'air libre et téléphona à Kite d'une cabine :

— Kite à l'appareil.

— Inspecteur... Clément... Je vous appelle de la station de métro.

— Ah... Et alors... Chiant comme on le pensait ?

— Non, non ! Pire ! Je dois avoir attrapé la crève par-dessus le marché !

— Bon, et sur le meurtre ?

— D'après les premiers éléments, il y a très peu de chance de retrouver l'assassin. La station et la rame étaient bondées.

— OK, donc demain on classe le tout ?

— Il y a pas mal de chance, en effet... (Une pause.) Et vous, de votre côté ?

Clément entendit Kite soupirer.

— Bof ! Rien. À l'église je n'ai rien pu voir de nouveau, car les scellés étaient mis et puis je ne suis même pas allé à la bijouterie...

— Hicks et ses balais à chiottes y étaient ?

On appelait les jeunes inspecteurs de la brigade de psychopathologie criminelle les balais à chiottes, car ils portaient tous les cheveux très courts et en brosse.

— Non, mais j'ai eu un accident avec la Rover...

— Oh merde ! Que de la tôle, j'espère ?

— Ouais, la porte côté conducteur a été carrément pulvérisée...

Il lui raconta rapidement les circonstances de l'accident, puis reprit :

— Bon, ce soir, tu ne fais pas la garde avec moi. Mais après tes cours, tu reviens à l'appartement. S'il y a quelque chose d'important, je passe te prendre.

Clément se mordit la lèvre et pria.

— Oui bien sûr, inspecteur. Sans aucun problème...

138

— OK, bon, demain je me donne la matinée pour récupérer, alors on se retrouve au New Yard à 14 heures, ça va ?

Clément approuva la décision de son supérieur. Ça lui laisserait une matinée supplémentaire avec Mary. Sur ce, ils se saluèrent et Clément redescendit prendre son métro, direction Finchley Central.

20

Quand l'homme sortit de son bureau, il ne gagna pas directement le parking par l'ascenseur. Il préféra le rejoindre par l'extérieur. La raison de ce détour était simple : il voulait se tenir au courant des dernières nouvelles concernant ses meurtres. Juste savoir si le Yard avait quelques indices. Il devait bien y avoir un autre flic à Scotland Yard en quête d'une célébrité d'un jour pour vendre le morceau aux journalistes. Le sergent Kelling l'avait bien fait hier.

Confiant, l'homme sortit de l'immense hall en marbre de l'immeuble et s'arrêta quelques instants sur le large perron. Il regarda vers sa droite, là où se trouvait d'habitude ce vieil homme à la barbe rousse qui vendait l'*Evening Standard* à la criée. Joie, il y était ! L'homme, sans même boutonner son imperméable, se dirigea vers lui et lui tendit une pièce de cinquante pence, sans un mot. Le vendeur s'empara d'un exemplaire de la dernière édition et le tendit à l'homme avec sa monnaie, sans un mot. Il mit ses pièces dans la poche intérieure de son manteau et plia en deux le journal pour le glisser à l'intérieur de sa sacoche en cuir noir.

La pluie s'était arrêtée de tomber depuis maintenant une bonne demi-heure. Seule la pellicule translucide recouvrant la chaussée et les trottoirs témoignait de sa chute ininterrompue depuis le début de la journée. L'homme regarda la forme qu'avait la lune ce soir. Mais il ne la vit pas ; elle était probablement cachée par un de ces nouveaux gratte-ciel qui commençaient vraiment à pourrir le quartier.

Il gagna alors l'entrée du parking souterrain en passant devant la petite cabane censée abriter le gardien, apparemment absent. « Encore en train de cuver sa bière et son whisky avec son collègue de l'immeuble d'en face aussi poivrot que lui... », pensa l'homme. Mais il n'avait pas le temps de s'appesantir sur le sort de ce raté. Il devait maintenant se concentrer entièrement sur sa soirée. Sur ce meurtre qu'il allait perpétrer avec une joie qu'il espérait plus forte encore qu'avec Lucy.

Il remonta tout le parking vers sa Mercedes, qu'il garait toujours sur sa place réservée. Elle se trouvait bien loin de l'ascenseur et de l'entrée, mais il s'en fichait, car il était homme à respecter les règles que la vie en société imposait. Toutes, sauf celle de ne pas tuer son prochain. Celle-là, il avait le droit de la transgresser. Après ce qu'on lui avait fait dans le passé ! L'homme cliqua sur sa télécommande et entendit le bruit caractéristique de l'ouverture des loquets. Il pénétra à l'intérieur après avoir pris soin d'enlever son imperméable qu'il allongea sur le siège arrière. Posant sa serviette à côté de lui, il s'empara du journal et le déplia.

Un article à la une retint immédiatement son attention.

L'AFFAIRE DU MEURTRE DE LA BIJOUTERIE REBONDIT !

À l'heure où nous finissons de boucler cette édition, on apprend, de sources non officielles, que l'affaire du meurtre atroce de la jeune Lucy Chambers, retrouvée étranglée et énucléée hier, a connu de nouveaux développements.

L'homme sentit des coups sourds résonner dans sa poitrine. Il continua néanmoins sa lecture.

Le New Scotland Yard serait parvenu à établir un lien entre ce meurtre et le meurtre de miss Eleanor Stout, lundi soir, dans la petite chapelle de Savoy Row (nos éditions datées du 23 décembre). Ce lien, dont la nature n'a pas été précisée à la presse, aurait décidé Mr Edward Forbes, directeur de la Brigade criminelle, à reconsidérer l'affaire. L'inspecteur-chef Barlow, et par conséquent l'inspecteur Paul Kite, impliqué dans la tuerie de triste mémoire ayant causé la mort du petit Mark Thomson, ont été déchargés de l'enquête. Cette dernière a donc été confiée au superintendant Hicks, et à ses jeunes limiers de la brigade de Psychopathologie criminelle [suite en page 5].

Quelle honte ! Mais pour qui te prennent-ils ? Un débutant ? Un enfant qui s'amuse ?

L'homme tenta de se calmer. Il sentait le sang affluer vers son visage. Un bourdonnement inhabituel lui remplit les tympans. Il jeta le journal sur le siège avant et se massa délicatement les tempes.

« Calme-toi ! Calme-toi ! tu as besoin d'être calme ! Pense à ce soir... Ils ont choisi de te sous-estimer ; eh bien, ils vont voir ce qu'ils ne veulent plus voir ! Un meurtre atroce, sanglant ! Ils ont retiré l'affaire a Kite qui était pourtant, lui, expérimenté ! »

L'homme tenta de se rappeler les termes exacts de l'article : « au superintendant Hicks et à ses jeunes limiers ».

Mon Dieu ! quelle honte ! vraiment... « jeunes limiers ».

Il se calmait au fur et à mesure que son esprit reprenait le dessus, au fur et à mesure qu'il répétait les gestes qu'il accomplirait ce soir. Cherchant à se détendre encore un peu plus, il alluma la radio. C'était le bulletin d'informations de 18 heures de la BBC. Cela suffisait bien ! Il appuya sur la touche du scanner automatique. L'autoradio chercha puis s'arrêta sur une station musicale. « *Angie, Angie, we can say we never try, Angie, Beautiful...* » Les Rolling Stones ! Il détestait. D'un geste brusque, il éteignit le poste. Décidément, aujourd'hui, il traversait une journée remplie de contrariétés. Mais tous paieraient ! Ce soir, il se promit de n'avoir aucune, mais aucune pitié. Sur ce, il démarra.

21

Le métro tardait à arriver. Mary et Clément étaient assis sur un banc en bois dans la charmante station « aérienne » de Finchley Central. Cette station avait toujours fasciné le jeune

Français, notamment son hall d'accueil et son guichet, dans cette vieille maison restaurée où l'on prend l'escalier qui devait, à l'origine, descendre à la cave et qui, aujourd'hui, permet de rejoindre le quai direction Londres centre.

La nuit était maintenant entièrement tombée. Heureusement, la pluie avait cessé. Lorsque Clément était allé chercher son amie à la danse, il pleuvait de grosses gouttes. Ils étaient revenus chez Mary, qui avait pris une douche salvatrice. Clément, lui, s'était juste séché les cheveux en écoutant la radio.

C'est Mary qui entendit la première le bruit du métro passant l'aiguillage desservant la station. Elle entraîna Clément et ils montèrent à bord du métro main dans la main. Trouvant facilement deux places côte à côte sur de vieux sièges orange foncé aux motifs douteux, Clément entreprit de faire le récit détaillé de sa journée au Yard. Le jeune fille l'écoutait distraitement. Il pouvait prendre son temps : Mary et lui avaient bien une demi-heure de trajet jusqu'à Leicester Square.

Une fois arrivés, Mary voulut absolument savoir où Clément l'emmenait. Ce dernier ne répondit pas. Ils sortirent de la station et passèrent devant la *Photo Gallery* pour rejoindre la petite rue de Slingsby Place. Là, son ami s'arrêta. Elle l'imita et en profita pour changer son petit sac à main d'épaule. Il semblait chercher du regard quelque chose. Un restaurant ? En effet, une fois l'enseigne repérée, Clément reprit sa marche, tenant fermement Mary par la main. Il avait décidé d'emmener son amie dans un restaurant chinois dont il avait eu l'adresse par son voisin de palier à Fulham.

— Alors, c'est ici ? demanda Mary.

— Oui. Tu aimes bien le Chinois ?

— Quelle question... Tu me prends pour une raciste ?

Clément se pencha vers elle et l'embrassa dans le cou. Il y avait quelques nuances de la langue française que Mary ne maîtrisait pas encore complètement.

— Non, bien sûr ! Je veux dire la cuisine chinoise...

Mary sourit à son tour et, pour toute réponse, poussa la porte du restaurant.

L'endroit était accueillant rien que par sa décoration. De nombreuses lithographies chinoises étaient fixées sur un magnifique lambris rouge. Au plafond, les lampions traditionnels pendaient. Au fond, près de la porte des toilettes, prenait place un immense aquarium rempli d'une multitude de poissons exotiques. La salle était encore vide et Mary et Clément purent ainsi choisir leur table. Ils optèrent pour celle collée à l'aquarium. On leur tendit alors des cartes.

— Mary...

Elle releva les yeux et fixa son ami.

— Oui ?

— Mary, laisse-moi choisir si tu le veux bien, car on m'a donné de bons tuyaux sur ce restaurant...

— OK, pas de problème...

Le serveur arriva presque immédiatement.

— Vous avez choisi, Mademoiselle, Monsieur ?

— Oui, déclara Clément. Nous prendrons pour commencer des raviolis de crevettes, numéro 21, puis des seiches à la pékinoise, numéro 52, pour finir avec des beignets de pommes au caramel, numéro 75.

144

— Et comme boisson, Mademoiselle, Monsieur ?

— De l'eau plate, s'il vous plaît.

Ils tendirent tous deux leur menu au serveur qui s'éloigna et fit sonner une petite cloche devant le passe-plat de la cuisine.

— Tu sais, Clément, ce soir, c'est moi qui t'invite...

— Non, il n'en est pas question, c'est moi...

— Mais c'est toujours toi !

— Oui, car je touche ma paye d'inspecteur en France. Et le loyer ne me bouffe pas tout, loin de là. Ça a été vraiment cool de la part de l'ami de ton père pour l'appart. J'espère qu'on pourra un jour le remercier...

— Au fait, tu ne l'as jamais rencontré depuis octobre ?

— Non, répondit Clément. Ton père s'est occupé de tout...

— Bien sûr que tu pourras le remercier !

Mary fixa les yeux de son petit ami et les trouva doux. Ses fins sourcils blonds les faisaient étonnamment ressortir. Quel charme ! Ses manières étaient toutes contenues. En fait, elle trouvait Clément beau garçon. C'était un délicieux flirt, « un bon coup » comme disait sa meilleure amie.

Mary ne comprenait pas l'attachement que lui portait Clément. Elle n'avait donné aucun signe censé lui faire croire à une aventure sérieuse. Le jeune Français jouait-il la comédie en se prétendant amoureux, croyant ainsi la séduire ? Était-il encore de ces mecs qui s'accrochent dur comme fer au romantisme, qui n'ont pas bien mesuré l'évolution de la condition féminine ? « Avant, les femmes se contentaient de faire un bon mariage, avait plaisanté sa professeur de danse. Maintenant elles se contentent simplement d'un bon coup ! » Mary était bien trop jeune pour se construire un avenir. Elle vivait une passion charnelle avec un beau garçon. Un flic.

— Clément, tu m'aimes vraiment ? demanda la jeune fille à brûle-pourpoint.

— Bien sûr, Mary... Pourquoi cette question, as-tu des doutes ?

— C'est-à-dire que, quelquefois, j'ai l'impression que tu joues au romantique, que tu te forces à te comporter comme ça avec moi.

— Vraiment ?

— Oui, c'est étrange... (Mary observa une pause.) C'est comme quand tu me dis que tu n'es pas dans ton trip de flic... Tu as l'air à cran ce soir.

Clément fit une légère grimace. Il n'avait pas envie d'en parler. Pas ici.

— Mary, parlons d'autre chose, s'il te plaît...

La jeune fille se sentit mal à l'aise.

— Tu évites toujours le sujet et tu me reproches après de ne jamais parler sérieusement de nous ! Je ne sais jamais où tu en es de tes interrogations. L'autre soir, tu n'as pas voulu me parler du théâtre, mais à chaque fois tu ne manques pas de me rabâcher tes journées d'enquêtes !

— C'est mon job, se défendit Clément. Tu ne peux pas me reprocher d'en parler !

— Avant l'affaire de 87, mon père racontait tous les soirs ses journées à ma mère. Elle l'écoutait avec passion, papa se demandait même si elle ne notait pas des détails dans un carnet. Il ne prenait pas son boulot au sérieux, il faisait son job en se disant qu'il était au centre de la comédie humaine tous les jours... Et puis il y a eu les meurtres de ce pédophile. Papa rentrait le soir en gueulant, il frappait maman quelquefois, il ne me parlait plus, jetait des objets par la fenêtre sans raison, découchait pour rentrer soûl au petit matin. Ça lui a coûté deux mois d'internement en hôpital psychiatrique. Maman était enceinte à l'époque. Elle a fait une fausse couche. J'avais 8 ans à l'époque.

Mary semblait avoir les larmes au bord des yeux. Clément lui prit la main. Elle se laissa faire.

— J'ai quelquefois du mal à admettre que mon père est encore flic. Tu comprends ce que je veux dire ? Quand tout ça s'est calmé, il nous avait promis d'arrêter, de lâcher le Yard. Et puis il s'est mis dans la tête qu'il devait se racheter, qu'il donnerait sa démission quand son nom serait réhabilité par les journalistes. Il me dit souvent : « Après cette affaire, je plaque tous ces cons et je me remets à la musique. » Mais il continue...

Clément sentit qu'il devait prendre la parole maintenant.

— Tu ne vois en moi que le flic, n'est-ce pas ?

L'absence de réponse ne laissait planer aucun mystère sur les sentiments de la jeune fille. Éprouvée par son père, elle ne voulait pas lier une relation sérieuse avec Clément de peur d'avoir à subir les affres de la copine de flic. Ne pas s'attacher, considérer Clément comme un corps ne l'engageait nullement. C'était là que Mary se trompait un tant soit peu.

Le jeune Français commençait à saturer de la routine du Yard. Depuis qu'il avait revu son ami Sébastien à Paris, il doutait de nouveau. Son copain d'enfance et de planches commençait à vivre du théâtre. Le démon allait-il de nouveau enflammer Clément ? Était-ce une erreur ? Replonger dans le milieu...

Il ne voulait pas aborder le sujet avec Mary. Que pourrait-il bien lui dire au juste ? Il était dans un flou qui n'avait pourtant rien... d'artistique ! Et comment réagirait son amie devant une telle annonce ? Le croirait-elle ? Ses sentiments évolueraient-ils ? Lui qui rêvait d'une paisible *love story* était confronté à sa première affaire de cœur...

Cette conversation le poussait trop à cogiter. Ils se faisaient du mal. Il fallait réagir... Sortir une phrase quelconque, neutre... Couper le fil de l'échange pour ce soir... Partir...

— Avant de commencer avec ces satanées baguettes, je vais aller me laver les mains...

Clément se leva et se dirigea vers la porte indiquant les toilettes. Il avait surtout besoin de se passer un peu d'eau sur le visage et la nuque. Digérer les paroles de Mary également. Une minute plus tard, il rejoignit Mary qui observait le manège des poissons dans l'aquarium.

— Mary ! chuchota-t-il sur un ton empressé. Il faut absolument que tu ailles voir les toilettes...

— Pourquoi ?

— Tu verras...

— Si c'est parce qu'elles sont sales, ça n'est pas la peine de...

— Non, non, bien sûr... C'est plus drôle que ça...

Mary se leva à son tour et se dirigea vers la porte. Elle tourna la poignée et pénétra à l'intérieur de la pièce. Surprise ! C'était le séjour des propriétaires ! Les enfants et les parents étaient tous rassemblés sur le canapé en train de regarder la télé. Des tartines de chocolat traînaient au milieu de papiers sur la petite table devant le canapé. Le grand-père semblait manger son bol de soupe. Mary se sentait gênée. Tout à coup, un petit garçon lui indiqua la pièce du fond tout en lui déclamant, très fier de lui :

— Les toilettes, c'est par là !

Pour se donner une contenance, Mary s'y rendit.

Une minute plus tard, elle avait réintégré la salle de restaurant où l'attendait un Clément hilare. Mary ne tarda d'ailleurs pas à l'imiter. Chassez l'artificiel, il revient au galop. C'est donc dans un concert d'éclats de rire que le serveur fut accueilli, surpris, avec ses deux petits paniers-vapeur de raviolis.

22

Jude Parlour avait fini son service relativement tôt aujourd'hui. À 5 heures de l'après-midi, elle avait déjà déserté l'hôpital de Chelsea. Mais elle ne comptait pas rentrer chez elle tout de suite. Avec Dorothy, la jeune réceptionniste et sa confidente quasi exclusive, elles se rendirent ensemble dans le centre de Londres, du côté de Piccadilly Circus, pour s'octroyer une soirée paisible entre femmes.

Ce soir, David n'avait pas pu se libérer. Il était encore de garde pendant toute la nuit. Décidément, on n'épargnait vraiment rien aux jeunes internes... Jude devait penser à ne pas rentrer trop tard. Sa demi-sœur, jeune fille au pair à Los Angeles, devait l'appeler vers 22 heures. Mais d'ici là, elle avait tout son temps.

Elle avait demandé à Dorothy de lui rappeler d'acheter pour David, au cas où elle l'oublierait, le dernier best-of de Genesis. Et elle rajouterait de son côté une petite surprise... Un caleçon humoristique, avait-elle pensé... Ou un tee-shirt avec une inscription grossière... Lui qui était si réservé... Il fallait le voir défaire la blouse de Jude... Un vrai animal... Mais Jude ne s'en plaignait pas : elle aimait cela et puis elle était amoureuse... C'était merveilleux... Si nouveau...

Elle avait souri pendant tout le trajet de bus en écoutant le récit de la journée de Dorothy. Elle avait vraiment le chic pour raconter les histoires !

Lorsqu'elle se sépara de Dorothy, qui regagna son appartement des Docklands, elle était très satisfaite et avait passé un très bon moment. Ainsi, à 21 h 55, elle tournait la clef dans la serrure de son petit loft de Gilston Road. Elle retrouva son coin cuisine dans le même état où elle l'avait laissé la veille au soir.

Jude s'assit sur son canapé blanc avant de commencer son rangement. Elle décida d'attendre le coup de fil de sa demi-sœur avant de s'y mettre. Elle en profita pour s'arrêter quelques instants sur l'aménagement de son petit appartement : elle en était si fière !

Certes le loyer bouffait déjà la moitié de sa paye, mais elle s'était toujours promis, lors de son adolescence, de vivre dans un appartement à elle, spacieux et fonctionnel. Elle avait trop souffert dans le F2 de sa mère, avec son beau-père, son frère et sa demi-sœur. Elle s'était toujours juré de s'installer dans un logement avec une douche individuelle et des toilettes à elle, pas sur le palier...

Elle s'était donc offert la location de l'appartement ainsi que l'ameublement qui l'accompagnait : un canapé blanc, sur de la moquette blanche, des murs peints en blanc, une table blanche aux formes modernes, une cuisine tout équipée blanche et une chambre aux tons... foncés. En blanc, cela lui aurait trop rappelé une chambre d'hôpital. Elle avait donc elle-même collé un papier peint bleu foncé et ne se servait pour son lit que de parures sombres.

D'ailleurs, ce contraste avait beaucoup plu à ses anciens amants. Et David l'adorait ! Surtout cette clarté de tous les instants dans la salle de séjour, et pourtant, elle ne comportait qu'une seule grande fenêtre donnant sur la rue.

« Dring, dring... »

Le regard de Jude arrêta son vagabondage et se fixa sur la porte.

« Dring, dring... »

Mais qui pouvait bien venir à cette heure ?

« Dring, dring... »

Oh, mais non ! C'était le téléphone. Jude confondait encore les deux sonneries. Elle décrocha le combiné et reconnut immédiatement la voix de sa demi-sœur.

Clément enleva le manteau de Mary aussitôt entré dans l'appartement, qui était conçu de telle façon que le séjour n'était accessible qu'au bout du couloir où se trouvaient les portes de sa chambre, du placard, de la cuisine et de la salle de bains. Il lui fit faire la visite des lieux, puis ils s'assirent sur le canapé.

Ils n'avaient pas bu une seule goutte d'alcool de la soirée et pourtant Mary et Clément avaient de plus en plus chaud. Clément avait quitté son sweat-shirt et était assis de telle sorte que son corps formait un parfait angle droit avec le canapé. Mary, elle, avait replié ses jambes dans la position « du lotus » après avoir défait ses Doc Marten's. Ils plaisantaient, riaient de bon cœur.

Leur conversation du restaurant était bien loin. Ils savaient ce pour quoi ils étaient ici. Ce pour quoi ils étaient ensemble. De temps en temps, l'un ou l'autre se penchait, réclamant un baiser. Ils ne fuyaient pas. Continuaient. Jusqu'à ce que les gestes rejoignent les baisers et qu'ils se serrent l'un contre l'autre, partageant la chaleur de leurs corps. Ce consentement par silences échangés était le liant de leur histoire.

Clément aurait voulu dire non, se lever du canapé, dire à Mary qu'il ne pouvait plus se contenter que de cela. Mais il n'en eut pas le courage. À l'inverse, il passa une main avide sous le pull de son amie.

Au même moment, un homme tenant à la main un gros sac à dos anormalement rond, sonnait à la porte d'un appartement du 11, Gilston Road.

Jude entendit une nouvelle fois la sonnerie. Cette fois-ci, elle en était sûre, c'était bien la porte. Elle se dirigea vers l'entrée tout en se demandant qui pouvait bien venir lui rendre visite à cette heure-là ? Il était tout de même plus de 11 heures ! Et si David avait pu se libérer de sa garde ? S'il avait eu la possibilité de la reporter à un autre soir, où Jude serait également de service à l'hôpital ?

Le cœur plein d'une hypothétique allégresse, elle poussa la poignée et ouvrit la porte. Un homme d'une quarantaine d'années se tenait debout, les pieds sur son paillasson « *Welcome* ». Il était vêtu d'un imperméable vert et portait un sac à dos à la main. Jude s'étonna : elle ne connaissait pas cet homme.

L'homme n'attendit pas longtemps sur le palier. La belle Jude vint lui ouvrir presque immédiatement. Elle était belle dans ce jean qui lui seyait parfaitement et dans ce joli sweat-shirt rouge qui s'harmonisait à la couleur châtain de ses cheveux. Elle était belle, sa Jude, et il lui sourit dès qu'elle entrouvrit la porte. Mais il lut un étonnement sur son fin visage. Il n'avait pas le choix, il devait absolument agir dans la minute. D'un coup sec de la pointe du pied, il tapa violemment dans le bas de la porte. Jude se cogna le front sur la serrure intérieure et tomba à terre. Elle ne comprenait rien de rien. Elle sentit juste son corps s'enfoncer mollement dans l'épaisse moquette blanche recouvrant le sol. Elle se toucha le front par réflexe comme pour savoir si elle saignait. Mais aucune trace rouge n'apparut sur le bout de ses doigts. Ouf ! Elle qui détestait la vue du sang...

L'homme entra précipitamment dans l'appartement et referma la porte de sa main gantée. Sa jolie petite Jude s'était peut-être blessée. La sotte. Il ne voulait pas qu'elle se fasse mal. Il ne voulait pas voir de plaie sur son front lumineux. Mais heureusement, elle était indemne. Alors, sans même attendre qu'elle se relève, l'homme posa son sac à terre et se jeta sur elle. Saisissant son cou.

Descendant ses mains et sa bouche tout le long du corps habillé de Mary, Clément s'attarda pendant quelques instants sur son cou. Il le lécha avec application, tentant de recouvrir chaque centimètre carré d'un baiser. Encore et encore, il descendit plus bas, passant ses paumes ouvertes sur la poitrine, le ventre, les cuisses de sa petite amie. Elle se laissait faire avec dévotion ne se sentant pas encore capable de prendre la moindre initiative. Elle soupirait calmement, passant la main dans les cheveux de Clément, puis la retirant lorsque ce dernier descendait trop bas. Chacune de leurs étreintes avait un goût de nouveauté.

C'était pourtant son troisième meurtre, mais l'homme éprouva une sensation toute nouvelle alors qu'il serrait ses gants noirs autour du cou de sa Jude. Si, au début de leur contact, elle n'avait pas pris conscience de la situation, encore sous l'emprise de son choc avec la porte, maintenant elle se débattait vigoureusement et cela plaisait forcément plus à l'homme. Elle ne parvint tout de même pas à crier, même si ce n'était pas l'envie qui lui manquait. Mais l'homme serrait son cou avec un force inouïe.

Elle avait l'étrange impression que sa tête s'était désolidarisée de son corps. À peine pouvait-elle bouger les yeux pour voir le visage de cet homme qui était en train de la tuer. Elle allait mourir dans cet appartement qu'elle aimait tant. Loin de cet homme qu'elle aimait tant. Dans les bras de cet homme qu'elle n'avait même pas eu le temps de haïr. Car en trente-cinq secondes, Jude avait cessé de vivre. L'homme lâcha le cou de la jeune fille et accompagna la chute de son dos sur le sol. Jude était morte maintenant. L'homme pouvait prendre son temps.

154

Mary sentait monter en elle un désir intense. Elle avait l'impression d'avoir devant elle non plus Clément, mais un simple jouet de chair. Elle allait s'en servir pour se donner du plaisir comme lorsque, plus jeune, elle jouait à la poupée. Elle entraîna Clément dans sa chambre et se coucha sur le lit, ordonnant à son compagnon de la déshabiller. Il s'exécuta avec dévotion.

Des paroles résonnaient avec insistance dans sa tête... Des paroles récurrentes qu'elle aurait aimé ne pas entendre : « Tu fais moins le malin, petit flic ! C'est toi qui m'obéis, hein ? Allez, pose ton flingue sur la table et écarte les bras comme sur les pare-brise des voitures... »

Clément avait quitté ses habits et elle observa la silhouette adulte dans l'obscurité, ne distinguant que les contours, évitant ainsi tous les défauts. Elle sentit qu'il s'allongeait près d'elle quand ils échangèrent leurs sueurs. Une odeur de corps s'installa dans la pièce. Mary gémit pour l'appeler. Il vint. Elle ne s'était jamais sentie aussi vivante.

Jude était bien morte. Elle avait vu passivement sa vie défiler devant ses yeux pendant ses dernières secondes, lorsqu'elle tentait d'aspirer encore un peu de cet air dont elle se fichait bien maintenant. Et c'est cette dernière image qui la fit presque pleurer. Cette image fixe devant ses yeux... Ce visage d'homme qui la regardait avec son sourire. Ce visage d'homme qui ne la reverrait jamais plus, qui ne se poserait jamais plus sur son ventre. Le visage de David, son jeune amant.

Clément laissa à Mary l'initiative. La jeune fille goûta chaque endroit du corps de son jeune amant avec application. Rien n'aurait pu l'arrêter en cet instant. Son visage était tendu par l'excitation. Elle aimait la texture de la peau de Clément. Elle aimait qu'il la prenne de ses habiles mains pour la retourner. Elle se faisait manipuler en sachant parfaitement qu'elle gardait le contrôle total des opérations. Un gémissement de gêne et son ami ne serait pas assez courageux pour continuer... Il stopperait net, déçu, fâché et tenterait de trouver un subterfuge, un autre plaisir à lui infliger. Si elle l'encourageait d'une main dans les cheveux, ou même plus passivement, en écartant ses lèvres, il continuerait son exploration, comme un aventurier ne cherchant qu'à s'échiner sur son corps. Le désir fou du jeune homme ne trouvait de réponse que dans le sien. Ils n'étaient plus que des boîtes à hormones animées.

Une décharge d'adrénaline plus tard, l'homme se releva de l'endroit où il venait de déposer Jude. Il contemplait l'épaisse moquette blanche aux gros brins. Cela devait probablement bien absorber le sang, ce genre de texture. L'homme se dirigea vers son sac à dos et en sortit chaque objet : d'abord l'archet du violon qu'il posa sur le canapé non loin, le couteau qu'il garda dans ses mains, puis la grosse sphère qu'il avait bien pris soin de gonfler durant le long moment qu'il avait passé à attendre sa victime.

Il devait la tuer à 20 heures et elle n'était revenue qu'à 22 heures... Et encore, peut-être attendait-elle quelqu'un. L'homme trouva donc plus prudent de laisser s'écouler encore une bonne heure avant de sortir de sa voiture.

Mais maintenant, il était tranquille.

Il revint vers Jude. Prenant sa respiration, il se pencha vers son corps et entailla doucement le haut de son cou.

Mais ça n'allait pas du tout ! Ce miroir sur pied qui réfléchissait son image devant lui l'énervait prodigieusement. Il ne voulait pas se voir lorsqu'il levait les yeux du cadavre de sa Jude. S'emparant de sa main gauche d'un cendrier en terre se trouvant sur une table basse toute proche, il l'envoya, d'un ample mouvement circulaire, se fracasser contre le miroir qui se brisa en mille morceaux. Tant pis pour le bruit, l'homme voulait se mettre dans les meilleures conditions possibles. Déjà qu'il avait bien chaud avec cet imperméable... Se concentrant, il posa de nouveau son couteau sur le cou de Jude. Juste en dessous de la mâchoire.

Ils avaient tous les deux très chaud. De fines plaques de transpiration ponctuèrent leurs nudités en mouvements perpétuels. Des brûlures ou des cloques ne manqueraient pas d'apparaître suite aux frottements qu'ils faisaient endurer à leurs corps. Puis disparaîtraient. Mary cambrait ses reins, faisait ressortir ses seins. La violence n'avait pas sa place ici, même si leurs silhouettes ne cessaient de se cogner, de se frapper. Le contact de leurs peaux était comme la rencontre d'un caillou et d'une flaque d'eau. Couverte par leurs cris. Si forts. Vibrants. Ils bouillonnaient. Leur sang s'agitait avec force pour servir leur plaisir.

Un épais filet de sang rouge-noir coulait avec abondance sur la moquette. L'homme venait de finir de trancher la tête de Jude. Elle ne tenait plus au tronc maintenant que par la colonne vertébrale. C'était la chose qui embêtait le plus l'homme. Graver des lettres sur un front, extraire des yeux de leurs orbites ou bien trancher le cou de femmes ne l'effrayait pas plus que ça. En revanche, être obligé de briser cet os le remplissait à l'avance d'une peur qu'il ne s'expliquait pas. Peut-être était-ce parce qu'il n'était pas un barbare... Pourtant en ce moment, il se sentait libre de toute convenance. *Alea jacta est*.

Il tint le couteau par la partie inférieure de son manche, s'apprêtant à fracasser l'os à l'aide de son extrémité. Levant le couteau bien haut, la lame vers le plafond, il abattit son bras. L'os céda immédiatement. Il ressentit lui-même un curieux malaise à la base de son cou, mais n'y prêta que peu d'attention. La tête de Jude était maintenant entièrement séparée de son corps. Heureusement que l'homme avait pensé à lui fermer les yeux tout à l'heure... Mais il s'en voulait tout de même un peu : ce geste brusque, même s'il était nécessaire, n'allait pas du tout avec le rythme de la chanson qui se jouait en ce moment dans sa tête.

Ils étaient là, maintenant, sur ce lit aux draps froissés. Tout oublier pour ne garder que l'instant. Comment faire autrement ? Ils étaient égoïstes et y prenaient plaisir. Guidés par un cerveau en roue libre qui ne reconnaissait et ne conjuguait que quelques verbes : écarter, entrer, sortir, s'appuyer, changer, caresser, serrer, se taire. Ils auraient pu murmurer, gémir, parler, crier, hurler. Mais ce serait déjà trop « couple », pas assez « coup ». Ils se retinrent.

158

L'homme ne se retint pas de sourire lorsqu'il déposa la tête de Jude sur le canapé, près de l'archet de violon. Puis, sans se départir de sa joie, il alla s'emparer du globe gonflable. Le tenant fermement entre ses deux mains, il l'amena près du corps de Jude et le posa à la place de la tête, en haut de ce cou flétri où se dessinait une multitude de filaments rouges. Baignant dans une mare de sang, la sphère bougea quelques instants puis se stabilisa, légèrement vers la droite. L'homme recula pour voir la scène de loin, comme la verraient ces imbéciles du Yard. Il ressentit, avant même de se retourner, une excitation vertigineuse.

Mary mordait ses lèvres roses, les yeux maintenant fermés, ses cheveux éparpillés sur le traversin. Clément, lui, ne voyait plus rien autour de lui. Il ressentait simplement ce plaisir physique auquel tout être humain avait droit. Un bien-être qui les faisait exister. Dont ils ne pouvaient se priver.

L'homme se retourna sur le pas de la porte et contempla sa nouvelle mise en scène. Splendide ! Magnifique ! Quelle bonne idée avait-il eue ! Et ce contraste des couleurs : rouge et blanc ! Le Yard serait fier de lui. Et il connut alors ce paroxysme physique qui l'avait déjà envahi lorsqu'il avait porté la main sur cette bonne vieille Eleanor, lorsqu'il avait fini de tuer la mignonne Lucy et maintenant lorsqu'il quittait la charmante Jude. Il nota qu'il arrivait à se retenir de plus en plus longtemps.

Après un dernier regard pour Jude, il éteignit la lumière et ferma la porte. Le pantalon de l'homme se détendit peu à peu au fur et à mesure de sa descente vers Gilston Road.

Clément resta de longues minutes allongé près de Mary, lui caressant les cheveux et les mains qu'elle avait croisées sur son ventre. Elle lui souriait avec ce sourire qu'il aimait tant. Puis, radieux et honteux à la fois, Clément se leva et gagna, toujours en tenue d'Adam, la salle de bains. Mary regarda ses petites fesses fermes qu'elle n'avait en fait que très peu vues. Et elle s'endormit presque aussitôt. Clément en profita pour ramasser ce bout de latex qui traînait négligemment sur le sol.

L'homme regagna sa voiture sans difficulté, avec son sac ne contenant plus que le couteau taché de sang. Une fois derrière le volant, il sortit ses gants de cuir noir de sa poche intérieure d'imperméable. Il les avait négligemment roulés en boule une fois la porte refermée. Et des gants froissés, c'était une chose qu'il n'appréciait vraiment pas. Mon Dieu, quelle soirée ! Il regarda sa montre : pas loin de minuit moins le quart. C'était l'heure de rentrer et d'aller se coucher seul dans son lit.

Il espéra qu'aucun bruit ne viendrait de la cave ce soir, il était fatigué et n'avait aucune envie de descendre. Se frottant les mains pour les réchauffer, il s'assura que le sac était bien à côté de lui et tourna la clef de contact. L'homme pensa à son prochain meurtre, dans deux jours. Mais pas de précipitation, il devait déjà profiter de celui-ci.

En attendant, il démarra et plongea dans la nuit.

160

Clément revint s'allonger près de sa petite amie endormie. Il rejeta sur eux un drap pour que leurs corps nus et encore transpirants ne prennent pas froid. S'emparant de la main droite de Mary, il plongea à son tour dans la nuit.

Samedi 27 décembre 1997

23

L'inspecteur Paul Kite, accoudé à la machine enfin réparée, tenait à la main un gobelet en plastique rempli de café. Il veillait au Yard depuis 7 heures du soir et ne s'était accordé que deux pauses : une pour aller se restaurer vers les 11 heures, puis celle-ci.

Quand l'agent de faction lui avait demandé sa destination, règlement oblige, il lui avait confié se rendre dans un petit restaurant qu'il appréciait tout particulièrement, près de Putney Bridge. C'était là qu'il emmenait souvent Michelle quand il était encore jeune inspecteur. Cela faisait une trotte depuis le siège du Yard, mais il avait besoin de prendre un peu de distance. Sa nuit agitée, puis l'enquête le rendaient nerveux, très nerveux. Presque aussi nerveux que pendant cette affaire de juin 87...

Kite n'avait rien appris de plus sur l'affaire dans l'après-midi et ses conclusions n'avaient pas avancé d'un pouce depuis hier. La nuit ne s'annonçait pas sous de meilleurs auspices. Rien à se mettre sous la dent depuis le début. Pourtant, Kite sentait que quelque chose pouvait arriver. Il s'était fait cette remarque en début de soirée : nous étions, il y a encore quelques minutes, vendredi. Lundi, Eleanor ;

mercredi, Lucy... Deux jours. Et mercredi plus deux égale... vendredi. Mais que pouvait bien valoir ce calcul ? Souvent, les tueurs évitaient de suivre un schéma trop logique, car ils se sentaient alors plus vulnérables. Il n'y avait qu'à se rappeler juin 87. *Non ! Ne te rappelle pas* ! Le meurtrier avait étalé ses trois horribles crimes sur plus d'un mois... *Non !*

Kite but la dernière gorgée de café qui restait dans son gobelet et le jeta dans la poubelle, du moins dans son intention, car le gobelet atterrit sur le sol. Avec un juron, Kite se baissa et retenta sa chance. En plein dans le mille cette fois. Il préférait cela, car il accordait beaucoup de crédit à ce genre de détail. Heureusement qu'il avait une vie de famille à côté de son boulot.

Pour Clément, les soirées devaient être bien longues... À moins que son jeune stagiaire lui cache quelque chose et fréquente une jeune fille... Décidément, c'était la période ! Déjà qu'il soupçonnait sa fille d'avoir un galant. Il en avait parlé en début de soirée avec Andrew Barlow :

— Tu sais Andrew, commença Kite sur un ton confidentiel, je crois que Mary fréquente...

Un sourire était apparu sur les lèvres de son supérieur.

— Comment ça ?

— Je ne sais pas... Une supposition. Je me demande si elle ne sort pas avec quelqu'un. C'est bien normal après tout pour un père de se demander ce genre de chose...

— Bien sûr Paul, répondit Andrew, qui, lui aussi, avait une fille mariée et déjà mère de deux enfants.

— Tu comprends, depuis un mois et demi

166

maintenant, presque systématiquement, elle va coucher chez son amie Anna après la danse...

— Hum...

— Alors, naturellement, j'ai demandé aux parents d'Anna, que nous connaissons bien, si Mary dormait bien chez eux...

— Naturellement, ajouta son ami d'un ton ironique.

— Oui, répondit Kite sur la défensive. Je ne leur ai pas montré ma carte de police, bien sûr ! Enfin bref... Elle ne dort que très rarement chez eux... Moins que ce qu'elle veut bien nous faire croire...

— Eh bien ?

— Eh bien, voilà ! Rien de plus ! Simplement j'espère qu'elle ne fait pas de bêtises... Et sa mère qui ne s'inquiète pas le moins du monde...

Barlow n'était pas étonné par la réflexion de Kite. Dix ans auparavant, lorsque sa fille avait le même âge que Mary, il se rappelait avoir poussé une gueulante mémorable quand elle avait voulu inviter son petit ami à dormir à la maison. « En tout bien tout honneur, papa ! Un sur le lit, l'autre sur un matelas par terre. » Maintenant, il repensait à tout ça avec nostalgie. Et dire qu'étant jeune, il se plaignait de la rigidité des parents de ses petites amies !

— Tu sais, Paul, Mary est sérieuse. Et puis il faut arrêter de se voiler la face ! Tu n'en as jamais parlé avec elle ? Juste évoqué le sujet ?

Kite avait secoué la tête négativement.

— Ne jamais en parler, c'est se voiler la face, avait continué son supérieur. Tu continues à croire qu'elle ne fait rien en refusant de dialoguer avec elle...

Andrew avait raison après tout. L'inspecteur en parlerait à Mary un de ces jours. Il faudrait juste choisir le moment. Depuis quelques mois, sa fille semblait plus distante de lui et il ne s'expliquait pas cette attitude. Kite oublia cette conversation quand la porte de la salle de repos s'ouvrit en grand. Un agent se tenait debout dans l'embrasure.

— Inspecteur Kite, un appel dans votre bureau... Urgent... La police de Chelsea...

Kite ne fit ni une ni deux et se précipita à la suite de l'agent.

— Urgent... Pour moi... La police m'a demandé nommément ?

— Non, ils ont demandé un inspecteur de la criminelle. Et puisque vous êtes le seul sur qui j'ai pu mettre la main...

Kite accéléra subitement. Et si son curieux pressentiment...

Quelque chose de grave venait de se passer à Chelsea, au 11, Gilston Road. On venait de retrouver le cadavre affreusement mutilé d'une jeune fille dans son appartement. Et la police locale préférait prévenir un inspecteur du New Yard pour le dépêcher sur les lieux. Ainsi, son intuition ne l'avait pas trompé. Le tueur devait être méthodique à l'extrême. Un meurtre tous les deux jours. Jude Parlour. C'était le nom de la jeune fille assassinée.

S'emparant en vitesse de son manteau, il se dirigea vers la porte. L'affaire rebondissait, il n'avait pas le temps de téléphoner à Clément, mais il ferait un petit détour par Fulham pour aller le chercher. Il était sûr que son jeune adjoint lui en voudrait s'il se rendait seul sur les lieux.

168

Le grand panneau NEW SCOTLAND YARD devant l'immeuble tournait encore et toujours quand Kite passa devant au volant de la Rover. Les nombreuses lumières de la ville agressèrent ses yeux pendant quelques centaines de mètres. Il prit la direction de Fulham alors que l'air glacial de la nuit pénétrait allégrement dans l'habitacle de la Rover par l'immense ouverture laissée par la porte arrachée. Mais peu importait, il fallait aller vite...

Un bruit. La sonnette. Un bruit de sonnette. Clément ouvrit un œil, puis l'autre, et se leva avec précaution. Nom de Dieu ! Qui pouvait bien sonner à cette heure ? Il se retourna. Heureusement, Mary dormait toujours.

Arrivé près de la porte, il plaça un œil devant le judas. Un Kite à la mine patibulaire se trouvait là, le doigt prêt à réappuyer sur la sonnette.

— Oh merde ! murmura-t-il. Le père Paul est là !

Il ouvrit la porte en grand et laissa passer l'inspecteur.

— Désolé, Clément, mais il y a du nouveau. Un nouveau meurtre à Chelsea.

Clément, encore dans les vapes, attendit la suite. Kite lui résuma rapidement l'appel reçu du commissariat de Chelsea.

— Allez ! Du nerf ! Dépêche-toi ! On file...

L'inspecteur s'interrompit et tendit un doigt vers le pubis de son jeune adjoint.

— Prends tout de même le temps de passer un caleçon, car le fond de l'air est frais ce soir...

Clément s'aperçut de sa nudité. Dans un réflexe de pudeur inutile, il se retourna et fonça vers sa chambre.

— Je vais prendre un verre d'eau à la cuisine, annonça Kite d'un ton goguenard.

Une fois réhydraté, il rajusta sa veste et son pantalon et jeta un coup d'œil dans le salon. Il s'arrêta net.

— Tiens, tu t'es acheté une paire de Doc Marten's ? On dirait le même modèle que Mary a eu pour Noël...

Un léger frisson parcourut le dos de Clément, qui enfilait son jean dans la salle de bains.

— Oui, répondit-il un poil trop vite.

Kite fronça les sourcils.

— Tu les as peut-être prises un peu trop petites alors...

Clément chaussait du 46.

— Oh ! Mais ce n'est pas pour moi... C'est pour ma sœur. Pour son prochain anniversaire, ajouta-t-il cette fois-ci plus calmement.

— OK ! Peu importe d'ailleurs, on a du boulot ! Allez ! En route !

Clément ramassa son manteau par terre et suivit Kite, qui sortait au pas de course de l'appartement. Une fois Kite engagé dans l'escalier, il claqua la porte. Sortie de scène. Changement d'acte imminent. La charge va commencer. C'était étrange cette sensation, mais Clément avait presque l'impression de prendre part à un scénario tout droit tiré d'un film policier. Et à en juger par l'excitation qui montait en lui, ça n'était pas pour lui déplaire. Toutes les réponses autrefois fuyantes se précisaient presque à son insu.

Kite le ramena à la réalité rapidement :

— Tu aurais pu me demander comment j'ai réussi cette prouesse inouïe de venir sonner à ta porte sans avoir à utiliser l'Interphone...

Clément ne répondit pas. Pas encore assez

réveillé tout de même. Son corps réclamait sa théine habituelle.

— Ballot ! C'est Robert qui m'avait donné le code lorsque j'ai signé le bail pour toi... Eh ben, ça promet ! Moi qui voulais un adjoint perspicace, je vois qu'au saut du lit, ça n'est pas vraiment le cas...

Clément chercha dans le guide de Londres l'emplacement exact de Gilston Road. Kite, très nerveux, suivait à la lettre ses indications précises et, en moins de dix minutes, ils furent sur les lieux. Kite gara sa Rover contre le pare-chocs d'une voiture de police qui avait laissé allumés ses gyrophares horizontaux. Les nombreuses lumières clignotantes devaient empêcher les riverains de dormir.

Kite remarqua un grand nombre de visages agglutinés derrière les fenêtres des maisons voisines. Il se dirigea vers l'officier de faction devant la porte du 11 et se présenta tout en montrant sa carte. Clément fit de même.

L'agent scruta avec attention leurs papiers et laissa ensuite passer les deux enquêteurs, qui ignoraient à quel étage se rendre. Mais ils n'eurent pas de mal à trouver. Des flics avec et sans uniforme s'étaient attroupés devant une porte au second étage. Clément entendit même quelques bruits de flash venant de là. Ils commencèrent alors leur montée. Kite, nerveusement, se grattait les poches qu'il avait sous les yeux.

— Inspecteur Kite, New Yard. Inspecteur stagiaire Bellanger, nous avons été appelés probablement par un de vos collègues pour venir constater le décès de la victime.

Un rictus échappa à l'agent chargé de garder l'arrivée au second étage.

— Oh, vous savez, je crois que personne n'a besoin de venir constater le décès... Il ne fait pas le moindre doute...

Il laissa passer Kite et Clément qui étaient maintenant à deux mètres tout au plus de la porte. Un silence relatif régnait sur les lieux. Pourtant, six personnes s'y trouvaient. Kite s'étonna de voir déjà tant de monde. Il entendit cette fois le bruit d'un appareil photo qui rembobinait sa pellicule. Le labo était déjà sur place ! À cette heure ! La police de Chelsea avait fait des prodiges. À ce moment, un homme d'une trentaine d'années, crâne rasé, vêtu à l'identique de Clément, se dirigea vers l'inspecteur Kite et lui tendit la main.

— Inspecteur Kite ?

— Oui.

Il serra distraitement la main de Clément.

— Bonsoir. Je suis l'inspecteur adjoint Brockley. C'est moi qui vous ai appelé. Merci d'être venu si vite... C'est très gentil de votre part, surtout que votre collègue le superintendant Hicks, que je viens de joindre à l'instant, ne va pas tarder...

Kite marqua le coup. Clément aussi. Le superintendant Hicks avait dû être indisponible une dizaine de minutes auparavant et on avait alors appelé la brigade criminelle « classique ».

— Je me suis un peu emporté tout à l'heure. Mais les consignes sont strictes. (Il déplia une feuille de papier sortie de sa poche.) Il faut contacter le service de psychopathologie criminelle pour tout meurtre perpétré dans Londres et dans sa proche banlieue. Mais vous devez vous-même avoir reçu la note...

172

— Bien sûr, c'est moi qui l'ai rédigée, répondit Kite sur un ton acerbe que ne saisit pas bien l'inspecteur adjoint Brockley.

— Oh, bien sûr...

Kite l'interrompit immédiatement, ne voulant plus entendre sa voix sirupeuse de premier de la classe.

— Pouvons-nous néanmoins accéder au lieu du crime ?

Le ton sur lequel Kite posa la question n'appelait qu'une seule réponse.

— Oui. Mais je vous préviens, il faut avoir le cœur bien accroché.

Il s'écarta. Clément, qui contemplait distraitement la cage d'escalier au papier peint beige et au carrelage de la même couleur tout en écoutant la conversation, n'aimait pas beaucoup cette dernière phrase : « avoir le cœur bien accroché ». Serait-ce bien plus horrible que les deux yeux de Lucy sur la table de nuit ? Et de cette tête sans expression, sans regard...

Oui. Il aperçut la tête sur le canapé près de l'archet du violon posé sur un coussin qui semblait être gonflé de sang. Puis il vit ce corps avec ce grotesque globe posé sur l'épaule droite. Et toujours ce sang, dont un homme avec une petite mousseline sur la tête et un masque sur le visage effectuait un prélèvement. Clément agrippa l'imper de Kite, qui se tenait lui aussi debout sur le pas de la porte, les yeux écarquillés.

Une bouffée d'odeur fade de nourriture à moitié digérée lui emplit la bouche. Et cette odeur de sang chaud, Kite la détestait plus que toute autre. En décembre... Ou en juin...

L'inspecteur et son jeune adjoint n'avaient aucunement envie de rencontrer le superintendant Hicks et sa bande de jeunes écoliers. Ils étaient donc descendus immédiatement après avoir discuté quelques instants avec un autre inspecteur, qui les avait mis au courant des divers et rares renseignements que la police avait été pour l'instant en mesure de rassembler : l'identité de la victime, son âge, sa profession, l'adresse et le numéro de téléphone de ses parents, qui étaient apparemment injoignables... Mais le labo étant déjà sur les lieux, l'heure de la mort avait pu être fixée avec précision aux alentours de 23 heures, ainsi que la cause de la mort de Jude Parlour : strangulation. On pouvait encore apercevoir des traces sur son cou. Quant aux autres informations, Kite et Clément devraient attendre jusqu'au lendemain les résultats du labo. Kite avait vraiment l'impression qu'on le prenait pour un con. Comme s'il ne s'en doutait pas !

Il posa une dernière question que son jeune adjoint, à peine remis, venait de lui souffler à l'oreille : Qui avait prévenu la police de ce drame ? L'inspecteur adjoint, qui avait vraiment réponse à tout, leur apprit qu'un voisin aurait entendu un bris de verre important vers les 11 h 20 venant de l'appartement de Jude. Il aurait alors attendu une vingtaine de minutes pour voir si cela se calmait, puis était allé frapper chez Jude. Mais personne n'avait répondu et il avait donc contacté la police par le 999 habituel.

Kite et Clément regagnèrent la Rover, craignant l'arrivée imminente de Hicks. Clément prit place sur le siège avant. Une fois à l'intérieur, il enfouit ses mains dans ses poches et colla son menton à sa poitrine. Si sa nausée avait bien diminué, il n'arrivait pas à effacer de son esprit l'image de ce corps surmonté d'une carte ronde du monde ! Quelle bizarrerie ! Quelle folie ! Kite, lui, n'eut pas besoin d'ouvrir la porte pour se laisser tomber derrière le volant. Il avait l'air aussi choqué que son jeune adjoint.

Il avait beau avoir vu d'autres cadavres dans sa carrière... Celui du jeune Mark... *Arrête tout de suite !* Il ferma les yeux pendant quelques secondes et posa les mains sur le volant. Respirant fort, Kite fixa le pare-brise et s'aperçut qu'il s'était remis à pleuvoir. Ça promettait avec la portière absente !

— Clément... Tout va bien ?

La question lui parut idiote.

— Bof, lui répondit en français Clément sans relever la tête.

— Bon... Je pense que le mieux maintenant, c'est que je te dépose à Fulham...

La tête sur le canapé.

— ...Tu ne me parais pas en état de passer le reste de la nuit au Yard...

L'archet de violon posé sur ce coussin gorgé de sang.

— ...Qu'en penses-tu ?

La moquette blanc et rouge.

— D'accord, fit Clément dans un murmure.

Ce corps intact jusqu'au cou.

Il était vraiment choqué. Bien plus qu'avec la découverte du corps de Lucy. Il savait que cette image allait l'obséder pendant longtemps. Mais ce qui l'énervait le plus, ce qui lui faisait adopter cette position de repli sur lui-même, c'était le fait de ne pouvoir rien faire, cette passivité forcée... Cette sensation étrange qui l'avait durement remis à sa place de simple spectateur alors que, tout à l'heure, dans la voiture, il avait l'impression d'être un des vrais acteurs de ce drame.

Si seulement ils pouvaient trouver quelque chose, un détail qui les mettrait sur un semblant de voie. Ce salaud était un rusé. Il ne laissait vraiment rien derrière lui. Et c'est cela qui minait le plus Clément, cette impuissance devant ce monstre qui devait se prendre pour un surhomme. Pensez donc ! Tuer trois personnes sans que l'on vous inquiète... Beaucoup le voudraient. Lui le faisait. Trop, c'était trop. Il n'entendit pas Kite démarrer. Simplement, il sentit un vent froid glisser le long de son visage.

Kite se dirigeait vers Fulham. Il n'avait pas trop envie de rentrer au Yard lui non plus... Il mit la radio en fond sonore. C'était le tube de Natalie Imbruglia, *Torn*. Kite se laissa bercer par le rythme léger de la chanson : « *Nothing's fine I'm torn. I'm all out of faith, this is how I feel. I'm cold and I am shamed lying naked on the floor.* » J'ai froid et j'ai honte, étendue nue sur le sol...

Cette sphère à la place de la tête.

— Inspecteur, vous pouvez changer ? demanda Clément sur un ton suppliant.

Kite poussa la cassette que contenait déjà l'autoradio. La voix de Paul McCartney résonna dans la voiture. C'était *Hey Jude* des Beatles. Jude ! Le même prénom que la victime ! Décidément, la musique lui en voulait ce soir...

Hey Jude, don't make it bad, take a sad song and make it better...

Kite connaissait les paroles par cœur. Mais il

ne chanta pas. Pas envie. Clément releva doucement la tête. La chanson continuait.

Ce globe posé sur ses épaules si fines.

*And any time you feel the pain, hey Jude,
refrain, don't carry the world upon your shoulder...* Ne porte pas le monde sur tes épaules. À
chaque fois que tu sens la douleur, chante
Jude... Chante...

Clément sursauta et poussa un cri d'étonnement. Kite prit peur et stoppa immédiatement
la voiture sur le bas-côté. Ils étaient à la hauteur
du stade de football de Chelsea.

— Ça ne va vraiment pas, Clément ? Tu veux
que nous descendions quelques instants ?

Clément ne répondit pas et appuya sur le bouton rembobinage de l'autoradio. Puis il le relâ-
cha. À nouveau la chanson :

*And any time you feel the pain, hey Jude,
refrain, don't carry the world upon your
shoulder...*

Kite ne comprit pas tout de suite l'utilité de
la manœuvre. Ce n'est qu'au bout de la troisième fois qu'il remarqua le sens des paroles.
Clément avait les yeux grands ouverts, les lèvres
fermées.

— Ne porte pas le monde sur tes épaules !

Il répétait la phrase en anglais, puis la tradui-
sait en français...

Kite fit alors le rapprochement. Il revit la
mise en scène macabre. Avec en fond sonore la
chanson des Beatles, ses paroles... Non, c'était
incroyable... Sa respiration s'accéléra subitement. Et si Clément venait de « mettre l'oreille »
sur le fil conducteur du tueur. Jude... Voyons...
Et Lucy... Oh non ! Ça n'était pas possible : *Lucy
in the Sky with Diamonds*... Et Eleanor... Kite

ne chercha pas bien longtemps, il était un fan invétéré des Beatles. *Eleanor Rigby*, bien sûr...

— Inspecteur, vous avez saisi ? demanda Clément d'un ton redevenu assuré.

— Bien sûr... Je crois, bredouilla Kite. C'est fou... Il faudrait vérifier les paroles des autres chansons...

— Des autres chansons ?

— Oui, *Eleanor Rigby* et *Lucy in the Sky with Diamonds*...

Clément ne comprit pas tout de suite.

— Nom de Dieu, murmura-t-il.

— Clément ! On rentre à la maison.

Kite ne proposait pas. Il ordonnait.

— On file chez moi pour vérifier tout ça... Tu coucheras à Finchley et...

Clément était partagé. Devait-il vraiment aller chez l'inspecteur pour ressasser les images et les paroles ? Mais il avait peut-être découvert quelque chose d'important ! OK, c'était décidé : Kite allait être ravi, il l'accompagnerait à Finchley. Il était sûr que Mary comprendrait sa décision. Il lui téléphonerait demain matin pour tout lui expliquer.

— OK, allons-y !

Kite voyait que Clément allait mieux. Il défit sa ceinture de sécurité.

— Je vais téléphoner à Kelling pour qu'elle vienne me relever de ma garde. Elle sera si fière, cette noix, qu'elle acceptera... Ne bouge pas !

Kite se dirigea vers la cabine BT située sur le trottoir opposé. Une fois à l'intérieur, il introduisit une pièce dans la fente et composa le numéro du sergent qu'il connaissait par cœur.

— Allô, lui répondit une voix pâteuse.

— Nancy ? C'est Paul Kite. Il faut absolument

178

que vous veniez au Yard me relever, car je ne vais pas pouvoir finir ma garde...

Le sergent Kelling mit quelques secondes à répondre.

— Un problème, Paul ?

— Non. Bon, vous rappliquez ?

— Bien sûr. Le temps de pa...

Kite raccrocha immédiatement et courut vers la voiture. Clément avait repris du poil de la bête. C'était visible, il regardait droit devant lui. Il venait de découvrir quelque chose. Il fallait maintenant vérifier si ce quelque chose dépassait le stade de la coïncidence.

Vite, Paul, vite, roule vers Finchley, je veux savoir...

— Il n'y a pas d'autres chansons des Beatles sur cette cassette ?

— Non, je ne crois pas. (Il s'empara de la cassette d'une main, l'autre tenant le volant.) C'est une cassette de Mary. Une compilation...

Vite, Paul, vite...

— J'ai un livre à la maison avec l'intégrale des paroles des chansons des *Fab Four*. Tu connais ce surnom ?

— Oui.

— Bon... Et j'ai aussi tous leurs albums...

Ils remontaient Warwick Road, déserte en cette heure avancée de la nuit. Clément tapait ses paumes sur ses genoux. La voiture avait beau glisser le long du bitume noir, lui, il était en pleine lumière.

24

L'homme ne prit même pas la peine de se brosser les dents. Il était si pressé de se blottir dans ses draps bleus, son Discman près de lui, qu'il oublia même de retirer ses lentilles de contact. Avant d'entrer dans son lit, il vérifia que tout était bien là, sur sa table de nuit : son verre d'eau sucrée, son Discman, ses écouteurs et son double CD bleu. L'homme se frotta le ventre avec douceur et enleva son caleçon. Il était nu, et pouvait enfin écarter la couverture et le drap pour pouvoir pénétrer dans son lit.

Le contact froid du tissu sur sa peau lui procura une sensation agréable. Il aimait penser que, dans quelques minutes, ses draps seraient à la même température que son corps. Qu'ils lui donneraient chaud, le protégeraient. Comme à son habitude, l'homme mit une application particulière à glisser ses mains et ses pieds aux extrémités du matelas, là où la chaleur de son corps ne viendrait jamais. Il voulait une parfaite homogénéité de la température. C'était un rituel indispensable pour passer une bonne nuit.

Une fois ce cérémonial effectué, il s'empara de son lecteur de Compacts-Discs et introduisit les petits écouteurs au plus profond de ses conduits auditifs. Ils ne devaient surtout pas tomber pendant la nuit. Car l'homme, comme après ses deux premiers meurtres, allait s'endormir avec sa musique. Et se réveiller avec. C'était sa règle du jeu, par plaisir d'abord et par superstition ensuite. Il pourrait penser à nouveau à ce cadavre qu'il avait mis tant d'application à décorer. Sa petite Jude qui devait probablement le voir en ce moment.

Oh, Jude ! N'es-tu pas fière de moi ? Ne t'ai-je pas rendu un fier service ? Ne t'étais-tu jamais aperçue de ton calvaire ?

L'homme étendit les bras à l'horizontale et serra les jambes. Il pensait à son corps nu cloué sur une croix imaginaire. Alors, un son puissant lui emplit les oreilles. Ce rythme au piano, cette voix... Quelle sobriété ! Et puis ces percussions discrètes pour le deuxième couplet... Juste le tempo qu'il faut pour serrer le cou d'une femme. Ces chœurs lointains. Et cette accélération guidée par les battements sur le caisson d'une batterie. Il faut serrer plus fort... Accélérer absolument... Même si la voix ne s'emporte pas, on sent ce changement dans le rythme... Puis on revient aux simples percussions.

Là, Jude était morte : c'était le moment de la pause.

Reprise : la voix plus traînante, un léger écho aux paroles. Il faut prendre du recul. Surtout que tout s'emballe par la suite. Plus de paroles, juste de simples onomatopées chantées sur le même rythme. Au milieu, un cri répété d'une voix rauque. C'était le moment où il avait donné le coup de couteau sur l'os de la colonne vertébrale. En fait, pensa l'homme couché dans son lit, ça n'était pas tant hors du rythme qu'il l'avait pensé sur le moment ! Et les onomatopées continuaient jusqu'à la fin. L'homme avait mis cette chanson en boucle, toute la nuit. Cette fois-ci, il décida de s'attarder sur les paroles.

Il se rappelait son hésitation de ces dernières semaines lorsqu'il préparait encore ses meurtres. Allait-il lui mettre ce globe sur la tête ou bien faire pénétrer sous sa peau divers objets ? Il avait opté pour la première solution et en était très satisfait.

181

L'homme était vraiment content de lui. Cette journée s'achevait en apothéose. Aujourd'hui, il n'allait pas travailler et aurait donc toute la journée pour faire le deuil de son troisième meurtre et pour préparer calmement le quatrième. Voire le cinquième, qu'il allait probablement offrir au Yard en même temps. Deux pour le prix d'un ! Franchement, il se trouvait bien trop généreux avec ces imbéciles de flics.

Perclus de fatigue, il sombra facilement dans le sommeil.

Si Jude avait réellement pu voir son bourreau, comme il semblait le croire, elle n'aurait pas été plus étonnée que cela d'observer sa tête endormie dépassant à peine des draps. Elle aurait entendu ce murmure qui sortait des écouteurs enfoncés dans les oreilles de l'homme. Mais surtout, elle aurait vu ce Discman en marche sur la table de nuit, avec l'inscription REPEAT sur son écran digital juste au-dessus du numéro 13, celui de la chanson qui devait accompagner son assassin toute la nuit. Si Jude avait été dans la pièce, elle aurait, par simple curiosité, retourné la boîte du CD vide. Connaître les goûts musicaux de ce sadique lui aurait semblé amusant. Elle aurait alors été bien surprise. En face du numéro 13, son prénom. *Hey Jude*. C'était idiot, mais Jude aurait pensé que son meurtrier n'était pas le genre d'homme à écouter les Beatles. Et pourtant.

25

— Inspecteur...

— Oh ! Abandonne le grade, Clément. Appelle-moi Paul.

— Paul, ce lien paraît tout de même incroyable.

— Incroyable ? Peut-être... Mais j'ai de plus en plus l'impression que tu as tapé juste là où il fallait...

L'inspecteur du New Yard était, en compagnie d'un Clément revigoré, sur le perron de sa maison. Il cherchait ses clefs.

— Merde ! J'ai dû oublier mon trousseau au Yard ! Je suis parti si précipitamment ! (Il marqua une pause, les mains sur les hanches.) Je vais être obligé de réveiller Michelle... Et avec cette foutue sonnette, je vais aussi réveiller la Jenkins ! Quelle merde !

Clément commençait à grelotter sur le perron. Kite s'en aperçut et se décida à appuyer sur la sonnette. Il serra les dents et ferma les yeux dès qu'il entendit les premières notes reproduisant la célèbre cloche de Big Ben.

— J'espère qu'elle a entendu... Si je suis obligé de sonner une deuxième fois...

Clément jeta un regard vers la maison d'à côté, celle des Jenkins. Une mince lumière venait de s'allumer à la fenêtre donnant sur la maison des Kite.

— En tout cas, précisa Clément, Mrs Jenkins n'a pas tardé...

Kite regarda dans la même direction que son assistant.

— Pfuiff ! Quelle vipère !

À cet instant, ils entendirent des bruits de serrures venant de l'intérieur du pavillon.

— C'est moi, Michelle ! Dépêche-toi...

Les bruits ne s'accéléraient pas pour autant. Quinze grosses secondes plus tard, Michelle fit son arrivée sur le perron, vêtue d'une simple robe de chambre.

— Paul ?

Elle tenta d'ouvrir son champ de vision à plus de vingt degrés.

— Clément ? À cette heure ?

Kite lui annonça :

— Écoute-moi, un troisième meurtre a eu lieu ce soir... Et sur le chemin du retour, je crois bien que Clément a eu, comme qui dirait, une illumination...

Michelle écoutait avec le maximum d'attention que lui octroyait son cerveau encore endormi. Ils étaient maintenant tous dans le hall. Son mari et Clément enlevaient leurs manteaux.

— Le lien principal entre les meurtres serait les Beatles ! L'assassin tuerait selon certaines paroles de leurs chansons...

Kite s'emportait tout seul dans l'entrée. Michelle se demanda si elle n'était pas en train de rêver, tout simplement. Son mari qui la réveillait à près de 2 heures du matin pour lui balancer des choses dont elle ne comprenait pas un piètre mot.

— Paul, je retourne me coucher. (Puis vers Clément :) Bonsoir Clément. Et s'il t'énerve trop, n'hésite pas à l'assommer...

Michelle essaya d'envoyer un clin d'œil à l'adresse de Clément, mais n'arriva pas à relever sa paupière une fois fermée.

— C'est ça... Dors bien... Viens, Clément, on va se faire un peu de café et on ira au salon.

Ils se dirigèrent vers la cuisine, où Kite mit la

bouilloire en route et sortit d'un placard un petit bocal de café lyophilisé.

— Je sais, il va être dégueulasse, mais bon... ça t'aidera à te tenir éveillé.

Clément hocha la tête. Il n'avait peut-être dormi qu'une petite heure, cependant il ne ressentait aucune fatigue. Kite reprit, décidément bien plus prolixe depuis cette découverte.

— J'ai réfléchi un peu sur le trajet jusqu'ici. On va tout de suite aller vérifier, mais je crois bien qu'il est question d'une église dans la chanson *Eleanor Rigby*. Et puis pour Lucy, les diamants tout autour d'elle...

Kite s'empara de deux tasses, y versa un peu de poudre et ajouta l'eau bouillante. Une odeur corsée emplit immédiatement leurs narines.

— Prends ta tasse. On va directement au salon.

Clément était impressionné par la discothèque du couple Kite. Vinyles, CD, cassettes, tous les supports avaient leur place. Kite farfouillait à la fois dans les disques et dans les quelques livres de la grande bibliothèque remplic principalement de cassettes vidéo.

— Eh bien ! Vous avez une drôle de discothèque, Paul ! s'exclama Clément qui avait déjà remarqué la présence de nombreux disques d'artistes francophones, dont une dizaine du seul Jacques Brel.

— Et encore, avec tout ce que Mary a dû emmener en haut ! répondit Kite à genoux près d'une pile de CD apparemment en attente de classement.

Il se dirigea vers la chaîne hi-fi et déposa cinq disques sur le meuble.

— Je n'arrive pas à mettre la main sur plus

de cinq disques des Beatles... Alors qu'on devait les avoir tous. À force de les prêter à tout le monde...

Il tenait à la main un gros livre au format de bande dessinée.

— Tiens, assieds-toi. On va regarder là-dedans...

Clément put lire le titre du bouquin : *The Beatles : the Ultimate Reference Book*. Kite rejoignit son stagiaire et ouvrit le livre entre eux deux.

— Ce qui est énervant, c'est cette présentation en partitions ! Il faut lire les paroles sur ces toutes petites lignes...

Clément était étonné de la présence d'un si gros livre de partitions chez les Kite.

— Mary joue d'un instrument ? demanda-t-il.

— Non, pourquoi ?

— Ce livre s'adresse d'abord aux musiciens.

— Oui, Michelle joue du piano. Et moi aussi, j'ai fait quelques années de solfège. C'est un peu grâce à cela que l'on s'est rencontrés... Dans le groupe de musique que j'avais formé à l'université avec un copain. On s'appelait les Fab Five ! J'étais fou des Beatles à l'époque...

Clément feuilletait le livre. Il s'arrêta à la première chanson qu'il trouva. Il s'agissait de *Eleanor Rigby*. Kite se concentra et ils partirent tous deux à la recherche d'une phrase qui confirmerait leur espoir. Soudain, Kite pointa un doigt vigoureux vers la fin de la partition, froissant du même coup la page.

— Écoute, Clément, écoute : *Eleanor Rigby died in the church and was buried along with her name. Nobody came*[1].

1. Eleanor Rigby mourut dans l'église et fut enterrée avec son nom. Personne ne vint.

Tous deux partageaient les mêmes images. Clément n'avait pu voir le cadavre mutilé de miss Stout, mais il se rappela le récit détaillé de Kite.

— Et fut enterrée avec son nom... Ce nom qu'il lui avait gravé sur le front...

Kite et Clément étaient tous les deux dans un état d'excitation tel qu'ils renversèrent presque ensemble leurs tasses de café, voulant tous deux introduire dans le lecteur le CD où se trouvait la chanson. Kite y arriva le premier. Clément revint vers la table et tenta d'éponger la mare de liquide qui s'était répandue sur la table et coulait déjà sur la moquette beige clair.

— Laisse, Clément... Écoute plutôt !

La chanson emplit la pièce d'un coup. *Eleanor Rigby* ne comportait pas d'intro. Dès la première seconde, les violons, les altos et les violoncelles martelaient leur supériorité. Mais plus que sur le rythme, Clément et Kite se concentrèrent sur les paroles chantées par Paul McCartney. Et effectivement, Eleanor était bien enterrée dans une église avec son nom. Une fascination étonnante se lisait sur les visages des deux enquêteurs.

— Lucy maintenant, proposa Clément.

À ces mots, Kite retira le CD rouge du lecteur et introduisit le CD de l'album *Sgt Pepper's Lonely Hearts Club Band*. Chanson numéro trois. *Lucy in the Sky with Diamonds*. Clément suivit les paroles avec un doigt sur le livre.

Picture yourself in a boat on a river...

Les deux ampoules dans les yeux. Les yeux. La lumière. La lumière dans les yeux.

Cellophane flowers of yellow and green, towering over your head.

Non, non, mais il fallait trouver.

Les yeux de lumière.

Look for the girl with the sun in her eyes and she's gone, Lucy in the sky with diamonds.

C'était ça ! *Le soleil dans les yeux de Lucy !*

— Cet homme est vraiment un timbré ! s'emporta Kite. C'est complètement fou d'aller chercher toutes ces conneries pour commettre des meurtres ! Ce salaud doit prendre ça comme un exercice de style, ça n'est pas possible autrement... Aucun mobile valable ne pourrait l'expliquer...

Clément n'écoutait que d'une oreille. Il pensait déjà à la journée du lendemain. Comment allaient-ils pouvoir reprendre cette affaire du métro après ces découvertes fantastiques ?

— Inspecteur, euh... Paul, ne pensez-vous pas que l'enquête pourrait nous être confiée à nouveau après ce que nous avons découvert...

Les yeux de Kite se mirent à briller.

— Et pourquoi pas ? En tout cas, merci Clément ! C'est toi qui es à l'origine de cette judicieuse association d'idées.

Kite était vraiment sincère. On l'entendait à son ton.

— Donne-moi ta tasse, Clément, je vais aller préparer un autre café.

Clément la tendit et se leva du même coup pour se diriger vers la chaîne hi-fi. Il voulait réécouter à la suite les trois chansons. Peut-être allait-il être à nouveau inspiré ? Et s'il y avait un lien entre ces trois chansons ?

Le jeune inspecteur entendit le bruit du lecteur qui recherchait la plage de *Eleanor Rigby*. Puis les instruments à cordes à nouveau. Heureusement que les lumières de la pièce étaient allumées car, il ne savait pas pourquoi, mais il

188

éprouvait une indicible peur devant la brutalité du rythme.

Jusqu'à une heure avancée de la nuit, ils écoutèrent, confortablement assis sur le canapé, d'autres chansons des Beatles. Clément connaissait comme tout le monde les Fab Four. Il n'était pas à proprement parler un fan, même s'il trouvait que certains morceaux étaient vraiment de pures merveilles. Ce soir, il avait comme l'impression, en comblant un tant soit peu son manque de connaissances sur le fameux groupe, d'appréhender l'énigme. Tenter de résoudre une série de meurtres en écoutant de la musique n'était pas particulièrement ce à quoi s'attendait Clément en entrant dans la police. Kite se fit en lui-même la même remarque. Car ils ne parlèrent que peu, ne sachant encore trop quoi dire devant l'invraisemblance de la situation.

Kite et Clément éprouvaient la sensation d'être en dehors du temps. Dans cette pièce remplie de sons au milieu d'une nuit glaciale et pluvieuse, alors que la plupart des gens devaient être en train de rêver, eux nageaient dans une réalité qui était bien plus délirante. Du moins Clément eut la prétention de le penser. Il tentait d'imaginer l'assassin évoluant chez lui, dans son salon, au rythme de la musique. Il se représentait le lieu avec force détails sans pour autant en saisir véritablement la forme. Comme lorsque, dans un roman, on pénètre dans un lieu qui n'est pas décrit par l'auteur. On invente alors une image similaire d'un lieu familier que l'on connaît et on s'y rattache pour toute la durée de l'histoire. En ce moment, par exemple,

Clément voyait l'homme évoluer dans cette maison même. Pourquoi ? Il ne le savait pas...

Kite semblait fatigué. Ses paupières se fermaient peu à peu. C'était compréhensible, il avait si peu dormi la nuit précédente... Mais cela l'étonnait néanmoins. Dans un moment pareil, avoir envie de dormir ? Son corps réclamait ses heures de sommeil en retard. Et puis de toute façon, ça ne servait à rien de lutter : que pouvaient-ils faire ici, cette nuit, dans ce salon ? Kite pensa à la journée qui l'attendait demain. Dès son arrivée au Yard, il irait voir le vieux Forbes, s'il n'était pas parti en week-end dans sa maison de Stoke-on-Trent. Mais après ce troisième meurtre, il se doutait bien que le vieux ferait acte de présence au Yard. Ne serait-ce que pour faire bonne figure devant ses copains du ministère de l'Intérieur...

— Je vais m'allonger, Clément, dit Kite en se levant.

— Vous avez sommeil ? s'étonna son jeune adjoint.

— Pas toi ?

— Avec tout le café que vous m'avez fait boire... Je n'en prends jamais, d'habitude.

— Bon, eh bien, occupe-toi comme tu veux !

Kite se dirigeait vers la porte quand il se retourna vers Clément. Il eut l'impression que ses jambes étaient en coton tant il avait envie de s'allonger.

— Mary a eu sa console pour Noël. Va voir dans sa chambre si tu veux.

— OK, mais je vais rester là pour l'instant ; j'ai bien envie de dresser une liste de toutes les chansons des Beatles avec, pour titre, un nom ou un prénom.

Kite approuva de la tête, ne se sentant même

pas la force d'actionner ses poumons, ses cordes vocales, sa langue et les muscles de sa mâchoire. Il sortit et le jeune Français se retrouva seul dans le salon.

Clément se leva pour aller changer le CD dans le lecteur et revint s'asseoir, le livre de partitions ouvert devant lui. S'emparant d'une feuille de papier vierge et d'un stylo à bille, il commença à feuilleter l'ouvrage page par page. Au bout d'une trentaine de minutes, il avait lu les paroles des chansons contenant dans leur titre un nom propre. Et il avait dressé une liste.

Kite enfila rapidement son pyjama et se glissa sous les draps, dans le petit espace qu'avait bien voulu lui laisser sa femme. Il se frotta les yeux et se mit sur le flanc, côté mur. Cette histoire des Beatles ! Pourquoi donc exécuter un tel plan ?

Soudain, une pensée traversa son esprit. Charles Manson, le tueur d'Hollywood... Celui qui avait assassiné, entre autres, Sharon Tate, la femme de Roman Polanski... Ne voyait-il pas dans le *White Album* des Beatles des prophéties concernant sa vie ? Et si le meurtrier d'aujourd'hui était un fan, un nostalgique de Manson ? S'il avait décidé de finir le travail, c'est-à-dire de tuer selon les chansons des albums *Red* et *Blue* ? Kite tenta de retrouver la date des meurtres de Manson. 1970, estima-t-il. À l'époque, il avait 13 ans et découvrait les Beatles. Mais il n'avait pas le souvenir de meurtres calqués sur des paroles de chanson. Manson avait simplement pris le *White Album* comme un appel à une révolution que sa folie avait décidé de mettre en route. Kite n'en était pas sûr.

Il se promit de vérifier dès demain matin. C'était étrange, mais Kite se trouvait bien plus calme, bien plus en harmonie avec lui-même. Le radio-réveil indiquait 3 heures et 13 minutes. Il était temps de s'endormir. Kite s'abandonna en priant pour connaître un sommeil, un vrai.

Clément relut sa liste pour la énième fois. Deux noms avaient tout de suite attiré son attention. Kite et Michelle. C'était une drôle de coïncidence que ces deux noms se trouvent sur la liste ! Kite pour la chanson *For the Benefit of Mr Kite* et Michelle pour la chanson éponyme.

Clément se promit de le faire remarquer à Kite. Il reposa la feuille et s'étira en bâillant bruyamment. Son coup de blues d'après le meurtre s'était envolé. Il allait parfaitement bien et n'avait qu'une envie, continuer l'enquête. Il se leva et prit la direction de la cuisine. Il n'avait aucun mal à évoluer dans la maison, car il la connaissait maintenant presque par cœur. Il grignota quelques sablés écossais pur beurre en restant debout contre le meuble de l'évier. Il jeta un coup d'œil sur le mot qu'avait laissé Kite à l'intention de sa femme. Il se demandait comment il allait occuper les deux heures qui lui restaient à veiller seul avant qu'une présence ne vienne lui tenir compagnie. Il finit son dernier biscuit et s'essuya les mains sur son jean.

Demain matin, il faudrait absolument qu'il téléphone à Mary et la prévienne. En attendant, il décida de se rendre dans sa chambre. Il sortit de la cuisine et emprunta l'escalier à la moquette verte. Une fois en haut, il ouvrit la première porte à gauche. Rien n'avait changé depuis sa visite en début de soirée. Le lit n'était pas fait. Les draps et la couverture étaient sens dessus dessous. Par terre, une multitude de livres scolaires traînaient en désordre. Son placard à vêtements était à moitié ouvert. Seul son bureau était bien rangé. Elle ne devait pas s'y asseoir souvent.

Clément s'imaginait Mary allongée par terre, sur le ventre, les jambes repliées en arrière et croisées, mordillant un stylo entre ses lèvres, un cahier devant elle. La parfaite petite Lolita.

Il s'assit alors sur le lit et regarda plus attentivement le contenu du placard renfermant tous ces vêtements qu'elle portait sur sa peau. Ses tee-shirts, ses pulls, ses jeans, ses petites jupes qu'il découvrirait au printemps... Il détailla le reste de la chambre : les posters au mur (The Cure, The Cranberries, John Lennon), la chaîne hi-fi et tous les disques autour, la petite télé et la console Playstation en dessous.

Clément se rejeta en arrière dans le lit. Il était allongé dans le sens de la largeur, ses genoux formant un parfait angle droit avec le bord du lit. Il imaginait Mary dans cette chambre, seule, allongée sur ce lit, accrochant ses posters, s'habillant le matin, travaillant par terre, écoutant de la musique, pleurant, riant, criant, chuchotant... Les yeux de Clément se fermèrent peu à peu. Lui qui ne devait pas s'endormir allait sombrer dans le sommeil. Il s'allongea normalement dans le sens de la longueur. C'était une sensation étrange de penser qu'une fois de plus il passait la nuit sans Mary. Mais cette fois-ci, comble du paradoxe, il allait s'endormir dans le lit de Mary seul, alors que son amie dormait paisiblement sous ses draps, seule également. Clément eut l'impression de sentir encore son parfum et s'endormit paisiblement. L'affaire de ce *serial singer* lui parut soudain loin, bien loin... Rideau et surtout pas d'applaudissements. Pas de bruit.

26

Au moment de se défaire des draps et de la couverture, Kite éprouva une curieuse impression. Il se sentait mouillé et froid. D'abord, il crut qu'il avait de nouveau uriné dans son pantalon de pyjama, mais la sensation d'humidité s'étendait de son dos à ses jambes. Il posa une main sur son visage avant même d'ouvrir les yeux et il sentit qu'une fine pellicule d'eau glacée recouvrait son front. Prenant peur, il se raidit tout en ouvrant grand ses yeux. La lumière lui fouetta les pupilles, puis son regard embrassa les grandes pelouses givrées du Victoria Park de Finchley. Il pensa tout d'abord à un rêve, un cauchemar supplémentaire. Après tout, un de plus ou un de moins, ce n'était rien de bien important pour sa santé mentale... Mais le froid était bien présent et il remarqua que ses bras nus portaient de larges marbrures.

Les images de sa soirée lui revinrent en mémoire. Il était rentré tard avec Clément et ils avaient cherché à confirmer la folle théorie de son stagiaire sur les Beatles. Les meurtres sur le schéma des paroles de chansons... C'était cela ! Ensuite, il avait sagement gagné son lit et s'était endormi auprès de Michelle... Alors pourquoi se réveiller au milieu du parc qui faisait face à son domicile ? C'était inouï ! Bien sûr, cela lui était

194

déjà arrivé au tout début de son mariage, et notamment la nuit où il avait arrosé la naissance de Mary avec les copains du Yard ! Il avait égaré ses clefs et n'avait eu comme solution que de dormir à la belle étoile... Mais Mary était née en juillet !

Kite commença à grelotter lorsqu'il prit conscience des raisons de sa présence dans ce lieu. Somnambulisme. Bien sûr... Comme la veille... Ou plutôt, pire que la veille. Son esprit nocturne ne l'avait pas simplement emmené dans le salon, mais lui avait fait ouvrir la porte pour sortir s'allonger dans le parc ! Cela devenait du délire... Presque irréel... Si un ami lui avait raconté une pareille mésaventure, il se serait empressé d'appeler un médecin du Yard pour savoir si cela était bien sensé. Kite voulut regarder sa montre, mais elle n'était pas à son poignet. Le froid lui mordait douloureusement la chair. Il eut une furieuse envie de se gratter les jambes. Le parc était désert. Ce ne pouvait être une indication pour l'heure. Avec cette température, personne n'allait se risquer dehors pour son plaisir.

Kite se leva péniblement. Il repéra un panneau indicateur et sut alors que quelques dizaines de mètres seulement le séparaient de la sortie la plus proche de son domicile. Son pantalon de pyjama était trempé. Il utilisa sa manche pour s'essuyer le visage. Il se sentait nauséeux, sale. Sans bien regarder devant lui, il entreprit de rejoindre le chemin de terre. Le contact de ses pieds nus sur l'herbe accentua l'impression de froid.

Il ne fit qu'un mètre avant de trébucher sur un objet. Se relevant sans même avoir le courage de jurer, il se retourna et découvrit sa guitare posée sur le sol. Sa guitare ? Pas besoin de se frotter les yeux... Il savait bien que c'était elle... Un autocollant à l'effigie de John Lennon était posé sur la caisse de résonance. Il s'imagina la scène dans un hoquet de désespoir. Devenait-il fou ? Pas seulement déprimé, mais bien fou ? Faisait-il des choses insensées sous l'emprise du sommeil ? Il avait dû descendre prendre sa guitare au garage avant de déverrouiller la porte et de venir s'allonger dans l'herbe du parc... Peut-être avait-il joué l'intro de *I Feel Fine* avant de se rendormir pour de bon ?

Des sanglots au bord des lèvres, il se saisit de son instrument et prit la direction de la maison. Il avait réussi à dissimuler à Michelle sa première nuit de somnambulisme, mais ce serait plus difficile avec celle-ci... Déjà il pourrait s'estimer heureux s'il s'en sortait sans une angine. Et puis, après tout, Michelle avait le droit de savoir que son mari n'allait pas très bien, que cette affaire lui bouffait la santé, comme celle de 87...

Il traversa la rue sans même s'assurer que Mrs Jenkins ne soit pas en train de guetter à la fenêtre et ouvrit la porte en grand. Elle claqua contre le mur. Michelle accourut presque aussitôt dans le couloir.

— Mary ?

Elle se reprit, les yeux écarquillés.

— Paul ! Qu'est-ce que tu fais là ? Je croyais que tu étais déjà parti comme hier ? Qu'est-ce que tu fabriques à cette heure avec...

Elle sut, au rictus de son mari, qu'il n'était pas nécessaire de continuer, sinon Paul allait se mettre à sangloter à peine le seuil franchi. Elle

196

alla vers lui et le frictionna avec vigueur tout en fermant la porte.

— Tu vas aller prendre un bain bien chaud. Tu es gelé... proche de l'hypothermie... Depuis combien de temps tu traînes dehors habillé comme ça ?

— Quelle heure est-il ? articula difficilement l'inspecteur.

— Dix heures passées. Paul, tu m'inquiètes... Va prendre ton bain. Clément est là. Tu es revenu avec lui hier dans la nuit. Il est en train de prendre son petit déjeuner.

Paul Kite, à l'évocation du prénom de son stagiaire, sembla reprendre des couleurs.

« Ainsi il me reste quand même un peu de mémoire », murmura-t-il entre ses lèvres gercées.

— Je vais demander à Clément de joindre le Yard pour leur dire que tu ne vas pas aller travailler aujourd'hui...

Kite réussit à chuchoter de ne pas le faire. Et, comme un zombie, il se dirigea vers l'escalier, soutenu par sa femme.

Clément était en train de finir son bol de muesli lorsque Kite fit son entrée dans la cuisine. Michelle le suivait. Il portait un costume de ville et avait la mine plutôt fatiguée.

— Je vais vous faire une omelette au bacon et du café, annonça Mrs Kite alors que l'inspecteur étreignait chaleureusement un Clément éberlué.

— Clément ! commença l'inspecteur. Rassure-moi... Nous sommes bien rentrés tard hier soir et puis je suis allé au lit alors que tu es resté en bas...

Clément hocha le tête.

— Tu as dormi ensuite ou tu es resté dans le salon ?

— J'ai été me coucher dans le lit de Mary, répondit le jeune Français sans comprendre vraiment le but de cet interrogatoire. Il ne précisa pas qu'il avait également téléphoné à Mary pour lui dire où il se trouvait. Il l'avait réveillée, mais de toutes les façons, il se devait de la prévenir. Il était parti en coup de vent hier soir après leur début de nuit.

— Lorsque je suis descendu tout à l'heure, j'ai vu que la porte sur la rue était ouverte, ajouta Michelle. J'ai cru que vous étiez déjà partis au boulot. Et puis Clément est descendu quelques secondes avant ton arrivée !

Kite avait tout raconté à sa femme alors qu'elle lui faisait couler son bain. Il recommença pour son jeune stagiaire. Cela lui faisait du bien de parler. Et tant pis s'ils perdaient une demi-journée ! Selon Michelle, il avait bien dormi quatre longues heures dans le parc ! Il n'en revenait pas, il avait dormi dans le parc pendant tout ce temps sans même qu'un passant le réveille ?

Au fur et à mesure qu'il avalait son omelette et buvait son café, sa frustration diminuait. Son corps reprenait le dessus et il aurait presque éprouvé une impression de bien-être si une sensation glaciale ne persistait pas sur ses cuisses. Le plus étrange était qu'il n'était pas plus que cela fatigué... Peut-être parce qu'il avait enfin partagé ses émotions... Ou bien parce qu'ils tenaient enfin un début de piste... Cette histoire de Beatles méritait d'être creusée... Mais il fallait maintenant que Clément et lui trouvent quelque chose à quoi s'accrocher vraiment... Le mobile du tueur par exemple... Cette idée de chanson était alléchante, mais...

La sonnerie du téléphone fit sursauter Kite, qui laissa du même coup involontairement tomber un morceau d'omelette dans sa tasse. Il pesta tout en se saisissant du combiné. Michelle était en train de lui masser délicatement les épaules.

— Kite.

Il avait repris sa voix normale. Seule une petite note éraillée subsistait.

— Bonjour Paul ! Nancy... Quelque chose ne va pas...

— Ah ! Je suis occupé, sergent. Je vous passe mon adjoint...

Il tendit le combiné à Clément en mimant une grimace.

— Sergent Kelling ?

— Clément ? Tu n'es pas au Yard ? Il y a un problème ? Et pourquoi es-tu chez Paul ce matin ?

Clément nota le ton ironique de la remarque.

— Nous arrivons tout de suite. Je vous rappelle que nous étions de nuit hier.

— Moi aussi...

Le ton n'avait rien de commode. Le jeune Français se rappela alors que le sergent les avait remplacés dans la nuit.

— ... et j'aimerais bien pouvoir rentrer chez moi avant le déjeuner...

— Je vous ai dit que nous arrivons dans une demi-heure tout au plus, sergent, répéta Clément, ulcéré par la voie stridente de la jeune femme.

À ce moment, Kite se mit à hurler tant qu'il pouvait.

— Qu'est-ce qui se passe donc ? aboya Kelling.

Le café venait de couler le long de la table pour recouvrir presque entièrement les cuisses de Kite.

— Rien, rien du tout, sergent Kelling. D'ailleurs je vais être obligé de vous laisser...

Sur ce, Clément lui raccrocha au nez pour la seconde fois en quelques heures. Kite était en train de bondir avec énergie dans la cuisine. Il se mordait la langue pour ne pas crier trop fort. Michelle lui demanda de se calmer et de s'asseoir. Elle diagnostiqua une légère brûlure. En laissant sa femme lui passer de la pommade, Kite pria pour que la journée se finisse mieux qu'elle n'avait débuté...

27

L'homme, en ce samedi matin, s'était levé de très méchante humeur. Il n'avait rien entendu à son réveil. Plus aucun son ne sortait de ses écouteurs. Il s'était inquiété immédiatement et demandé s'il n'était pas devenu sourd pendant la nuit. Mais non, il entendait le vent souffler sur la toiture. Alors ? Que s'était-il passé ? Il se pencha vers sa table de nuit. Son Discman était arrêté. Il tenta d'appuyer sur la touche PLAY, mais un message apparut alors sur l'écran digital : *Low Battery*. Il avait oublié de vérifier l'état d'usure des piles de son appareil favori.

À ce moment précis, il se haïssait. Il aurait le courage de se faire mal, il se donnerait des coups de poing sur le torse et sur le visage, il s'enlèverait quelques ongles de ses doigts, il se priverait de manger, de boire. Mais il se savait bien incapable d'accepter de tels supplices. Lui, il pouvait les infliger. Pas les subir. Comme dimanche soir, quand il avait été obligé de sévir dans la petite pièce de la cave. Il avait mis en œuvre sa politique de brimades, d'humiliations. Car personne ne devait savoir. Personne.

De toute la matinée, l'homme ne desserra pas les dents. Lorsqu'il lava dans l'évier le couteau sur lequel séchaient des plaques du sang de Jude, il ne dit pas un mot et ne siffla même pas. Quand il passa à la machine à laver ses vêtements de la veille au soir, dont certains portaient eux aussi la trace de son forfait, il ne s'accorda pas non plus le droit d'allumer la radio. Il devait être puni pour son manque de précaution. C'était la première fois en cinq ans qu'une pareille mésaventure lui arrivait.

Vers les 11 heures, l'homme s'octroya une pause. Il s'assit à la table de cuisine et se prit la tête à deux mains. Il devait penser aux prochains meurtres. Absolument. Cet après-midi, il devait régler quelques questions concernant des affaires personnelles, mais il décida de s'accorder le début de la soirée pour les évoquer sérieusement. Ne plus rien laisser au hasard.

L'homme avait mal à la tête depuis son lever, mais s'était refusé à prendre une quelconque aspirine. Devant l'insistance de la douleur, il finit tout de même par en prendre une, effervescente, qu'il fit fondre dans un verre. Il le but d'un seul coup et cela lui laissa un désagréable goût salé et piquant dans la gorge. Pour ne plus y penser, il prit l'initiative de descendre le plateau-repas à la cave. Il n'attendrait même pas qu'on le lui réclame.

Posant le verre d'eau habituel et une tranche de cheddar sur un énième plateau, il se dirigea vers le sous-sol. C'est alors que Paul lui barra la route. Voulant lui serrer la main, l'homme envoya le plateau au diable et étreignit avec force la poigne de McCartney. Il ne pouvait en croire ses yeux, ses oreilles. Paul lui parlait de sa voix douce, on eût presque dit qu'il chantait... Il le félicitait pour ses trois premiers meurtres et lui demandait de ne pas s'arrêter en si bon chemin... De commettre son quatrième, bien sûr, pour mettre un point final à son chef-d'œuvre, mais de ne pas hésiter à aller un peu plus loin... Il invita le Beatles à venir s'asseoir dans le salon, sans succès.

Aller un peu plus loin, soliloquait McCartney, c'était ne pas forcément s'arrêter au prénom dans les titres... Leur œuvre était si riche et l'homme la connaissait si bien qu'il lui serait aisé de s'offrir un autre plaisir... Puis Paul McCartney s'écarta et s'engouffra dans la buanderie.

L'homme resta statufié pendant un bon quart d'heure. Il se rendait compte de sa chance, de son immense fortune d'avoir été conseillé par un de ses hôtes en personne. Cela faisait si longtemps qu'ils ne lui parlaient plus... Il se savait maintenant sur la bonne voie. Plus aucun doute possible. Les larmes aux yeux, il alla préparer un nouveau plateau-repas.

Une inquiétude s'empara de l'homme une fois devant la porte blanche. Pas un bruit. Il frappa plusieurs coups. Au bout d'une bonne minute, il entendit enfin un long râle d'où semblait s'échapper une intense douleur. Il respira : ouf, la mort n'avait pas encore frappé. Il ouvrit et posa le plateau près de l'entrée. Une odeur infecte lui chatouilla les narines. Il referma vite la porte et se passa une main sous le nez ; il tentait de chasser cette terrible puanteur.

Oh non... Plus besoin, mon Dieu. Laissez-moi sans rien. Je ne veux plus manger. D'ailleurs, je n'ai plus aucune dent. À peine puis-je me traîner sur le sol hideux de cette pièce pour atteindre le verre d'eau qu'il m'est impossible de porter à ma bouche. Vous le savez pourtant, mon Dieu, il m'a broyé toutes les phalanges. Je suis obligée de renverser le verre sur le plateau pour laper avec ma langue blanche les quelques gouttes que la terre ne boit pas. Libérez-moi, mon Dieu, de cet habit de souffrance, de ce corps qui a cessé depuis longtemps d'être le mien. S'il vous plaît, mon Dieu, j'implore votre pitié.

L'homme regagna le rez-de-chaussée et continua sa montée vers l'étage. Cette odeur l'avait vraiment dégoûté. Comment pouvait-on être si sale ?

Il fit couler le robinet d'eau froide dans son jacuzzi tout en se déshabillant. Il voulait se laver des impuretés dont il s'était probablement imprégné dans la cave. La télécommande de sa chaîne hi-fi en main, il pénétra dans la baignoire. Il sentit le contact de l'eau froide sur son corps. Cela lui procurait une sensation unique, comme si on lui glissait des plaques en fer à la fois au-dessus et en dessous de la peau.

L'image obsédante de Paul McCartney dansait dans son esprit au rythme d'une de ses mélodies... Paul était vivant ! Pour lui, Paul avait toujours été vivant ! Il n'avait jamais cru tous ces racontars sur la prétendue mort de son idole. Il se rappelait encore cet après-midi froid de novembre 69 où un hurluberlu du Speaker's Corner avait brandi la pochette de l'album *Abbey Road*, son préféré, en expliquant les circonstances de l'accident de voiture qui aurait carbonisé McCartney en 66.

« À gauche de la photo, un cimetière ! Regardez ! Le groupe accompagne Paul vers sa demeure éternelle ! Je n'invente rien ! John est en blanc, c'est le prieur ; Ringo est en noir, c'est le croque-mort ; et George est en jean, c'est l'esprit des Beatles... Regardez bien le sosie de Paul maintenant... il est pieds nus ! Pieds nus ! C'est comme ça qu'on enterre les morts en Inde ! Et il tient sa cigarette de la main droite, alors que *notre* Paul est gaucher ! »

L'homme se rappelait cette harangue comme s'il l'avait entendue hier. Pour lui, les rumeurs, comme tout fan qui se respecte, devenaient réalité ! « À droite ! Vous voyez tous que la voiture de police est une fourgonnette de la morgue municipale... Et à gauche, lisez la plaque d'immatriculation de la Beetle : LMW 28 IF. Living McCartney Was 28 IF [1]. Et *notre* Paul aurait été dans sa 28e année à la sortie de cet album. » Et l'orateur reprenait sa théorie en boucle...

L'homme s'enfonça encore un peu plus dans l'eau de sa baignoire. Il avait passé le week-end entier prostré dans sa chambre en réfléchissant à cette atroce théorie. Paul serait mort et un sosie le remplacerait... Il avait fondu en larmes, refusé de s'alimenter pendant près d'une

1. Vivant, McCartney aurait 28 ans SI.

semaine. Sa mère avait appelé un médecin qu'il avait injurié...

Il s'était mis à la recherche d'autres indices, espérant n'en trouver aucun... Il réécoutait tous leurs albums un gros casque sur les oreilles... Et puis il en découvrit : des paroles d'abord...« Living is easy with eyes closed »[1] dans *Strawberry Fields Forever*, « He blew his mind out in a car »[2] dans *A Day in the Life*, « We were talking about people who hide themselves behind a wall of illusion. Never glimpse the truth »[3] dans *Within You, Without You*, puis des murmures à la fin de certains morceaux... John Lennon qui glisse un faible « I buried Paul »[4] à la fin de *Strawberry Fields*, qui chuchote un « Paul is dead, miss him, miss him »[5] dans *I'm so Tired*. Et les vinyles qu'on repassait à l'envers et qui étaient censés reproduire le bruit exact de la tôle froissée...

Son meilleur ami, également fan du groupe, lui disait de ne pas se faire de bile, que tout cela était faux, que Paul ne pourrait jamais mourir... Mais que penser de la pochette de *Sgt Pepper* avec cette tombe sur la pochette et de cette guitare en forme de P posée dessus ? Et de cette poupée rousse ressemblant à Jane Asher, l'éternelle fiancée de McCartney, qui tient dans la main l'Aston Martin de l'accident ?

Seul son meilleur ami avait le droit de pénétrer dans sa chambre. Il le rassurait en lui

1. Il est facile de vivre les yeux fermés.
2. Il a explosé dans une voiture.
3. Nous parlions des gens qui se cachent derrière un mur d'illusion et qui n'aperçoivent jamais la vérité.
4. J'ai enterré Paul.
5. Paul est mort, il me manque, il me manque.

disant que le groupe était entré dans le jeu des prédicateurs... Qu'ils s'étaient tous amusés à semer ces éléments... L'homme avait quelquefois l'impression que son ami essayait également de se convaincre lui-même, mais ces discussions lui avaient fait du bien... Il était reparti du bon pied, jusqu'à la séparation du groupe, jusqu'à l'assassinat de Lennon... Mais c'était aujourd'hui que la réponse lui était venue. Paul McCartney lui était apparu et cela le remplissait d'une fierté sans bornes.

Il observa à la dérobée son sexe entre cette touffe de poils pubiens roux. Cette couleur qu'il détestait et qui lui imposait la teinture mensuelle de ses cheveux. Et ce sexe dont il ne s'était jamais servi pour satisfaire une femme. Ce pénis qui ne connaissait que l'onanisme. Tout du moins jusqu'à lundi dernier. Car, depuis lundi, l'homme n'avait même plus besoin de se toucher pour se procurer ce plaisir qu'il méritait au même titre qu'un autre. Il suffisait de tuer. Et contrairement à l'acte d'amour, l'acte de tuer ne lui faisait pas peur, ne le répugnait pas.

Son corps s'adaptait peu à peu à la température de l'eau. Il tendit alors la télécommande vers la chaîne. C'était le même disque que celui de mercredi soir. Il pressa le bouton commandant le lecteur de CD. La touche RANDOM. Lecture aléatoire. Il s'en fichait, car il aimait toutes les chansons du double album *Blue* des Beatles, qu'il possédait en quintuple exemplaire. Le lecteur cherchait au hasard la première plage, la première chanson qui allait emplir la salle de bains de l'homme. Ce serait la douze. *Lady Madonna*. Comme une prémonition.

28

Une fois arrivé dans le bureau, Kite s'adressa à Clément. Il avait repris toute sa confiance. Il ne doutait pas que l'affaire pourrait de nouveau leur être confiée après leur découverte.

— Je vais aller informer la vieille momie de notre piste... Avec un peu de chance et s'il a bien pris sa bonne dose de laxatif ce matin, il devrait pouvoir arranger le coup pour que nous soyons à nouveau sur l'enquête...

Son jeune stagiaire hocha la tête en signe d'approbation.

— Au fait, inspecteur, lança Clément. Il y a quelque chose de très drôle sur la liste que j'ai dressée hier soir. Votre femme et vous en faites partie...

— Oui, je sais... Je t'en ai déjà touché un mot dans la nuit... Notre groupe... Les Fab Five... Je t'expliquerai ça au calme tout à l'heure. On fera monter une pizza...

Il sortit du bureau sans même prendre la peine de quitter son imperméable.

Le bureau de Forbes se situait au quatrième étage. Kite emprunta l'escalier de secours pour s'y rendre. Il ne voulait pas prendre le risque de rencontrer quelqu'un dans l'ascenseur. Le bureau de Hicks et de sa brigade se situait également au quatrième. Et Kite n'avait absolument pas envie d'échanger ne serait-ce qu'un regard avec l'un de ses membres. Une fois arrivé sur le palier des ascenseurs, il prit à gauche pour se rendre directement dans le bureau de Forbes. De nombreuses plantes vertes bien entretenues fleurissaient le couloir sombre.

Kite arriva enfin devant la porte du bureau de la secrétaire du vieux Forbes. Il ne savait pas si elle serait là ce matin. D'habitude elle prenait son samedi. Kite frappa une fois à la porte et attendit une réponse, les mains déjà posées sur la poignée de la porte.

— Entrez...

Kite prit sa respiration et poussa la porte. S'il y avait sa secrétaire, il y avait le vieux Forbes.

— Bonjour Kathleen, commença Kite.

Cette dernière lui répondit d'un sourire gêné. Kite regarda l'intérieur du bureau. Trois personnes, un homme, deux femmes, se tenaient debout près de la lourde porte capitonnée de tissu rouge, seul accès au bureau de Forbes. Ils se sentirent obligés de saluer l'inspecteur d'un bonjour peu convaincant. Kite leur répondit et se tourna vers Kathleen.

— Il faut absolument que je parle à Mr Forbes. J'ai une information très importante au sujet des derniers meurtres de...

Les trois intrus haussèrent imperceptiblement leur tête et du même coup leur attention. Kathleen se décala de façon qu'ils ne puissent pas la voir et posa son doigt levé contre sa bouche :

— Chut ! marmonna-t-elle. Mr Forbes est occupé en ce moment et il doit recevoir ces trois personnes du *Sunday Times* le plus rapidement possible... Faites une note, inspecteur Kite...

Kite quitta son imperméable et le mit sur son bras droit replié.

— Non ! Je ne peux pas attendre, c'est au sujet des meurtres de...

— Oui, oui, je le sais bien, inspecteur, mais... (Kite jeta un regard appelant à la générosité de

208

son interlocutrice.) Bon, je vais voir ce que je peux faire, mais je ne vous promets rien...

Elle posa son stylo, chaussa ses lunettes et se dirigea vers la porte capitonnée en demandant pardon aux trois journalistes qui mouraient d'envie d'interroger Kite.

— Vous êtes l'inspecteur Kite ? demanda une jeune fille asiatique aux longs yeux noirs.

Kite ne répondit pas. À peine susurra-t-il un « merde ! » Les journalistes cessèrent immédiatement leurs sourires et se replongèrent dans l'étude des couleurs du papier peint hideux. Trois minutes plus tard, la porte rouge s'ouvrit enfin. Forbes en sortit avec, sur ses talons, sa secrétaire visiblement fière d'elle.

— Je suis à vous dans quelques minutes, mesdames, monsieur, dit-il de sa voix de castrat.

Il s'avança vers Kite et tendit sa main aux os saillants. On aurait dit le bras d'un squelette avec une montre. Forbes prit l'initiative de la conversation en poussant Kite dans le couloir.

— Dépêchez-vous, Kite... J'ai un travail énorme...

Kite s'humecta les lèvres et commença son récit :

— C'est au sujet des meurtres de ces femmes... Je crois que nous tenons, mon stagiaire français et moi, une piste sérieuse...

Il attendit quelques instants la réaction de Forbes, qui se grattait le nez en observant l'état pelliculaire du haut de sa veste.

— Paul, j'ai dit à votre ami Barlow que vous étiez tous déchargés de l'affaire... Je ne vais pas changer d'avis maintenant.

Un jeune flic, sa carte accrochée à la ceinture, passa devant Forbes et lui adressa son plus beau sourire de fayot.

— Si vous avez quelque chose à dire, adressez-vous directement à Hicks. Son bureau n'est pas loin et il doit y être actuellement... Quant à moi, je vais être obligé de vous laisser, car il faut absolument que je prépare un discours rassurant pour le diffuser dans la presse. Et puis il y a ces trois jeunes journalistes que je dois recevoir... (Il leva un doigt ridé vers le ciel.) Ordre de là-haut. Du 10e...

— Mais c'est à vous que je veux en parler, pour savoir ce qu'il m'est autorisé de faire..., insista Kite.

— Non, non et non ! martela Forbes. Hicks est également votre supérieur hiérarchique, vous pouvez donc aller le voir et tout lui expliquer.

Ses veines du cou grossissaient à vue d'œil.

— C'est que je me demandais si nous ne pourrions pas reprendre part à l'enquête...

Forbes manqua de s'étrangler.

— Vous êtes fou, Kite ! Avec la tournure que prend l'affaire dans l'opinion publique ? Vous voulez ma tête et celle du New Yard tout entier ? (Il marqua une pause devant le regard soudain vide de l'inspecteur.) Excusez-moi de vous parler ainsi, Kite, mais je suis très énervé par cette affaire : elle me fait même rater un week-end à Stoke. Mais vous devez comprendre qu'il m'est impossible de vous confier ce dossier après la... (Il s'arrêta, ne voulant pas retourner plus le couteau dans la plaie : il savait Kite très sensible à ce sujet.) Continuez plutôt ce crime du métro... Cela doit bien amuser votre jeune Français, cette histoire de meurtre-suicide, n'est-ce pas ?

Kite ne prit même pas la peine de répondre et tourna le dos au vieux directeur. Forbes aurait voulu donner une petite tape amicale sur l'épaule de Kite, mais ce dernier ne lui en laissa même pas le temps. Il réintégra alors son bureau où les trois journalistes commençaient sérieusement à s'impatienter. Kite reprit son chemin vers les escaliers.

À peine arrivé dans le hall, il vit la silhouette de Hicks se faufilant dans le couloir de droite. Allait-il l'appeler ? Il fit un pas et pensa alors à Clément. S'il parlait, ils n'avaient que très peu de chance de refaire partie de l'équipe. Et quand bien même, ils joueraient les seconds rôles et tout le succès reviendrait à cette clique de jeunes trous-du-cul. Kite s'abstint de héler Hicks et, d'un pas plein de détermination, se dirigea vers les escaliers.

— Quelle bande de faux derches !

Kite rentra dans le bureau sans même faire son célèbre geste à la James Bond. Clément compulsait des feuilles et un gros livre posés avec ordre sur le bureau.

— Pourquoi vous êtes revenu si tôt ? Qu'est-ce qui se passe ?

— Ils n'ont même pas voulu m'écouter ! Je leur ai dit que nous avions découvert peut-être *le* lien entre les trois meurtres, mais je n'ai même pas pu exposer notre théorie...

Son stagiaire fronça les sourcils.

— Le vieux Forbes s'en fichait comme de son premier dentier ! Le vieux connard !

— Qu'est-ce qu'on fait alors ? questionna Clément visiblement perplexe devant le récit de son chef.

— On continue, bien sûr ! On ne lâche pas le morceau ! Tous les deux...

— Et le meurtre du métro ? demanda Clément

— Rien à battre. Si Nancy n'a rien à foutre, elle n'a qu'à aller s'en occuper...

Il n'y avait rien à ajouter.

Après avoir commandé la pizza par téléphone, l'inspecteur Kite jeta enfin un coup d'œil sur la liste que Clément avait composée la nuit dernière :

> *Michelle*
> *Eleanor Rigby*
> *Docteur Robert*
> *Sgt Pepper's Lonely Hearts Club Band*
> *Lucy in the Sky with Diamonds*
> *Being for the Benefit of Mr Kite*
> *Lovely Rita*
> *Lady Madonna*
> *Hey Jude*
> *Martha my Dear*
> *Rocky Raccoon*
> *Julia*
> *Sexy Sadie*
> *The Ballad of John and Yoko*
> *Maxwell's Silver Hammer*
> *Mean Mr Mustard*
> *Polythene Pam*

Il avait fait un inventaire, qu'il espérait exhaustif, de toutes les chansons composées et chantées par les Beatles comportant un nom ou un prénom dans leur titre. Elles étaient donc au nombre de dix-sept.

Kite reposa la feuille devant lui et réunit ses deux mains devant sa bouche.

— Je te dois bien une explication sur cette liste et sur nos prénoms, car cela ne tient pas du simple hasard ! À l'université, en 1976, j'ai monté avec l'aide de trois autres copains, et de l'amie de l'un d'eux, un groupe : les Fab Five. Nous avions, dès le départ, défini les « règles » du groupe. La première était simple, nous devions toujours être cinq... Un de plus que les vrais Fab. La deuxième règle compliquait un peu le tout : il fallait obligatoirement avoir un rapport entre son nom ou son prénom et l'une des chansons des Beatles...

— C'est incroyable ! coupa Clément.

— Oh ! Moins que tu ne le crois, Clément..., reprit Kite. Beaucoup de groupes du même genre existaient en Angleterre à l'époque... Et peut-être même à l'étranger... Les personnes de mon âge avaient dans les 6 ans lorsque les Beatles sont nés... C'est l'âge où l'on commence à s'intéresser à la musique. Quand les Beatles se sont séparés, nous avions 14 ans et nous étions encore trop jeunes pour vraiment exprimer notre passion... Lorsque nous avons commencé à mûrir, les Beatles étaient déjà séparés. Tous les groupes d'amateurs qui ont fleuri à l'époque exprimaient cette frustration d'adolescents, bercés par les Beatles depuis toujours et qui n'ont jamais pu assister à un seul de leurs concerts, ou qui n'ont jamais pu faire la queue pendant des heures pour acheter leur dernier album...

» Pour mon groupe, on se réunissait tous les lundis soir après les cours et on essayait de jouer et de chanter le répertoire des Beatles et d'autres artistes de l'époque. C'était vraiment un petit groupe sans prétention. Et puis un jour, l'un des fondateurs du groupe a quitté l'université définitivement. Le groupe a bien failli ne jamais se relever de son départ. Pensez-vous !

Les Fab Five de l'université de Liverpool n'étaient plus que quatre ! Nous avons donc passé une annonce dans la gazette du campus, mais aucune candidature ne nous est parvenue. Pas une seule sérieuse du moins. Jusqu'à ce qu'un de mes copains, le proprio de ton appartement de Fulham justement, qui prenait des cours de secourisme, nous informât que la jeune formatrice s'appelait Michelle et était une fan des Beatles.

Il sourit et reprit :

» En tant que fondateur du groupe, j'ai été la voir un soir après son cours et lui ai parlé de nos petites réunions du lundi soir. Et ni une ni deux, elle a accepté tout de go. Elle était si jolie et si sympa. Certes elle était de six ans notre aînée, mais elle chantait si bien... Il fallait l'entendre ! Et puis je suis tombé amoureux d'elle...

— Quelle rencontre ! se réjouit Clément. En somme, c'est un peu grâce aux Beatles que vous vous êtes rencontrés...

— On peut dire ça, oui... (Kite semblait songeur.) Mais, stop ! Maintenant, il faut réfléchir sérieusement à cette liste... Voir si l'on peut en tirer quelque chose...

— D'abord, il faut recenser tout ce qu'on peut trouver en commun sur les meurtres et les victimes, commença le jeune Français.

— Ce qu'il faudrait absolument trouver, l'interrompit Kite en posant les mains sur son bureau, c'est le mobile de ces meurtres, ce qui a poussé ce sadique à interpréter les paroles de ces inoffensives chansons en véritables mises en scène macabres...

Kite repensa à Charles Manson. Tout à l'heure, il irait à la librairie *Murder One*, sur

214

Charing Cross Road, pour acheter un livre sur le sujet. Il reprit :

— Est-ce un fan des Beatles ? Un anti-Beatles ? Quel lien a-t-il avec eux ?

— Oui..., reprit Clément. En fait, il faudrait savoir si cet homme aime ou hait ce groupe. Les victimes n'ayant, au premier abord, aucun lien entre elles, l'homme ne doit pas viser une personne particulière, mais bien les Beatles eux-mêmes... Ce pourrait être un jaloux, un frustré... Quelqu'un qui a souffert des Beatles... Directement ou indirectement.

Kite fronça sévèrement les sourcils. Tout ceci n'avait ni queue ni tête. Il fallait reprendre les éléments un par un et tenter de les expliquer.

— Il existe donc plusieurs similitudes que l'on retrouve lors de chaque meurtre. Pour les victimes d'abord, strangulation suivie d'une mise en scène où le meurtrier procède à une dégradation physique d'une partie du corps de la victime : le front pour Eleanor, les yeux pour Lucy et le cou pour Jude.

Clément prenait quelques notes sur une feuille qui traînait sur le bureau. Kite continua de suivre son raisonnement.

— Deuxième similitude, on a retrouvé près de chaque cadavre un élément d'instrument de musique : des cordes de guitare aux poignets d'Eleanor, un triangle de percussionniste dans la bijouterie de Lucy et un archet de violon sur le canapé de Jude. Ce qui confirme en somme notre hypothèse que l'homme est un mélomane : les meurtres ont bien un lien direct avec la musique.

— De plus, les instruments de musique sont différents à chaque fois, ajouta Clément.

— Exactement. Troisième point commun

entre les trois victimes, elles sont toutes trois célibataires...

— Nous n'en sommes pas sûrs pour Jude, intervint Clément.

— Oui, en effet, mais on peut le supposer. Partons sur cette base. Le meurtrier tue donc des femmes célibataires en laissant près de leur cadavre un élément d'instrument de musique... Pouvons-nous, rien qu'avec ça, associer un mobile ?

Le silence envahit le bureau. Clément pensait que ce lien était primordial. Célibataire... Single... Célibataire... Single...

Kite entendit le monologue de son jeune adjoint. *Single*. Il ne savait pas pourquoi, mais chaque fois qu'il pensait à une personne célibataire, il revoyait cette pauvre miss Lonelyhearts de *Fenêtre sur Cour*, le film d'Alfred Hitchcock. Cette pauvre petite femme qui habitait au rez-de-chaussée de l'immeuble et qui faisait semblant de recevoir quelqu'un chaque soir en dressant la table pour deux et en jouant la comédie. *Single*. Miss Lonelyhearts...

— *Lonelyheart* ! s'exclama Kite tout en regardant son stagiaire avec insistance. *Lonelyheart* ! répéta-t-il. *Sergeant Pepper's Lonely Hearts Club Band* ! L'orchestre des cœurs solitaires... des célibataires... (Kite n'en revenait pas et se passait une main insistante sur le menton.) Cet homme est un cinglé ! Il tente probablement de constituer un orchestre de jeunes femmes célibataires...

— Vous ne croyez pas que tout ça semble tiré par les cheveux ? demanda Clément qui venait de cesser d'écrire.

— Qu'est-ce qui est tiré par les cheveux ? Sa démarche ou nos déductions ? Tu trouves déjà normal que la première intuition que l'on ait eue sur un homme soit due à une cassette dans un autoradio ? Et ces mises en scène grotesques issues de l'interprétation des chansons, trouves-tu cela normal ? Qu'est-ce qui semble normal chez eux ? (Kite montait l'intonation de sa voix à chaque question.) Crois-tu que c'était un comportement normal de foutre un petit môme drogué dans un sac pour provoquer la police afin qu'elle le déchiquette elle-même ?

Clément comprit l'énorme signification de la dernière phrase.

— Paul, du calme, répétait Clément.

Mais il ignorait les paroles de son stagiaire et continuait son monologue.

— Cet homme est probablement à l'égal de Charles Manson ou de Mark Chapman. (Devant la mine étonnée de Clément, il précisa sa pensée :) Manson était un fou qui a tué pas mal de monde, dont la femme de Polanski, Sharon Tate, dans la région de Los Angeles. Il disait lire des prophéties dans les paroles des chansons du *White Album* des Beatles. Je vais aller acheter sa bio tout à l'heure. Peut-être que je trouverai quelque chose dans la folie de Manson. (Il marqua une pause et se gratta l'intérieur des cuisses. Sa douleur le reprenait par endroits.) Mark Chapman est l'homme qui a tué John Lennon le 8 décembre 1980. Chapman était un fan fou des Beatles. Et il a tué à cause de cela. (Nouvelle pause.) Je me rappelle encore la scène le lendemain matin. Je descendais tranquillement pour prendre mon petit déjeuner et j'ai trouvé Michelle, la tête entre les mains, les yeux rouges. J'ai haussé le volume de la radio et la nouvelle m'a scié. Je ne voulais pas le croire. Je pensais à une manipulation du style de la mort de McCartney, mais la BBC ne plaisante que très rarement...

— Pourquoi Chapman a-t-il tué son idole ?

Paul haussa les épaules.

— Il parlait de remplir une « mission ». C'était un débile. Il n'a pas fui après son crime et il a sagement attendu la police en serrant dans sa main le livre de Salinger...

— *L'Attrape-cœur* ?

— Oui. Au procès, il a tout bonnement déclaré que ce meurtre était la seule façon pour lui de devenir plus célèbre encore que son idole. La drogue ne l'avait pas arrangé. Il s'identifiait complètement à Lennon. Il s'enregistrait avec un magnétophone ridicule en train de chanter ses chansons, il a épousé une femme d'origine asiatique comme John et sa Yoko. Je crois même qu'il avait démissionné de son dernier emploi de vigile en signant John Lennon !

Clément écoutait avec attention l'inspecteur. Il devina les conclusions plus ou moins cachées de Kite.

— Donc vous pensez que le meurtrier serait un fou s'identifiant non pas aux Beatles comme Chapman, mais à leurs chansons. Un *lonely-heart*, un célibataire frustré, qui en voudrait aux femmes en général et aux « femmes des Beatles » en particulier...

— Oui, on peut dire ça... Il pousse le vice jusqu'à tuer selon les « conseils » de ses idoles et, pour donner une finalité à l'affaire, essaye de constituer un orchestre de cœurs solitaires...

— Et il n'est pas près de s'arrêter, constata Clément. Il reste huit noms de femme. Soit encore, si l'on pousse le raisonnement jusqu'au bout, huit meurtres...

— Et on ne peut pas lancer dans les médias

une campagne demandant à toutes les femmes portant ces noms de rester cloîtrées chez elle !

— Bien sûr que non, soupira Kite. De toute façon, nous n'avons aucun pouvoir. Et comme je n'ai pas l'intention d'aller quémander du côté de Hicks... Et puis les gens ne prendraient pas cette mesure au sérieux... Va dire à Michelle de rester à la maison plus d'une demi-journée... Mais que pouvons-nous bien faire ? Nous sommes là assis le cul sur nos chaises... Il faudrait absolument retrouver cet homme.

— On peut toujours demander aux fans-clubs une liste de leurs membres, regarder sur Internet s'il n'y a pas un site qui recenserait les fans, les anti-Beatles...

C'était effectivement ce qu'ils avaient de mieux à faire cet après-midi.

— Tu pourrais peut-être aussi aller faire un tour du côté de Regent Street, ajouta Kite sur un ton désabusé. Je sais qu'il y a là-bas une boutique qui vend tout ce dont les fans des Beatles raffolent.

Kite ouvrit un tiroir et en ramena un petit prospectus jaune.

— *Beatles for Sale*, annonça-t-il. 8, Kingsly Street, juste derrière Hamleys... Tiens...

Il tendit le papier à son jeune adjoint.

— De toute façon, il ne faut pas se faire d'illusions...

Kite s'était tourné vers la fenêtre et regardait au-dehors les gens marcher dans la rue. Le vent s'était levé et décoiffait les têtes aux cheveux longs.

— La phase « je pense dans mon bureau et je fais des associations entre des chansons des Fab Four, un film d'Hitchcock et trois meurtres sanglants ; ainsi je trouve une petite partie du profil psychologique du tueur » est bien finie. Terminée. Maintenant, ça va être l'attente...

S'ils ne trouvaient rien aujourd'hui, ce qui était plus que probable, demain, il irait trouver le superintendant Hicks. Peut-être que Hicks aurait une idée lumineuse qui arrêterait le massacre. Car il y avait bien une chose à laquelle Kite ne voulait pas penser, c'était cette autre similitude entre les meurtres, cette unité de temps. Deux jours entre chaque. Dimanche, l'homme tuerait à nouveau. Et Kite n'y pouvait rien, même s'il allait voir Hicks et ses jeunes chiens fous. Il ne pourrait éviter ce meurtre, comme celui de la petite Pamela il y avait de cela dix ans. Il cessa de fixer la rue par la fenêtre, car le vide relatif au-dessous de lui accentuait sa nausée.

29

L'homme attendait patiemment la victime désignée par Paul McCartney ce matin. Il s'accordait là une petite récréation. Confortablement assis sur un banc, son chapeau rabattu au maximum pour que sa tête ne soit visible de personne, il avait peut-être l'air d'un clochard, mais n'en avait cure. Seul comptait son dessein. Paul l'avait autorisé à se débarrasser de cette fille. Il avait longuement hésité auparavant, ne pouvant l'inclure dans son plan. Non pas que sa mort ne lui soit d'aucune utilité. De cela, il en était persuadé. Elle était là pour lui rappeler son échec, le début de cette épopée. Elle était la représentation vivante de son mal-être.

À chaque fois qu'il la voyait, il ne pouvait s'empêcher de vomir. Cela était gênant. Bien gênant. Il l'embrassait à chaque fois avec un mal de ventre atroce. Son œsophage le brûlait comme jamais, attaqué de tous côtés par les acides qu'elle lui faisait sécréter. Il aurait aimé la tuer d'une façon atroce, mais il se contenterait de la poignarder entre ses seins. Dieu ! que ses seins étaient beaux ! Presque aussi beaux que ceux de sa maman... Dieu ! qu'elle était belle... Presque aussi belle que sa maman... Mais elle ne pouvait continuer à vivre. L'homme la poignarderait, car ainsi son assassinat ne serait pas rapproché de son chef-d'œuvre.

La voilà qui sortait de chez elle... Elle emprunta le trottoir, elle ne le vit pas... Il serra dans sa main le long couteau et se leva. La suivre de loin... Il s'était creusé la cervelle toute la matinée à son sujet. Les paroles de Paul lui revenaient à l'esprit : « Il n'y a pas que des prénoms dans les titres de nos chansons... Cherche bien la phrase et tu verras que tu pourras la tuer... »

Il n'avait pas mis longtemps à chercher, pas mis longtemps à trouver. Et ainsi, un couteau glisserait bientôt entre ses deux mamelons. Il se réprimanda tout en marchant. Entre ses mamelons... Il trouvait cette image d'un vulgaire... Allons... Il ne devait pas jouer au banal sadique. Son père devait mourir, cela, c'était planifié. Sa mère serait épargnée bien sûr... Comment pouvait-il en être autrement... Tuer le père et la fille, c'était déjà bien suffisant. Après, la sagesse viendrait l'envahir tout naturellement... Tout cela était écrit... pensé... calculé...

La jeune fille aux cheveux bruns ne se retournait pas vers lui. Elle portait un petit sac aux motifs incas que l'homme jugea grossier. Ils arrivèrent tous deux sur la route principale et rencontrèrent leurs premiers passants. La jeune fille entra dans un magasin de vêtements. L'homme attendit patiemment, lustrant de ses mains humides le manche du couteau. Quand elle sortit, il fit bien attention de ne pas rencontrer ses yeux d'un bleu divin. Le bleu de sa mère, pensa-t-il. Elle tenait maintenant à la main un autre sac. Ils continuèrent leur avancée. Elle marchait sans se presser, l'homme apprécia. La jeune fille pénétra dans un supermarché et acheta un magazine et deux ou trois barres chocolatées. L'homme, à travers la vitrine, ne la voyait qu'à moitié. Elle sortit, il lui emboîta le pas en restant à bonne distance. Il savait où elle se rendait. Il allait souvent là-bas en sa compagnie... en leur compagnie...

Le pub dans lequel il pénétra quelque trois minutes après l'arrivée de la jeune fille était d'un aménagement très moderne. Les traditionnelles boiseries avaient cédé la place à des grands pans de plastiques multicolores. L'endroit était principalement rempli de jeunes. L'homme s'accouda au comptoir et, tout en gardant son chapeau, demanda une pinte de John Smith. La jeune brune était à une table et papotait avec deux amies devant un verre de bière. Il devait attendre son heure. Une femme au pub passait obligatoirement par les toilettes au moins une fois. Il commanda une deuxième pinte. La dernière. Il ne devait pas être sous l'emprise de l'alcool pour commettre sa petite récréation.

Soudain, sa proie se leva. Posément, il reposa son verre et glissa les mains dans ses poches. Il devait agir vite et surtout silencieusement. C'est qu'il n'était plus seul face à ses victimes comme pour Eleanor, Lucy et Jude. L'homme se rappela une dernière fois la disposition des toilettes. Il l'intercepterait à la sortie, la bâillonnerait avec son bras et l'entraînerait dans le recoin sombre où était posé le téléphone. Alors, il lui larderait le torse de coups de couteau, une main fermement posée sur ses petites lèvres toutes roses... C'est curieux, mais il se serait cru plus émotif en de telles circonstances, plus ennuyé peut-être... Mais Paul lui avait insufflé la confiance nécessaire à son petit amusement.

Il s'ébroua et passa devant les deux amies de sa prochaine victime, puis il vint s'adosser au mur sombre pour l'attendre. Alors, elle sortit. Il vit son visage en sachant qu'elle ne pouvait voir le sien. Il vit ses cheveux, son corps, ses jambes, ses petites chaussures à lacets... Et il sut alors que le couteau ne pourrait jamais sortir de sa poche. La tuer elle, c'était la tuer, ELLE. Et l'homme ne s'en sentit pas la force. Une bouffée de sueur lui monta au visage. La bouffée des faibles. Il tomba presque à terre en regardant la jeune fille s'éloigner de lui, de la portée de sa lame... Ses jambes devenaient molles, ses bras devenaient flasques...

Il avait échoué ici, dans ce pub. Il avait essuyé son premier échec depuis qu'il était si heureux... Car le « Low Battery » de ce matin n'était qu'une broutille comparée à son impuissance devant elle. Il resta encore quelques minutes près du téléphone en attendant de retrouver un semblant de confiance, puis regagna le comptoir en prenant bien soin de ne pas se faire voir. Il paya, salua le serveur et sortit. Au-dehors, la nuit tombait presque. L'homme se surprit à pleurer. C'était bien la première fois qu'il pleurait de rage depuis qu'il préparait son chef-d'œuvre. Il regagna sa voiture alors qu'une rafale de vent détournait les larmes de ses joues.

30

La pizza n'avait pas eu beaucoup de succès. Paul Kite et son jeune lieutenant avaient gagné le parking. Direction Tottenham Court Road, non pas qu'ils aient décidé de reprendre en main l'affaire du meurtre-suicide qui leur passait bien au-dessus de la tête, mais parce que chacun allait pouvoir satisfaire ses envies dans ce quartier. Kite pourrait aller à la librairie *Murder One* et Clément pourrait se rendre au *Webshack*, un Web Café situé non loin, sur Dean Street, et qu'il connaissait pour s'y être rendu quelquefois.

Kite ne trouva aucune place libre dans tout le quartier et décida donc de remonter Tottenham Court Road sur cinq cents mètres pour venir se garer devant le poste de police du quartier. Là, il trouverait une place sans problème et ne serait pas inquiet au sujet de sa voiture laissée au regard de tous les passants. Ils se séparèrent donc devant le poste et se fondirent dans la foule dense qui confluait vers Oxford Street.

Clément avait trouvé un ordinateur libre dès son arrivée dans le Web Café. C'était une prouesse relativement rare pour l'endroit, qui ne comptait qu'une vingtaine de PC. Il était donc assis en face d'un écran de taille moyenne, sur une chaise sommaire. Dès son arrivée, il était allé chercher au comptoir du bar une tasse de thé Earl Grey. Il farfouilla ensuite sur le Net, lançant une recherche grâce à Yahoo ! Le jeune Français aurait aimé en profiter pour laisser un petit message dans la boîte à lettres électronique de Mary, mais il s'était dit que ce n'était vraiment pas le moment. Au *Webshack*, les places étaient chères. Et puis Kite l'avait remonté à bloc... Ils avaient tous deux un but désormais : retrouver ce fou. Dans la case, il tapa « The Beatles » et attendit ensuite quelques secondes. Pas moins de cent soixante sites lui étaient proposés en accès direct.

« On va rétrécir le champ de recherche », se dit Clément devant l'écran.

Il s'empara à nouveau de la souris et cliqua sur plusieurs boutons avant de saisir dans une zone de texte « Beatles fan-club ». Une nouvelle liste aussi impressionnante que la précédente apparut sur l'écran. Il pouvait commencer par enlever tous les sites Web des particuliers comme *Cheryl's Beatles Tribute* ou *Chris Collier's Beatles Page*... Il se privait clairement des sites pirates qui évoqueraient par exemple des affaires bizarres ayant un rapport avec les Beatles, mais sinon il allait y laisser et son temps, et son portefeuille.

Clément fixa attentivement l'écran.

— Commence donc par le... (il posa son doigt sur l'écran) *London Beatles Fan-Club*.

Clément cliqua sur le titre. L'ordinateur chercha l'adresse et s'arrêta sur le site *http://www.lbfc.demon.co.uk*. Il commença sa lecture.

Kite poussa la porte de la plus célèbre librairie de Londres spécialisée dans la littérature criminelle, *Murder One*. Visiteur pour la première fois de son existence, l'inspecteur du Yard, ne comprenant rien au rangement du lieu, avisa un vendeur pour lui demander conseil. Il interpella donc un petit homme chauve, avec de longues et épaisses moustaches noires. Son physique faisait penser à Hercule Poirot, pensa Kite. Hormis les moustaches qui ne satisferaient pas le véritable connaisseur de l'œuvre de Dame Agatha Christie.

— Bonjour, monsieur.

La voix de l'homme était très grave. Encore une autre différence avec Poirot et sa voix obséquieuse.

— Bonjour. Je cherche un livre qui parlerait de l'affaire Charles Manson. Une biographie de l'homme ou le récit de l'enquête... Quelque chose de pas trop aride, mais contenant pas mal de détails.

— Oui, bien sûr, monsieur, lui répondit le petit homme en réfléchissant.

Kite jeta un coup d'œil sur les rayonnages de la librairie qui avaient l'air extrêmement bien garnis.

— Attendez-moi une petite minute, monsieur... Je reviens.

L'homme descendit au pas de course le petit escalier menant au sous-sol. Il en remonta triomphalement une trentaine de secondes plus tard, tenant à la main un livre grand format.

— Voilà la bible, monsieur ! *Helter Skelter* : le bouquin qu'ont écrit conjointement le procureur de l'affaire, Vincent Bugliosi, et un journaliste américain, Curt Gentry. Il ne m'en reste qu'un vieil exemplaire. Mais rien n'a été fait de plus précis depuis ce livre, qui a d'ailleurs obtenu le prestigieux prix Edgar en 74...

Kite prit le bouquin des mains du petit homme et le retourna plusieurs fois, lisant la quatrième de couverture et remarquant la teinte jaunâtre de la tranche supérieure du livre.

— Il m'a l'air, en effet, extrêmement didactique... Quel est son prix, s'il vous plaît ?

L'homme gratta son crâne chauve et fixa Kite de ses petits yeux.

— Pardonnez-moi, commença le vendeur, mais vous ne seriez pas l'inspecteur Kite du New Yard ?

Kite écarquilla ses yeux de stupéfaction.

— Pardon ?

— Je sais que cela ne se fait pas, monsieur, mais n'êtes-vous pas l'inspecteur Kite ?

— En effet, mais...

Le petit homme lui tendit la main, un grand sourire aux lèvres.

— Oh, quelle surprise ! Bonjour inspecteur. (Kite, surpris, lui serra la main.) Je suis Richard Porter.

Ce nom rappelait vaguement quelque chose à Kite.

— Vous ne me reconnaissez pas ? reprit le vendeur. Richard Porter. Nous nous sommes rencontrés il y a dix ans, sur cette terrible affaire du « fou aux sacs blancs ». Je m'occupais de la rubrique Crime du *Telegraph* à l'époque...

Mais oui ! se rappela Kite. Porter ! Dieu qu'il avait grossi ! Il se rappelait bien le petit homme maintenant. Le *Daily Telegraph* avait été un des seuls journaux à ce moment-là qui avait pris la défense des inspecteurs de la police. Lorsqu'il s'était fait virer du journal pour avoir donné cette ligne éditoriale à contre-courant, il avait projeté d'écrire un livre sur l'affaire et avait rencontré Kite à ce sujet.

— Comment allez-vous ? demanda Kite. Vous êtes vendeur ici, maintenant ?

— Vendeur ? (Porter posa ses doigts sur ses larges hanches.) Vous rigolez ! Je suis le nouveau propriétaire de l'endroit...

— Eh bien, félicitations ! Déjà que la maison avait une très bonne réputation...

Porter sourit et invita Kite à pénétrer dans son bureau au sous-sol. Il serait très content si l'inspecteur acceptait de discuter un peu avec lui.

Le site du *London Beatles Fan-Club* était très bien réalisé et très complet. Déçu par l'absence d'une liste quelconque de ses membres, Clément se rabattit sur de nombreux articles décrivant les activités du fan-club et sur de nombreuses photos sur les lieux de la capitale britannique où travaillaient, vivaient et s'amusaient les Beatles. Avant de devoir libérer l'ordinateur, il nota l'adresse de la présidente du fan-club, une certaine Jane Goldblum, résidant au 5, Leighton Gardens. Voilà une adresse que Kite apprécierait probablement...

Vraiment, le temps passait très vite une fois branché sur le Web. Et on y trouvait des anecdotes toutes plus incroyables les unes que les autres : à la fin de *A Day in the Life*, les Beatles auraient murmuré à l'envers la phrase : « We'll fuck you like Superman [1] » avant d'inclure dans le dernier sillon quelques brefs instants de fréquence de quinze kilocycles que seuls les chiens peuvent entendre... *Penny Lane*, cette chanson au rythme si bon enfant, cachait également bien

---

1. Nous vous baiserons comme Superman.

228

son jeu : on parlait de *Fish and finger pie* [1], expression donnée pour obscène dans les rues de Liverpool, ou bien encore de *Fireman who keeps his fire engine clean* [2], que certains traduisaient vertement par le pompier qui astique sa lance...

Sur un autre site, le jeune inspecteur trouva des pages et des pages démontant les rumeurs de la mort de McCartney. Le *I burried Paul* de *Strawberry Fields* devenait un *Cranberry Sauce* [3].

Clément vida d'un trait le fond de sa tasse de thé froid et se leva. Tout cela était bien drôle, mais peu productif. Immédiatement, un jeune garçon boutonneux vint avidement prendre sa place.

En revenant vers la voiture, il se mit à repenser à l'épisode de ce matin. Ainsi Kite était somnambule. Il ne savait pas si c'était une habitude de son supérieur, mais il trouvait cela inquiétant. Depuis le début de ces meurtres, l'inspecteur n'était pas bien. Clément se doutait que les ressemblances plus ou moins lointaines avec l'affaire de 87 minaient Kite.

Depuis lors, Paul avait perdu son insouciance. Lui qui ne voulait jamais tomber dans le cliché du flic déprimé y avait été amené contre sa volonté. Son malaise se reflétait sur toute sa famille. Il n'y avait qu'à voir la façon dont Mary se comportait avec lui, Clément... Elle n'arrivait pas à le considérer par amour simplement parce qu'il était flic comme son père. Il se rappelait ses paroles de la veille : « Tu crois pouvoir

1. Littéralement : tarte au poisson et au doigt.
2. Le pompier qui garde sa pompe à incendie propre.
3. Sauce aux airelles.

me garder en me faisant jouir ? Je ne pense pas que tu sois le seul capable de le faire... C'est curieux, mais je ne crois pas être capable de me donner autrement à un flic. Tu baises comme un flic, Clément. »

Le jeune Français comprenait en un sens les propos de son amie. Il lui avait avoué ses véritables aspirations, sa vraie nature. Mais elle sentait qu'il prenait du plaisir à suivre une enquête, à rentrer tard, à ne pas se raser... Même si pour lui, tout cela n'était qu'un rôle... Kite... Kite et son amour des Beatles. Une pensée traversa l'esprit de Clément. Et si Kite était le meurtrier ? Il aimait suffisamment le groupe de Liverpool pour cela... Cette pensée le fit sourire... Ce n'était pas possible.

Résumons... Pour Eleanor, je ne sais pas où il pouvait être... J'étais à Paris. Pour Lucy, eh bien mercredi soir à 7 heures... Paul est venu me prendre à l'Eurostar de 8 heures, donc... Bon, admettons... Et pour Jude ? Il était au Yard... Il pouvait s'absenter... N'est-il pas sorti pour dîner ? ARRÊTE ! *Pour les trois meurtres, je ne pourrais pas lui servir d'alibi.* ARRÊTE ENFIN ! *S'il est somnambule, il peut tout aussi bien être schizophrène en pleine journée...* C'EST FINI MAINTENANT ? *Non, ça n'est pas possible que le Yard nous ait déchargés de l'enquête sur des soupçons de culpabilité. Ils doivent savoir Kite un peu instable, mais de là à...* STOP ! *Du reste il pourrait ne pas agir seul, il faudra faire attention à ses alibis... Il peut agir en groupe comme au temps de la fac...* TU VAS TE TAIRE ! *Et puis rappelle-toi les paroles de Mary... Il cherchait sa grosse affaire... Alors pourquoi ne pas se la créer ?* TU DIVAGUES !

Clément s'engagea dans Tottenham Court Road, décontenancé.

Kite pénétra à l'intérieur de la librairie *Dillons* sur Oxford Street, portant sous le bras le livre sur Manson que Richard Porter lui avait si gentiment offert. Kite s'était promis de revenir le voir bientôt. Il était vraiment content d'avoir rencontré cet ancien journaliste reconverti. Comme quoi ! Il ne fallait jamais faire de généralités sur une profession...

La librairie *Dillons* était pleine de monde. Kite voulait trouver un livre complet retraçant la carrière des Beatles, si possible avec bon nombre d'allusions aux chansons.

Quelques années auparavant, il avait entendu parler d'un bouquin qui révélait les « secrets de fabrication » des chansons du célèbre groupe de Liverpool. Mais il serait bien incapable aujourd'hui de s'en rappeler le titre. Il se fraya donc un chemin jusqu'aux étagères « Music ». Il n'aimait pas l'aménagement intérieur de cette librairie : trop sombre avec ses rayonnages noirs... Mais Kite n'avait pas le temps d'aller fureter ailleurs. Il passait un doigt sur la tranche des livres au fur et à mesure de l'avancement de sa recherche. Il commençait à avoir chaud, son imperméable encore sur ses épaules. Avec tout ce monde et le chauffage qu'il soupçonnait à son maximum, de fines gouttelettes de sueur apparurent sur son front et son nez. Ou était-ce à cause de tout ce temps perdu ? Soudain, Kite mit le doigt sur un beau livre au papier glacé : *The Beatles* de Steve Turner. C'était peut-être l'auteur qu'il cherchait. S'en emparant, il le retourna et détailla le texte présent sur le dos du livre.

Cela faisait bien un bon quart d'heure que Clément poireautait devant le poste de police de Tottenham Court Road, accoudé sur la Rover de Kite. Il s'était rendu à la boutique *Beatles for Sale,* mais n'avait pas su trouver l'accroche pour faire parler les propriétaires, qui plus est sans pouvoir leur montrer sa carte du Yard. Le jeune inspecteur se voyait mal demander une liste des acheteurs réguliers de la boutique ou bien une base de données des abonnés à un quelconque fanzine consacré au célèbre groupe. Il s'était alors contenté de chiner à travers les rayons du magasin regorgeant de CD, de cartes postales, de montres et même de blousons à l'effigie des *Fab Four.* Mais sa recherche s'avéra infructueuse... Clément espérait que Kite n'avait pas, lui non plus, chômé. Mais que pouvait bien faire l'inspecteur ? Il avait simplement deux livres à acheter... Cela ne devrait pas prendre tout ce temps... Le jeune Français commençait à trouver l'attente longue.

— Eh ! Excuse-moi, Clément ! Je suis en retard...

Il portait à la main un sac qui contenait, selon les estimations de Clément, deux livres grand format.

— Excuse-moi, fit Kite en se rapprochant et en baissant le ton. Mais j'ai rencontré un ancien ami journaliste et il m'a tenu la jambe un long moment.

Clément s'étonna. Avait-il vraiment entendu les mots « ami » et « journaliste » accolés dans la phrase de Kite ? Il en doutait, c'était si peu probable.

— Bon, as-tu trouvé quelque chose sur le Net ?

232

N'attendant même pas la réponse de son stagiaire, Kite s'engouffra dans la voiture.

— Bof ! Pas grand-chose...

Kite introduisit la clef de contact. Décidément, ils avaient vraiment un problème avec le temps. Ce temps qui passait bien trop vite et qui était si stérile. Kite jeta un coup d'œil sur l'horloge du tableau de bord de sa Rover. Déjà 3 heures et demie. Kite fulmina intérieurement. Ils piétinaient encore et toujours. Rien de concret et l'après-midi allait bientôt se finir. Et ce n'est pas l'adresse notée sur un bout de papier que venait de lui tendre Clément qui allait rassurer l'inspecteur du Yard. Certes, ils prendraient vers l'ouest, vers Kensal Green, pour aller rencontrer cette Jane Goldblum. Mais que pourrait-elle bien leur apprendre ? Elle allait leur donner la liste des membres du fan-club qu'elle dirigeait et ce serait tout. Ils ne seraient pas plus avancés avec une liste de noms recensant les fans « déclarés » des Beatles à Londres. Mais que pouvaient-ils espérer de plus ? Kite se voyait marcher dans la rue et croiser l'assassin à un coin de rue avec une inscription sur son front : « C'est moi le méchant ». Il se jetterait alors sur lui et le menotterait avec ses mains en attendant l'aide de ses collègues. Si tout cela était si simple... Mais il savait que son jeune adjoint et lui devraient faire preuve de patience... De beaucoup de patience...

L'homme s'était peu à peu remis en accord avec lui-même. En pensant et repensant à son échec, en le rapprochant des paroles de Paul McCartney ce matin, il s'était rendu à l'évidence la plus juste : son plan était sauf. Il n'y aurait pas de meurtres supplémentaires de femmes venant de ses mains. En somme, il avait raté une occasion, voilà tout... Tuer cette jeune fille lui avait souvent traversé l'esprit, mais il fallait se rendre à l'évidence : il ne pourrait pas la tuer. Il ne pourrait pas lever un couteau ou un revolver sur elle. Alors il s'était fait à cette idée en errant dans Londres le reste de l'après-midi. Il essuierait probablement les remontrances acerbes de McCartney, le musicien était connu pour son mauvais caractère et ses tendances à la mégalomanie, mais il se coucherait devant son maître pour se faire pardonner. Il avait déjà tout cogité pendant sa longue marche qui le conduisit dans le quartier de Soho. Certes, il y aurait du monde en ce samedi après-midi, mais, justement, c'était ce qu'il cherchait.

Lorsqu'il sortait d'une de ses crises intérieures, d'une de ces crises qu'il lui faisaient perdre confiance en lui, il voulait voir le maximum de corps et de visages. Il se prouvait ainsi sa supériorité en entendant la voix si peu distinguée de certaines femmes ou leurs grands éclats de rire vulgaires qui le dégoûtaient. Il éprouvait ce curieux besoin d'observer le visage de ces hommes, la cigarette au bec et le sweat-shirt d'un club de football sur le buste. De détailler leurs visages aux traits grossiers. Alors, il souriait et passait une main sur son menton parfaitement rasé. Sa supériorité ne faisait alors plus aucun doute, aussi bien physiquement qu'intellectuellement.

L'homme s'arrêta quelques instants devant le théâtre *Prince Edward*. Son imperméable vert le rassurait. Il savait qu'avec lui sur le dos, il ne s'énerverait contre personne. Il n'insulterait pas les jeunes le bousculant dans la rue, tous ces gens qui ne respectaient pas les règles de la vie en société, qui se fichaient éperdument de leurs semblables et vivaient égoïstement. Prenant la direction de Shaftesbury Avenue, il leva les yeux et remarqua la couleur grise des quelques nuages parsemant le ciel en cette fin d'après-midi. L'homme avait pour intention de se rendre chez ce petit disquaire qu'il connaissait bien et qui le fournissait en inédits. C'était un commerçant sérieux aux goûts sûrs et il lui faisait quasiment confiance les yeux fermés. Il s'en était même fait un ami. L'homme passa la langue sur ses lèvres. Avant, il devait acheter le journal pour se tenir au courant des derniers développements de l'affaire. Mais surtout pas le *Times*... Son journal favori l'avait trop déçu. Confiant, il paya le *Daily Telegraph* et le déplia tout en continuant son avancée.

Le titre à la une choqua l'homme :

LE CARNAGE DE CHELSEA.

Au-dessous était reproduite une photo de nuit du lieu du crime. On pouvait y voir, sous la seule lumière orange des lampadaires, de nombreux policiers s'affairant autour de voitures aux gyrophares allumés et d'une ambulance. La photo était légendée. L'homme rapprocha le journal de ses yeux et lut :

Le mélomane sadique avait choisi ce paisible immeuble.

Il s'arrêta net. Auraient-ils un semblant de piste ? Avalant l'air avidement, il déplia le journal et détailla l'article. Debout sur le trottoir, immobile, l'homme se faisait réprimander par les nombreux passants qui se cognaient involontairement à lui.

> Le meurtrier fou laisserait près de ses victimes un instrument de musique. Le superintendant Hicks du New Yard supervisant ces tragédies aurait laissé entendre qu'une guitare aurait été trouvée près du cadavre d'Eleanor Stout. Pour la jeune Lucy Chambers tuée mercredi soir, c'est un triangle de percussionniste que l'assassin aurait déposé près de son cadavre.

Puis, plus loin :

> L'enquête se dirigerait donc vers la piste d'un mélomane au mobile encore bien trouble.

Commençait alors la longue diatribe d'un ancien responsable du Yard qui devait arrondir ses fins de mois en vendant ses opinions insipides au journal. L'homme arrêta sa lecture et passa une main sur son front légèrement humide. Ces flics étaient vraiment incompétents. Mais il n'allait pas s'en plaindre.

La ruelle où se trouvait le magasin de disques était très étroite. L'homme s'y engagea. Une odeur de poisson frit lui vint aux narines. Il regarda le trottoir opposé et vit qu'il était encore jonché d'ordures diverses : emballages, légumes écrasés, boîtes de conserve... Ça n'était pas étonnant : les propriétaires de ce restaurant, dont les cuisines donnaient en face du magasin, étaient d'une malpropreté qui répugnait l'homme. Jamais il ne mettrait les pieds dans un tel endroit.

Jetant le journal dans une poubelle déjà pleine, il pénétra dans la boutique. Son ami disquaire vint le saluer presque immédiatement. Quelques personnes étaient penchées sur les bacs pleins de disques. L'homme nota leur mine médiocre. Il engagea la conversation, mais se rendit compte que son ami n'avait pas trop de temps à lui accorder. Vexé, il lui lança un « au revoir » timide et gagna la porte.

En fond sonore, il crut reconnaître la voix prétentieuse de Mick Jagger. Les Rolling Stones ! L'homme les détestait vraiment. D'une haine sauvage. Mais quelque chose lui disait de ne pas sortir encore de la boutique. Il se décala légèrement vers la droite pour laisser libre accès à la porte et resta debout, immobile, la tête levée et les mains dans les poches. Une lumière tamisée se diffusait dans la boutique avec une certaine difficulté. L'homme sentait avec écœurement cette odeur de transpiration propre aux petites gens. Qu'est-ce qui le poussait néanmoins à rester ? Peut-être les paroles de cette chanson qui emplissaient le petit local tout entier « *And could you stand the torture, And could you stand the pain, Could you put your faith in Jesus when you're burning in the flames* [1] ? » Quel rythme... Mon Dieu... Quel rythme ! L'homme pensa qu'il devait être intéressant de tuer en suivant la partition de ce

1. Pourrais-tu supporter la torture, pourrais-tu supporter la douleur, pourrais-tu mettre ta foi en Jésus si tu brûlais dans les flammes ?

morceau. Avis à un collègue amateur des Stones !

L'homme sortit de la boutique et affronta en pleine face une pluie battante. Avis à un collègue ! Il se réprimanda pour la seconde fois de la journée. Il ne pouvait avoir de collègue : il était cet unique génie qui avait mis seul au point ce scénario. Manson était un pauvre illuminé à côté de lui. Il se répéta en lui-même les paroles de cette chanson des Stones essayant de retrouver le rythme. « *Could you put your faith in Jesus when you're burning in the flames.* » Puis il secoua la tête. Ses cheveux noirs étaient lourds de pluie. Les Beatles étaient vraiment bien plus poétiques que les Stones... Il se serait mal vu mettre le feu à un cadavre. Il n'était pas un monstre, tout de même. Et c'était bien pour cela qu'il était unique.

L'homme continua sa marche. Fier.

31

L'entretien que Paul Kite avait eu avec miss Jane Goldblum, la présidente du *London Beatles Fan-Club*, il y avait de cela une bonne heure, avait été inintéressant au possible. À peu de choses près, ils avaient failli manquer la jeune femme qui partait dîner chez des amis dans la banlieue sud. Elle n'avait donc eu que peu de temps à consacrer à l'inspecteur du Yard. Clément était resté dans la voiture pour ne pas rendre l'entretien trop formel. Kite demanda à miss

Goldblum de lui communiquer la liste des adhérents du fan-club.

— Pourquoi, inspecteur ? Un de nos membres se serait compromis dans une affaire où la responsabilité du fan-club est en jeu ?

— Rien de tout cela, l'avait rassurée Kite. (Puis il ajouta sur un ton qui se voulait convaincant :) Ma visite d'aujourd'hui est une simple visite de routine qui a pour but de recenser le nombre d'adhérents de chaque association et leur identité « au cas où ».

— Vous me rassurez, avait ajouté miss Goldblum en laissant Kite pénétrer dans son appartement.

Elle lui avait alors simplement fourni la liste, mise à jour la veille, de ses membres, ainsi qu'une tasse de café. Le café était si mauvais que Kite, profitant d'une courte absence de son hôtesse, avait vidé le liquide chaud dans le pot d'une plante verte posée par terre près du canapé.

— Serait-il possible de nous revoir, miss Goldblum ? demanda Kite lorsque cette dernière revint dans le salon.

Elle fit une mine perplexe.

— Comment cela, inspecteur ?

Kite fit un geste évasif de la main.

— Je ne sais pas... Je peux revenir ici ou, si vous êtes à Londres dans la journée... J'aimerais que nous parlions un peu plus de votre association, vos actions, vos rencontres...

— Il ne devrait pas y avoir de problème, inspecteur. Mais puis-je vous poser une question ?

— Je vous en prie.

— Venez-vous ici à titre personnel ou bien vraiment professionnel ? demanda Jane Goldblum avec un malicieux sourire.

239

— Les deux, lui avait répondu Kite immédiatement.

Il ne savait pas pourquoi cette réponse lui
était venue à l'esprit. Peut-être pour donner raison à miss Goldblum. Tant et si bien qu'ils se
fixèrent un rendez-vous devant le *Virgin Mega-
store* de Marble Arch lundi à 6 heures du soir.

Kite et Clément étaient maintenant attablés
dans un pub très chic de Fulham. À travers la
vitre recouverte par endroits d'autocollants
publicitaires, Clément regardait la nuit noire
au-dehors. Il était près de 18 heures. Kite, las,
avait décidé d'abandonner l'enquête pour
aujourd'hui et voulait se retirer chez lui à Finchley pour compulser les livres qu'il avait achetés
aujourd'hui.

— J'en apprendrai bien plus avec eux qu'en
tournant en rond dans Londres à la recherche
d'une piste qui n'existe pas...

Kite rageait de ne pas avoir accès au rapport
du meurtre de Jude. Peut-être le meurtrier
avait-il laissé ou fait quelque chose qui, associé
à l'idée des Beatles, ferait avancer leur enquête
d'un bond. Il but une gorgée de Guiness et s'af-
faissa un peu plus sur la table.

— Qu'allez-vous bien pouvoir demander à
cette miss Goldeuh...

— Goldblum, l'aida Kite.

— Miss Goldblum, reprit Clément, quand
vous la rencontrerez lundi ?

Kite leva ses yeux vers lui.

— Je ne sais pas encore, mais cette femme
doit probablement connaître tous les coins de
Londres qui ont un rapport avec les Beatles...
En cherchant bien, à la fin de la semaine prochaine, nous aurons peut-être un peu avancé...

Et puis à ce rythme effréné, on aura trois nouveaux meurtres, soit trois fois plus d'indices...

Kite était aussi amer que la bière brune qu'il avait forcé son jeune stagiaire à commander.

— Vous ne pouvez pas avoir accès par un moyen ou un autre au dossier complet de l'affaire établi au jour le jour par Hicks et toute sa clique ? interrogea Clément.

— Non, du moins pas officiellement. Je n'ai pas la possibilité de demander « hiérarchiquement » le dossier à Hicks. (Pause accompagnée d'une rasade de bière.) Et puis n'oublions pas que dès le début de la semaine, Barlow, Giggs et Cie vont me demander des comptes sur cette merde dans le métro... Avec un peu de chance, ils vont bien trouver une autre connerie à nous refiler...

Kite marmonna un juron incompréhensible entre ses dents. Il se leva sans un mot pour aller vers le comptoir et en revint avec un verre de gin et une *lager* pour son stagiaire.

— Oh ! Je sais, ça n'est pas bien, mais je n'en boirai qu'un, promis... Mon beau-père préférait le whisky pour faire passer les pilules bien amères, comme le jour où Michelle lui a annoncé qu'elle allait vivre avec un jeune inspecteur anglais, de six ans son cadet, et sans le sou... Lui qui voulait absolument qu'elle aille vivre dans le sud de la France et qu'elle épouse un Français...

Clément écoutait, la tête dans son verre. Lui aussi était désolé de cet après-midi infructueux.

— Le jour où je lui ai annoncé la nouvelle de la naissance de Mary, il est tombé dans mes bras en pleurant et a insisté pour que je reste toute la soirée avec lui. Nous avons sifflé ensemble toute une bouteille de Jameson.

C'était la dernière fois que je le voyais vivant...
Il est mort d'une crise cardiaque en pleine partie de roulette au casino de Monte-Carlo un
mois après. C'était quelqu'un de rare... On avait
fait un pacte entre nous. On s'était promis que
le prochain whisky que l'on boirait après la disparition de l'un ou de l'autre, ce serait tous les
deux, là-haut, en trinquant. En attendant, je
marche au gin ! Mais je dois t'embêter avec tous
ces souvenirs...

— Non, au contraire, répondit Clément avec
sincérité. Je suis très touché par la confiance
que vous m'accordez. C'est même un pcu
comme si je faisais partie de la famille...

Visiblement ému, Kite sourit et passa la main
dans les cheveux blonds de Clément. Depuis le
début de cette affaire, il le considérait non plus
comme un simple stagiaire efficace, mais bien
comme un fils, comme ce fils qu'il n'avait
jamais eu à cause du drame de 87, lorsque
Michelle avait fait une fausse couche pendant
sa longue dépression. Le caractère de Clément
le fascinait également. Le jeune homme était
indiscernable et il aimait les « personnages
gris », comme il les appelait, les personnages ni
blancs ni noirs.

— Ah, mon bon Clément ! reprit l'inspecteur.
Le climat porte aux confidences, tu ne crois
pas ? Regarde... On se croirait dans un film noir
avec cet éclairage tamisé, ces tables vides et la
plantureuse serveuse au comptoir !

Clément embrassa la pièce du regard et revint
river ses yeux dans ceux de Kite.

— Oui... L'alcool également... Ne nous le
cachons pas... Je vais prendre un gin comme
vous. Je reviens.

242

Kite sourit et sortit de son portefeuille un billet de dix livres.

— Tiens... Reprends-moi un verre aussi.

— Non, je vous invite. Pour une fois !

Quand il fut revenu à la table, la conversation reprit. Clément se voulait loquace. Et pourquoi ne pas expliquer tout à Paul Kite ? Si son niveau d'anglais le lui permettait, il le ferait.

— Vous parliez de confidences, Paul. C'est à mon tour. J'ai appris que vous avez vendu la mèche en ce qui concerne mon passé de comédien...

Kite allait interrompre le jeune homme.

— Non ! Ne dites rien. Ce soir, *je* parle. (Il insista sur le pronom.) J'ai envie de vous confier la raison pour laquelle j'ai tout arrêté à Paris.

Il but cul sec le verre de gin sous le regard ahuri puis protecteur de Kite.

— Le théâtre a toujours été ma passion, commença-t-il. Depuis ma jeunesse en fait. Et ce devait être ma vie... À 10 ans déjà, je montais sur les planches poussé par mon père, lui même grand amateur de théâtre et comédien amateur. J'ai suivi des cours au collège, puis j'ai fait partie d'une troupe au lycée. On me disait doué. Mon prof en Terminale, un soir, m'avait dit que j'avais de réelles capacités. Le soir, j'étais rentré, tout fier de l'annoncer à mes parents. Ils m'écoutèrent calmement, puis mon père se leva, déclama une tirade de Roméo et Juliette et me serra fort dans ses bras. Rien qu'en y repensant, j'en ai la gorge serrée.

» Puis j'ai eu mon bac avec mention. Mes parents n'ont pas voulu que j'arrête mes études complètement. Alors je voguais de casting en casting quand les cours de la fac m'en laissaient le temps. Avec Sébastien, mon meilleur ami, on a écumé pas mal de boîtes de prod... Lui avait arrêté ses études et ne se consacrait qu'à ça. En trois ans, j'ai décroché trois rôles minables... Lui en a décroché le double et a été obligé de travailler à mi-temps pour joindre les deux bouts. Mais pas de gloire à l'horizon... On nous regardait de haut comme si l'on était des incapables, alors que personne ne nous demandait de faire nos preuves... Je n'ai pas supporté cette situation. J'ai déprimé. Où était la gloire si souvent promise ? Tous mes rêves se sont écroulés. Je ne serais jamais célèbre, je ne recevrais jamais d'Oscar. Je ne trouvais plus aucun goût à mes études, alors j'ai tout foutu en l'air. Il fallait me trouver un boulot... Partir loin même...

» Sébastien et mes parents ont tenté de me raisonner, de m'inculquer une dose de patience... J'ai tout plaqué, passé le concours d'inspecteur et accepté l'offre de partir vous rejoindre. Un pays étranger et une activité à temps complet, loin de celle à laquelle je me destinais à l'origine, me sont apparus comme le meilleur moyen de faire le point et de repartir de zéro. Qui plus est, je ne risquais pas d'être tenté de reprendre le collier ici...

Clément s'interrompit. Kite l'écoutait paisiblement. Il continua.

— Et puis j'espérais rencontrer quelqu'un. Construire une relation durable qui me stabiliserait complètement.

Le jeune Français s'arrêta à nouveau. Était-ce le moment de le dire ? De l'avouer à l'inspecteur ? Cette pensée le traversa. Lui parler de Mary et de leur liaison. Il s'imaginait la réaction de Mary si elle était avec eux : « Tu vas faire ta déposition, Clément... C'est ça ? » Mais Kite prit les devants.

— Ne t'inquiète pas pour ça ! Tu as encore du temps !

Il avait choisi pour lui. L'annonce était reportée.

— La semaine dernière, à Paris, j'ai assisté à une pièce dans laquelle jouait Sébastien. C'était la première fois depuis longtemps que j'allais au théâtre et que je le voyais. Depuis, c'est étrange, mais je sens que ma passion tente de me rattraper. J'y pense de plus en plus et le reste me semble quasiment fade...

— Fade ?

— Oui... Sauf l'enquête peut-être... J'ai tant l'impression de composer un personnage d'inspecteur pendant les recherches que ça me paraît intéressant...

— Ainsi tu vois les choses comme ça ?

Kite se gratta le front, puis passa une main sur son visage.

— Bien sûr, tout cela est normal, reprit-il. On ne peut probablement jamais se débarrasser d'une passion. Elle reviendra encore et toujours. C'est comme ça que je vois les choses. Tu as été déçu de l'attitude de certaines personnes dans le milieu, peut-être même as-tu été déçu du milieu. Mais je ne sais pas si c'est une raison pour tout arrêter ! Surtout d'une manière aussi brusque ! Quand on a des ambitions, il faut toujours s'y tenir et tu sais ce que cela me coûte de te tenir un tel discours, n'est-ce pas ? Tu te doutes que ces paroles ne sont pas des paroles en l'air... Crois-tu que ça ne m'a jamais traversé l'esprit de rendre ma carte du Yard après l'horreur de 87 ? J'ai même voulu redémarrer mes études et demander à Robert de me prendre dans son cabinet d'avocats... D'être quasiment à mon compte comme lui et ne pas avoir à subir la frustration de petits chefs... Car leur frustration déteint sur toi et après tu es fini ! Quand je vois la carrière de Robert et sa bonhomie ! Plus épanoui que lui...

Clément rebondit sur les paroles de Kite.

— Nos histoires ont peut-être quelque chose de semblable en effet... Mais la vôtre est terrible, car ce n'est pas vous qui avez décidé d'arrêter ! On ne vous a pas laissé le choix !

Kite approuva.

— Oui, c'est sûr, mais dans ton cas on parle d'aspirations artistiques... De quelque chose chevillé en toi, que tu sens comme la seule chose possible, le seul aboutissement que tu as à donner à ta vie professionnelle... Tu devais rêver d'un milieu qui ne te juge que sur ton talent et tu te retrouves dans un monde glauque de politicards et de financiers de l'art où le copinage règne en maître.

— J'ai l'impression de revivre une discussion avec mon père !

— Et il avait raison de te pousser à persévérer ! Si les gens autour de toi et surtout toi, en fait, te disaient que tu avais du talent, alors...

— Mais les refus m'ont fait si mal !

— Et puis ? Tu en essuieras pendant longtemps avant que tu puisses dire « merde » à un metteur en scène. C'est la *Règle du jeu*, comme dirait notre ami Renoir.

Clément nota la référence cinéphile d'un Kite qui le sidérait d'honnêteté.

— Dis-toi bien, Clément, que tu dois toujours faire tes preuves, accepter l'attente ! Tout ne peut dépendre de ton seul talent, car il y aura toujours des décideurs faillibles... Tu ne peux pas arriver et dire : je suis le meilleur, donnez-moi tout de suite le rôle de Roméo... Même si au plus profond de toi, tu ressens, et c'est naturel, cela... Dis-toi qu'une réussite que tu cherches est mille fois plus fastueuse qu'une réussite que l'on t'offre ! Après, l'injustice est toujours possible, mais tu auras fait le maximum et tu partiras au moins la tête haute en laissant la leur fichée dans la merde ! Mais dans ton cas, pas de tout ça ! Tu dois réussir ! Je veux que tu réussisses ! Voilà...

Il n'y avait pas grand-chose à ajouter. Un court silence s'installa avant que Kite, n'appelant aucunement son jeune stagiaire à la réponse, regardât sa montre et se levât.

À la sortie du pub, l'inspecteur voulut raccompagner son jeune adjoint jusqu'à son appartement, mais ce dernier déclina l'offre.

— Demain, vers les 10 heures au Yard. Je serai probablement là-bas avant... Tu veux que je te téléphone vers 9 heures pour te réveiller ?

Clément répondit par l'affirmative.

— Tu as projeté quelque chose ce soir ? demanda Kite

— Rien de spécial... Dans l'état où je suis..., argumenta Clément sans en rajouter.

Il se passa une main sur la figure. Au même moment, ils entendirent le tonnerre gronder au loin, vers le centre de Londres.

— Eh bien ! Ça doit être le déluge dans le centre ! D'ici à ce que ça nous arrive..., lança Kite.

Ils se serrèrent la main plus longuement que d'habitude et l'inspecteur monta dans sa voiture.

En chemin, Clément s'acheta un bol de nouilles chinoises lyophilisées au supermarché

Safeway près de chez lui. Une fois arrivé dans son appartement, il fit chauffer de l'eau. Il espérait trouver un petit mot affectueux de son amie, mais elle ne lui avait rien laissé. Il était plus de 9 heures du soir lorsqu'il s'assit sur le canapé, devant sa télé. Il avait bien sûr repensé à la discussion du pub. Il en était encore tout bouleversé. Son esprit n'arrivait pas à fixer un autre sujet. Même Mary lui semblait loin... Il alluma sa console, l'esprit chargé de remords...

Avant de regagner sa demeure de Finchley, l'inspecteur Kite prit la décision de rendre visite à son ami Robert, qui serait à même de lui remonter le moral en débouchant une bonne bouteille de vin blanc français qu'il gardait au frais dans sa sublime cave aménagée et ne débouchait qu'avec une infime parcimonie. Il n'avait néanmoins jamais refusé un verre à son plus vieil ami. Kite gara sa voiture devant le grand portail en fer forgé et, sans même prendre le soin de fermer à clef les portes de sa Rover, se dirigea vers la sonnette. Son doigt pressa le bouton à quatre reprises avec, à chaque fois, le même insuccès.

— Bon Dieu de bon Dieu ! Je commence à avoir le palais rudement sec !

Mais personne. Kite hésita à laisser un mot accroché sur un des pics du portail, mais se ravisa au dernier moment. Il regagna sa voiture tout en se disant qu'il allait devoir garder sa soif pour lui jusqu'à son arrivée à Finchley. Robert devait être encore au boulot. C'est pourquoi il rentra chez lui en vitesse, allumant, pour la première fois, la sirène et le gyrophare alors qu'il n'était plus en service. Après un bref séjour dans la cuisine, où il se prépara deux sandwiches au fromage qu'il fit descendre avec deux canettes de Guiness, Kite monta embrasser sa fille qui travaillait studieusement dans sa chambre avec, comme à son habitude, la musique à fond.

Il lui demanda si sa soirée chez Anna s'était bien passée. Elle lui répondit oui sur un ton qui intrigua Kite. Il se changea alors et passa un jean et un polo léger. Il faisait très chaud dans la maison et Kite se demanda s'il n'allait pas baisser le chauffage d'un ou deux degrés. Michelle l'attendait dans la salle de séjour en lisant le livre qu'il lui avait offert pour Noël.

— Bonsoir... Comment vas-tu ?

Il se dirigea vers elle et l'embrassa sur la joue.

— Bien, lui répondit sa femme. Et toi ? Mieux que ce matin ? Tu t'es un peu calmé ?

— Calmé oui... Je suis complètement à plat...

— Pourquoi donc ? demanda Michelle en posant son livre refermé sur la table basse.

— Cette foutue enquête qui n'avance pas. Nous en sommes toujours au point mort et tu ne peux pas savoir à quel point ça m'énerve...

— Tu veux qu'on en parle ?

— Non, répondit fermement Kite qui s'était juré de laisser Michelle à l'écart de ses investigations depuis 1987. Son détachement à l'époque vis-à-vis de la fausse couche de sa femme l'avait profondément marqué. En dépression, il ne s'était pour ainsi dire jamais occupé d'elle, ni même n'était allé la voir à l'hôpital.

— Comme tu veux... (Elle reprit son livre sur ses genoux.) Au fait, tes cuisses vont mieux ?

Kite y repensa pour la première fois depuis l'incident.

— Oui, bien mieux. Mais il serait bon que tu me remettes un peu de pommade. Juste pour bien assurer le coup.

— OK, je t'en mettrai tout à l'heure.

Kite approuva et embrassa à nouveau sa femme sur la joue. Il s'assit alors sur le fauteuil mou en tissu vert qui appartenait jadis à son père et ouvrit le sac contenant les bouquins. Il ne voulait pas parler de sa conversation avec Clément. Elle n'appartenait qu'à eux deux. Kite se sentait bien.

— Tu as fait des achats ? questionna gentiment sa femme.

— Plus ou moins, répondit-il évasivement.

— Demain, tu vas travailler ? demanda-t-elle.

— Bien sûr ! Avec ce qu'on a sur le dos, tu peux être sûre que nous...

— Nous ? l'interrompit Michelle. Tu ne vas quand même pas embêter Clément un dimanche... Invite-le plutôt à déjeuner...

— C'est impossible, nous devons absolument aller au Yard demain...

— Paul ! Tu ne crois pas que tu exagères ? Depuis qu'il est rentré, il n'a pas eu une seule demi-journée à lui...

Kite se renfrogna et se rejeta dans son fauteuil.

— J'ai l'impression que tu es jaloux de nous ! Dis-lui que je l'invite demain et que nous serons très contents de l'avoir à déjeuner.

Kite leva la tête vers sa femme.

— Bon... s'il veut, bien sûr... Et Mary et toi vous me le rendez pour l'après-midi sans faute...

Le ton imposait une réponse positive.

— Reste manger ici, Paul... Tu as bien le temps d'aller au Yard ensuite...

— Pour l'après-midi sans faute, répéta Kite.

Sa femme soupira.

— Je dois l'appeler demain matin du bureau pour le réveiller. Je le lui dirai à ce moment-là...

Il semblait attendre une réponse de sa femme, qui était déjà replongée dans son livre. Kite fit de même et ouvrit le pavé consacré à l'affaire Charles Manson. Si l'assassin de ces trois femmes l'avait pris pour exemple, il trouverait probablement des choses intéressantes à ce sujet.

Ça ne cadrait pas du tout ! Kite venait de survoler les trois cents premières pages de *Helter Skelter* (qui était d'ailleurs le titre d'une chanson des Beatles) et se rendait compte une fois de plus de l'inutilité de sa démarche. Il lisait les pages en diagonale en tentant de cerner les passages spécifiques ayant trait aux Beatles et à leur implication dans la folie de Charles Manson. Car Manson était bien un fou mystique, rien de plus. Sur cela au moins, l'opinion de Kite était forgée.

Il reposa le livre et s'empara de la tasse de café que Michelle lui avait apportée avant de partir se coucher. C'étaient donc de simples messages que Manson croyait entendre dans le *White Album* des *Fab Four*. Il ne s'était aucunement servi d'une chanson pour mettre en scène ses meurtres atroces. Il voyait dans *Helter Skelter* (Le Grand Chaos) une prophétie sur la fin prochaine et violente de la société, dans *Piggies*, un appel au meurtre des policiers et dans *Sexy Sadie*, un hymne à une de ses compagnes, Susan Atkins. Deux autres morceaux du *White Album* venaient compléter le tableau : *Blackbird*, censé appeler les Noirs à la révolte et *Revolution 9*, que Manson considérait comme naturellement inspiré par le chapitre 9 de l'Apocalypse selon saint Jean.

Kite bâilla. Il n'était pas loin de 11 heures !

Bientôt, une nouvelle journée commencerait. Une nouvelle journée qui serait encore remplie de frustrations. Kite ferma les yeux pendant quelques instants. Il irait bien mettre un disque dans le lecteur CD de la chaîne hi-fi. Mais il aurait juste voulu du rythme et une voix. Pas de paroles : il aurait trop peur de les entendre et de les comprendre. Tout d'un coup, il se leva « Un disque de Michelle, un artiste français... Voilà ce qu'il me faut. » Il farfouilla plusieurs minutes dans la discothèque ne sachant pas quoi choisir. C'était la première fois qu'il voulait écouter un disque français. « Tiens, Georges Brassens... Il m'a l'air d'avoir une bonne tête avec sa pipe et sa grosse moustache... »

Il s'empara du CD et l'introduisit dans la platine. Puis il retourna s'asseoir. *Frénétique l'une d'elles attache le vieux maréchal des logis et lui fait crier : « Mort aux vaches ! Mort aux lois ! Vive l'anarchie ! »*

Kite était satisfait : il ne comprenait pas un mot des paroles et le rythme sec de la guitare lui convenait parfaitement. Il ouvrit donc le deuxième livre, celui-là entièrement consacré aux Beatles.

« Les secrets de toutes leurs chansons », annonçait le titre. Kite avait l'impression de s'être tout de même fait un peu berner. Certes le livre contenait de belles photos, mais il n'apprit vraiment rien de nouveau. Il s'intéressa particulièrement aux chansons de la liste, survolant les autres. Et puis encore plus précisément aux trois chansons ayant inspiré les meurtres.

Eleanor Rigby, écrite par Paul McCartney, parlait d'une vieille fille chargée de nettoyer une église après les mariages. Cruelle ressemblance, se lamenta Kite. Une anecdote à propos de cette chanson était à noter : on avait retrouvé, non loin de l'endroit où McCartney et Lennon s'étaient rencontrés pour la première fois, la tombe d'une réelle Eleanor Rigby. Paul McCartney avait toujours démenti avoir écrit la chanson tout en pensant à cette tombe.

Pour *Lucy in the Sky with Diamonds*, il y avait cette polémique autour des initiales de la chanson. LSD, comme cette drogue que Lennon reconnaissait consommer. En fait, le titre aurait été inspiré par un dessin que Julian Lennon, le fils de John, aurait ramené de l'école et qui aurait représenté une camarade de classe, Lucy O'Donnell, dans les nuages avec des diamants autour d'elle. Aujourd'hui, ce n'était plus un simple dessin, mais une réalité, et non plus Lucy O'Donnell, mais Lucy Chambers.

Quant à la troisième chanson, *Hey Jude*, McCartney l'aurait écrite en pensant à ce même Julian Lennon, alors partagé entre son père et sa nouvelle compagne Yoko, et sa mère Cynthia qui entamait une procédure de divorce. Paul McCartney aurait donc écrit cette chanson, dans une première version, sous le titre *Hey Jules*.

Kite soupira bruyamment. *C'était bien le moment pour ces anecdotes de concierge !* Ses paupières lui pesaient énormément. *Résiste !* Il ne fallait pas qu'il s'endorme... *Résiste ! Il te reste encore des pages à lire !* Mais le livre lui échappa des mains et il sombra dans un sommeil qu'il espérait calme, sans rêve, sans sortie nocturne. Un sommeil d'homme, pas de flic...

La première vision fut celle d'un Paul McCartney avec sa célèbre coiffure « sixties ».

Paul... Nous avons le même prénom... Oh, Paul... Peux-tu m'aider à me relever ? Sers-toi des cordes de guitare que cet enfant de pute a enroulées autour de mon poignet... Viens, Paul... N'aie pas peur... Tu vois bien que je me vide de mon sang... John est déjà parti, tu ne voudrais pas que je parte le rejoindre, dis-moi... Paul, aide-moi ! Les entailles sur mon front me font un mal affreux... Ça me lance horriblement... J'ai l'impression de perdre l'esprit, Paul. Et si je perds l'esprit, qui t'écrira de si belles chansons ? Paul, vite ! J'étouffe sous cette masse de terre qui contracte ma poitrine... Si tu ne te presses pas, je vais perdre mes poumons... Et qui te chantera Eleanor Rigby *? Qui, Paul ? Réponds ! Réponds, Paul ! Qui ?*

Le cadavre de Paul chantait : « *Eleanor Rigby died in the church and was buried along with her name. Nobody came.* »

Paul Kite continua son chemin.

Ringo Starr le fixait avec ses orbites vides. Il était habillé tout de noir, comme le fond de ses trous infects au milieu de son visage.

Paul... Viens me voir, toi qui le peux... Je t'attendais... Tu vois ces deux sphères là-bas près de cette belle vitrine scintillante... Va les prendre... Prends-les... Prends-les, Paul ! Tu dois m'aider, sinon qui jouera de la batterie dans le groupe ? Déjà que nous avons perdu ce pauvre John en bas de son immeuble... Remarque, je ne sais pas si je n'aurais pas préféré mourir comme lui. Imagines-tu seulement un instant, Paul, la douleur qu'implique l'énucléation d'un être vivant ? Mais vite... Sinon je perdrai la vue à jamais et alors...

Dépêche-toi, Paul ! Cours ! Là-bas, près de la vitrine des diamants !

Le cadavre aveugle de Ringo chantait : « *Look for the girl with the sun in her eyes and she's gone, Lucy in the Sky with Diamonds.* »

Paul Kite continua son chemin.

Le corps de George Harrison ne prêtait aucune attention à la venue de Paul Kite. Seule sa tête, à plusieurs mètres de distance, fixait l'homme qui marchait.

Désolé, Paul... Mais tu es ma seule chance de survie. Si tu ne fais rien, les Beatles seront par deux fois orphelins... D'abord John et ensuite moi... Paul, je ne te demande qu'une seule chose, écoute bien... Tu ramasses la tête par laquelle sort le son de ma voix et tu la remets sur ce corps par là qui est le mien... Il me faut ma chair, Paul ! Il me faut mon corps ! Mes poumons pour chanter, mes mains pour jouer de ma belle guitare et écrire ces chansons que tu aimes, Paul... Fais-le, Paul ! Ne sois pas égoïste ! Fais-le pour tous les fans du monde entier ! Pour toi et pour tous les fans du monde entier !

La tête coupée de George chantait : « *And any time you feel the pain, Hey Jude, refrain, don't carry the world upon your shoulder...* »

Paul Kite stoppa net et se réveilla dans un sursaut.

Il tomba littéralement de son fauteuil et haleta de longues minutes, agenouillé sur le sol. C'était atroce ! Ces visions cauchemardesques de ses idoles défigurées. Il n'en pouvait plus... Il souhaitait que tout cela finisse bientôt. C'était décidé : demain, il raconterait tout ce qu'il savait à Hicks. Tout. Et il poserait deux semaines de congés. Les deux nuits précédentes avaient été assez éprouvantes, pas besoin de pourrir les autres avec ces meurtres... S'il continuait, s'il ne lâchait pas les rênes, comment se passerait sa prochaine nuit ? Il s'endormirait dans son fauteuil et rêverait de visions inhumaines, des corps de Michelle et de Mary affreusement déchiquetés par ce sadique sans visage... Ou bien même se lèverait-il pour s'emparer d'un hachoir et démembrer sa petite famille ? Kite sentit les larmes lui monter aux yeux. Il se leva et regarda par la fenêtre. De fins flocons de neige tombaient enfin sur Londres. Et Kite pleura. Cela faisait si longtemps qu'il n'avait pas vraiment pleuré... Il attendit quelques instants, seul, le sel sur ses joues.

Quand plus tard il monta se coucher, il s'allongea, nu, près de sa femme. Michelle sentit la présence de son mari. Elle lui saisit alors un bras et le posa sur sa chemise de nuit, à l'endroit de sa poitrine. Et ils firent l'amour.

33

L'homme était assis à son spacieux bureau qui touchait presque son lit. Sa chambre était plongée dans une obscurité que perçait seulement une applique, juste au-dessus du bloc de papier qu'il était en train de remplir. Sa main dérapait sur le papier. Quelquefois les feuilles se froissaient. D'autres fois, elles se gondolaient quand il y posait ses paumes moites pour reposer son poignet. Il devait finir ce soir. Il le devait absolument. Car ainsi, demain, il serait libre.

Longtemps, dans sa jeunesse, puis plus tard, il avait écrit sous l'emprise de la drogue, du LSD, mais tout cela était terminé. L'acide lysergique diéthylamide l'avait aidé à accepter sa condition, lui avait fait oublier ses désillusions. Mais il y avait un temps pour tout. Il avait commencé en 1971, sept ans après que Bob Dylan eut initié son groupe favori à cette drogue « à la mode », emboîtant ainsi le pas aux autres groupes comme les Pink Floyd et leur Syd Barrett.

L'homme se rappelait parfaitement sa première fois : il avait dilué les comprimés dans son café, comme l'avaient fait Lennon et Harrison pour leur première fois. Cela lui avait donné une grande confiance en lui. La même réaction que ses idoles.

John Lennon avait vu son ego décupler sous l'effet de la drogue, George Harrison était parti pour sa quête spirituelle, Paul McCartney alla même jusqu'à déclarer que la drogue avait fait de lui quelqu'un de plus honnête et qui a vu Dieu. Seul Ringo Starr, qu'il n'aimait pas plus que cela, n'avait pas vu l'utilité du LSD.

L'homme se rappela les reproches de sa mère qui mettait néanmoins la main au porte-monnaie pour acheter ses doses. Elle avait toujours reproché aux Beatles leur publicité datant de 1967 dans le *Times* dénonçant la loi interdisant l'utilisation de la marijuana. La BBC avait immédiatement censuré *A Day In the Life* et

Lucy In the Sky with Diamonds suite à cette prise de position.

L'homme posa son point final alors que son stylo était à court d'encre. Il était heureux que sa confession se termine ainsi.

La chambre bleue. Sur le bureau, un calepin entier noirci d'une écriture monotone et soigneuse. Dans le lit, un homme aux cheveux noirs et au nez aquilin, aux pommettes saillantes et aux oreilles sans lobes. Et sur son visage, un rictus.

Dimanche 28 décembre 1997

33

— Marre de ce jeu de merde !

Clément jeta violemment sa manette de jeu par terre et se leva du divan. Il avait beau se vautrer sur le canapé, torse nu et en caleçon, rien n'y faisait : il n'avait pas sommeil. La télé avait succédé à la lecture, puis la console, puis les pensées... Ah, ces pensées ! Le doute l'assaillait comme jamais auparavant. La conversation avec Kite l'avait tout chamboulé. Il ne croyait pas le bonhomme capable de faire preuve d'autant de lucidité sur ce qui lui était arrivé et sur son avenir.

Non pas qu'il considérât l'inspecteur comme un être superficiel, bien sûr, mais parce qu'il voyait Kite comme quelqu'un de renfermé, refusant d'évoquer ses affaires personnelles. En revenant de Paris, Clément avait senti un imperceptible changement, non pas dans son attitude, mais dans sa façon de penser. Il sentait qu'il n'allait plus prendre de plaisir dans le train-train quotidien du Yard.

Puis les discussions avec Alexander et Mary avaient ajouté à ses propres réflexions une sorte de certitude. Il ne doutait plus que sa vie passât par le théâtre. Kite avait fini par le convaincre en lui faisant dire que, si l'affaire de ce *serial singer* le passionnait, c'était d'abord parce qu'il avait l'impression de faire partie du générique d'un film au scénario tordu.

Clément alla à la cuisine et se servit un verre d'eau. À présent, sa relation avec Mary s'éclaircissait... Elle ne voulait pas aimer un flic... Il n'en était pas vraiment un en somme... L'affaire en cours l'enflammait, d'accord, et il y avait de quoi ! Peut-être allait-il la résoudre, y mettre un point final grâce à ses réflexions et au concours de Kite. Il se présentait là le bon côté des choses, mais il y avait le revers de la médaille : s'il reprenait le théâtre, serait-il à même d'aimer Mary comme maintenant ? La question méritait d'être posée.

Pendant ses années de lycée et de fac, il avait eu quelques relations passagères avec des jeunes filles qui aimaient l'acteur en puissance, la grande gueule dénuée de toute timidité, toujours premier pour flamber en public. Et lui les aimait à travers l'image qu'elles renvoyaient de sa personne. Tout n'était qu'artificiel, leurs relations se résumant souvent même au simple plaisir sexuel... Justement le tour qu'avait son histoire avec Mary et qu'il ne supportait pas ! Alors ? Londres lui servirait-il de leçon ? Quand lui choisissait un flirt simplement sexuel, tout allait bien, mais quand l'autre le faisait, il ne l'acceptait pas ! Mary allait changer d'optique, il en était sûr, et cela le ragaillardit.

Dans son appartement de Fulham, ce soir, il se sentait un peu seul, mais son esprit s'était calmé. Toutefois, il n'avait pas sommeil. Il allait se replonger dans cette affaire qui, vraiment, le passionnait. Kite aurait été content de voir son stagiaire reprendre du poil de la bête. Il devait douter de la motivation du jeune homme après le ton de leur conversation. Et il ne voulait pas que l'inspecteur du Yard se déprime et doute de lui. Après tout, il devait beaucoup à Kite !

Et s'il jetait un coup d'œil au gros livre sur les Beatles qu'il avait ramené du Yard ? Il s'en empara et se rassit sur le divan.

Il lut entièrement les textes de *Lucy in the Sky with Diamonds*, *Eleanor Rigby* et *Hey Jude*. Et s'il tentait de parcourir aussi la chanson des *Lonely Hearts* ? Avec leurs déductions fantasques de l'après-midi, la chanson pourrait avoir un lien, elle aussi, avec l'affaire. *Lonely Hearts*. Célibataires. Il chercha dans l'index le numéro de la page où se trouvait la partition de *Sgt Pepper*. Il commença la lecture.

It was twenty years ago today, Sergeant Pepper taught the band to play.
C'était difficile de lire le texte de la chanson sur ces partitions.
So may I introduce to you the act you've known for all these years, Sergeant Pepper's Lonely Hearts Club Band.
Il était bien incapable de lire la partition et aurait bien voulu entendre la chanson et son rythme. Il la relut une fois encore et ses premières phrases retenaient son attention. Et si le meurtrier avait poussé son délire jusqu'à se mettre en scène lui-même ? Clément traduisit le premier vers :
Il y avait vingt ans aujourd'hui, Sergeant Pepper apprit au groupe à jouer.
Puis la suite :
Donc laissez-moi vous présenter le spectacle que vous connaissez depuis toutes ces années,

l'orchestre des Cœurs Solitaires du Sergeant Pepper.

Ça semblait plus littéral que littéraire, mais ça suffisait amplement...

— Continuons dans le délire..., chuchota-t-il penché sur le livre.

Le meurtrier se serait servi de cette chanson spécifique, car les paroles lui correspondaient. Il fallait peut-être chercher *vingt ans* plus tôt le mobile de ces meurtres. L'assassin aurait attendu vingt ans avant d'agir rien que pour coller à cette chanson. Vingt ans. Voilà peut-être une autre piste. Il soupira :

— Complètement fou...

» OK, reprenons, mon petit Clément... Comme dans les romans policiers... Avec logique... Imagine que le meurtrier, en plus de mettre en scène les meurtres qu'il commet grâce aux paroles des Beatles, aille même jusqu'à y trouver son mobile... Imagine donc que ce pervers veuille reconstituer l'orchestre du Sergeant Pepper, car ses motivations collent à cette chanson. En somme, il se serait passé il y a vingt ans quelque chose dont il veut se venger. Et il commettrait alors des meurtres ? Pourtant, il n'est pas question directement de mort violente, de crime dans ces chansons... Question d'interprétation, de dérèglement psychique... Et si on pousse le bouchon un peu plus loin, il se peut que l'homme s'appelle carrément Pepper ! Il aurait souffert de son nom après que les Beatles en eurent fait une chanson... En quelle année a été écrite *Sgt Pepper* ? Vite, Clément, cherche... Si Sgt Pepper *a été écrite en 77, ça collait ! 77 plus 20 égale 97.*

Clément consulta le livre.

— 1967 ! Merde ! 30 ans !

» Calme-toi, Clément... Tout n'est pas perdu, il se peut qu'il ait été trop jeune en 1967... En 77, on pouvait encore se moquer de lui. Kite t'a bien dit qu'à cette période, les Beatles étaient encore en pleine gloire, même séparés... Son motif serait alors clair, il tuerait aujourd'hui des femmes célibataires ayant le même problème que lui : celui de porter le prénom de femmes chantées par les Beatles. Si ça se trouve, il se prend même pour un sauveur... Et si tu appelais Kite, Clément ! Tu as peut-être une fois de plus mis le doigt sur un élément important... Très important... Non, bien trop tard, Kite doit dormir et puis cette hypothèse n'est pas sérieuse. Il doit y avoir une autre explication. En tout cas, si ta théorie se tient, Kite ne peut être le meurtrier... *Kite*, c'est un « cerf-volant », ce n'est ni du poivre ni une autre substance épicée... Et puis tu voyais Paul ensevelir une vieille dame avant de lui graver le front au cutter ? Tu voyais bien ton Kite se pencher vers une jeune fille qui aurait pu être sa fille pour lui enlever les yeux avant de les remplacer par des ampoules électriques ? Imagine l'inspecteur du Yard, ne serait-ce qu'un instant, séparant une tête d'un corps et faisant ainsi preuve du plus parfait sadisme. Certes, être un gentil père de famille ne garantit pas contre le meurtre... Mais Kite est-il un bon père de famille ? Mary est-elle équilibrée ? Tu as toujours des doutes, Clément. Ils sont loin, enfouis, mais tes doutes subsistent... Et tout cela parce que tu as appris que ton supérieur aimait les Beatles et était dépressif ! Crois-tu qu'il soit le seul sujet de Sa Très Gracieuse Majesté fan des Beatles et dépressif ? Allons ! Un peu de bon sens... Tu n'as rien de concret pour l'instant... Juste des suppositions... Et c'est bien plus excitant, n'est-ce pas ?

Clément avait pourtant les yeux brillants d'excitation comme hier soir dans la voiture de l'inspecteur. C'était sûr maintenant, il ne trouverait plus le sommeil. Il s'habilla rapidement et décida de sortir dans le centre pour ne pas passer la nuit dans le silence. Il irait au *Zoo Bar* sur Leicester Square. C'était Mary qui lui avait fait découvrir l'endroit lors de leur toute première rencontre et c'est là qu'ils avaient passé leur première soirée à Londres ensemble.

Une fine pellicule de neige recouvrait le trottoir devant l'immeuble. Vu l'heure tardive, Clément devrait attendre le bus de nuit qui le conduirait jusqu'à Piccadilly Circus. Il allait passer la nuit dans ce bar-discothèque pour ne rentrer qu'au petit matin, la tête pleine de son et de musique. Cette nuit, comme la précédente, le *serial singer* ne chanterait plus dans la tête de Clément.

35

Quand Kite descendit de sa Rover accidentée, il remarqua les légers flocons de neige qui s'étaient déposés sur son imperméable pendant son trajet. Il était d'une humeur maussade ce matin. Bien plus grave, il était désabusé. Après avoir pris hier soir la décision de rencontrer le superintendant Hicks pour l'entretenir sur cette idée des Beatles, il ne trouvait plus aucune motivation susceptible de le faire avancer. S'il venait au Yard ce matin, et qu'il n'appelait pas plutôt Hicks, c'était simplement pour rédiger un semblant de dossier contenant le nom et l'adresse de Jane Goldblum, ainsi que toutes les paroles des chansons ayant servi à inspirer l'assassin. Il s'était levé en reculant ce matin et ne devait son départ qu'aux encouragements de Michelle à qui il s'était décidé à raconter toute l'histoire, hier soir, avant de s'endormir.

Kite ouvrit la porte de son bureau et vint directement s'asseoir sur sa chaise sans même accrocher son imperméable sur le portemanteau. Il le jeta négligemment sur la table de son jeune stagiaire. Clément ! Il ne le verrait même pas ce matin ! Pas même sa présence pour lui remonter le moral... Mais Michelle avait raison : il tirait peut-être un peu trop sur la ficelle et son jeune adjoint devait être bien fatigué. Un doute l'envahit soudain... Se désintéressait-il de l'enquête ? Non, il ne le croyait pas. « Mais pourquoi tant de doutes ce matin, Paul ? Pourquoi te poses-tu toutes ces questions ? Contente-toi de rédiger ton rapport, va le porter à Hicks et évacue cette affaire de ton esprit... Tu iras la suivre de loin chez ton nouvel ami Richard Porter, le libraire... »

— Oui..., soupira Kite la gorge nouée. Mais il est l'heure que j'appelle mon Clément...

C'était la première fois depuis bien longtemps qu'il se parlait à haute voix. Il décrocha le téléphone et composa le numéro de l'appartement de Fulham.

C'était d'accord. Il avait accepté avec joie. Michelle et Mary auraient donc Clément à déjeuner. Et lui serait seul dans son bureau avec un pauvre *fish & chips*. Kite avait demandé à brûle-pourpoint à son jeune adjoint si l'enquête l'intéressait encore sans toutefois lui préciser son intention d'abandonner l'affaire. Il avait eu la plus belle réponse qu'il pouvait espérer : cette idée du Sergeant Pepper et de cette longue attente de vingt ans. Pourquoi ne pas le croire ? Il allait joindre cette nouvelle supposition au dossier de Hicks. Si avec cela Hicks n'en tirait pas quelque chose... Résigné, il s'empara d'un stylo et glissa une feuille de papier à l'en-tête du Yard devant lui.

Mais où était donc ce livre avec les paroles des chansons des *Fab Four* ? Clément l'avait bien emporté hier matin... Il devait l'avoir laissé au bureau. Kite eut beau balayer la pièce du regard, il ne trouva rien. Et encore une contrariété de plus ! Non vraiment... Il allait devoir plonger dans sa mémoire pour écrire les paroles des chansons concernant l'affaire. Quelle tuile ! Soudain, son nez se mit à saigner. Un mince filet de sang coulait le long de sa bouche et continuait sur son menton. Il s'en aperçut trop tard pour éviter que cette goutte vienne s'écraser en plein milieu de la feuille qu'il était en train de rédiger. Il bascula sa tête vers l'arrière, fou de rage. En se tenant le nez d'une main, il froissa la feuille avec l'autre et la balança le plus loin possible. Il ne lui en aurait pas fallu beaucoup plus pour sortir de son bureau et ne plus y revenir avant longtemps.

36

L'homme s'était levé tôt, car il avait choisi de tuer le matin. Ça n'était pas une lubie de sa part, mais simplement l'aboutissement du spectacle qu'il préparait depuis tant d'années. Vers 9 heures, il était descendu dans sa cave et avait apporté le plateau habituel. Ce n'était plus une odeur qui s'échappait de la pièce, mais bien un relent infernal, qui lui avait fait regretter ses tranches de pain de mie de son petit déjeuner. Ce curieux mélange de bile et de pain à peine mâché lui était revenu dans la bouche et il avait vomi tout cela à l'intérieur de la pièce surchauffée.

Malade, un goût amer sur le palais, il était remonté tout de suite sans même prendre le soin de refermer les trois verrous. Il s'était abondamment rincé la bouche avec de l'eau fraîche et s'était passé une serviette mouillée sur le visage et le cou. L'homme avait eu au moins le bonheur de constater que sa désillusion de la veille était oubliée, pardonnée même. Paul McCartney n'était pas venu le réprimander cette nuit. Du reste, il n'avait croisé aucun des quatre Beatles ce matin et cela avait plutôt tendance à l'inquiéter. Pourquoi ne venaient-ils pas l'encourager pour le clou de son spectacle ? Et puis il se dit que tout cela était fait exprès. Ils le laissaient se concentrer au maximum, sans venir le distraire. Ils savaient ce que signifiait d'entrer en scène pour la dernière fois.

L'homme ne paniquait pas. Les Beatles viendraient le féliciter là où son spectacle se terminerait. Il leur avait expliqué son plan des dizaines de fois et les quatre vedettes connaissaient bien l'endroit. Il en était sûr.

L'homme régla les derniers détails du crime de ce matin. Ou plutôt de ce midi, car l'épisode de la cave allait le retarder. Il n'était pas question qu'il prenne le volant dans cet état. Il s'empara de son sac à dos vide, qui avait contenu avant-hier le matériel pour sa Jude. Posé sur la table, il le remplit avec application. Il glissa deux minces pipeaux irlandais sur le côté gauche du sac. L'homme n'avait pas pensé à mettre de gants ce matin, mais aujourd'hui, il s'en fichait par-dessus tout. Calmement, il se saisit de trois poupées miniatures et les rangea bien au fond. Il avait eu un mal fou à trouver des poupons de plastique semblables à ceux qui avaient fait scandale sur la couverture jamais publiée de la compilation américaine *The Beatles Yesterday and Today*. Elle représentait les quatre stars assises avec, tout autour d'elles, des têtes et des corps de bébés.

Le groupe voulait alors se séparer de son image de gentils garçons. Hélas, l'album ne sortit pas avec cette pochette et le disque devint ainsi le seul microsillon des Beatles à perdre de l'argent. L'homme en possédait une reproduction en très grand format sur le mur de la chambre d'amis. Tout en pensant aux sourires de ses idoles sur l'affiche, il ferma alors son sac et se rappela les détails de son plan. N'avait-il rien oublié ?

Il repensa à la vision de la cave, à la vision de cette femme encore vivante allongée par terre sans aucune pudeur, sa robe sale relevée laissant dépasser cette gaine qu'elle portait encore malgré toutes les livres qu'elle avait dû perdre... Et quelle vulgarité encore, ce soutien-gorge à moitié dégrafé qu'il voyait par l'échancrure béante de sa robe... Sur le côté droit du sac à dos, l'homme glissa un revolver aux reflets brillants muni d'un silencieux.

37

Une fois douché et habillé, Clément ferma à clef la porte de son appartement et prit la direction de la station de Fulham Broadway. Il était 10 heures et demie et il prévoyait un trajet d'une cinquantaine de minutes jusqu'à Finchley. Les rames de métro étaient bien moins fréquentes le dimanche. Pendant son long trajet monotone, il continua sa courte nuit de sommeil, que Kite avait stoppée avec son coup de téléphone. Il était rentré tôt ce matin, les oreilles ravagées, mais cette sortie lui avait fait énormément de bien. Quand il arriva dans la petite gare en plein air de Finchley Central, la neige s'était arrêtée de tomber. Un vent glacial soufflait maintenant et il se félicita de s'être chaudement couvert. Bâillant une fois encore, il espéra que la journée serait calme et sans contrariété. Sinon, sa légère gueule de bois ne passerait jamais.

Clément sortit de la station, remonta l'immense Ballards Lane et bifurqua dans The Ridgeway pour couper à travers le Victoria Park. C'était un raccourci qu'il connaissait depuis peu et qui lui faisait gagner à chaque fois dix bonnes minutes. Les pelouses du parc étaient recouvertes de neige, mais les allées avaient été dégagées. Que la neige était belle sous ces petits rayons de soleil perçant les nuages ! La quiétude naturelle de l'endroit envahit peu à peu son esprit tourmenté. À peine fit-il attention à ce groupe de gamins jouant au foot les mains gantées, des cagoules enfoncées sur la tête et dont une des passes hasardeuses avait failli projeter le ballon sur sa tête. Empruntant une des sorties est du parc, il arriva quasiment en face de la demeure des Kite. Il s'apprêtait à sonner lorsque Mary apparut à la fenêtre de sa chambre et l'informa qu'elle descendait lui ouvrir. Clément lui répondit d'un clin d'œil. Cette visite serait probablement la seule chose agréable de la journée... Devant la porte, il se mit à siffloter la mélodie de « *Je m'voyais déjà en haut de l'affiche* ». Inexplicablement ?

— Reprends un peu de salade de fruits, Clément... Je vois que tu louches dessus depuis cinq minutes...

Michelle accompagna sa remarque d'un sourire amical. Ils avaient tous bien apprécié le repas préparé cette fois-ci par la maîtresse de maison en personne. Mary avait été la principale animatrice de la conversation. Elle essayait par cet inhabituel bagout d'évacuer son stress. Clément lui avait confié ses probables intentions avant le déjeuner et la jeune fille ne savait pas par quel bout prendre la chose. Parler pour ne pas penser, telle semblait être sa mécanique pour ce déjeuner. Ils abordèrent alors le sujet épineux de Paul. Michelle avait relevé quelques symptômes d'avant sa dépression.

— J'espère que tout ça va bientôt s'arrêter, continua-t-elle.

Son sourire s'évanouit d'un coup.

— Il vous a mis au courant de l'affaire des trois meurtres ? s'enquit Clément.

— Oui... Il n'arrivait pas à trouver le sommeil et il m'a raconté en quelques mots...

Clément posa une main sur celle de Mary et lui expliqua brièvement de quoi il s'agissait. Mary était abasourdie.

— Je comprends pourquoi il est si lunatique en ce moment... Ça doit lui rappeler son affaire du tueur de 88.

— 87, corrigea sa mère. Oui... Je crois bien que ça le met dans un état pas possible. Et encore, heureusement que tu es là. S'il n'avait pas son jeune stagiaire avec lui... Et toi, que penses-tu de tout ça ?

Clément prit la parole :

— C'est évidemment un peu incroyable au premier abord, mais c'est une théorie tout à fait plausible... Le seul ennui, c'est que nous ne nous occupons pas officiellement de l'affaire. Et c'est vraiment difficile de travailler dans ces conditions... Nous n'avons pas accès aux rapports, aux derniers indices... à la...

— Peut-être, l'interrompit Mrs Kite. Mais vous connaissez ce qui a inspiré au meurtrier ses crimes... Et c'est énorme...

— D'autant plus, ajouta-t-il, que j'ai peut-être trouvé un mobile possible hier dans la nuit.

Mary n'en revenait pas : c'était inconcevable, ces meurtres sur le thème d'une chanson des Beatles.

— Vraiment ? s'étonna Michelle. Tu as prévenu Paul ?

— Bien sûr.

— Alors ça fera une pièce de plus au dossier...

Clément fronça les sourcils.

— Au dossier ?

— Oui. Il est en train de monter un dossier

sur l'affaire pour le remettre au superintendant...

— Mais il ne m'a absolument rien dit ce matin ! s'étonna Clément.

— Il me l'a confié hier dans la nuit... Il en avait vraiment marre. Il m'a expliqué qu'il avait beaucoup hésité... Maintenant, si tu as mis un autre élément en évidence, il se peut qu'il ait changé d'avis... Peut-être ferais-tu bien de le rappeler ?

Le bureau de Kite ne répondait pas. Il devait être parti déjeuner. Le jeune inspecteur revint vers la table.

— Et quel est ce dernier indice, alors ? demanda Mary.

— Bof, lui répondit Clément. Ce n'est pas grand-chose en fait... Simplement une extrapolation du début de la chanson *Sgt Pepper's Lonely Hearts Club Band*.

Sous les regards insistants et attentifs de ses hôtesses, Clément détailla son hypothèse :

— Le titre évoque déjà un orchestre de célibataires. Et justement, toutes les victimes étaient célibataires. Avec les instruments que l'on a retrouvés près des cadavres, on peut faire le rapprochement avec le groupe qu'évoque la chanson. Maintenant, si l'on considère que le meurtrier a aussi cherché à s'identifier à une chanson — et c'est là le plus important —, il aurait choisi celle-là. Et si sa démence est sans limite, il peut même avoir suivi mot à mot les paroles de la chanson... Ou si l'on va encore un peu plus loin, s'appeler lui-même Pepper et se désigner comme le chef d'orchestre...

— *It was twenty years ago today, Sergeant Pepper taught the band to play*, récita Mary.

274

— Exactement, continua le jeune Français. Il aurait donc attendu vingt ans avant de commettre ses meurtres simplement pour être « dans le rythme ». Ce qu'il faudrait, c'est retrouver ce qui se passa ce jour-là, en 1977... Le 22 décembre 1977, pour être plus précis. Soit vingt ans jour pour jour après ce quelque chose qui pourrait bien être son véritable mobile... Le 22 décembre 1997 étant le jour du premier meurtre, celui d'Eleanor Stout...

Michelle écoutait attentivement l'explication.

— Je sais, ajouta Clément. Ça paraît vraiment tiré par les cheveux, mais vu que cette histoire l'est du début jusqu'à la fin...

Il se passa la langue sur ses lèvres sèches et regarda autour de lui. Mary et sa mère avaient le nez dans leur assiette. Le silence était de rigueur. Michelle le rompit après quelques dizaines de secondes. Sa voix semblait empreinte d'une légère inquiétude :

— C'est vraiment étrange et ça ne peut être qu'une coïncidence, bien sûr... Mais le 22 décembre 1977, c'est la date exacte de notre premier flirt, Kite et moi...

Mais oui ! Le soir du premier meurtre, Kite et sa femme allaient partir au restaurant comme à leur habitude.

— C'est vraiment une drôle de coïncidence..., constata Clément. Vraiment drôle...

Ce groupe de musique où il fallait se nommer comme dans les chansons ? Y aurait-il un lien ? Kite !

C'est Kite. C'est Kite le meurtrier... Bien sûr... Il mène une double vie depuis quelque temps. Il n'est pas plus somnambule que toi ! Il vous possède tranquillement ! Voilà la vérité ! Il a dû louer un appartement ou une maison dans

Londres pour être plus libre et y séjourne une fois seul la nuit, ou le jour... En ce moment, il n'est pas au Yard, bien sûr ! Il est sagement en train de tuer sa quatrième victime... Pamela ou bien Martha, peu importe ! Et ensuite... Ensuite... Il reviendra chez lui et étranglera sagement Michelle, ma belle. Ce sont des mots qui vont si bien ensemble... La coïncidence ne peut exister... Kite est lié à ces meurtres commencés le jour de son anniversaire de rencontre avec Michelle. Il a déjanté, pété les plombs... Il est devenu schizophrène ! Tu entends, Clément... Tu as travaillé avec un schizophrène pendant toutes ces semaines...

Clément sentait son esprit se liquéfier. Bientôt, il ne serait plus ici. C'était un peu la même impression que l'ivresse, lorsque l'on s'arrête de boire juste avant d'être malade à en vomir. Sa tête tournait sous les effluves de la suspicion... Il n'osait poser la question à Michelle, cette question qui dédouanerait l'inspecteur... Son emploi du temps du lundi 22 décembre, le jour du premier meurtre...

— Et... lundi..., bégaya-t-il, comment était Paul... Je veux dire l'inspecteur...

— Oh, énervé bien sûr, répondit Michelle. Mais il y avait de quoi ! Nous avons failli arriver en retard au restaurant pour notre anniversaire. La circulation était infernale pour revenir sur Londres... Nous avions passé la journée chez mon frère à Ashford.

— Toute la journée ? Et vous êtes allés directement au restaurant ? hurla presque Clément.

— Oui... Mais pourquoi ? En fait nous n'avons pas été au restaurant, mais directement sur les lieux du meurtre. Paul avait été rappelé. Il était très énervé de rater notre sacro-saint

276

dîner annuel... Je suis rentrée en métro et lui est rentré plus tard...

Sans la fatigue qui pesait sur lui, Clément se serait bien levé pour étreindre la femme de Paul. Elle venait d'innocenter son mari. Kite n'était pas à Londres pour le premier meurtre ! Le jeune Français s'en voulut d'avoir soupçonné l'inspecteur. Comment en était-il arrivé là ? Il devait maintenant réagir. Kite devait être au Yard en train de rédiger son rapport sur l'enquête pour le transmettre à ses supérieurs. Il fallait à tout prix trouver... Couper l'herbe sous le pied de ces arrivistes... Clément tenta de se remémorer les confidences de Kite sur leur petit groupe.

— Ma question va vraiment vous paraître idiote, s'excusa-t-il par avance, son self-control retrouvé. Mais vous vous êtes bien rencontrés à l'université dans un petit groupe de musique...

— Oui... Paul t'a raconté ça ?

— Un groupe où il fallait obligatoirement se nommer ou se prénommer comme dans les titres de chansons des Beatles ?

— Oui, bien sûr...

— Et... Non, vraiment c'est idiot... Mais y avait-il un membre qui s'appelait Pepper ?

— Non, aucun...

La tension retomba d'un seul coup. C'était une sensation étrange, mais Clément avait eu l'impression que tout le monde partageait ses espoirs. Michelle continua d'un ton maintenant plus assuré :

— Il y avait Paul « Kite » pour *Being for the Benefit of Mr Kite*, Pamela Turner pour *Polythene Pam*, un Maxwell... Je ne me rappelle plus trop bien son prénom... Irvin, je crois, pour *Maxwell's Silver Hammer* ; et puis Robert, le seul que Paul voit encore... Lui c'était pour *Docteur Robert*, je crois... Tout simplement... Et moi pour *Michelle*...

— Robert, ce n'est pas l'ami avocat de Paul qui me loue l'appartement ? demanda Clément.

— Si, bien sûr, répondit Mary avant sa mère. Quelqu'un de très gentil... Nous sommes restés très proches...

— C'est grâce à lui que j'ai pu rencontrer Kite, continua Michelle. Il suivait les cours de secourisme que je dispensais à l'université de Liverpool. Un jour, il m'a proposé de rejoindre le groupe. (Elle ferma les yeux.) Je crois bien qu'il était tombé amoureux de moi... Mais il n'en a jamais reparlé... Depuis, on se voit souvent.

— Il vit seul, demanda Clément.

— Non, avec sa mère.

— Pas marié ?

— Non, célibataire.

Première contraction de l'estomac.

— Et il aime toujours les Beatles ?

Clément menait cela comme un véritable interrogatoire. Il n'aimait pas son ton. Pas plus que la tournure que prenaient les événements.

— Je pense... Non, en fait, j'en suis sûr... Il a acheté, il y a dix ans je crois, la maison qui avait appartenu à Paul McCartney dans St John's Wood.

Clément se rappela avoir vu une photo de l'imposante maison sur le Web.

Seconde contraction de l'estomac.

— C'est tout de même incroyable, toutes ces coïncidences...

— Coïncidences avec quoi ? demanda Michelle, étonnée.

— Avec les meurtres... Les vingt ans de votre

rencontre et le fait qu'il soit amoureux de vous, c'est un mobile. Son adoration des Beatles expliquerait sa façon de procéder...

— C'est impossible ! Vraiment ! Robert est un des avocats les plus compétents et respectés de toute l'Angleterre... On le voit souvent... Paul est même passé hier le voir et...

— Mais au fait, demanda Clément, la peur au ventre, quel est son nom de famille ?

— Pungent. Robert Pungent.

Pungent. Clément traduisit immédiatement. « Épicé, relevé... poivré. » Mary sursauta. Michelle resta bouche bée.

Troisième contraction de l'estomac. Plus forte, celle-là.

— Il faut téléphoner à Kite ! s'écria Clément. Mais Kite n'était toujours pas là.

Ainsi donc, tout cela pourrait être à l'origine d'une simple vengeance personnelle ? De la vengeance d'un homme bafoué par un autre homme ? Tout ce chemin, toutes ces déductions réfléchies ou spontanées pour ce résultat si simple, si familier ? Mais alors ? Si tout cela se vérifiait, il fallait faire attention pour Michelle, Mary et Kite... Après sa petite démonstration de force, l'homme pouvait très bien se mettre à viser les personnes plus directement concernées par sa folie meurtrière.

Il n'y avait pas une minute à perdre. Enfin du concret, un nom, une adresse, de l'action. Une situation non plus frustrante, mais inquiétante... Comme si le passage de l'état de spectateur à celui d'acteur se faisait dans la douleur. C'était bien la première fois que Clément rechignait à entrer en action. Peut-être tout simplement parce qu'il n'était pas sur scène, mais justement dans la réalité ? Néanmoins, il ressentait une forte excitation. Sa fatigue de la nuit s'était entièrement évacuée. De l'adrénaline pure devait circuler dans ses veines.

— Mrs Kite, pouvez-vous me trouver l'adresse exacte de Robert Pungent ? demanda Clément.

Michelle Kite était plutôt calme. Comme Mary d'ailleurs. Elles devaient toutes les deux digérer cette supposition. Elles n'avaient ni envie de l'affirmer ni envie de l'infirmer. Juste savoir la vérité. Robert... Ce gentil Robert... Si attentif avec sa douce maman... Michelle alla chercher son sac à main et saisit son petit carnet.

— Pungent... Non... J'ai dû l'inscrire à Robert... (Elle tourna les pages en vitesse.) Robert, 7, Cavendish Avenue, quartier de St John's Wood.

— Mrs Kite, serait-il possible de vous emprunter votre Clio pour m'y rendre ?

Michelle n'hésita pas et sortit les clefs de son sac.

— Tu y vas sans Paul ? Remarque, il vaut peut-être mieux...

— Si vous pouvez le joindre, l'interrompit autoritairement Clément, racontez-lui toute l'histoire. Et dites-lui que je le rejoins au Yard le plus vite possible...

— Mais va au Yard tout de suite... Tu verras avec lui...

Non, Clément voulait se rendre à St John's Wood. Seul. Mais en fait, qu'allait-il bien pouvoir dire à ce Pungent ?

Quatrième contraction de l'estomac.

Il décida donc de partir. Clément embrassa les lèvres de Mary avec passion sans lui dire un seul mot. Un geste pour Michelle et il était

280

dehors, près de la voiture. Dégageant avec ses mains nues la neige du pare-brise de la Clio, il n'avait maintenant plus qu'une hâte : se débarrasser de cette douleur à l'estomac qu'il savait associée à son anxiété bien légitime.

À l'instant même où Clément allait tourner la clef de contact, il vit Mary bondir de la maison son anorak à la main. Elle semblait lui crier quelque chose. Il baissa la vitre et se pencha légèrement vers l'extérieur.

— Clément ! Attends-moi, je connais la route...

Clément n'en croyait pas ses oreilles. Son amie voulait venir avec lui !

— Mais je la trouverai ! Reste là !

Mary avait la main sur la poignée de la porte.

— Ne sois pas idiot ! Non seulement je connais le chemin, mais en plus je connais la maison et son propriétaire... Robert nous ouvrira...

Clément sentait la situation lui échapper confusément. Les arguments de Mary lui semblaient justes, mais si Pungent était le tueur, alors... Il fallait prendre une décision rapidement car sa petite amie se glissait sur le siège.

— Non ! Mary, j'y vais tout seul...

Il poussa Mary hors de la voiture en posant une main énergique sur ses fesses et claqua la portière. La jeune fille manqua tomber à la renverse. Il ne s'excusa pas et tourna la clef de contact avec détermination. Rien. La portière se rouvrit alors et Mary prit place à côté de son compagnon.

— 1277...

— Quoi ! hurla Clément, énervé.

— 1277... Le code pour faire démarrer la voiture.

Mary tapa le code sur le cadran situé derrière le levier de vitesse. Clément soupira et la fixa droit dans les yeux. C'était fou. Ses yeux exprimaient une parfaite détermination. Comme les yeux de Kite le soir de la découverte du corps de Jude... Clément abdiqua et démarra. Décidément, Mary était imprévisible. Mais il l'aimait bien trop pour lui reprocher son entêtement. Son énervement diminua peu à peu. Clément conduisit vite car ils avaient assez perdu de temps comme ça. À cet instant, il aurait aimé avoir une sirène et un gyrophare. Et cela n'avait rien, mais vraiment rien de puéril.

38

En rythme, Robert, n'oublie surtout pas le rythme...

Robert Pungent sonna à la porte de ce petit appartement situé dans la rue Princes Place. Il portait à la main son sac à dos rempli soigneusement dans la matinée. Il n'avait rien omis, il en était sûr.

Alors, tu vas m'ouvrir, enfin ? Je suis là pour ton bien ! Je ne te veux aucun mal !

La porte ne comportait pas de judas. Il entendit un bruit de pas. Bruit était synonyme de parquet ou de carrelage. La femme n'avait donc pas de moquette. C'était bête car Robert adorait la moquette. Mais pour cette délivrance-là, il avait juste besoin d'un lit. Un lit où il pourrait étendre cette femme avec douceur après lui avoir serré les chairs du cou. La porte s'ouvrit en grand.

Oh Dieu ! ce qu'elle était belle dans cet ensemble sport ! Un peu enveloppée, mais si distinguée.

Robert Pungent lui adressa un bref sourire qui décontenança la femme. Elle resta tétanisée de longues secondes. Il eut même le temps de refermer la porte et de la pousser dans l'appartement. Elle n'eut aucune réaction. Pungent était contrarié. Mais il se rassura. Avec ce qu'il allait lui faire maintenant, il était sûr qu'elle allait remuer... Peut-être crierait-elle même ?

C'est le début de la chanson, Robert, et dépêche-toi, car elle est très courte, celle-là... à peine deux minutes vingt... Et elle est si rythmée... Tu vas devoir te surpasser... Mais je te fais confiance...

Pungent profita de la courte introduction sans paroles pour se saisir du cou de cette femme. Elle se mit tout de même à se débattre. Ses petites jambes potelées battaient l'air... mais bien trop vite...

Tu n'es pas dans le rythme, ma chérie...

Il serra de plus en plus fort et sentit le contact du cuir chaud sur sa peau. Il aimait cela. Commençaient alors les paroles. Premier couplet avec, dans le fond, ces petits balais que Ringo remuait sur sa batterie et qui étaient vraiment pratiques pour garder le rythme dans la tête. La femme commençait vraiment à suffoquer, ses joues roses devenaient rouge sang. Pungent continua à serrer.

Là... Voilà... Tu as bien compris... Ralentis encore un peu et tu seras parfaitement dans le rythme...

Fini. La femme était morte. Les yeux révulsés.

Pungent, qui ne supportait toujours pas cette vision, lui rabattit les paupières. Puis, il jeta un coup d'œil à l'appartement. Spacieux, confortable, décoré avec goût... Encore une fois, il ne s'était pas trompé. Il repéra la chambre d'un seul regard et porta le corps sans vie de la femme sur son lit. Il revint ensuite prendre son sac à dos, qu'il emmena dans la chambre.

Oh ! Quelle sobriété ! Ce simple piano pendant ces couplets chantants !

Une fois revenu dans la chambre, il ferma les rideaux jaune canari d'un seul geste et regarda cette femme sur le lit. « *Lying on a bed, listen to the music playing in your head.* [1] » Il ouvrit son sac à dos et s'empara d'une flûte. Il attendit tranquillement le début de cette courte période instrumentale entre les couplets deux et trois, puis enfonça avec conviction un pipeau dans l'oreille droite de la femme. Même chose dans son oreille gauche avec l'autre pipeau. Pungent était satisfait.

Reprends maintenant... Reprends le couplet... Vite, car la fin est proche...

Robert ne savait pas s'il allait oser le faire. Il s'était demandé pendant des mois quelle était la meilleure solution. Et même maintenant, il hésitait encore. Mais cette incertitude le gênait moins qu'une autre... Parce qu'elle n'avait aucune conséquence directe sur son œuvre. Il se répéta ses deux solutions dans la tête. « *Baby at your breast, wonders how you manage to feed the rest* [2] » ou « *Children at your feet, wonder*

---

1. Étendue sur un lit, écoute la musique qui se joue dans ta tête.
2. Un bébé contre ton sein, il se demande comment tu parviens à nourrir les autres.

how you manage to make ends meet [1] ». Il s'était dit que cela dépendrait de sa condition du moment. Et là, Pungent n'avait pas envie de voir les seins de cette femme. Alors, avant que la chanson ne se terminât dans sa tête, il prit dans son sac les trois poupées de porcelaine et les posa une à droite de la jambe droite, une à gauche de la jambe gauche et l'autre au milieu des deux jambes que l'homme écarta quelque peu en fermant les yeux.

Recule-toi, Robert... Recule-toi et admire ton ultime œuvre avec ces femmes... avec tes femmes !

Pungent prit du recul et ouvrit à nouveau les rideaux. Une lumière faible, mais suffisante pénétra dans la pièce et éclaira le corps entier de la femme. Il se retourna, la bouche ouverte.

Ça y est ! Tu jouis ! Oh, Robert, tu jouis... tu jouis...

Robert Pungent sortit de la chambre, ferma la porte de l'appartement et passa le porche de l'immeuble. Il sifflait.

Dans le petit appartement, étendus sur le lit, cette tête où deux flûtes étaient plantées et ces pieds où trois poupons étaient jetés, appartenaient bien à Madonna Estevez, l'attachée culturelle de l'ambassade du Chili à Londres. À *Lady Madonna...*

---

1. Des enfants à tes pieds, ils se demandent comment tu parviens à finir le mois.

Paul Kite avait longtemps hésité avant de sortir déjeuner à l'extérieur du Yard. Le dossier était encore loin d'être fini. Mais de toute façon, Hicks revenait au bureau vers 15 heures. C'était du moins ce que son imbécile d'assistante avait dit à Kite. « Mais je ne sais pas s'il aura le temps de vous recevoir... Mr Hicks est très occupé en ce moment. Sur cette affaire des meurtres en musique... » Kite avait essayé d'en savoir plus, mais la jeune femme avait été intraitable. Elle lui avait juste confié que la brigade craignait un nouveau meurtre aujourd'hui. « Tous les deux jours, c'est le schéma récurrent. » Kite revoyait le visage encore juvénile de l'assistante. Elle souriait d'un air complice comme pour affirmer sa supériorité d'information. « Si elle savait, cette cruche... » Mais il n'avait pas envie d'être désagréable aujourd'hui... Il n'en avait même pas le courage.

Kite décida donc de s'accorder une pause déjeuner à l'extérieur. Il n'avait pas très faim et en profiterait pour s'aérer les poumons. Cette matinée studieuse l'avait tué. Il se demanda s'il n'aurait pas mieux fait de rentrer à Finchley pour déjeuner avec Michelle, Mary et Clément. Mais s'il se sentait capable de faire le trajet aller, il n'aurait pas le courage de faire le trajet retour. Il remonta, sous un pâle soleil, Victoria Street vers Westminster Abbey.

Clément gara la Clio devant la lourde clôture du 7, Cavendish Avenue. Il s'était transcendé au volant de la petite voiture française, aidé en cela par l'impression de toucher bientôt au but... Ce but qui clôturerait sa carrière de flic... Et puis Kite était innocent, c'était cela le plus important — soulageant, surtout...

Les deux jeunes gens n'avaient mis que dix minutes pour couvrir les quinze kilomètres séparant Finchley de St John's Wood. Mary avait guidé avec précision son petit ami durant tout le trajet. Elle était très excitée de prendre part à cette curieuse expédition. Se pourrait-il que Robert Pungent, le meilleur ami de son père, riche et distingué avocat, soit le terrible meurtrier ?

Mary repensa aux nombreuses fois où Robert l'avait prise sur ses genoux quand elle était petite, aux nombreuses fois où il venait à l'improviste l'enlever de la maison familiale pour lui offrir le cinéma plus le restaurant, toutes ces fois où il l'avait emmenée au pub de Finchley pour lui payer une bière... Robert... C'était aussi lui qui avait été le plus attentionné quand sa mère avait fait une fausse couche juste après la terrible épreuve de 87... Son père était en dépression et Robert s'était occupé de tout, allant même jusqu'à prendre des vacances pour veiller Michelle des journées entières... Robert... « Toi, l'homme aux gestes si doux, toi le rêveur qui idéalises l'amour..., est-ce possible que tu sois le monstre que tout le Yard recherche ? Plus que quelques secondes... »

Clément et Mary mirent tous deux pied à terre

en même temps, les yeux à la recherche du portail d'entrée. Il faisait vraiment froid dehors.

— Bon..., commença Clément. Que fait-on maintenant ?

Il fixait la clôture, les yeux plissés, tentant de repérer une quelconque ouverture lui permettant d'apercevoir la maison. Cavendish Avenue était apparemment une rue très calme. Aucune voiture en stationnement.

Le jeune Français leva les yeux. Il vit de nombreux troncs dépouillés, dont les fines ramifications grises bougeaient dans le vent.

— C'est plutôt lugubre...

Mary hocha la tête et se dirigea vers le haut portail terminé par de grosses piques.

— Nous allons sonner tout simplement, conclut-elle, comme si tu venais *enfin* le remercier pour l'appartement... De toute façon, il sera si content de me voir qu'il nous ouvrira sans problème.

— Oui... Tout ça en admettant qu'il est innocent... Parce que sinon, ça va être un autre son de cloche...

— Et qu'est-ce que tu veux bien qu'il nous fasse ? Qu'il nous séquestre ?

— Ne plaisante pas, la réprimanda Clément, angoissé à l'extrême.

Non sans appréhension, Mary appuya sur la sonnette. La maison devait être éloignée de la grille car ils n'entendirent pas le moindre son. Trois minutes passèrent, Mary pressa à nouveau le bouton. Rien. Ils commençaient à grelotter.

— Le portail n'est peut-être pas fermé ? suggéra la jeune fille. Souvent, dans les grandes demeures, les proprios ne prennent même pas la peine de...

Et, sans attendre la réaction de son compagnon, Mary posa ses mains nues sur le métal froid. Elle poussa et, effectivement, le portail s'entrouvrit.

— *Let's go !* lança-t-elle triomphalement, en soufflant sur ses paumes.

Clément la suivit, sans desserrer les dents. Il était bien trop médusé par la détermination de sa petite amie.

L'immense façade blanche de la demeure impressionna le jeune inspecteur. « Vraiment ! Pungent doit être plein aux as pour s'offrir ce truc, en plus de tous ses appartements... », pensa-t-il.

Une fois le portail franchi, on apercevait la villa au bout d'une longue allée de gravillons bordée d'arbres. Ils remarquèrent deux traînées de cailloux légèrement écrasés sur toute la longueur du chemin.

— Il doit probablement garer sa voiture ici..., dit Clément en montrant les traces sur le sol.

S'approchant de la porte noire au gros bouton doré, il sentit son mal de ventre qui se manifestait encore et toujours. Que faisaient-ils là ? Ils étaient bien inconscients d'oser se rendre chez l'un des meilleurs amis de Kite pour déterminer si, oui ou non, il était à l'origine de trois meurtres sanglants... Pourtant quelque chose les poussait irrésistiblement vers ce Pungent... Cet amoureux bafoué, fan des Beatles... Tout était si fou... Et si Clément n'avait jamais entendu *Hey Jude* dans la voiture de Kite... Où serait-il aujourd'hui ? Probablement pas en train de déranger un éminent citoyen britannique — de surcroît prestigieux avocat d'affaires...

Clément effaça rapidement toutes ces pensées de son esprit juste à temps pour voir Mary frapper trois coups sur l'imposante porte. Rien. Encore trois autres coups. Toujours rien.

— Tu vas peut-être me dire que, dans ce genre de demeure, les propriétaires laissent la porte ouverte parce que...

Mary fit signe à Clément de se taire et tourna la grosse poignée.

En vain.

— Il fallait tout de même pas espérer ce genre de truc, ironisa Clément.

Mary porta un doigt à sa bouche et dit d'un ton excessivement sérieux :

— Il faut entrer là-dedans.

— Tu es folle ! Violation de domicile ! Je ne sais pas ce que ça coûte dans le droit anglais, mais je me rappelle bien ce que ça coûte dans le droit français... Et je n'ai pas envie de...

— Tais-toi donc... Et réfléchis ! Il doit bien y avoir une fenêtre ouverte ou...

— En plein hiver !

Mary haussa les épaules et enfouit ses mains plus profondément dans les poches de son anorak. Quel froid ! Elle aurait dû prendre une écharpe avant de partir.

— Ou bien, continua Mary, imperturbable, la porte de la cave... Faisons le tour de la maison.

Ils s'exécutèrent. Au moins, cela les ferait bouger.

— Attends ! Pas si fort... Je n'arrive pas à glisser ce bout de bois...

Mary s'énervait car son ami tremblait. Elle avait réussi à convaincre son compagnon que la porte extérieure menant à la cave semblait bien vieille et qu'il était probablement possible de faire sauter le verrou.

— Il suffit de la pousser simplement un peu, lui avait expliqué Mary, et je glisserai un bout de bois jusqu'au loquet du haut. Ensuite, un bon coup vers le haut et le tour est joué... C'est encore une chance qu'il n'ait pas cadenassé toutes les serrures... Regarde les points des autres verrous...

Mais Clément ne regardait pas. Il était totalement sidéré par l'esprit pratique de sa compagne. Comme dans un autre monde, au milieu d'une splendide villa anglaise et s'amusant à faire sauter les verrous d'une porte d'un riche avocat — ami de la famille Kite de surcroît.

— Mais, Mary, tu es vraiment timbrée ! On ne va pas fracturer cette porte de merde ! C'est de la folie... Qu'est-ce qui t'arrive ?

Clément repensait à leur nuit et à la douceur fruitée de sa peau.

— Je veux connaître la vérité ! répondit-elle. La vérité... Et s'il faut en passer par là...

Elle se tourna vers Clément.

— Je te signale quand même que maman, papa et moi sommes concernés par cette affaire, si tes conclusions sont justes...

Clément soupira. Elle avait raison. *Il faut te concentrer maintenant, oublier ton mal de ventre et pousser la porte en bois même avec tes mains tremblantes.*

— Vas-y ! Là... Ouais, comme ça ! OK...

Mary prit une bouffée d'air et remonta sa main avec force vers le haut. Le bâton heurta la petite serrure qui ne céda pas.

— On recommence..., souffla-t-elle.

« Heureusement que personne ne nous voit

grâce à cette haute clôture et aux arbres »,
pensa Clément dont le tremblement des mains
persistait.

Nouvelle tentative. Cette fois-ci, la serrure
céda. Mary jeta le bâton à terre et entra la première dans la cave, son camarade sur ses talons.
Une odeur désagréable remplissait l'atmosphère glaciale. C'est la première chose que les
deux jeunes compagnons remarquèrent. Ils ne
voyaient rien car la simple lumière du jour
n'éclairait qu'une petite surface devant la porte.
« Les fenêtres devaient être calfeutrées », pensa
Clément. Ils avancèrent pas à pas, se tenant par
la main. Soudain, un grognement rompit le
silence.

— Quoi ? chuchota Mary à l'adresse de son
ami. Tu as encore peur...

— Non ! Je n'ai pas peur... Pourquoi as-tu
grogné ?

— Je n'ai pas grogné... Ce n'est pas toi ?

— Non.

De nouveau, un grognement. Plus épais.

— Merde... Ça vient de là, je crois...

Clément marcha à tâtons vers la droite, d'où
semblait provenir le bruit.

— Mary... Essaie d'allumer cette putain de
lumière...

Elle s'exécuta, passant ses mains sur le mur.
Elle commençait à perdre un peu de son assurance.

— Je n'arrive pas bien à me rendre compte
des distances... Je vais essayer de trouver un
interrupt...

Clic !

Un néon, fixé au plafond en plein milieu de la
pièce, clignota avant de diffuser une puissante
lumière. Mary et Clément clignèrent des yeux.

Leur stress diminua de moitié. Balayant l'espace du regard, ils constatèrent qu'il y avait là juste une petite table et, au fond, une porte d'un blanc brillant.

— C'est étrange, cette porte..., s'étonna Clément. Regarde, elle semble bien neuve à côté de ces deux murs de briques...

— Je ne sais pas ce qu'il y a derrière, mais, regarde... Trois serrures ! Et elles sont toutes ouvertes...

De la lumière sous la porte... D'habitude il n'allume jamais... Et puis quel est ce bruit venant du dehors ? Oh ! Une ombre de pied derrière la porte... Et si quelqu'un d'autre était là... Il n'a pas eu le temps de fermer les serrures tout à l'heure... Il faut que j'arrive à crier... Mais j'ai la gorge si sèche...

Un gémissement atroce transperça la porte blanche. Clément et Mary se figèrent, tétanisés.

— Qu'est-ce que c'est ?

Le jeune inspecteur hésita à tourner la poignée. Mais il le fit. Mary s'avança prudemment derrière lui. Une bouffée fétide les frappa en pleine face.

Ils détournèrent rapidement la tête après s'être rendu compte du spectacle qui s'offrit à leurs yeux dans cette petite pièce surchauffée. Un corps, vivant à en juger par les gargouillements, gisait dans une mare d'excréments et d'urine. Il s'agissait à n'en pas douter d'une vieille dame. Sa robe souillée ne couvrait plus que partiellement sa peau recouverte de taches immondes. Des cheveux blancs humides étaient collés sur son front. Les deux jeunes gens ne purent soutenir cette scène plus de quelques secondes. L'odeur insupportable leur donnait la nausée. Ils avisèrent un escalier montant vers ce qui devait être le rez-de-chaussée, s'y engouffrèrent en vitesse. Il fallait fuir...

Mais qui était cette femme ? La mère de Pungent ?

Mais que s'est-il passé ? Ai-je bien entendu ? Ou est-ce ma seule oreille restante qui me jouerait des tours ? Des mots en français... Mon Dieu, je dois rêver... Ou je dois me rapprocher de vous... Oh, mon Dieu, je sens un courant d'air froid me chatouiller le ventre... Est-ce vous ? Venez-vous me prendre enfin après toutes ces heures de grand supplice ? Et toute cette lumière qui envahit mon tombeau... Pardonnez-moi, mon Dieu, je peux juste la deviner d'un œil car l'autre n'est plus dans mon orbite... Quand mes mains m'y autorisaient, j'y mettais un doigt pour bien m'en rendre compte... Oh, mon Dieu, est-ce vous qui fuyez dans l'escalier ? Restez, mon Dieu... Je vous en prie... Venez me délivrer...

Accoudés au radiateur du grand hall de l'entrée, Mary et Clément reprirent peu à peu leurs esprits. Une chose était maintenant sûre... Pungent était bien un fou.

— C'est atroce..., hoqueta Mary. La vieille femme en bas, je crois bien que c'est sa mère...

— Vite, va appeler une ambulance.

Mary ouvrit au hasard la première porte devant elle. La cuisine. Un bref coup d'œil lui fit voir un téléphone mural. Elle appela les urgences pendant que Clément, le visage blanc comme un linge, explorait le rez-de-chaussée. « Pourvu que l'on ne trouve rien d'autre », pensa-t-il.

Mary précisa bien à son interlocuteur d'entrer dans la cave, puis raccrocha précipitamment pour composer avec fébrilité le numéro du bureau de son père au Yard. Il fallait le prévenir... Mais il n'était toujours pas là, toujours pas revenu de sa pause déjeuner. Mary jura tout ce qu'elle connaissait en français et rattrapa son camarade qui était monté à l'étage.

— C'est immense, ici ! cria-t-il. Tu as prévenu les urgences ?

— Oui.

— Et le Yard ?

— Oui, mais papa n'est pas là...

Clément arrêta sa prospection et se tourna vers son amie.

— Et alors ? Ça n'a plus aucune importance... Appelle n'importe qui...

— Ah oui... Nous sommes censés être ici peut-être ? Si ça se trouve, Robert est juste coupable d'avoir séquestré sa mère...

L'image leur revint. Clément sentit un flot de bile lui remonter dans l'œsophage. Il vomit dans le couloir du haut, face à la chambre bleue de Pungent.

— Merde ! jura-t-il tout en s'essuyant la bouche avec un mouchoir en papier.

— Redescends attendre l'ambulance... Je vais me charger de visiter les autres pièces.

— Merci...

Clément était fier de son amie. Elle semblait moins impressionnée que lui. Il se sentait bien maladroit en ce moment... C'était Mary qui prenait le contrôle des opérations. Était-ce à dire qu'elle était meilleure comédienne que lui et pouvait jouer avec plus de sang-froid ?

Mais non, arrête ! Tu n'es pas dans un film, mais dans la réalité ! Cela confirme bien tout : elle est beaucoup plus douée que toi pour la réalité. Elle a les pieds sur terre et ne voit pas tout à travers une caméra !

Mary ouvrit une porte. Au loin, ils entendirent une sirène d'ambulance. L'hôpital de St John devait être tout proche. Sans même prendre le temps de regarder l'intérieur de la chambre, Clément descendit l'escalier quatre à quatre. Mary, elle, continua seule son exploration. Sur ce bureau immense là-bas, il y avait un bloc de papier. Intriguée, elle s'approcha.

Le Requiem, Seigneur... Enfin, j'entends le son du Requiem... Ce bruit me fait tant de bien, mon Dieu... Merci encore... Je vous aime...

Clément guida les deux ambulanciers et le médecin vers la cave en leur expliquant du mieux qu'il pouvait l'état de la vieille dame. Il leur avait montré sa carte du Yard pour justifier sa présence, mais les trois hommes n'avaient pas semblé y accorder la moindre attention. Avec professionnalisme, ils embarquèrent la veille femme. Avant de partir, le médecin vint rassurer Clément en lui disant qu'elle s'en sortirait...

— Mary ! Mary !

Il se tenait en bas de l'escalier du rez-de-chaussée.

— Qu'est-ce que tu fous ? Viens... On va au Yard, il n'y a pas de temps à perdre... Pungent n'est pas là. Il risque de rentrer bientôt et on

296

pourra l'interpeller avec ton père... Mais qu'est-ce que tu fous, dépêche-toi, merde ! J'en ai marre de gueuler...

Clément avait les nerfs à vif.

Mary était assise sur le lit bleu de Pungent. Elle était en train d'essayer de déchiffrer les pages remplies d'une écriture minuscule. Elle se montra à l'interpellation de son ami.

— Tu l'as trouvé sur le bureau de sa chambre ? demanda Clément en feuilletant rapidement le bloc-notes.

— Oui, comme je te l'ai dit... Ça a tout l'air d'être une sorte de journal intime...

Clément redonna le carnet à Mary. Ils arrivèrent à la Clio et s'y engouffrèrent. Ils tâchèrent de se tenir bien droit pour éviter le contact de leurs tee-shirts trempés de sueur.

— J'ai juste feuilleté... Il y parle de lui et de ses victimes. Robert est vraiment l'assassin, Clément...

Mary avait envie de pleurer. Son Robert était un monstre... Des images de son enfance défilèrent devant ses yeux.

— OK, alors direction le Yard et le plus vite possible... Il faut absolument le cueillir quand il reviendra ici... Ou même avant, car s'il découvrait l'absence de sa mère...

Il démarra. Au même moment, de fins flocons de neige se remirent à tomber. Mary sécha ses yeux humides et rouvrit le journal. Et rien que la première phrase lui glaça le sang.

Cette jouissance que je refusais par les femmes m'est venue par le meurtre. Hier, un troisième assassinat a été commis. Ce fut encore meilleur qu'avec les précédents.

Demain, une quatrième femme mourra, dans son lit, calmement, et alors je jouirai. Tout est si normal... Pourquoi serais-je différent ? Parce que je tue ? La belle affaire... Moi, il y a vingt ans, on m'a détruit l'âme. Cette âme que je chérissais tant, que j'entretenais avec ferveur dans les chapelles, chez moi, à toute heure du jour et même de la nuit... Cette âme que je voulais rendre belle en prévision du moment où il ne me resterait plus qu'elle... Et le 23 décembre 1977, c'est l'inverse qui s'est produit. Mon âme m'a quitté. Je restais juste avec mon corps. Et vivre avec son corps seul, c'est un pénible calvaire...

Je suis entré à l'université de Liverpool en 1976. Ce fut très dur pour moi de quitter Londres et de me déraciner de cette ville où s'était déroulée toute mon enfance. Je me promis d'y revenir le plus tôt possible, une fois mes études terminées. Comment allais-je bien pouvoir survivre dans cette affreuse ville de briques qu'était Liverpool ? Une chose me rassurait néanmoins : Liverpool était la ville natale des Beatles. Oh ! John, Paul, George et Ringo, si vous n'aviez pas été là, je me serais jeté du Royal Liver Building. Pas un doute à ce sujet.

Le premier week-end après mon installation, je me suis rendu devant la maison natale de John. Et c'est ici que Paul Kite m'a accosté pour la première fois. « Je t'ai déjà vu à l'université, non ? Tu es en droit ? » Moi, je n'avais pas envie de répondre à ce petit homme au visage poupon et au fort accent de la région, mais j'ai quand même acquiescé d'un laconique : « Oui, je suis en droit... ». Ce serait aujourd'hui si facile de dire que cette courte phrase allait être à l'origine de trois et bientôt quatre meurtres. Je n'aurais jamais dû parler à Paul. Pourquoi n'ai-je pas eu le courage de détourner la tête et de continuer ma visite ? Pour ma lâcheté, il paiera.

Nous sommes vite devenus les deux meilleurs amis de l'université (« du monde » était barré. C'était, à ce point de la lecture, la seule rature du manuscrit). On ne se quittait jamais pendant la journée, car nous suivions les mêmes cours. Moi, je désirais ardemment devenir un grand avocat de droit pénal. Les grands procès criminels m'avaient toujours fasciné. Lui, il voulait embrasser une carrière d'avocat comme son père et reprendre son cabinet.

J'ai alors appris une grande leçon : il ne faut jamais juger un homme sur sa première impression, car derrière son visage maladroit, Paul cachait une personnalité explosive, mélange de douceur et de colère. Il savait être gai, triste, calme, excité... Moi qui n'étais qu'un pauvre Londonien loin de ses fumées et de ses bus rouges, j'admirais... oui... je l'admirais. Et puis, il y avait notre folle passion commune pour les Beatles. J'avais tout de suite rejoint le groupe de Kite. Avec lui, j'en étais un des fondateurs. « Les Fab Five », c'était sensass, non ? Il y avait avec nous une fille, son ami et un autre garçon. Tous fans des Beatles, tous portant le nom ou le prénom d'une chanson. Robert Pungent, m'avait dit Kite, était un nom extraordinaire. Robert pour Dr Robert et Pungent pour *Sgt Pepper* et même *Mean Mr Mustard*... Je n'avais jamais fait attention qu'il y avait autant d'épices dans les Beatles. Pauvre Paul ! S'il se doutait alors à quoi cette ressemblance me servirait...

Nos réunions du lundi devenaient, au fur et à mesure de nos progrès à la guitare, le summum de la semaine. Je les attendais avec une joie incommensurable. Car les soirées qui suivaient étaient si plates.

Je n'ai jamais été dans la même chambre que Paul. Pendant mes cinq années d'études, j'ai partagé ma chambre avec Steve, un grand blond aux yeux dorés dont toutes les filles se disputaient le bras (le bras ! Que mon écriture semble naïve). Il n'était que très rarement dans son lit et les fois où il était présent, c'était avec une fille qu'il amenait en douce. Autant dire que nous avons échangé cinq mots tout au plus en cinq ans. Le soir, je restais seul, accoudé à mon bureau, rédigeant mes études de cas et apprenant mes manuels de droit. Paul vivait aussi en ermite. Il ne sortait de sa chambre que très rarement. C'était quelqu'un de très studieux et très travailleur. Il n'était pas plus attiré que moi par la gent féminine. Nous exécrions ensemble ces personnes comme Steve ou tous ces autres mâles qui profitaient des jeunes étudiantes pour les dépuceler avec fierté. Je me rappelle un jour où un professeur avait confisqué à un élève de notre classe une liste où étaient recensés en colonne le nom, l'âge et la description des jeunes filles avec lesquelles il s'était satisfait. Paul et moi, nous condamnions sévèrement ce comportement.

Et vint ce jour de l'année 1977. C'était un 8 novembre. Je m'étais inscrit à un cours de secourisme organisé par la Croix Rouge Internationale. La première séance eut lieu le lundi, mais cela ne me posait plus aucun problème, car le groupe venait d'être dissous. Un des membres (le chanteur, de surcroît) venait de quitter l'université pour des raisons obscures et nous avions tous juré que le groupe ne fonctionnerait plus si nous n'étions pas précisément cinq. Alors Paul et moi, nous nous sommes mis à la recherche d'un nouveau membre. Vainement. Pendant deux mois, je crois, il n'y a pas eu de répétition le lundi. Paul, moi et les autres, nous allions alors au pub prendre un verre, mais cela ne remplaçait évidemment pas le groupe.

Alors, j'ai rencontré Michelle. Ma Michelle.

C'est elle qui donnait les cours de secourisme. Elle venait de finir sa faculté de médecine. Michelle. Déjà à l'époque, j'aurais tué pour elle. Je suis allé la voir à la sortie du gymnase pour lui demander d'où venaient ce prénom et ce nom à consonance française. Elle m'a alors souri pour la première fois et je me souviens encore aujourd'hui de la blancheur de ses dents, contrastant avec le rose pulpeux de sa bouche. Elle m'expliqua que son père était français et sa mère anglaise. Le soir même, nous sommes allés prendre une bière au pub des étudiants. J'ai peut-être passé là la plus belle soirée de mon existence d'âme. Elle adorait les Beatles... Charmante coïncidence, ce prénom et sa passion pour le groupe originaire de Liverpool ! Dès le lendemain, je l'ai retrouvée au cours et je n'avais d'yeux que pour elle. J'observais pour la première fois en détail un corps de femme. Je m'arrêtais sur ses seins lorsqu'elle mimait les mouvements respiratoires d'urgence ; sur ses reins quand elle écrivait au tableau en tenant la craie entre ses doigts si fins... Je tentais d'imaginer son corps nu sous cet uniforme de la Croix Rouge. Mais j'avais si peu d'expérience en anatomie féminine — j'entends anatomie des formes, basée seulement sur quelques photos érotiques et un film du même acabit — que j'avais peur de salir son corps en l'imaginant nue dans toutes ces effrayantes positions.

Le troisième soir, je l'ai présentée à Paul, car elle acceptait de faire partie du groupe. Quelle joie ! Même quand les cours de secourisme seraient finis, je pourrais continuer à la voir... Kite ne semblait pas emballé par Michelle au premier abord. Il la trouvait « trop vieille ». C'est vrai qu'elle était déjà âgée de 26 ans à l'époque... Mais Paul changea rapidement d'avis lors de notre première répétition.

Michelle sidéra tout le monde par le timbre de sa voix. Mon Dieu... Si vous aviez pu l'entendre chanter « *I want to hold your hand* »... J'avais l'impression qu'elle chantait juste pour moi... D'ailleurs, j'avais demandé à changer de place et à me rapprocher sur le devant avec ma guitare. J'étais ainsi plus près d'elle. Kite n'y voyait aucun inconvénient. Il devait se douter de la nature de mes sentiments, mais ne fit jamais une seule remarque à ce sujet.

Plusieurs fois, j'ai invité Michelle au pub. Mon travail s'en ressentit et je fus obligé de laisser la première place à Kite dans toutes les matières. J'étais attentionné à son égard... Je l'avais fixée droit dans les yeux pendant de longues secondes. Elle n'avait pas détourné la tête... Oh, mon Dieu...

Un soir, alors que nous revenions ensemble du pub, j'ai voulu tendre la main vers la sienne et la lui prendre en douceur... Mais je n'ai pas eu le courage... J'idéalisais jour et nuit notre union future, je faisais semblant dans mon petit lit d'avoir Michelle près de moi et je chuchotais le soir sous mes couvertures des mots doux à son attention...

Je répétais sans cesse à haute voix le matin, en me rasant la barbe rousse, ce « Michelle Pungent », trouvant la consonance fort belle. J'ai même demandé à mes parents qu'ils m'envoient de Londres une méthode de « Français rapide » juste pour l'épater un peu plus... Je voulais tout le temps la voir, je l'invitais donc au cinéma tous les jeudis soir. Pour payer nos sorties, sans rien dire à mes parents, je faisais la plonge le midi à la cafétéria. Cela dura un mois. Puis un jour, elle m'annonça qu'elle ne pouvait plus venir au pub et au cinéma avec moi... J'étais réduit à la voir pendant la seule répétition du lundi...

Alors, j'ai appris la nouvelle. Il neigeait ce

23 décembre et je devais retrouver Paul quelques instants dans sa chambre avant de rentrer à Londres chez mes parents pour les fêtes. À part les cours et les répétitions, je ne voyais plus guère Paul. Ses résultats étaient en baisse alors que les miens étaient sur une pente ascendante. J'en déduisais qu'il était probablement amoureux... J'imaginais volontiers nos mariages, moi au bras de Michelle et Paul au bras d'une femme quelconque. Mais la vérité était tout autre.

Et en ce 23 décembre 1977, Paul Kite m'a volé mon âme en me laissant...

41

ma seule chair définitivement inapte à aimer. Aimer avec son seul corps revient à haïr sa seule âme.

Robert Pungent venait de quitter sa Lady Madonna derrière lui. Il marchait vers St James's Park en laissant, dans la fine couche de neige recouvrant les trottoirs, l'empreinte de ses chaussures. Pungent souriait. Il était fier de la confession que trouveraient les flics dans sa belle chambre bleue. Il arriva dans le célèbre Mall. Jetant un coup d'œil sur sa droite, il aperçut Buckingham Palace. Il repensa à cette journée du 22 décembre 1977 :

Quand j'arrivai dans la chambre de Kite, je vis qu'il n'était plus à l'aise avec moi... Il ne me gratifia même pas d'une de ses plaisanteries habituelles sur mes cheveux roux ou sur son voisin de chambre. Il se contenta de me faire asseoir sur son lit. Et il m'apprit que, bientôt, Michelle serait allongée là. Oh, bien sûr ! Il ne me l'apprit pas dans ces termes-là... Il était bien trop respectueux d'elle et même de moi.

Je me levai d'un bond et restai debout face à lui. Cela faisait déjà deux semaines qu'il voyait Michelle en soirée. Pour moi, ça n'était pas possible. Je l'aimais toujours, plus que jamais. Puis il me décrivit ma Michelle, il me confia qu'il aimait passer la main dans ses cheveux et lui caresser l'épaule. Moi, je n'avais jamais osé ce geste... Je lui demandai alors sans ambages s'il était sorti avec elle. La réponse tomba sèchement. Oui. Hier soir. Et dire que moi, j'étais à ce moment-là *seul* dans ma chambre en train de rédiger un devoir de droit pénal. Jamais je ne pourrais reprendre un devoir de pénal. Mes jambes lâchèrent d'un coup et je suis tombé sur le sol froid de la petite chambre. Paul se précipita vers moi et m'aida à me relever. J'avais uriné dans mon pantalon. Il m'ordonna de me déshabiller et me prêta un de ses slips et un de ses pantalons. Puis il vint vers moi et posa une de ses grosses mains sur mon épaule. Ce n'était pas la peine, Paul, j'avais bien compris, tu sais... Nous sommes si semblables... Mais savais-tu, Paul, que, ce soir-là, tu avais ruiné non seulement ma carrière d'avocat pénal, mais, plus grave encore, la vie de quatre femmes qui allaient mourir vingt ans plus tard jour pour jour.

Tu m'as raccompagné dans ma chambre. Je me suis couché tout habillé. Je ne voulais pas affronter ce corps qui, à présent, était le seul témoin de mon existence. J'ai éteint la lumière, mais je n'ai pas pu m'endormir. Je pensais à toi, Paul, et je ne te haïssais même pas... Je perdais la notion de sentiment et c'était pour moi une preuve de mort spirituelle.

Sanglotant, j'ai saisi le crucifix sur ma table de nuit et l'ai jeté rageusement sur le mur d'en face. Si mon voisin de chambre avait été là, peut-être l'aurais-je étranglé...

Pungent emprunta la Horse Guards Road qui longeait St James's Park sur toute sa largeur. Malgré le froid, de nombreux couples avec des enfants se promenaient sur les petits chemins du parc. Pungent aimait penser à cette herbe verte que recouvrait la neige fraîchement tombée. Il ne savait pas pourquoi, mais il aimait. Oui, depuis peu, il avait réappris à aimer...

J'ai brillamment fini mes études de droit public économique et je suis entré immédiatement à *Norton Rose* dans la City. Je continuais à voir Kite régulièrement pendant tout ce temps et je me suis même rendu à « l'inauguration » de leur maison de Finchley. Moi, je vivais seul avec maman dans son appartement de Chelsea. Papa était mort. Et elle ne voulait pas un seul *penny* de moi. Alors, j'ai commencé à acheter des appartements un peu partout. Je gagnais très bien ma vie, d'autant plus que, pendant l'année 1987, j'ai ouvert mon propre cabinet avec cinq autres confrères. Kite, lui, était rentré dans la police parce qu'il ne voulait pas « travailler avec ces pourris-de-fric d'avocats ». Si j'avais épousé Michelle, peut-être aurais-je eu le courage d'arrêter mes études et de faire vraiment quelque chose qui me plaisait... Du droit pénal... ou même écrire... Ma vie monotone continuait, couvée par cette mère que je n'aimais plus. Je n'avais que la musique et la lecture pour m'évader de ce monde tiède. J'écoutais en boucle tout le week-end l'intégrale des Beatles, seul dans ma chambre au papier peint d'adolescent. Jusqu'au jour où j'eus l'occasion d'acquérir LA maison de mes rêves. Cette maison de Cavendish Avenue, près du studio d'Abbey Road, où avait habité Paul McCartney et où Ils se réunissaient tous après leurs sessions d'enregistrement. Maman eut le cœur brisé de quitter l'appartement de Chelsea, mais elle ne voulait pas m'abandonner. Moi, je m'en fichais bien.

Nous avons emménagé rapidement. Il n'y avait pas de travaux à faire, les anciens propriétaires, très soigneux, avaient tout laissé en l'état des « années McCartney ». Et c'est à cette période, je crois, que le déclic s'est produit...

Robert Pungent aurait bien aimé s'arrêter, mais il n'en avait pas le temps. S'il avait pu, il serait allé vers Duck Island et aurait observé, paisiblement assis sur un banc froid, ce couple et leurs petits gamins heureux. Il les aurait entendus crier et chahuter dans la neige avec leur père riant aux éclats. Il aurait souri à la vue de leur mère regardant son petit monde avec bonheur. Depuis le début de la semaine, Pungent était vraiment heureux. Cela faisait si longtemps que cela ne lui était pas arrivé.

Penser, à chaque fois que je m'asseyais sur la lunette des toilettes, que Paul et les autres l'avaient probablement fait avant moi, me faisait rêver. Puis Ils sont venus à moi. Ils me sont apparus un soir. Paul s'était glissé derrière le piano et avait commencé à improviser une mélodie. George était à la guitare, John tranquillement assis à mon bureau se triturait l'esprit pour coller de jolis mots sur le doux refrain... Seul Ringo restait debout, désœuvré. J'avais compris. Le lendemain, je suis allé acheter une batterie chez *Rose-Morris* et nous avons ainsi passé des soirées merveilleuses, envoûtantes.

Souvent, John prenait la place de Paul au piano. Ils m'ont laissé quelquefois jouer un peu de guitare, ou écrire quelques paroles sur le papier... Quand je racontais cela à maman, elle me disait que je voyais des fantômes, qu'elle n'avait jamais entendu les instruments. Je la rassurais. Je lui disais que les fantômes ne jouent pas de la musique, et puis que sa surdité devait être importante... Je l'avais installée dans une petite chambre du bas, près de la cuisine. Moi, j'avais pris l'immense chambre du haut et l'avais fait entièrement tapisser de bleu.

Quand tout fut fini, j'avais invité mes collègues, Michelle, Paul et leur fille chez moi. La soirée s'était bien passée. Kite semblait vraiment impressionné par ma nouvelle demeure. J'avais regardé Michelle en essayant de la trouver à nouveau désirable. C'est vrai que je faisais encore attention à elle. Ne l'avais-je pas veillée pendant la dépression de Kite au moment de sa fausse couche ? Mais ce n'était pas par amour, plutôt par devoir et parce que Paul était et reste mon meilleur ami. En ce jour où je pendais ma crémaillère, elle avait 41 ans. Malgré ses traits encore très expressifs, je n'arrivais plus à éprouver le moindre sentiment à son égard.

Je me sentais condamné à mourir vierge et, ce soir, à nouveau seul dans cette grande maison, j'étais plus bas que terre... Ma Michelle ne m'attirait plus. J'ai écouté la chanson éponyme des Beatles et je n'arrivais même pas à me rappeler son visage. Et j'ai pleuré.

Depuis quinze ans, cela ne m'était pas arrivé une seule fois. Même quand mon père est mort d'un cancer. Il était alors dans le coma et ma mère, à son chevet, m'avait dit de lui dire « au revoir ». Cela m'avait paru ridicule, mais je l'avais fait. Une larme avait coulé le long de sa joue flétrie. Ma mère avait pleuré sans discontinuer pendant une journée et une nuit. Moi, je n'avais pas versé la moindre larme.

Or, ce soir, j'ai pleuré.

Ces larmes sur cette chanson me firent tellement de bien. Je laissais le disque tourner. C'était le disque deux du *Red Album* des Beatles. Arrivèrent la chanson *Eleanor Rigby* et ses terrifiants violons. Je ne saurais encore aujourd'hui dire pourquoi, mais sur cette musique, j'imaginai le meurtre de Kite. Était-ce cette même sonorité, ce même rythme que la scène de la douche dans *Psychose* ? Je me voyais dans une église en train de serrer son cou entre mes mains, en train de lui taillader le visage en suivant la cadence des altos... Un désir meurtrier m'habitait. Un sentiment clair m'était apparu : je voulais *tuer* Kite. Je haïssais Kite. Ce fut un nouvel instinct pour moi. Mon premier instinct d'homme depuis cette scène de la chambre à l'université où ma vessie s'était vidée devant Paul.

Je me suis déshabillé. Il fallait que je me regarde dans un miroir. Ce serait incroyable si je pouvais supporter la vision de mon corps. Mais si ! J'ai passé mes mains sur ma peau nue. C'était bien la résurrection de mon âme dans ce corps qui m'appartenait à nouveau. Nu, je suis descendu voir ma mère pour lui demander un petit crucifix. Elle me le donna en marmonnant quelque chose à propos de mon indécence. Mais elle devait être contente de ma réconciliation surprise avec le protestantisme. Cette nuit-là, je me suis masturbé cinq fois.

Pungent sortit de St James's Park et continua sa route vers le sud. Au loin, il voyait le haut de Westminster Abbey. Il se racla la gorge à plusieurs reprises et, avisant une poubelle, enfouit son sac à dos vide bien au fond. Il reprit sa marche en tâtant la poche intérieure de son imperméable. La forme allongée du silencieux le rassura.

J'aurais voulu me venger de Kite tout de suite, le tuer la nuit même d'un coup de couteau en plein cœur. Mais une telle vengeance n'était pas digne de ma nouvelle assurance, de mon nouveau génie. J'ai donc pris la décision d'attendre encore cinq ans. 1997, vingt ans après leur premier flirt. Je pourrais alors reconstituer cet orchestre aux noms de chansons qui avait causé ma mort durant quinze longues années. Le 22 décembre 1996, je me suis mis à la recherche de victimes potentielles. Il me fallait quatre femmes célibataires. Je n'ai pas eu à aller bien loin. Jude était infirmière dans le service de cardiologie de maman. Quand j'emmenais maman, je pouvais la voir, elle, avec ses beaux seins, ses belles jambes. Je l'ai donc inscrite sur ma liste en troisième position.

Eleanor serait la première. C'était bien normal... Ce sont ses violons qui m'ont redonné la vie. Je l'ai découverte au hasard d'une conversation dans un magasin où quelqu'un cria son prénom. Comble du bon goût, miss Stout était dame de paroisse dans le quartier de Covent Garden. Moi qui devais la tuer dans une église ou une chapelle...

Pour Lucy, ce fut encore plus simple. J'ai regardé sur le registre du commerce dont nous disposions au cabinet et j'ai lu qu'une Lucy Chambers avait ouvert une bijouterie près d'Oxford Street. Quelle chance ! Avec plein de diamants autour d'elle...

Pour la suivante, Madonna, c'est à un cocktail de charité que je l'ai rencontrée. Nous n'avons pas bavardé une seule seconde ensemble, mais j'ai bien retenu son nom.

Voilà en fait cette idée de génie... Reconstituer ce groupe virtuel. Le *Pungent's Lonely Hearts Club Band*. Kite serait alors chargé de l'affaire et je pourrais enfin me mesurer à lui. Face à Face.

Je ruminai ma vengeance jusqu'à dimanche dernier où, pour moi, tout commença vraiment. Maman voyait bien que je mijotais quelque chose. Je me promenais nu dans la maison et j'écoutais les mêmes chansons à longueur de journée, le volume à fond. Et puis elle m'avait vu acheter des petites poupées, une sphère gonflable... Son air fureteur m'énervait, je fus obligé de la punir. De toute façon, je la détestais de plus en plus. Son corps décrépit était hideux... Ses rides multiples m'horripilaient... Je l'ai cloîtrée à la cave dans une petite pièce que j'avais spécialement aménagée avec chauffage et porte bien cadenassée. Mais avant de l'y emmener de force, je devais me faire une idée précise sur certaines choses. Sur ces choses qu'il m'était impossible d'ignorer. Un œil se laissait-il facilement se déloger de son orbite ? Ou encore : comment pouvait-on faire pénétrer un pipeau irlandais chromé à l'intérieur d'un conduit auditif ? Seule maman pouvait m'aider à trouver les solutions. Je l'ai donc droguée à son insu samedi soir et pendant la nuit, j'ai tout essayé. Ce fut terrible ! Non pas parce qu'elle est ma mère — cela je m'en fichais éperdument —, mais parce qu'elle s'est réveillée juste à l'instant où je venais d'extraire son œil. Elle a poussé un cri horrible. J'ai dû marteler plusieurs fois sa tête avec le plat de ma main. Elle s'est évanouie. J'ai alors glissé le pipeau dans son oreille. Son tympan fragile céda immédiatement. Profitant de son inconscience momentanée, je l'ai traînée à la cave. Je m'étais occupé tant bien que mal de sa plaie à l'œil qui, par miracle, ne saignait plus. Tant mieux, car je ne voulais pas qu'elle meure... Si au moins elle s'était appelée Pamela, Julia ou Martha... maman aurait été à même de figurer dans mon orchestre magique.

C'était bien de se sentir à nouveau capable

d'aimer et de haïr. Oh, Michelle... Un soir de septembre dernier, quand je t'ai vue dans une robe de soirée mauve... je t'ai désirée comme jamais auparavant. J'aurais voulu te saisir par les hanches et embrasser tendrement tes lèvres maquillées. De ce baiser que je n'ai jamais osé... Et puis j'ai pensé à ton mari... Il m'inspirait une telle répulsion... Comme ta fille d'ailleurs, dont la moitié aurait dû m'appartenir. Bien calé dans un fauteuil, je me suis amusé à la détailler des yeux... Elle est à moitié belle, ta fille... Comment serait-elle si j'avais été le père ? Ou peut-être aurions-nous eu un petit garçon, Michelle ? Un petit John...

Ah ! Mary... Je peux bien l'avouer ici : j'ai voulu me débarrasser d'elle, de tout ce qu'elle représentait, mais je n'ai pas pu. Paul McCartney m'avait presque ordonné son meurtre. « Il n'y a pas que nos titres qui contiennent des prénoms. » Te souviens-tu de notre morceau préféré, Michelle ? *Let It Be*. « When I find myself in times of trouble, Mother Mary comes to me, speaking words of wisdom. Let It Be... [1] » Mother Mary... Daughter Mary... Mary, dans ce pub où je lui ai tant de fois payé un verre de Coke, puis une pinte de bière... J'avais un couteau dans la main et la main dans la poche. Ma main n'a pas pu bouger. J'ai regardé ta fille et puis ton visage s'est substitué au sien. Tu étais là devant moi, sortant des toilettes, comme lors de nos soirées dans les pubs de Liverpool... Je n'ai pas eu le courage de la saigner. Je n'ai pas eu le courage de tuer ton enfant.

Les femmes que j'ai tuées n'auront pas d'enfant. Je leur ai rendu un fier service ! Porter le

1. Quand je suis dans une période de troubles, la Vierge Marie vient à moi, parlant les mots de la sagesse. Ainsi soit-il.

nom des chansons des Beatles peut mener à la mort... C'est un calvaire qu'elles ignorent. Moi, j'ai eu la chance de revivre, mais elles ? Ainsi, c'était fait, elles étaient mortes et c'était bien pour elles aussi.

Robert Pungent déboucha dans la grande rue. Il marqua une petite pause et détailla la façade du grand bâtiment. Sordide. Pas comme sa belle demeure de Cavendish Avenue. Mais ça n'avait vraiment rien à voir. Il reprit sa marche et croisa un groupe de cinq femmes, en train de rire aux éclats et portant à la main des sacs de Vivienne Westwood, la célèbre couturière londonienne. Pungent serra les dents. « Encore ces femmes mariées à de riches enfants de putain. » Il tenta de se maîtriser. Il les haïssait. « Il faut voir ces femmes portant un orgasme sur leur perpétuel sourire. » Il reprit la route menant à son but.

Kite et moi dérogions à la règle des autres étudiants putrides de l'université, qui ne pensaient qu'à satisfaire leurs instincts. Michelle, ce sont deux êtres purs qui t'ont aimée...

Je me rappelle aussi Steve, mon compagnon de chambre qui, tous les samedis et dimanches soir, ramenait des filles dans son lit. Je me souviens de ces cris, de ces halètements obscènes... Je tentais de ne pas les écouter, de fermer mes oreilles, les doigts crispés sur le petit crucifix que je glissais sous ma couverture. Mais à l'époque, mes mains descendaient ostensiblement vers le bas de mon ventre, sur mon sexe gonflé de honte. Si je pouvais résister à l'envie de posséder une femme, j'éprouvais la nécessité de vivre cette sensation douce et acidulée de l'orgasme au creux de mes reins. Je ne te connaissais pas encore, Michelle, car après, lorsque les halètements revinrent, je laissais mes mains bien en évidence sur la couverture et je les fixais. Elles ne bougèrent jamais.

Kite et moi ne comprenions pas l'attitude de nos compères étudiants face à leurs besoins insatiables. C'étaient des lâches, des impatients, incapables de refouler leurs sentiments. Et plus tard, ces mêmes hommes, grands pontes du droit ou de la finance, continuent dans cette même voie grâce aux paquets de fric qu'ils amassent et qu'ils considèrent comme un instrument de pouvoir et de puissance sexuelle. Ah... Comme je les exècre... Comme Garbes, mon associé, qui me raconte le lundi son week-end, où il reçoit ses enfants dans sa maison de campagne, avec sa nouvelle maîtresse. Il nous explique que tout va bien dans le meilleur des mondes, et que les enfants ne sont pas choqués de trouver « une nouvelle femme à papa ». Mais qu'en sait-il ? Il ne leur parle qu'avec son portefeuille... À chaque fois que Garbes m'en parle, une sourde haine envahit tout mon être, j'aurais aimé pouvoir le frapper, lui broyer ce sexe honteux qui réclame le sang que son cœur oublié lui fournit. Cette ordure avait considéré sa première femme comme un simple déversoir... Comme un container à gosses... Parce que, pour faire bonne figure dans la société, il faut être marié et avoir des enfants. Ce genre d'homme ne vaut rien. Amourette sans lendemain... Comme au théâtre... Un coup, puis un autre, puis encore un autre et rideau.

Si seulement Michelle était tombée sur ce genre de pénis, elle en serait vite revenue et aurait demandé réparation avec moi... Malheureusement, elle avait choisi mon double, Paul. Qui a un cœur. Mais je m'emporte et il est bientôt l'heure de conclure...

Pungent passa devant le panneau qui indiquait son but et pénétra à l'intérieur de l'immeuble. Aimablement, il renseigna l'hôtesse d'accueil qui lui demandait la raison de sa visite. Lui adressant un petit signe de remerciement, il se dirigea vers l'escalier. Pendant sa montée, il caressa son revolver à travers le tissu...

> Aujourd'hui, dimanche 28 décembre 1997, ce n'est pas un simple jour dans ma vie. C'est *mon* jour. Qu'Ils me pardonnent, mais ce dimanche restera à jamais mon *Bloody Sunday*[1].

Robert Pungent attendit que le couloir soit vide avant de s'y engager. Il regarda attentivement les petites plaques fixées sur les portes. En face de l'une d'elles, il stoppa. À travers la vitre opaque, il entrevit une silhouette floue assise derrière un bureau. D'un calme serein, il posa sa main sur la poignée.

42

Kite entendit le grincement caractéristique de la poignée. « Allons bon ! À peine revenu, il faut que l'on vienne m'emmerder... » Il leva à contrecœur la tête de son rapport, tout en gardant le stylo à la main. Robert Pungent se tenait dans l'embrasure.

— Robert... Que fais-tu ici ?

Kite se détendit et, sans se lever, invita son ami à rentrer.

1. Dimanche sanglant.

— C'est drôle de te voir là... Tu vas rire, mais hier, je suis passé à St John's Wood pour me faire payer un verre de vin blanc, sans t'y trouver...

Il paraissait réellement content de revoir son vieil ami. C'était bien la première fois que celui-ci lui rendait visite au bureau.

— Mais qu'est-ce que tu as ? Tu es devenu muet...

Kite observa la figure de Pungent. Elle était rouge vermeil. Il aperçut à la racine de ses cheveux bruns la véritable couleur rousse, la couleur de leurs années d'université... Il observa aussi ce long imperméable vert qui lui descendait jusqu'aux pieds.

Pungent attendit quelques instants et sortit de sa poche le revolver muni d'un silencieux. Il fixa intensément le visage de Kite. Il ne voulait pas tirer tout de suite. Non. Il voulait attendre de lire la réaction de surprise sur le visage de son ami, de son meilleur ami, qu'il haïssait plus que tout autre. Il tira.

Kite reçut la balle en plein milieu du cou. Elle dessina instantanément un petit cratère d'où s'échappait un épais filet de sang. L'inspecteur s'écroula sur le bureau, la tête sur le dossier ouvert. Le sang continua de couler et se mêla à l'encre noire.

Robert Pungent rempocha son pistolet et battit l'air avec sa main droite pour enlever la petite odeur de poudre. Il avait raté son tir. Mais il n'avait pas la force de tirer une seconde fois. Son meilleur ami... Paul... Il espéra que cette balle suffirait. Il regarda le corps inerte. Il aurait préféré voir cette belle tache rouge ailleurs que sur ces feuilles de papier. Sur cette belle neige blanche qui commençait à tomber par exemple. Pungent sortit du bureau.

43

Mary n'avait pas encore fini la lecture du carnet de Pungent lorsque Clément arrêta brusquement la petite Clio en face de l'entrée du Yard. L'agent de faction se dirigea vers eux et reconnut immédiatement le jeune stagiaire, qu'il salua d'un geste de la main. Les deux jeunes sortirent de la voiture et se ruèrent à l'intérieur.

— Les escaliers..., souffla Clément à l'adresse de son amie.

Ils s'y précipitèrent sous le regard amusé de la réceptionniste, qui se demandait pourquoi ils étaient si pressés. Au moment de mettre le pied sur la première marche, Clément dévisagea un homme brun vêtu d'un imperméable vert qui descendait. Son estomac se contracta soudainement sans qu'il sache vraiment pourquoi.

Mary bouscula tout le monde sur son passage. Il la rattrapa en montant les marches quatre à quatre jusqu'au second étage. En coup de vent, Mary et Clément, la fille et le fils d'adoption de l'inspecteur Kite, ouvrirent à la volée la porte de son bureau.

LE SANG SUR LE BUREAU. LE CORPS IMMOBILE DE KITE. Et ce bruit dans leurs crânes comme quand ils se réveillaient après un mauvais rêve. Cette sensation d'être en dehors du temps.

316

Ils se jetèrent sur lui. Lui parlèrent doucement. Lui caressèrent les cheveux.

44

Robert Pungent vérifia que son manteau était
bien boutonné avant de sortir du Yard et s'engagea dans Victoria Street. Sa demi-fille et le
jeune stagiaire de Paul avaient un peu raté leur
entrée, pensa-t-il. Pungent sentait le silencieux
tiède à travers son pull et sa chemise. C'était un
peu comme s'il était à même sa peau. Mon Dieu,
comme il se sentait heureux en ce moment ! Il
sifflotait entre ses lèvres l'introduction d'une
célèbre chanson de son groupe favori. Puis, il
entama la première phrase : *For the benefit of
Mr Kite, There will be a show tonight at Scotland
Yard*[1].

Qu'Ils lui pardonnent d'avoir un tant soit peu
changé les paroles, mais c'était si beau comme
cela...

Pungent refit le chemin jusqu'à sa voiture
garée près de chez Lady Madonna. Roulant
tranquillement vers sa demeure, puis la dépassant pour continuer sur Circus Road.

Un peu plus loin, il stoppa sa voiture tout près
du passage piéton sur lequel Ils avaient marché
pour la couverture de leur album *Abbey Road*.

1. À l'intention de Mr Kite, il y aura un spectacle ce
soir à Scotland Yard.

Il ouvrit la portière, sortit et alla s'allonger en plein milieu de la rue recouvrant ainsi une partie des larges bandes blanches. Il voyait au-dessus de lui des arbres sans feuilles et, autour, les figures étonnées des rares passants.

Robert Pungent se trouvait *bien*. Il n'entendait aucune musique se jouant dans sa tête. Ses oreilles sans lobes frémirent sous le vent, et de fins flocons de neige vinrent se déposer sur ses yeux fermés. Alors, il sortit lentement son revolver et posa le bout du silencieux sur sa tempe droite. Et, d'un mouvement sec du doigt, il pressa la détente.

Composition réalisée par NORD COMPO

Imprimé en France sur Presse Offset par

BRODARD & TAUPIN

GROUPE CPI

La Flèche (Sarthe).
Imp. : 6786 – Edit. : 10243 - 04/2001
ISBN : 2 - 7024 - 3028 - 7
Édition : 01